Playing Ball

SHAE CONNOR

KATE MCMURRAY

KERRY FREEMAN

MARGUERITE LABBE

Published by
Dreamspinner Press
5032 Capital Circle SW
Suite 2, PMB# 279
Tallahassee, FL 32305-7886
USA
http://www.dreamspinnerpress.com/

ISBN: 978-1-62798-175-0
Digital ISBN: 978-1-62798-176-7

Printed in the United States of America
First Edition
September 2013

Table of Contents

One Man to Remember

KATE MCMURRAY

"You can keep the things of bronze and stone and give me one man to remember me just once a year."

—Damon Runyon

Chapter 1

New York City, 1927

THE flower vendor on Forty-Third Street displayed a riot of brightly colored roses and carnations. Walt wiggled his fingers as he tried to choose.

"Whaddya think of these orange carnations, Mr. Selby?" asked the florist.

Walt loved them, truth be told. He fingered the yellow rose pinned to his lapel, already starting to wilt a little. "They are lovely," Walt said. "Such an unusual color."

"They're five cents each, but for you, I'll take a nickel."

Walt chuckled and fished a coin out of his pocket. He tossed it at the florist and then plucked one of the bright orange carnations from its vase. He threw the yellow rose in a bin and fastened the carnation to his lapel.

He strolled back to the *Times* building, enjoying the warm spring weather and the brief respite from the chaos of the newsroom. And chaos it was, because as soon as he stepped off the elevator, he was swarmed.

From the shouting and excitement, Walt was able to discern that Babe Ruth had done something—worn a new hat to a club the night before, by the sound of it, although Walt kept listening, hoping for something baseball-related—and that some kid playing for the Giants had hit two home runs the day before.

He took off his fedora and ran a hand through his hair. "Pipe down, fellas. One story at a time."

It was Reinhold who said, "Who cares about what the Babe wore last night? Aside from Selby, I mean." He smirked, and it wasn't an altogether friendly expression. "I hear this kid uptown could be the next Babe Ruth, only he doesn't like the press much."

"Really?" Walt asked, his interest piqued. "If he doesn't like the press, he's not much like Ruth."

Reinhold nodded. "He's quiet, I mean. Doesn't talk much. Avoids reporters. But he hits like Ruth."

"No one hits like Ruth," said Louis.

"What's the kid's name?" asked Walt.

"Little-something. Littleton?" said Reinhold.

"Littlefield," said Louis, derision in his voice. "He's not for real, though. He had one lucky game."

Still, one lucky game was enough to get Walter Selby's attention.

THE very next afternoon, Walt caught the Third Avenue El uptown and walked to the Polo Grounds, enjoying the anonymity of mass transit but not especially enjoying the odd looks some of Harlem's rougher residents kept shooting him. He pulled his hat down so the brim covered his eyes, but he supposed there was no hiding the crisp gray suit nor the flower pinned to his lapel—a purple carnation today—nor the shiny shoes.

Not that Harlem shunned fashionable people. Far from it; Walt knew from personal experience that the well-dressed congregated on the streets all over the neighborhood. He had been sneaking uptown for years to catch the jazz shows at the Cotton Club, and those nights were always full of the most splendidly appointed people.

But perhaps he would have been rendered inconspicuous if he'd worn a little less color on the trip uptown to see the Giants play. His red tie probably did not help matters.

Reasoning that it was too late to do anything about it now, he walked into the stadium and headed for the press box. Ken Smith from the *Graphic* was standing and gazing out at the field.

"You hear about this kid from Ohio?" Smith asked.

"Yep. You think what they say is true?"

Smith shrugged. "Probably a lot of malarkey. Kid just had a good day."

Walt took off his hat and ran a hand over his hair. He glanced at the clock, seeing by the time that the first pitch must have been imminent. He replaced his hat and adjusted his lapels, and then he pulled his notepad and a pencil from his pocket. "Were you here for the game the other day?" he asked.

Smith nodded. "I was. It was something to see, but the kid is clumsy. Luck was all it was. He doesn't have the same beauty as Gehrig or the panache of the Babe. He's a twenty-six-year-old boy from Ohio who had a good day. That's all."

Walt decided to refrain from judging for the time being. Instead, he watched the game begin. He could hear manager John McGraw shouting from the Giants' dugout, although the sound was soon overwhelmed by the roar of the crowd as the game got underway. Walt walked to his typewriter and ran his fingers over the keys as he listened to the radio fellas starting their broadcast. He sank into his chair with a sigh, prepared to watch and churn out a story about the game.

Skip Littlefield was again substituting for Freddie Lindstrom at third base, but he'd been put late in the batting order, so he didn't go up until the second inning. As he stepped up to the plate, Walt leaned forward to watch.

"Hey, Ken, you got those binoculars?"

Smith raised an eyebrow but obliged Walt, handing over the pair of binoculars he kept in the press box. Walt took them and fiddled with the focus until he could see Littlefield clearly. The kid held the bat loosely in his hand. He pulled off his cap, revealing a head of thick, dark-blond hair. He wiped his brow with the back of his hand before he pulled the hat back on. This was a kid in tremendous condition, with a body that looked powerful and impressive even under the loose uniform. Walt was hit with a wave of arousal, something not altogether welcome in the context of the baseball game, but still, this was a kid who had *it*. Even when he was concentrating on the game, Skip Littlefield exuded a sexuality that resonated with Walt, got his blood pumping.

He wanted to say something to Ken Smith, but kept his mouth shut.

The kid swung the bat a few times, just to warm up, and then he walked up to the plate. He narrowed his eyes at the pitcher and tilted his head as if he were making a complicated calculation. He took his batting stance, bending his body at the waist and raising the bat. The pitcher wound up and threw the ball. Walt heard the *klok* of the bat hitting the ball, and then he watched that ball soar over to left field. It wasn't a home run, but it was a solid hit, and the outfielders couldn't get to it in time. Littlefield ran and made it to second base before the Phillies got a handle on the ball. When Walt focused the binoculars on Littlefield again, he had hardly broken a sweat. He stood there with his hands on his hips, his facial expression neutral, maybe even expectant, like this was exactly the outcome he'd planned.

It wasn't just luck. That was abundantly clear to Walt.

"A base hit," Smith said dismissively. "A lucky shot."

Walt stayed quiet. He wanted this story more than anything. The Giants had a secret weapon in a young rookie who could hit the ball like it was his destiny. Walt felt that in his gut. But he waited out the game, watching until the fifth inning, when Skip Littlefield did it again. He missed in the seventh, but got another hit in the ninth.

Hang Ken Smith, Walt thought. *This was not luck. That was skill. Genius.* The next Babe Ruth was here in upper Manhattan, and that was a story Walt wanted to write.

JOHN "SKIP" LITTLEFIELD was not a smart man. He knew this about himself, so it wasn't a matter of shame so much as fact. There was a reason he was here on a ball field and not writing books in a tower at Harvard—or whatever they did at Harvard; it wasn't like he'd ever been there. He hadn't finished school, actually. Didn't need it, was what he figured, since the plan had always been to go work for his father, who currently owned a repair shop near their home outside Columbus, Ohio. But then it had turned out repair jobs did not come easily to Skip, and he couldn't quite understand the mechanics of the automobiles his father had lately taken to fixing. And that had left Skip somewhat adrift.

But Skip had always been good at baseball. He'd played for the school team back when he was still in school. He played with the guys from the repair shop on a team called the Upper Arlington Bolts, a play, Jimmy from the shop had explained, on both the sorts of bolts you used to fix things and lightning bolts, which he'd drawn on the front of each cap before he'd issued it to a teammate. Skip was better at leading his baseball team to victory than he was at repairing cars, that was for certain. Then, one day, a man in a fancy suit pulled him aside after a game and asked if he'd like to play baseball for money.

Five years later, here he was, sitting in the dugout at the Polo Grounds in New York City of all places. He didn't care much for the city. He shared an apartment on Third Avenue with two other guys from the Giants, and that was all right, but there was never any silence. Even if his roommates weren't beating their gums at each other, there were cars and sirens and people talking outside almost constantly. Skip was surprised to find he missed Ohio, too, which was funny because Ohio had never offered him much except opportunities for failure. At least here people thought he was pretty swell because he could hit a baseball.

"Skip, you're on deck," said Mr. McGraw.

Rogers Hornsby was standing near the edge of the dugout. He slapped Skip on the back and said, "Hit it out of the park," in his Texas twang.

Skip took a bat and swung it experimentally. He liked the weight of this one, a little heavier than the bat he'd used in the previous inning. He watched Mel Ott bat; Ott hit the ball right into the first baseman's glove. Skip had already figured out that the Phillies weren't playing well when balls were hit near left field, so slugging the ball to the right was a good way to get an out.

He walked up to the plate and eyed the pitcher. Skip didn't know the guy's name, but he'd been watching those pitches from the dugout all through the game. The man liked a fastball, couldn't really throw anything else effectively. His curveball was slow and tended to go out of the strike zone. Skip had gotten a single in the second inning, but he was more prepared now. He knew if he hit the ball toward the unattended part of the outfield, he should be good for another base hit.

And so, the pitcher squatted and squinted at Skip, then he wound up, and then he pitched. It was a fastball headed right for Skip's left hand, so Skip shifted, swung the bat, and connected with the ball, sending it out toward left field just as he wanted, and then the ball just kept going, past the outfielders running for it, and into the stands. Skip ran, but knew he didn't really need to, that ball was gone. Home run.

In the locker room after the game, Skip's roommate Joe slapped his back. "That was a hell of a hit," he said.

"Thanks," said Skip.

Joe leaned back against his locker. "Don't wait up for me tonight. I've got another date with Estelle."

"Oh?"

Joe grinned. "I'm gonna marry that girl. She's… she's swell."

Skip laughed. "Swell?"

"I don't know what else to call her. She's a sheba. Like Clara Bow. But even prettier."

Skip didn't like these bull sessions, but he recognized how important they were. His friends wanted to talk about their romantic adventures, and he understood that desire, but he himself kept mum. He didn't have much to share lately, for one thing, but he also knew that if he were honest about his own desires, his friends would be horrified.

"Good luck," he said to Joe.

Skip changed clothes and headed out of the locker room. In the hall, he saw a man in a dark suit with a pink carnation pinned to his lapel. The man was handsome. He looked wealthy, his clothes expensive, and that made him entirely out of place in a baseball stadium. Skip planned to walk past him, but then the man said, "Mr. Littlefield."

Skip was surprised. He'd kept such a low profile he couldn't imagine anyone would know his name. He turned to the man. "Yes?"

The man smiled. "I'm Walter Selby."

"All right."

A look of surprise came over Mr. Selby's face. "I'm a sports reporter for the *Times*."

That made Skip's heart seize. "Oh. Nice to meet you."

Mr. Selby smirked. "Calm down. You're getting too excited."

Skip let out an exasperated sigh. He recognized the sarcasm, but he had no interest in talking to a reporter.

"I've heard you don't like the press," said Selby, "but all I want is a little bit of your time. I—there's something really special about you. I was at yesterday's game too, you know, and watching you play is really something else. I'd like to interview you for my paper."

"Oh, no. I couldn't possibly—"

"I see such potential in you. Obviously the big story this summer is that Murderers' Row in the Bronx, but we could change the narrative, write a new story. Ruth has been at this a decade. He's having a hell of a season now, yes, but soon he'll be the past. You could be the future."

"Mr. Selby—"

"Let me buy you dinner. We'll talk about baseball. I won't print anything you don't want me to print."

"I'm just not sure it's a good idea."

Selby took a notepad and a pencil from his pocket. He scribbled something on the pad and then ripped off that sheet of paper. He handed it to Skip, who almost shoved it in his pocket without a glance. Instead, he took a deep breath and looked. There were a lot of words there, and they all started to swim together a bit.

"The Penguin is a speakeasy off Times Square," Selby said under his breath. He pointed to a word that started with a P on the page. "Meet me there tomorrow night. I'll buy you a cocktail. All right?"

"I'm not sure—"

"No one knows who you are, if you're worried about being recognized in a place that serves hooch. And besides, if the Sultan of Swat, Babe Ruth himself, shows up anywhere else in Times Square, all the reporters will go there. I just want to talk about baseball, honest. That can't be too difficult, can it?"

Skip looked at the jumble of words on that piece of paper. "Tell me the address of the place again."

Instead of the look of triumph Skip expected to see, a frown crossed Selby's face. "Fifty-Sixth Street. I wrote it right there." He pointed.

Skip recognized the numbers. He *could* read, a little. He put together which was the street the club was on and which were the cross streets and he nodded, though he also committed the address to memory. Just in case.

"So you'll come?" asked Selby.

Skip looked up into the face of this man who seemed so interested in him. He didn't know what to make of the attention he was getting. The man *was* very good-looking, the sort of man Skip had sometimes lusted after before he moved to New York. Nothing like that could happen here and he knew that, but part of him held out some hope.

"I… yes. I'll be there."

Selby grinned. "Fantastic."

Chapter 2

WALT leaned against the brick facade of a Times Square building and watched Babe Ruth get out of a cab. The Bambino was wearing a clean white suit with a matching fedora tilted at a jaunty angle. Walt always found the contradiction of Ruth—the expensive clothes on the odd, triangular body, with the craggy face that looked like it had been in too many bar brawls—to be quite interesting. But there were plenty of reporters in New York dying to follow Ruth around. Walt had another story to pursue.

The Penguin Club was around the corner. It wasn't Walt's favorite Times Square establishment. It was a little bland, but that was why he'd chosen it—it was safe. He couldn't imagine a kid like Skip would do well in the sorts of places Walt really liked to go. He was skittish in the baseball stadium; Walt couldn't imagine him calm in one of the racier clubs.

He pulled his fedora down over his eyes and slunk down Fifty-Sixth Street. The Penguin was a little off the beaten path—another reason Walt had chosen it—and tonight, Walt wanted to fade into the background a bit, to observe instead of be observed.

He spotted a figure walking down the street from Sixth Avenue and knew immediately it was Skip. He walked with a dancer's grace, something Walt had noticed at the stadium. As he came closer, Walt saw he was wearing a brown suit a couple of seasons out of style and a battered bowler hat that didn't really go with the suit. These were forgivable offenses, Walt decided, since he did look pretty great out of a baseball uniform.

"Why, Mr. Littlefield," Walt said as Skip walked up to him. "You're a real sheik outside of the ballpark."

It was too dark to see if Skip was blushing, but Walt imagined from the way he ducked his head that he was.

"I'm still not really sure about this," Skip said.

"One measly drink won't do any harm."

Walt gestured for Skip to follow him. He knew the password, although the door was being watched by a big six named Anthony, with whom Walt had once had a brief and tawdry affair. Luckily, they were still on good terms.

"How are ya, Walt?" Anthony greeted him.

"I'm just ducky. This is my friend John."

Skip tilted his head, but then extended a hand to Anthony, who shook it.

Anthony said, "You boys can go on in. Although, Walt? If you're looking for something to do later, Carmela's performing at that little place off Forty-Third tonight."

Walt nodded. He loved Carmela's show, but he was sort of wishing this interview would go long enough for him to miss it. And he certainly knew better than to think Skip would be interested in a show like Carmela's. "I'll keep that in mind," Walt said.

As Walt led Skip into the speakeasy, Skip said, "Who is Carmela?"

Walt chuckled. "Would it terrify you if I told you she is a female impersonator?"

Skip tilted his head again, as if he were taking that in. "Like a man in a dress?"

Walt nodded. "Carmela is in fact an Italian fella named Carmine who I've known for years. He's… well, he's something, to be sure. But his brother owns a bunch of the Times Square establishments, plus a few other places downtown, so he has plenty of performance venues."

Skip seemed more intrigued by this than put off, which was not the reaction Walt had been expecting. "What does he do in his show?"

"Dances, tells jokes, that sort of thing. Like a one-man vaudeville act. Why do you ask? Do you want to see it?"

Skip shrugged. "Just wondering."

What an interesting man Skip was turning out to be. The lack of literacy had given Walt pause back at the stadium. Walt's handwriting wasn't so abysmal that it couldn't be deciphered, so Skip's hesitancy over the words said a lot. But he still had found the place. Asking about school was on Walt's agenda for this evening. He didn't know much about Skip except that he was very attractive—he had a round face with a narrow nose and surprisingly plump lips atop that athletic body, and as he removed his hat, he displayed a thick head of wavy blond hair—and he played baseball as well as or better than many of the best ballplayers in the city. He was also, apparently, barely literate and intrigued by the idea of a show like Carmela's. Walt was fascinated.

Walt led him over to a table in the corner, a shadowy spot Walt liked because it meant he could see everything without being in the middle of it. Sometimes he chose one of the grander booths closer to the band and held court, but tonight, he wanted to talk to Skip and he didn't want to share.

The band struck up a clunky version of "Tea for Two," a song that didn't lend itself well to the current conflation of instruments, but Walt was able to mostly tune them out and focus on his subject. Skip, for his part, looked around the room, raking his gaze over the decor, the people, the band. Tonight, Ruthie Dixon, a charming flapper girl whom Walt knew mostly from years of hanging around the clubs in Times Square, was sitting on a table in the corner with her legs crossed at her knees, laughing uproariously with the crowd of men who had gathered around her.

"Quite a place," Skip said.

"This is nothing. Some of the clubs in this town are not to be believed. There was a blow at this place on Fifty-Third the other night, most spectacular thing you've ever seen."

"You come to the speakeasies often?"

Walt shrugged. "Often enough. You ever been to one?"

"My roommates brought me to one when I first moved here. But I ain't even been in New York that long. Only since April."

Walt could concede that three months in New York wasn't really enough time to see much. "You like what you've seen so far?"

"I guess. It's… it's not like Ohio."

Walt laughed. "I've never been to Ohio, but I can imagine."

When Matthew came over to the table, Walt was embarrassed to have recognized yet another person in the establishment and wondered what Skip must think of him now. Matthew just winked and said, "Can I get you fellas something to drink?"

"What have you got?" Walt asked.

"I'd stick with the rum. It's the real McCoy. There's whiskey, too, but I think it's the hooey from that barrelhouse downtown. Tastes like formaldehyde."

"Rum it is, then. Two of whatever's good."

Matthew nodded and walked off.

Skip laughed and shook his head. "Every bar in my hometown closed when Prohibition started. Every one. You can still get cider from some of the farms just outside town, and wine at church, but otherwise, there's nothing."

"But in New York…."

"Yes. First night I was here, my roommate Joe pulled out a bottle of something. I'd only been drunk once before, when I was seventeen and some friends and I got into my daddy's supply. He tanned my hide for that." Skip laughed lightly and shook his head.

"I rarely get blotto. I just like a drink now and then."

"Sure."

Matthew came back and slid two highball glasses onto the table. Walt paid for the drinks.

"You don't have to," Skip said.

"My pleasure. Besides, I invited you out."

They spent the next half hour discussing Skip's origins—life in Upper Arlington, Ohio, and his failed career as a mechanic, mostly—and Skip put away two cocktails before his lips really started loosening up and he confessed, quietly, "Baseball is the only thing I've ever been good at."

"That can't be true."

"I was no good at school. Some kids take to reading like it's the most natural thing, but I see a bunch of letters on the page and I can't always make sense of them. I mean, sometimes I can, but sometimes all the letters just look upside down and backwards." He shook his head.

"What is it about baseball that you like?" Walt asked, interested in this phenomenon with the letters but not wanting to pursue it just yet. It seemed a sore subject.

"I don't know. It's easy. All you gotta do is hit a ball with a bat and catch. It helps if you can run pretty fast, which I guess I can. If the Giants want to pay me to do that, I'm not going to argue with them."

"You have to know that it's not really that easy. There are other men who get paid to play baseball who can barely hit a ball. I know you've only played in a half-dozen games now, but your batting average is higher than Ruth's."

Skip frowned. “That can’t be true.”

“It is true. Ruth’s average is currently about .350. Yours is closer to .400.”

Skip waved his hand. “Oh, I don’t much abide by the numbers. What do numbers tell you?”

Walt was surprised by how dismissive he was. “The numbers tell you everything. The numbers show you that Ruth, Gehrig, and Combs could probably win a game all on their own, but then you throw Koenig, Meusel, and Lazzeri into the mix and that team is unstoppable. The numbers show you there has never been a team like that. The numbers also tell me that you, Skip Littlefield, hit just as well as any of those guys, but nobody knows it because the Giants are not the story this year. The Yankees, the Babe, goddamn Murderers’ Row—that’s the story this year.”

Skip put a hand over his mouth and shook his head. He dropped the hand slowly. “I don’t want to be a story.”

“But you are! Can’t you see that?”

Skip rolled his eyes. “Mr. Selby, you can’t possibly—”

“Call me Walt.”

Skip sighed. “All right, Walt. Look, I appreciate this, I really do, but I’m happy with the Yankees stealing all the headlines. I don’t want people to pay attention to me. I just want to play baseball.”

Walt took a sip of his drink, let it sit on his tongue, and tried to decide how to respond. It was rum mixed with some kind of juice, which was a shame because the rum really was very good, from what Walt could taste of it. “Why is that? It’s rare to find a talented person in New York who doesn’t want to become famous. It’s hard to find *anyone* in New York who doesn’t want to become famous.”

Skip squirmed in his chair. “I would like to keep my privacy.”

“Understandable.” Although, there it was. With seven words, Skip had irrevocably hooked Walt, because now Walt wondered what secrets Skip was keeping.

THE third drink was probably a mistake.

Skip likened his will when drunk to the way the floorboards in his father’s Model T warped after he left it out in the rain. He felt soft and easy to bend. Walt Selby could probably kick a hole right through him, and Skip would be happy to let him.

Because for all that Walt was still trying to get Skip's story, which Skip didn't like much, he was also really nice to look at. Walt had close-cropped dark hair that seemed to be thinning a little. Sometimes he pulled a little pair of spectacles out of his pocket when he needed to read or see something better, and Skip thought the way they sat on the edge of Walt's long nose was cute. Everything else about Walt was long, too—his face, his fingers, his whole body, as if he were a normal person stretched out like taffy. Then there was the gray suit he was wearing, the red rose pinned to his lapel, the red tie at his neck in almost the same color. The cut of the suit was a little different from what Skip was used to, everything fitted just so, as if it were sewn just for Walt, which it probably had been. Skip didn't know what kind of money newspaper reporters made, but if it was enough to keep Walt in hooch all the time, he probably made a decent wage.

Well. Skip knew better than to gaze too long at Walt. He tried to concentrate on the band playing.

It sure was hard to focus with all that alcohol swimming through his body.

The waiter, who seemed to have makeup on his face like a woman, came by the table again and smiled at Walt in a way Skip didn't like. Then he said, "Another round, fellas?"

Walt looked at Skip and smiled. "No, I think he's had enough. Thank you, though, Matthew."

Walt's smile caused warmth to spread through Skip's body. Or maybe that was the booze.

Walt escorted Skip out of the speakeasy a few minutes later. Walt shook hands with the muscle at the door, and Skip didn't like the way that guy looked at Walt, either. Skip stumbled out onto the street and wondered when he'd become so possessive. Walt was definitely not his. Walt would surely be horrified to learn Skip had been sort of thinking about him that way.

Skip stumbled over something on the sidewalk. Walt caught him and propped him up. Skip definitely liked the feel of Walt's arms around him, but they were gone too soon.

"Where do you live, doll?" Walt asked. "Can I escort you home or get you a cab?"

Panic flooded Skip. This night couldn't end yet. He wasn't ready to let Walt go. "You didn't get your story," he said as a way to stall.

Walt smirked and leaned against a lamppost. "I got a story."

"What is it?" Skip grunted and crossed his arms. "That I'm some yokel from Ohio who doesn't know bull about anything except baseball?"

Walt's face fell. "What? No, that wasn't what I thought at all."

"You want to know why I don't want anyone to write about me?" Skip said, feeling a weird swell of anger now. "Because all I am is baseball. There's nothing else to say. I couldn't finish school because all I see when I look at a book are words swimming around on the page. I'm stupid. That's all there is to it. So I thought I could be a mechanic, but I'm no good at that either. I couldn't make sense of how the parts fit together and I work too slow. I don't have a wife or a sweetheart or kids or nothing either. But baseball... that's the one thing I can do. So put that in your goddamn story. Skip Littlefield is a dummy who is only good for hitting a baseball."

Walt pushed off the lamppost and stepped forward. "Skip, stop it. That's not what I think at all."

"What else is there to print?"

"Top of the ninth, two men on base, you go up to the plate. What do you do?"

That took Skip off guard. "What does that have to do with anything?"

"Just pretend. Answer the question. Game's tied and you're in the position to hit the game-winning run. How do you handle it?"

Skip decided to play along, even though he didn't understand this line of questioning. "Who am I playing?"

"Does it matter?"

"Yes."

Walt smiled. "Uh. Any team. Let's say the Robins."

Skip mentally ran through the Robins' lineup. "They're weak in right field and their second baseman is a slow runner. So I'd hit the ball in that direction. If the pitcher throws me a fastball, I might be able to use the speed to get a good grip on the ball and send it into the stands, but if not, the Robins are more likely to miss the catch if I hit it toward right field."

Walt gaped at him for a moment. "Just like that?"

"Just like that. Their starting pitcher, the one with the light hair, what's his name?"

"Jesse Barnes."

"Yeah, Barnes. His career is ending soon. His fastball is pretty slow. Hard to get a home run off of him. The ball doesn't hit the bat hard enough. Plus, he tends to pitch high. So if I were at the plate, I'd angle the bat up. Bob McGraw hits them right at you, so you have to be prepared for that. And that relief pitcher, um… what's his name?"

"Cantrell?"

"Sure. He's good, but he can be sloppy. If you catch him on a sloppy day, you can't hit anything he throws and it's better to get a walk."

Walt gaped at Skip for a moment. "Reverse the situation. Say you're in the field. Third base. Herman's at bat."

"Herman?"

"Tall, skinny guy. Long face. First base."

"Right, okay. Sorry, I have trouble with the names. He's a slugger, yes?"

"Yes."

Skip nodded, thinking about it. "He's a slugger but doesn't hit a lot of home runs. So you tell the outfield to be ready for him. Then you gotta make a choice. Do I want the ball? Herman gets a lot of RBIs. So I want to get the guy out before he gets to third or home. If he hits it toward me, I take it and toss it to second or first, go for the double play. But he's unpredictable, so if he hits it toward first, maybe you try to get him out there."

The smile on Walt's face widened. "You want to know what I'd write about you?"

"What?"

"That Skip Littlefield is a nice guy who keeps things close to the vest, but he's a goddamn genius when it comes to baseball."

Skip nearly laughed at how absurd that seemed, but he swallowed it. "That's ridiculous."

Walt shrugged. "That's how I see it."

A small crowd of people walked between Skip and Walt. They were speaking excitedly—Skip could have sworn he heard someone mention Babe Ruth and Jack Dempsey in the same breath—and then they bustled into the Penguin. When they were gone, Walt was back leaning against the lamppost.

"Let me get you a cab," Walt said.

That's how I see it.

No one had ever called Skip a genius.

"I don't want to go home yet," Skip said.

"All right. What shall we do instead?"

"This friend of yours. The man who wears dresses. Is his show good?"

Walt furrowed his brow. "The act is pretty great, yes. You want to see it?"

"Maybe."

"I'll take you, but only if you go to enjoy the show. Carmela doesn't need anyone gawking at her like she's a freak. She's there to sing and dance."

"I won't gawk."

"All right. Let's go."

They walked south on Seventh Avenue. Skip followed along and tried not to seem overwhelmed, even though he was. Times Square was so bright and loud and a little dangerous, with cars driving every which way and what seemed like hundreds of people milling around on the sidewalk. As they got closer to Forty-Third Street, Skip saw people pouring out of the Paramount Theater, signaling a show had just ended. He thought about the moving picture he'd seen there not long ago, though he couldn't remember the plot so much as the experience. They didn't have theaters like the Paramount in his little town in Ohio. There was a theater in Columbus that showed moving pictures sometimes, but he'd had to travel to get there. He liked movies more than plays or musical revues because it was easier to see everyone and follow what was happening.

And there went his mind, wandering off again.

Skip focused on Walt walking ahead of him, and then they stopped at a black door. Walt eyed Skip with an odd expression.

"You're sure about this?" Walt asked.

Skip nodded. He was drunk enough to be sure.

The abrupt change in lighting as they pushed into the club made Skip light-headed for a moment. He put out his hand, which landed on Walt's arm. Walt seemed solid enough, so Skip curled his hand around Walt's bicep and was led to the ticket counter. An Ethel—a fella in a brightly colored flouncy shirt with kohl lining his eyes—stood behind the counter, leering at Walt. Skip gave Walt a little bit of a tug.

"You're not chickening out on me, are you?" Walt asked.

"Not a chance."

"Come on, then."

Walt handed the ticket fellow a couple of bills and soon they were ushered into one of the tiniest theaters Skip had ever seen. It wasn't even really a theater so much as a room, approximately the same size as Skip's apartment, with four round tables lined up in front of the stage and rows of mismatched chairs lined up behind them. The tables were all occupied, and a smattering of the seats were filled. Walt led Skip to the middle of the rows of seats, so Skip sat and waited to see what would happen.

Something occurred to Skip's addled brain as he watched the sort of men who took up space in the theater. Some of them were effeminate men, like the fella at the counter, but not all of them were. Skip glanced at Walt, at the fashionable suit and the rose on his lapel, and he started to wonder.

"Can I ask you something?" Skip said.

"I'm all ears, dollface."

The nickname irked Skip a little, but he supposed what Walt was implying—that Skip had a face like a woman's—was not something Walt intended as insulting. He might even find it desirable. For confirmation, Skip whispered, "Do you know many men who desire the company of other men? Instead of women, I mean."

Walt looked so shocked that Skip immediately regretted asking the question. It was a foolish thing to ask. There was no way a man like Walt—a handsome, successful man—would know anyone like that, nor would he want to be spending time with a man like that. Skip was so horrified he'd even said anything that he began to stand to leave. He figured he could just walk out of the theater and put this whole night behind him.

Walt put a hand on Skip's thigh, keeping him in his seat.

"Why do you ask?" Walt said.

Why had he asked? Skip wasn't sure. He tried to make his mind focus on something, but it was swimming now. He looked around him. He hadn't known many men like himself. There had been Billy, the neighbor's son, with whom Skip had fooled around as a teenager, but that hardly counted since Billy was married to a pretty girl named Rosemary now, and by all accounts as happy as he'd ever been. Otherwise, in Skip's experience, the few men he knew like himself had congregated at a club in Columbus that sometimes had female impersonators. Maybe it was the hooch talking, but it seemed logical that a club like this would have men like that, too.

Skip wasn't willing to give that much away, however. "Forget I asked."

"I do know a few," Walt said.

Skip was astonished. Then he glanced around and figured this was also a foolish reaction. Walt was, after all, in this sort of club, and based on that earlier conversation Skip had witnessed, it was not Walt's first time here. Skip thought back on all of the men they had run into that evening, from the strongman at the door of the Penguin to the Ethel selling tickets into this theater, and how all of them had given Walt "the look." Skip wondered how often Walt returned that expression.

The alcohol made him brave enough to ask, in a whisper, "Are you one of them?"

Skip's heart pounded while he waited for an answer.

"Yes," Walt said softly. "As are you, if I'm not mistaken."

Skip had trouble catching his breath, so he nodded. Walt leaned in close enough that Skip could feel Walt's breath on his face. The moment was heavy, the air in the room suffocating in the way only a hot New York night could be, and Skip was about to say something—anything—but then the lights on the tiny stage flashed on.

A woman walked on stage and drawled, "Darlings," to the audience. She was a large brick of a woman in a rectangular flapper gown covered in sparkly tassels and sequins. She was a little bowlegged and she had an Adam's apple. Skip couldn't figure out who Carmela thought she was kidding.

She immediately broke out into song. After a few bars, Skip recognized it as a Gershwin tune called "The Man I Love," a song he'd been quite fond of after hearing it performed on one of his first nights in New York.

Thinking about the lyrics made Skip acutely aware of the man sitting next to him, a man who inspired feelings of arousal and possession in Skip, a man who had called him a genius not that long ago.

After the show, Skip used the men's room and then met Walt outside, where he was talking to some man. They were laughing about something together. As Skip approached, Walt made eye contact and then somewhat abruptly said, "Well, I should be going. It was great to see you, though, Rob."

The show had been uproarious, funny, and entertaining, and not at all what Skip had expected, and he wanted to talk about it, but now that the alcohol was dissipating, he was suddenly quite tired. This Rob fellow walked away, leaving Walt and Skip alone on the sidewalk.

"Well," Walt said. "I suppose I understand better why you didn't want to be interviewed."

Skip shook his head. "The one thing I didn't want anyone to know, and you found it out anyway. I should be terrified, but somehow, I trust you."

"I want you to trust me, Skip. I promise I won't print anything more than what I told you before. You guard your privacy, which I respect, but you're some kind of savant when it comes to the game. My not printing much about your personal life will give you an air of mystery. Fans will like that. They'll find it intriguing. And besides, my goal as a sports reporter is to report on the game. Fans like the stories about the Babe, sure, but they care about runs and RBIs, too."

"Thank you." Skip shoved his hands in his pockets and looked toward Seventh Avenue, toward the bright lights of Broadway. "I guess I should go home."

"Can I help you get a cab?"

Skip had been planning to take the subway up to his place on West Seventy-Third Street, but he nodded.

Walt took a step toward him. "Before you go, I just wanted to say that I had a nice time tonight. I'll say that in my article. There's something really special about you, Skip, and I want people to see that."

Skip could hear his father's voice bouncing around in his head. He could hear every time someone told him he'd never amount to anything. But Walt clearly saw something else in him. There was something so strange about that.

Or there was still enough alcohol buzzing through Skip that everything seemed weird.

He was confused briefly, but then Walt stepped forward and extended his hand. Skip reached to shake it, but then thought better of it. Instead, he did what he'd been longing to do since they'd spoken quietly in the theater.

He leaned up on his toes and kissed Walt.

Skip could feel Walt's surprise, but then Walt kissed him back and put a hand on his waist. It was magic, the way their lips came together, and there was a sexual charge to it, too. Something pricked at the back of Skip's mind, that he should be more cautious, but then, Walt was kissing him, too, so….

They were kissing on a street. Two men kissing. In the middle of a busy city.

Skip pulled away and looked at Walt.

"I'm sorry, I—"

"Oh, it is quite all right," Walt said. He glanced toward Times Square. "Well, as much as I'd enjoy getting arrested for indecency, perhaps the best course of action is to get you home, where you can sleep this off. Are you playing tomorrow?"

"Travel day. We're going to Boston."

Walt nodded. "I'd like to see you again after you get back. And not for another story."

Skip wanted that too, more than anything. "Yes."

He followed Walt back toward Times Square, where Walt managed to hail a cab and usher Skip into it.

"So, when you get back," Walt said.

"You know where to find me."

Chapter 3

SKIP woke up to someone pounding on his door.

"Skip!" a voice shouted. It took him a moment to realize it was his roommate Mickey. "Skip, we have to leave soon to catch the train. Get up!"

"All right! I'm awake!"

Skip sat up. It took a moment for the pain to blossom, and then his head throbbed. Dear Lord, what had he done the night before?

He remembered in a flash: the speakeasy, all those rum cocktails, Carmela dancing across the stage.

Kissing Walter Selby.

That got Skip out of bed in a hurry. He hopped up and scrambled into whichever clothes were closest—some wool trousers and a white shirt that could probably stand to be laundered—and then poked around for his billfold and hat. He stumbled down the hall and managed to shave, at least. He seemed somewhat presentable by the time he met Joe and Mickey at the front door.

"Wild night?" Mickey asked with a little bit of a sneer.

"Too much rum, I guess," Skip said.

"You're not hiding a dame under your bed, are you?" asked Joe. "Because we're gonna be gone for a few days. You might want to let her out."

Mickey guffawed.

Skip couldn't think of a witty reply, so he just shrugged and said, "No girls under the bed."

On the train ride up to Boston, Skip's mind was focused almost exclusively on Walt, reliving the night before, alternately thrilled by what had happened and horrified by his own behavior. He fretted that all of it was a scheme on Walt's part to get Skip to admit to something he didn't want to see in print, but that kiss had certainly felt genuine. Maybe it was foolish, but Skip trusted Walt. Maybe that trust was cemented with alcohol, but maybe Walt had earned it, too. Or maybe there was a printing press somewhere cranking out pages describing all of Skip's secrets.

He was glad he'd be out of town when the story hit the paper. He wasn't sure he could face it. Not that he'd even be able to read much of it, but he didn't want to deal with people's reactions. What if his teammates found out how broken Skip was? What if John McGraw found out? What if the team owners found out? They probably wouldn't let him play baseball anymore, and then where would he be?

To help stop fretting, he switched to thinking about the upcoming game against the Braves. He tried to recall what he already knew about the team. He hadn't played in that many games for the Giants, that was true, but he'd been watching games all season, so he knew each team's weaknesses, knew its strengths, knew which batters to watch out for, knew where to hit the ball.

Unfortunately, strategizing his game against the Braves made him think of Walt, too, of the questions Walt had asked. Walt had called him a genius. But how could that be true? Skip couldn't remember anyone ever calling him smart. His thoughts became confused and muddled the more he turned over the events of the previous night. He fretted about what Walt might print. He worried it would distract him from the game. He desperately wanted to see Walt again. Well, at the base of things, he wanted Walt fiercely, sexually, desired and craved him, got excited thinking about him. But he was terrified that getting involved with the man would only cause more problems. How would he explain absences to his roommates? What if they were seen together in public?

He managed to listen when his teammates started yammering on about the upcoming series and even managed to add something to the conversation. He listened when they talked about women. He felt anxious to at least get to their destination so he could think about Walt without it showing on his face. As conversation waned, he leaned back and closed his eyes, hoping to fall asleep.

WALT SELBY had lived in New York City all his life and sometimes felt like he'd seen everything during his thirty-four years on earth.

He'd been a boy when the subway opened, a university student when the *Titanic* sank, and a cub reporter for the *Times* when the US started shipping boys to the war in Europe. He'd survived his mother succumbing to influenza, he'd been an eyewitness to the bombing on Wall Street in 1920, and Times Square had become *Times Square* in his lifetime. He'd been getting his feet wet as a sports reporter the year Prohibition went into effect, though he still had a bottle of really good scotch that had been a gift from John McGraw after Walt had started covering the Giants. It sat unopened in his Greenwich Village apartment.

He'd been spending a lot of his downtime in the Times Square speakeasies for the past seven years, and he'd seen a hell of a lot there, too. He'd gotten caught up in raids, he'd seen a man poison himself with bad booze, he'd seen a couple of men get thrown out of a club for dancing together. He'd picked up sailors at the Hotel Astor; one had hit him hard enough to leave a bruise afterward. He'd once been picked up by a low-level mobster, and they had wild and imaginative sex in one of the most richly appointed houses Walt had ever seen. And after many years in the newspaper biz, he'd heard more secrets about New York's swanky set than he was really comfortable with knowing.

As a boy, he'd seen Christy Mathewson pitch. He'd seen Ty Cobb perform feats of sportsmanship that seemed superhuman. He'd seen Babe Ruth hit more home runs than he could count. He'd watched careers begin and end and begin again.

After all that, he shouldn't have been surprised by anything.

And yet Skip Littlefield surprised him.

Here was a quiet man who didn't want any part of the spotlight and yet was doing something extraordinary. That didn't astonish Walt any less now that he understood why Skip guarded his privacy so much. Walt couldn't get the memory of that night out of his brain—talking over drinks, walking along Seventh Avenue, laughing at Carmela, all of it. And that kiss still burned on Walt's lips. Had there ever been a kiss like that in the whole history of world? So sweet and yet so charged, spontaneous and open and just there on the street, and then it was over before Walt even got a chance to grasp onto it.

He strolled into the newsroom two days after their night out and saw the usual buzz of activity. Reinhold was hovering around Walt's desk as Walt got to it.

"Fluke!" Reinhold said. "You're such a fool, Selby. The new kid on the Giants you drooled all over in that article? Littlefield? He got totally balled up yesterday. Whiffed by every pitch thrown at him. Apparently McGraw is furious."

Walt scoffed. "That's not true."

Reinhold grabbed a newspaper off a nearby desk and slapped it on Walt's. It was open to the sports page. The headline said, "Giants Disappoint—Braves Win 5–2."

Walt read the story with some measure of distress. Reinhold had exaggerated—Skip had gotten a hit in the seventh inning, though he hadn't scored a run—but the game hadn't gone well. Walt was inclined to believe *this* was the fluke, that Skip had just had a bad day, but he was hesitant to voice that opinion out loud. "He'll be better today."

Reinhold turned around. "Hey, Louis! Can we get the Giants game on the radio?"

Fifteen minutes later, Louis had turned on the radio in one of the meeting rooms. The crackly broadcast came through well enough for those assembled to discern it was the top of the fourth.

"*Terry steps up to bat,*" the announcer said. "*First pitch. Terry swings and misses. Strike one. Second pitch. Oh, close one. Ump rules it a ball. Third pitch. Terry bunts! Oh, didn't see that coming. Terry's running. Welsh has the ball. He throws it to Bancroft. Bancroft throws to Fournier, but he's too late. Terry is safe at first.*"

"I like the New York announcers better," Reinhold said.

"Hush," said Walt.

The radio announcer said, "*Littlefield is coming up to the plate. He's the new kid from Ohio. Impressive stats so far, but he hasn't done much here in Boston. He takes the stance. First pitch is... oh, strike one! Swing and a miss. Second pitch....*"

Walt listened, his heart in his throat. He wished he could be at the game to see this. Not that he had any business interfering, but he couldn't help but think if he were there, he could see what was really going on."

"*And that's strike two!*" said the announcer.

Walt cursed under his breath.

"Tut tut," said Louis. "You're letting your team allegiance show. What happened to objective reporting?"

"I cover baseball in New York City. I'm allowed to root for the home team."

Louis grinned. "Aw, I'm just razzing you, Selby."

"*Swing and a miss again*!" said the announcer. "*Littlefield is out. This is just not his game.*"

Walt wondered if something was wrong with Skip. It seemed strange for him to be hitting this badly.

"When's the next home game?" he asked the assembled crowd.

"Tuesday," said Reinhold.

Walt made a mental note to make sure he was the one covering that game. He needed to see what was happening with his own eyes.

Chapter 4

WALT sat on the edge of his seat for most of the next game. From his vantage point behind third base, he could see into the Giants' dugout, and Skip was definitely there, looking forlorn. Walt had managed to get a word with John McGraw before the game; McGraw had said Skip would sit this one out unless they needed a pinch hitter late in the game. That Walt found this disappointing was an understatement; he really wanted to see Skip play. But after the dismal performance in Boston, Walt understood McGraw's decision to bench Skip.

Walt wasn't sure where his faith in Skip had come from, besides Skip's own analysis of the game. Walt supposed the proof was in the pudding—the series against the Braves notwithstanding, most of Skip's at bats were spectacular. Walt was confident that if Skip were given room to fly, he'd take off. Keeping him chained to the bench was not the best use of him. Then again, he was a rookie on a team with a lot of talent. If not this season, then next… assuming the Giants didn't let Skip go at the end of the season because of one bad series. Stranger things had happened.

It was a good game, well played and kind of a nail-biter, but the Giants ultimately pulled off a victory over the Pirates.

Walt spent a few minutes discussing the game with the other reporters in the press box, and then he walked with Charlie Segar of the *Mirror* to talk to a few players. He enjoyed listening to Segar talk; the man was from England originally, though he had spent most of his life in the US, so his accent was a little muddled. Walt had thought maybe it was an affectation at first—not that he judged, he thought as he fingered the purple lily on his lapel—but it didn't much matter now that they'd gotten to know each other. The bottom line was that Segar loved baseball, and he buzzed with enthusiasm as they walked together into the bowels of the stadium.

"Hell of a hit Roush got in the seventh," Segar said. "He may hit enough balls to justify his salary yet."

Walt chuckled. "I liked the way Harper looked this game. And Bill Terry and even Hornsby."

"I could have sworn Hornsby was going to retire last year, but he's still doing great things."

"It's a good team we've got here in Manhattan. Almost enough to make you forget the Bronx exists."

Segar grinned. "I'm going to go talk to McGraw. You need anything?"

"Nah, I'm fine."

Segar shook Walt's hand and walked away. Walt lingered in the hallway outside the locker room and caught players as they left, asking each a couple of questions about the game and dutifully writing their answers in his notepad. Since this was mostly a pretense, he wasn't sure how much he would use, but at least the Giants could discuss a victory instead of a defeat, and everyone seemed happy and enthusiastic.

He got stuck talking to Rogers Hornsby for nearly ten minutes while Hornsby talked his ear off about strategy. Walt started writing that story in his head—"It's clear Hornsby's interest is more in coaching than playing these days…."—but then he almost lost sight of the real reason he'd come to the locker room.

Skip walked out with a bag on his shoulder. When he caught sight of Walt, he stopped short and stared for a moment. Then, perhaps seeing that Walt was embroiled in this conversation with Hornsby, he took a deep breath and kept walking.

Walt said, "Would you excuse me?" and ducked away from the conversation before Hornsby could object. He glanced back and saw that Hornsby had already thrown an arm around one of the rookies, probably giving the poor kid advice.

Walt had to jog to catch up to Skip. He hooked a hand around Skip's elbow and pulled him to a shadowy spot off to the side of the hallway that led out of the stadium.

Skip's eyes went wide.

Walt's heart pounded. He took a deep breath and said, "Did you see the article?"

"About me?" Skip shook his head.

"It ran Thursday."

"I was in Boston."

"I know, but I thought maybe… well, I've got a copy. I can show it to you."

Skip bit his lip and nodded.

Walt almost offered to read Skip the story, but worried that would offend him. Instead, he said, "All good things, I promise. I think you're a savant when it comes to baseball."

"I don't know what that means."

"It's a French word. It means genius."

Skip shook his head. "McGraw didn't let me play today. He said maybe I could pinch-hit, but he put Ott in instead."

"I know." Walt added softly, "What happened in Boston?"

Skip grunted and looked down the hall, where Hornsby was now holding court before a gaggle of other players. "I can't talk about it here."

"Meet me tonight. Out somewhere. Just to talk. I promise I won't print anything."

Skip looked around, looked at anything except Walt, and then said, "Yes, I… yes. Where?"

"Speakeasy on West Third. Is it okay if I write it down?"

Skip nodded.

It had been a spontaneous decision to invite Skip to a place so close to his apartment. So Walt wrote down the speakeasy's address and drew a little map. "Take the Sixth Avenue El to Bleecker. It's not far from there."

Walt watched Skip stare at the map, apparently trying to decipher it. It occurred to him that Skip might have a learning disorder of some type. His intelligence was apparent, particularly when he talked about baseball, so it struck Walt as odd that he couldn't read well. But there had been a fascinating article Walt had read not long before about dyslexia that had detailed a teenager of normal intelligence who nevertheless struggled with reading. The scientist who wrote about the case thought the teenager had something wrong with his brain that made it difficult to process information correctly.

It brought everything Skip had said during their night together into clearer focus. Skip thought himself stupid, but he really wasn't.

"I think I can find it," Skip said.

"Worst case, you can ask for directions. Oh, I have a telephone, too. You can call me anytime. I wrote the number there at the bottom."

Skip folded the piece of paper and put it in his pocket. He looked over Walt's shoulder, so Walt glanced back and saw that Hornsby's party was breaking up.

"I'd better go," Walt said, "but I will see you tonight, all right?"

"A word, Littlefield!" Hornsby bellowed.

Skip nodded. The faintest of smiles danced across his lips. "Tonight. Yes." Then he went to talk to Hornsby.

Chapter 5

SKIP liked the elevated trains a little better than the subway, though he didn't think he would ever get used to the noise. At least the elevated trains were above ground, and the open windows let in plenty of air. In the subway, Skip always worried he would suffocate.

He got off the train at Bleecker and walked down the stairs to street level. He was immediately turned around. Three different streets all seemed to intersect at this spot, and Skip had no idea which turn to make.

He pulled Walt's piece of paper out of his pocket. Walt had even drawn a triangle with a cross on it, which helped Skip figure out that he should walk in the direction of the church on the corner. He took a deep breath and followed the directions.

He rounded a corner onto West Third Street and saw Walt standing there, leaning against the building's brick exterior. Even with his hat pulled over his eyes and a cigarette dangling from his lips, Skip would have recognized him. He knew the shape of Walt now, knew his stance, knew the details of his lanky body.

Skip cleared his throat. Walt looked up and smiled. He flicked at the brim of his hat with his finger, revealing his face. "Glad you could make it. I was worried you'd get lost."

"Your little map helped."

"I should hope so! I've lived in this neighborhood most of my life. Come on."

Skip followed Walt into what looked like a restaurant, but instead of stopping to eat, Walt led Skip to the back. There, Walt knocked on the door three times in quick succession and then twice slowly. A piece of metal slid across the top of the door and a set of eyes gazed out.

"Where were you last night?" said a voice from behind the door.

"The Ariston Hotel," said Walt.

The eyes disappeared. A moment later, the door swung open. Walt greeted the guy guarding the door amiably and then led Skip down a staircase. When they got to the landing, Skip asked, "Did you know that guy?"

"No. That's just the password procedure here."

The room was dimly lit, but before Walt even found them a table, Skip could tell he was in a room almost exclusively populated by men. There was a woman with a sweet, melodious voice crooning softly with a band in the corner, and another dancing with a man in front of the band, but otherwise, Skip didn't see anyone female.

That wasn't too strange. Skip had been to plenty of male-only spaces in Columbus. But he'd thought the women of New York were more free than that, were allowed in more places. He glanced back toward the man dancing with the woman near the band. He had a narrow waist and wide hips and some bulk at his chest that the white shirt he had on was fighting to contain. There was certainly no Adam's apple.

Where had Walt brought him?

They found an empty table and sat together. Walt did some kind of song and dance with a waiter, and soon enough they were supplied with glasses containing alcohol of some sort. Walt sniffed his and gave a tiny sip.

"The rotgut here is a little suspicious. I think it's whiskey," Walt said. "But I couldn't swear to it. It kind of tastes like it was made in a bathtub, soap and all."

Skip held the glass to his nose and sniffed it. It smelled off and was harsh on his nose. "Do you think this coffin varnish is safe to drink?"

"I don't see anyone dying."

Skip took a sip and thought there was something odd about the taste, like whiskey mixed with detergent. Maybe it would be better to just pretend to drink it and keep his wits about him, especially given what had happened the last time he'd gone with Walt to a speakeasy.

They were silent for a moment. Skip was hoping Walt would postpone asking about Boston, but naturally the next thing out of Walt's mouth was "So what happened in Boston? And don't say nothing, because I know that's not true."

"What do you mean?"

"I realize I've only seen you play once, but between seeing you and talking to you, I know you have a real aptitude for the game. I listened to the radio broadcasts of a couple of the games in Boston, and I could tell you weren't playing well. So what happened?"

Skip hesitated to answer. He wanted to be honest—and couldn't think fast enough to come up with a lie anyhow—but it was a lot to confess. Skip changed the subject. "What did you say in your article?"

Walt's eyebrows shot up, but then he nodded. "You want to know if you can trust me." He reached into his jacket and extracted a folded-up newspaper page. "Take a look."

Skip had to concentrate, but he read that the headline said, "New Rookie Could Be Giants' Ticket to Victory." He very slowly looked over the first paragraph, willing the words not to flip around on the page. "Skip Littlefield is a quiet man from Ohio, new to New York and wide-eyed to its splendors." He got stuck on that last phrase because he wasn't sure what it meant. He sighed and kept reading. "He also knows more about baseball and this year's NL teams than any other person in the game."

He continued to read, but kept getting frustrated, coming up against unfamiliar words and realizing it was taking him a long time. He glanced up at Walt, who was looking at him expectantly. That only served to make Skip more self-conscious.

Still, he was relieved. "You didn't say anything about—" Skip held a hand to his chest and then gestured toward Walt. He had already known Walt hadn't printed anything incriminating, because no one had said anything in the almost week since the article had been published, but it was nice to have that confirmed.

"I don't peddle in petty gossip, Skip. Well, not often, anyway. And I wouldn't print something like that. Partly because it would implicate me also, but partly because it's not fair and it's not anyone else's business."

Skip nodded and handed the article back.

"Did you finish it? I said a lot of nice things about you."

"I can't finish it." That was a hard thing to admit, but it would have taken Skip all night to read the whole thing.

Walt nodded. "Well. Maybe it won't amount to anything, but it's some good press, both for you and for the Giants. John McGraw liked the article."

"He did?"

"Yes. I talked to him before the game today. He has faith in you too, you know. He pulled you from the lineup because he thought you might have been overthinking something and you needed a break. But that's not it, is it?"

Walt had gotten them right back around to the question at hand. "No," Skip said.

Walt's face softened. "You can tell me."

Skip took a moment to think about whether he could trust Walt. He thought maybe he could. Plus, he wanted something to happen here. Something had to. This was the crux of his problem, the waiting and wondering and wanting, the not being able to tell what was right or what he should do.

"I was distracted," Skip said.

"By what?"

"You. I couldn't stop thinking about you."

IT HAD been a risk bringing Skip to Julian's. The speakeasy had been running out of the basement of the rotating restaurants at street level since Prohibition began, and somewhere along the line it had become the Village's haven for the queer set. Walt loved this place, though he hadn't come in a while, preferring to make himself seen in Times Square, thinking that lent him a mask of sorts to cover what he really wanted to be doing. Most of the faces in tonight's crowd at Julian's were strangers, but the people he did know were all people he trusted.

Walt sensed Skip knew what this place was about, and he seemed unfazed. Perhaps that was what gave him the courage to make his confession.

"Me?" Walt asked, still astonished.

"I was… confused."

"What confused you, exactly?"

Skip looked around the room. Walt didn't like this tendency of Skip's to look around when he was nervous, because it made it harder to read his moods. Then Skip said, "I was appalled by my own behavior that night we went out last week."

"Why? You did nothing embarrassing."

"Yes, I did. I made a complete fool of myself. I risked baseball, the only thing I'm any good at. I'm glad you wrote a nice story about me, but what if you hadn't? What if I got fired?"

"You won't. I wouldn't do that to you."

"I know that now. I didn't know that when I was on the train up to Boston. I just got to thinking about all the stupid things I'd let myself do. But more than that, I couldn't stop thinking about you and how much I wanted to see you again."

That was more like it. Walt smiled. "I thought about you a lot, too. Almost constantly."

"You did?"

"Yes. I wish I could have seen you play today."

"Maybe tomorrow."

"I'll be there."

Skip took a tentative sip of his drink. He winced and put it back down. "I need to do something about this."

"The bad hooch?"

Skip laughed and shook his head. "No. This… whatever I'm feeling. I don't like it."

"What did you have in mind?" Walt asked, wondering if his instincts were right.

"I don't know what to do."

"This place is safe," Walt said. "Everyone here is like us. You can be honest."

Skip looked around with a frown on his face. Walt looked too, hoping to understand what Skip saw. Walt saw men in couples or small groups, sitting around tables, talking or touching. The mood seemed somber tonight, which was unusual, but maybe it was the soft music from the band making everyone quiet and introspective.

"What is it that you want?" Walt asked. "If, for just a moment, the outside world did not exist, what would you want most in the world?"

Skip leaned back for a moment. Then he leaned forward. He spoke softly. "Baseball. And you."

Walt took a chance and kissed Skip. This kiss was just as magical as the first had been, one for the record books, as far as Walt was concerned. It was slick and hot and soft and sweet. Walt lifted his hand to cup Skip's cheek and leaned into it more, enjoying the way Skip pressed back, how their lips slipped together easily.

Skip pulled away and then looked around with wide eyes.

"No one is paying attention to us," Walt said, "and if they were, they don't care that we're two men. Stop worrying."

"It doesn't feel right to do that in public."

Walt understood that. "I'll tell you what we should do. I live two blocks from here. You should come with me to my apartment." At Skip's increasingly shocked and worried expression, Walt said, "Nothing will happen unless you want it to. We can have a drink or we can talk or we can do… other things."

Skip took a series of deep breaths. Walt's insides began to churn as he waited for Skip to make a decision. He wanted Skip, all right, wanted to get underneath the outdated suit and see what that body looked like. But there was something really special about this man, too, something Walt hoped to tap into. Skip intrigued him, kept him interested, kept him guessing. It was hard to surprise a man like Walt, and yet Skip had daily since the moment they'd met, even while he was out of town.

"Yes," Skip said. "Let's go. Before I change my mind."

Walt stood, picking up his hat as he did so. He adjusted the yellow carnation on his lapel so it stood just so. Skip stood too, smoothed the front of his jacket, and then picked up his own hat, the beat-up looking bowler that looked fifteen years old.

"We will discuss your wardrobe at a future date," Walt said.

"What's wrong with my wardrobe?"

"Maybe those old clothes got you by in Ohio, but this is New York."

Skip frowned and looked down at his shirt. Walt thought maybe he hadn't picked the right time to comment on Skip's sartorial choices. He chuckled, trying to lighten the air around them. "Come on."

They left Julian's and walked over to Sullivan, where Walt lived on the top floor of a three-story brick building tucked in off the street. It wasn't glamorous—not like the brownstone off Washington Square Park where he'd grown up—but it was his and it was private.

Walt let Skip into the apartment. Skip looked around, probably both taking it in and avoiding looking at Walt. That was all right; Walt was willing to let things build, to wait until Skip trusted him.

Skip ran his fingers along the edges of Walt's furniture, dragging his fingertips along the top of the sofa, over the little table where Walt ate sometimes, over the desk off to the side and the armoire where Walt kept off-season clothing. He peeked into Walt's rarely used kitchen and glanced toward the bedroom without getting near it. That was probably too dangerous. Walt was content to let Skip explore.

"My apartment is really different," Skip said. "Well, I share it with two other fellas from the team, so it's a mess all the time. This place is so tidy."

"Thanks. I like it." Walt fished for topics of conversation. "Ah. So I've been thinking—"

"I think we should have sex."

Walt's whole body shut down for a moment. "You… Are you sure?"

"What do they call people like us? Queers. Three-letter men. Fags. We're both fags. Right? That's why there's all this, I don't know, stuff… tension between us. I want you so much that it's all I've been thinking about for almost a week. I think we…. I think for me to get my mind back, we have to do this."

Walt wanted that too, but he was still floored by the request. "I appreciate your candor, Skip, I do. I'm glad you feel like you can say these things now that we're alone. And, Lord, I want that too, but—"

"I know I come across as an inexperienced country bumpkin, but I'm not—"

"I know."

Skip shook his head slowly, but then he lunged forward, framed Walt's face in his hands, and then kissed him fervently. Walt sank into it, tasting Skip and that cruddy moonshine from Julian's. He pulled Skip close until their bodies pressed together.

"This might just lodge me further in your brain," Walt pointed out. He smirked. "I am pretty handsome. You might never be able to forget me."

Skip smiled faintly. "Risk I'm willing to take."

Walt laughed. What a strange situation he'd found himself in. He kissed Skip again. They stood close enough together that, when Walt pressed forward and pulled Skip close again, he could feel Skip's hardness against his leg. Christ. No fooling around here. This moment was very real and a little bit dangerous.

No sense in beating around the bush. Walt steered Skip toward the bedroom. When it was clear there was little to no hesitation in Skip, Walt began to take his clothes off as if he were unwrapping a present.

Skip plucked the flower from Walt's lapel and tossed it away. He pushed Walt's jacket off, undid the buttons of his vest, tugged at his belt. Walt kissed Skip and continued to undress him, pulling off his shirt, and then undoing the button on his trousers.

When he got Skip down to his skivvies, Walt murmured, "Thank goodness that suit is off you. It's a terrible crime against fashion."

Skip laughed, though it came out sounding a little choked. "You really do care about what I wear."

"No, I care about good clothes. Which those are not. But no matter. You aren't wearing them anymore."

"Maybe we should get these nice clothes off you faster."

They tugged and wrestled until they were both nearly naked and panting on the bed. Walt kissed Skip deeply, ran his hand through Skip's wavy blond hair, pressed his erection against Skip's thigh. He wasn't sure exactly what Skip had in mind, though he didn't care that much. He'd do anything if it meant a night with Skip.

"I want to see…." Skip ripped off Walt's undershirt with no further explanation. He ran his hands up Walt's chest. "Yes," he whispered. "Yes, this is what I want." He moved one hand up Walt's back, up his neck, into his hair, and they kissed again, hot and sweet.

"What do you want?" Walt asked, his breath nearly gone.

"You."

"How do you want me?"

Skip looked up and caught Walt's eye. "I know sometimes men…. I'm not sure I can…."

"Only what you feel comfortable with."

Skip let out a breath and, somewhat to Walt's surprise, pulled Walt into his arms and hugged him close. "Like this. Just like this. Okay?"

The way their skin met, the heat of Skip's breath on Walt's neck, the tangle of limbs, all of these things made Walt's heart beat faster. He understood instantly what Skip wanted and he was happy to give it. "Yes. Like this."

They kissed. Walt hooked his thumbs into Skip's shorts and started to pull them down. As he peeled away the last of Skip's clothing, he took a moment to really look at his body. It was tight and athletic, strong, masculine. He had a dusting of light colored hair over most of his body, concentrated above his cock, which was hard and pink and beautiful. Walt groaned at the sight.

"So sexy," he murmured.

Skip took his turn undressing Walt the rest of the way. He ran his hands over Walt's exposed skin as he slid off his undergarments. He pressed his palms into Walt's chest, ran fingers down the dip in Walt's back, cupped his hands around Walt's ass. When Walt was naked, Skip kissed him again and wrapped a hand around his cock. Skip's hand was warm and calloused and felt so good around Walt's cock that he groaned and bucked against him. He had to take a deep breath to keep from getting carried away.

"Just like this," Skip repeated before kissing Walt again.

Skip thrust his hips against Walt's and then wrapped a hand around both of their cocks. That was everything right there, heat and smooth skin, and Walt was so aroused he ached. His need to find release hit him with an amazing urgency, and he began to thrust against Skip, pushing against his hand and his cock. Skip ground back, sliding against Walt. They found a rhythm and moved together, Skip stroking their cocks together with one hand and touching Walt's chest with the other while Walt ran his hands along any bit of Skip's skin that he could reach.

They fit together so well, Walt couldn't help but think. Skip kept making the sexiest little moans and grunts. The sound and the movement only served to increase Walt's arousal. His blood rushed and his hearing became radio static and then everything was Skip, just the man writhing in his arms, his lips parted and his hips searching for release. Walt put his arms around him and kissed him fiercely, bringing him closer, fusing their bodies together.

Skip let out a guttural moan. Walt tried to catch his gaze. Their eyes met, and Walt could see Skip was losing his hold on the situation. Then Skip's eyes rolled back and he stopped breathing. Walt felt him come, felt that release hot on his own skin. It was enough to send Walt over the edge, and soon release found him, pumped out of him, and he grasped at Skip as he lost his mind.

When Walt came back to himself, he and Skip were still clutching each other and breathing heavily.

Then Skip started to shake.

"Oh. Oh, baby, what is it?" Walt asked. "Shh, it's okay."

Skip pressed his forehead against Walt's collarbone. "That was… was that all right?"

Walt huffed out a laugh. "It was better than all right. What are you… was it bad? Did I hurt you?"

"No. No, Walt, I don't think you could hurt me. I just worried you might regret—"

"No. Never. I could never regret—I could never forget—being with you."

"Really?"

"Of course. Don't ever doubt that. I chose to invite you here knowing full well what would happen. I wanted you. I still want you. I want you to stay here tonight so we can be together again soon. I want to try different things and get to know your body and be with you in whatever ways are possible."

Skip closed his eyes and burrowed his face into Walt's neck. "Thank you," he whispered.

Walt wondered if there was a bad memory there, a coupling that had gone horribly, an abusive lover, if he'd gotten caught. "You're safe with me," Walt said, stroking Skip's hair.

"Walt," Skip said. "Oh, Walt. I…. I've never met anyone like you before."

Walt sighed happily, pulling Skip with him into the bed. "The feeling is mutual."

Skip settled into the bed, curling against Walt. "Just like this," he whispered.

"This is all there is."

"Mmm." Skip shifted a little, getting more comfortable. "I want all those things too, those things you talked about. I don't have your way with words, but I…. I want those things. With you."

"You just said it perfectly."

Chapter 6

THE rest of that July was a whirlwind. McGraw put Skip back in the Giants' lineup and he excelled, hitting the ball more often than not and earning a batting average close to .400. He was pretty good in the field too, making a key play against the Cubs one week and another the next week against the Cardinals. Walt kept saying he couldn't understand why none of the other papers had picked up on what a phenomenon Skip Littlefield was, but the Yankees' Murderers' Row was still dominating the headlines, and even Skip couldn't save the Giants from losing spectacularly a few times in the same period. Skip was overshadowed again when Ty Cobb got his four thousandth hit and that was all anyone could talk about for a few days.

Skip didn't mind. It gave him some freedom to behave how he wanted, to play baseball for the love of the game instead of to win, and to spend as much free time as he could with Walt. They went to clubs and speakeasies, they went to shows on Broadway, and they made love passionately in Walt's apartment whenever Skip was in town.

Skip's roommates started teasing him about all the nights away. Skip just shrugged and said he had a sweetheart who lived in the Village—technically true—and he didn't want to jinx a good thing by introducing said sweetheart to his friends just yet. Joe seemed to get that, since he'd been secretive about his girl Estelle when they'd first gotten together. Mickey had made a joke about how he didn't think Skip had it in him to be spending the night with a young lady—to which Skip had replied without thinking, "It's not what you think"—and then a lot of ribbing had ensued. The teasing made Skip uncomfortable, but it seemed mostly harmless.

One night, Walt took him up to the Cotton Club to hear Duke Ellington play. Skip had never seen anything like it. The floor show was a stage full of chorus girls with skin much darker than Skip's, who twirled around in a choreographed dance wilder and racier than anything Skip had ever seen before. When the audience was invited to dance, a pretty white girl asked Skip to go with her, and he obliged, although he would have rather danced with Walt. Still, he'd never heard jazz like this, and he'd never seen such marvelous dancing.

He was feeling giddy and overwhelmed as he sat with Walt at a table in the corner. "This is fantastic!" he said.

Walt smiled broadly. "I really love the music here. I'm happy you're enjoying yourself."

Skip sighed happily and sat back in his chair. He reached over and squeezed Walt's hand briefly before letting it go. The last week had been beyond belief, with Skip still wondering what Walt saw in him, why Walt wanted to spend so much time together. Not that Skip was complaining; he liked Walt a great deal and he was having a lot of fun.

"Did you see the *Mirror* today?" Walt asked.

"No." Skip laughed, because he knew Walt knew better.

"Oh, there was a story about the National League I enjoyed. A lot of predictions for the season. I thought it might be interesting to get your take on some of them."

"What were the predictions?"

"Pirates, Cardinals, Giants. Any of those could win the pennant. The Cubs are maybe in there, but probably not."

"Seems about right." Skip didn't think much of the Cubs' chances, but they were definitely a tough team to beat.

"You do know that the main reason the Giants are even in it is you."

Skip scoffed. "That's hardly true. There's Hornsby and Bill Terry and…." He let it go and looked at Walt. "You really believe that, don't you?"

"I'm apparently the only one who does. You've really got something, though. You'll go far. People will remember you."

Skip sipped his drink and shook his head.

"This reading thing," Walt said. "I've been thinking about it. You can tell me to buzz off, but I thought maybe…. I mean, you said the words jump around on the page sometimes, right?"

Skip wondered what that had to do with anything. He shrugged. "Sometimes." He decided to play like this situation didn't bother him, though he did not want to discuss reading with Walt.

"There are disorders, real problems in the brain that can cause that. That is, there's nothing wrong with you. Over time, you could learn to read better. You're not stupid. You're just… built a little differently."

This conversation was making Skip nervous. He looked around the room. Everyone seemed to be intent on their own conversations or the band or the flurry of activity on the dance floor. Skip lowered his voice. "How can you say that? I'm broken. Never amounted to anything. I can't fix things. I have trouble reading. I couldn't finish school. I want… the wrong things." And that was how he felt, deep in his soul.

Walt smiled. "You're not broken. I still believe now what I believed that first night we talked. You're a genius in some ways. Do you think I'm smart?"

"Of course."

"I can't fix a car. I've never even driven a car. Who needs one when you've got the subway?"

"Oh."

"I can't hit a baseball, either. Never was any good at the sport. I just like to watch it." Walt reached under the table and squeezed Skip's knee. "No one was put on this earth to be great at everything. Each of us has our own ability that makes us special. For you, it's baseball. But you're great in other ways too. You're sweet and caring and…." Walt looked around and lowered his voice. "You're sexy and funny and smart in your own ways. And you don't think of me as broken, do you?"

"No, of course not." Skip really didn't, either.

"Maybe we're both a little bit bruised and bent, but in similar ways, don't you think?"

Skip gazed at Walt, his heart in his throat. How could Walt see all these things in him? Had anyone ever seen these things in him?

"I wish I could kiss you right now," Skip whispered.

Walt smiled. "I wish that too. Maybe we should get out of here so we can go somewhere we can do that."

Skip laughed. "Maybe we could listen a little while longer. But thank you."

WALT brought Skip to the new Saks Fifth Avenue department store to buy a new suit. Walt offered to pay, but Skip insisted he buy it himself with his baseball salary. His rent was cheap in the shared apartment, and he was drawing a decent, although not great, salary from the Giants, so he had money squirreled away.

"Wide-leg trousers are fashionable this year," Walt explained as they walked together. "In the magazines, they say you should wear a white carnation tucked into the top buttonhole of your jacket, but you can see how well I follow that advice." Today, the flower vendor on Forty-Third Street had carnations in a deep violet color, so Walt had pinned one of those to his lapel before leaving Times Square to meet Skip.

"This is important to you," Skip said as he touched the sleeve of a lovely chocolate-brown suit jacket.

"I like fashion," Walt said. "Well, specifically, I like beautiful things. Present company included."

Skip blushed.

"I realize that, as an athlete, you don't have to have the nicest wardrobe. The public will forgive you if you wear that beat-up old bowler hat everywhere." Walt flicked at the brim of the hat, setting it askew. "But humor me. Let me dress you. You look good now, but think about how great you *could* look." Skip laughed and set his hat to rights.

"I don't really care," said Skip.

"Hmm." Walt didn't believe that. He did care, at any rate. "Well, it's summer. We need lighter fabrics. Maybe this gabardine."

And so they shopped. Walt enlisted the help of a handsome salesman who clearly knew what he was doing. They put Skip in several different suits, finally settling on a light-brown wool and a more classic black suit, both cut nicely. A tailor appeared and took Skip's measurements. Walt picked out a few Arrow shirts, showing the sharp points on the collar to Skip. He also bought a new straw boater hat with a bright red ribbon on it for himself. That last purchase was just for fun.

It brought Walt great pleasure to put Skip in more fashionable clothes and, as predicted, Skip was even more handsome in a nice suit instead of an old, worn suit or a baseball uniform. More than that, he was still bashful, blushing whenever Walt or the salesman complimented him, which Walt found endearing.

Walt wore his new hat outside and grinned at the sunshine and his companion. They walked down Fifth Avenue, looking for a place to eat. They stumbled into a cafeteria—half the places to eat in the city seemed to be cafeterias these days, much to Walt's chagrin—and ate a quick dinner.

It had been a nice day, Walt reflected as they rode the elevated train downtown to his apartment. Skip had been smiling through a lot of it.

"I hope you don't mind that I'm doing all this," Walt said. "I suppose I'm grooming you a little to be the next big *it* baseball star. How old is Babe Ruth now? Early thirties, I believe. And he wasn't much of a student either, as I recall. You and the Babe have a lot in common, actually. So who knows? In five years, that could be you."

Skip shook his head. "I'll never be like Babe Ruth."

"Why? You hit as well as he does."

"No, I mean… he's everywhere. The Sultan of Swat. That's what they call him, right?" Skip glanced around the train car. "Remember last week when we saw him? That getup was ridiculous. Who wears a fur coat in July? And the woman he was with was not his wife."

"True. I've seen photos of Helen, and that is not what she looks like." Walt smirked. "You're right. I can't imagine you parading around with women who are not your wives."

Skip laughed and shook his head. "I don't want that kind of attention. You know that."

"I do know that. But you could be a more quiet presence on the field, like Gehrig, and play well and get the accolades. Get stories written about you."

Skip's star shone so brightly. Walt understood why he didn't want to be in the spotlight, but he deserved credit for playing the game so well, more credit than a lot of the media were giving him considering he was still being labeled a fluke.

Skip kept shaking his head. "You see things in me that nobody else does. I just don't understand."

Walt shrugged. "It's a gift."

Chapter 7

AFTER a Wednesday game, John McGraw pulled Skip aside. They wound up in an office, seated with Mr. Thompson, who Skip recognized as one of the team lawyers. The bottom dropped out of Skip's stomach as he looked around the room, fearing a number of possibilities: he was being fired or traded; he might have to move out of New York and away from Walt; his affair with Walt had been discovered. He wiped the cold sweat from his brow and looked at McGraw, hoping this would be over quickly.

McGraw glanced at Mr. Thompson and waited expectantly.

"You've done some great things on this team," McGraw started.

This is it, Skip thought. *They're going to kick me off the team.*

Logically, he couldn't think of a reason why he would lose his slot on the team. He'd been playing well lately. He got along well with his teammates. He was queasy anyway. Thompson said, "The article about you in the *Times* was quite complimentary."

"Oh." Skip wasn't sure what he was supposed to say.

"It was good press for the Giants, certainly. And Walter Selby has always been a friend to the team."

Skip tried not to react to the utterance of Walt's name. He shifted in his seat, uncomfortable and now even more worried about the direction this was going.

"You've been seen around town with him a lot," Thompson said.

"We, ah, became friends after the article," Skip said. That seemed reasonable. He wasn't sure if these men would know more than that was going on with Walt. In Skip's experience, people tended not to jump to those sorts of conclusions, although now he worried it was simply his friendship with Walt that had gotten Skip in trouble. Maybe players weren't supposed to fraternize with the press. Maybe they were on to Walt.

"You're young and new to the city," said McGraw. "So you may not realize this. But Walt Selby is—"

McGraw closed his mouth abruptly and looked at Thompson, who shrugged. "They called him the Dapper Dandy for a while." Then, more slowly, Thompson added, "He does add a bit of style and class to the sport."

"He's a fag," McGraw said.

Skip felt like he'd been punched. He sat back in his chair, absorbing some of the venom in McGraw's pronunciation of that word. *Fag*. He'd just used it with Walt not that long ago, but it wasn't a friendly word, not in this context.

"I know this may come as a surprise," said Thompson.

"You know what that means, kid?" said McGraw. "Walt Selby, he's a swell guy, but at the end of the day, he spends time in the company of other men. You get it?"

"I understand," said Skip.

Thompson sat up and leaned forward. "Has he tried anything with you?"

"No. No, of course not," Skip said. "Just showed me around the city. Took me to a few shows."

"He's got his sights on you," McGraw said. "You gotta be careful, Skip. You're too trusting."

"You can't be seen with him anymore," Thompson said. "There will be talk. People will get ideas."

Skip bristled at that. He couldn't be seen with Walt anymore? How did going places with him in public matter? "But he's my friend."

"I appreciate that," Thompson said. "But during the regular season, when all eyes are on us? Particularly now that we're in the pennant race? The team doesn't need any negative press. It's bad enough that we have to compete with the Yankees for reporters' attention. If the story becomes a rumor about our rookie hitter and not about how well we're playing, that's bad news for the team."

"That big ape Ruth is stealing all the attention," McGraw said. "He's a clown, but the fans and the reporters like him. You do anything that brings bad attention to this team, well…."

"You understand our concern, surely," said Thompson.

"The owner will take action," said McGraw. "Hell, I'll do something. This team, we've beat the Yankees a time or two in the

World Series, and I intend to do it again. But that's not possible if you do something that will bring shame on the team."

Skip looked between the two men. He couldn't believe this was happening. "So you could fire me just for spending time with a friend?"

"Walt Selby is not your friend," said McGraw. "A man like that… he's not the sort of man one calls a friend."

Skip felt backed into a corner. He thanked McGraw and Thompson for sharing this information with him. In a daze, he walked back to the locker room and changed into street clothes. All the time he'd spent with Walt really experiencing the city flashed through his mind, all the dancing and shows and booze. He'd seen bands play marvelous music, he'd danced until his feet were sore, he'd gotten a little zozzled on moonshine, and through all of it, Walt had been at his side, steering the way and showing him things he'd never seen before. But now he couldn't be seen with Walt anymore?

As Skip suspected might happen, Walt was waiting for him when he left the locker room.

"I can't talk here," Skip said under his breath.

Walt nodded. "Did something happen?"

Skip shrugged. He couldn't get into it now, not when people were just around the corner who could watch him.

"Skip," Walt breathed.

"Not now."

It wasn't just that he didn't feel safe talking to Walt in the stadium. Skip couldn't handle this situation. He was inches from screaming at someone, from losing his grip, from losing his mind. He had too much dancing around his head, too many thoughts about what he should do and what he wanted. He wanted Walt, but he wanted baseball too, and when forced to choose one over the other, he couldn't decide which he wanted more.

So he walked out of the stadium.

AT HOME that night, Skip sat on the couch and listened to the radio while Joe and Mickey buzzed around. He realized he hadn't had a quiet night at home since he'd met Walt. It should have been a relief, but instead, he felt sad and a little empty. He'd used the public telephone in the hall and managed to catch Walt at home, but all he'd told Walt was "I can't tonight." Walt had tried to argue, and then he'd asked what was wrong, but Skip had just murmured, "Nothing," and hung up.

The apartment was hot. Joe joked about getting the older woman who lived in the apartment downstairs to make them some lemonade. Mickey told him not to be an idiot. Skip just sat on the sofa with a wet towel pressed to his head. He let the moderately cool water drip down his face, which gave him a little relief.

"No plans with your sweetheart tonight?" Mickey asked.

"Nah," Skip said.

"Sometimes you do need a break," said Joe. "I'm going to go see Estelle tonight, though. She wants to go to this speakeasy on the West Side that's supposed to have some really great white lightning. Rum right off the boats that are floating offshore. It's probably bull, but worth a shot, right? I heard Babe Ruth likes to drink at this place."

"The Bambino likes to drink any place," Mickey said.

"You boys want to come along?" Joe asked.

Mickey shrugged. "Sure, maybe. Where is this place?"

"Uh. Eleventh Avenue, I think. Off Fifty-Seventh Street."

"Think there will be any pretty flappers there?"

Skip laughed despite his sour mood. "Aren't all flappers pretty?"

Mickey balked. "No. Definitely not. There was this bird at the place Joe and I went last week.... What was that place called?"

"Dunno. I didn't like it, though. Pretty sure the Mob runs it."

Mickey shrugged. "The Mob owns most of the speakeasies, Joe. Don't be an idiot. Anyway, there was this bird, and she was tall as the Woolworth Building, and I thought, that's a doll I'd like to know. So I walked up to her and I says, 'I'm Mickey. I play for the Giants,' and so she turns to me, and... oh. What a face this girl had."

"She was a bug-eyed Betty," said Joe. His eyes were wide, like he was still a little traumatized by it. "That's why I love Estelle. She's a swell gal, but she's also beautiful."

"You're a lucky man," said Mickey.

"I mean, she's not *just* beautiful. She's really smart, too. We have a good time together."

Skip sighed. He pulled the towel away from his face. The little bit of remaining water was too warm to cool him off. "I'm not feeling so well, boys. I think I'll stay in tonight."

"Suit yourself," said Joe. "Go get dressed, Mickey. We'll find you a pretty girl for the night."

Joe and Mickey retreated to their respective rooms to change for the night. Skip stayed on the couch, wearing old pants and an undershirt, the water from the towel rapidly drying. He gave some thought to going out with Joe and Mickey. It could be fun. They'd gone out together a lot when Skip had first moved in. Mickey, who had a face only a mother could love, often struggled with talking to women, for all his bravado. Joe was so head over heels over Estelle that he hardly saw other women. Skip was happy to hang in the background, or to be polite to any women who approached him. He envied Joe and Mickey their desires, wishing he could make himself like women the way they did, but that part of him didn't seem to exist.

While part of Skip did want to go out that night and see what kind of trouble he could find, part of him also wanted to sit at home and wallow in the impossible decision he had to make.

He opted for wallowing. Joe and Mickey left a short time later. Skip turned up the volume on the radio.

Mr. Thompson—and John McGraw, for whom Skip had a lot of respect, even with his gruff demeanor—had basically given Skip an ultimatum. They couldn't have known what kind of bind they were putting him in. If Skip and Walt had been just casual friends, Skip would have been able to make that decision easily: baseball ruled Skip's life.

But Walt was not just a casual friend. Skip had never known anyone like Walt, had never had a regular thing with another man. He'd never had sex so good. He'd never had as much fun with anyone else. No one had ever seen Skip the way Walt did. When Skip was with Walt, he felt smart and good and handsome. He felt whole instead of broken. He felt better than he felt when he was alone.

How could he give up Walt? Walt made him a complete person.

But how could he give up baseball?

He spent the night brooding and listening to staticky jazz. Duke Ellington and his band took over the airwaves, reminding Skip of the nights he'd gone to the Cotton Club with Walt. He thought about nights spent with Walt listening to this kind of music live and in person, which made him think about nights spent in Walt's bed, making their own kind of music.

Skip felt sick at the idea of having to make a decision.

The music on the radio changed to a song Skip recognized as Gershwin's "The Man I Love." Skip closed his eyes and lay against the couch. The room was so hot it threatened to suffocate him, which only made Skip feel worse. He sank into the couch cushions. He listened to the song, heard the lyrics, and frowned.

Walt was the man Skip loved.

Love was supposed to be a good feeling, wasn't it? Something happy and joyful, something worth celebrating. But at the realization that he was in love with Walt, all Skip felt was sadness and fear. He felt broken again. There was no way for him to ever have what he wanted, no way for him to celebrate this love. Was there?

He had no idea what to do.

Chapter 8

IT HAD been two weeks since Walt had spoken to Skip at all. He was worried now, convinced something was terribly wrong. He'd tried to speak to Skip a few times at the stadium, but Skip had blown by him each time. He'd tried telephoning. In desperation, he'd even written a letter, albeit an ambiguously worded one he doubted Skip would or could read. Walt tried to piece together the last night they'd spent together, looking for where things had gone wrong, trying to figure out what he had done that had driven Skip away.

It was maddening not to be able to speak to Skip. Walt felt like some of the color had drifted out of his life. How could such a thing have happened? Walt wasn't a man who let himself get tied down. He'd had regular sex partners before, men he spent time with, romantic attachments, but none who'd affected him the way Skip did. In Skip's absence, he'd gone out the way he had before he met Skip, but it wasn't the same. He worked and did some of the best writing of his life. He still credited Skip with being part of the Giants' strategy for winning the pennant.

He left the newsroom and let himself feel some of the sadness he'd been keeping at bay ever since Skip had basically disappeared. It was so strange. Walt had really thought they had something.

He ran into Reinhold in the elevator. "Your carnation is looking a little droopy," Reinhold said, pointing at Walt's lapel.

Walt looked. Indeed, the petals were browning and wilting a bit. Then he realized it was the same yellow carnation he'd put there in the morning. "I suppose I forgot to change it."

Reinhold laughed. "Really, Selby? In the four years I've known you, that is the one thing you do like clockwork every day. You never have a droopy flower on your lapel. The Dapper Dandy always looks impeccable."

Walt bristled inwardly at the moniker and the teasing he was getting from Reinhold. Most days he could take it, he could even dish it out right back, but today he was not in the mood. He rubbed his forehead. "Guess I had a rough day."

"Giants lose a whopper?"

"They won today, actually." But Skip hadn't talked to him after the game. Again.

"Well, gosh, Walt. Did your mother die? Why the long face?"

"It's nothing."

He was saved from having to explain by the elevator opening. He gave a little wave and then hurried through the lobby and plunged into the Times Square traffic, leaving Reinhold behind.

Walt's apartment seemed especially empty when he got home. It looked sad, monochromatic, disappointing. Walt halfheartedly tidied it, but then gave up. He walked over to his bookcase and took a few books off it, hoping for a distraction. He had a copy of Fitzgerald's *The Beautiful and the Damned*, which he tried reading for a while, but he couldn't focus. He kept thinking about Skip and wondering what had gone wrong.

And then there was a knock at the door.

Walt had hope but low expectations as he went to the door, guessing his visitor was likely one of his neighbors needing something—money or a cup of sugar or whatever fool thing one of them could pester him about. He opened the door to Skip.

Skip looked bereft. His hair was mussed, he had dark circles under his eyes, and he looked even rougher than he had at the end of that day's game. The first thing he did was put his arms around Walt and hug him tight.

When Walt heard the gasp of someone who was about to start sobbing, he pulled Skip into the apartment and kicked the door closed.

"Oh, Skip. Oh, baby, I missed you," Walt murmured. "Where have you been?"

"Give me a minute," Skip said, his face pressed into Walt's shoulder. "Just let me hold you for a minute."

Walt held Skip right back, hugging him tightly and memorizing the moment: Skip's smell, the warmth of his body, the way he fit against Walt, the sounds he made. This felt fleeting, like Skip might be a figment of Walt's imagination, destined to disappear again quickly and leave Walt with empty arms.

Eventually, Skip pulled away and said, "I'm so sorry I haven't been able to talk to you. I still don't know what to say, but I had to see you. I couldn't stay away any longer."

"What happened?"

Skip began to pace. "Giants management said I can't be seen with you anymore because they know you're… well, you know what you are. I could lose my job if they catch me with you again, if we continue to draw attention to ourselves. They're making me choose, Walt. I have to choose between you and baseball."

Walt understood instantly. "They talked to you two weeks ago?"

Skip nodded.

"Oh, baby." Walt reached for him.

Skip stepped back. "John McGraw and the lawyers, they don't know what a sacrifice they're asking me to make. What they see when they look at me is a young, inexperienced boob who is new to the city and doesn't know the ways of the world. They see the kid they think I am being led astray by a man they don't approve of. They don't know the real truth, and I can't tell them. But I can't make this choice. It's all I've been able to think about for two weeks, and I just can't decide. I can't give up baseball, but I can't lose you, either."

"What exactly did they tell you?"

"I can't be seen with you." Skip began to pace. "They threatened me with my job if I continued to spend time with you in public. Said I couldn't get any bad attention, especially not with the way the Yankees are playing. John McGraw wants us to win another World Series and thinks I could cause problems if the press says bad things about me." He stopped moving and looked at Walt. "He called you a fag."

"I suppose that's not a secret."

Skip gaped at Walt. "It doesn't bother you that everybody knows?"

"It bothers me that people condemn us. My behavior has never hurt anybody."

Skip resumed pacing. "What can I do, Walt? Is there something I don't see?"

Walt gestured toward his sofa as a method of stalling while he thought about it. He waited for Skip to sit before he sat as well. He knew he couldn't make Skip give up baseball for his sake. It was not only unfair to Skip, it was unfair to the game. How could Walt presume to pull a player in his prime from the sport? On the other hand, he'd been miserable these past two weeks without Skip. How had this man burrowed his way into Walt's heart so quickly?

Well, the question didn't matter much now. The damage was done and Walt's heart was aching, not just with the potential for what he might lose, but for the decision Skip had been struggling to make.

Walt folded his hands in his lap, unwilling to touch Skip just yet in case he was unable to stop. "I've been covering sports in New York for six years, and I can tell you this: unless your name is Babe Ruth, nobody cares about you during the off-season. There are other sports for reporters to care about. More to the point, a lot of players leave town over the winter."

"All right. I don't see what that—"

"What we need is a temporary solution. So we aren't seen together during the rest of the baseball season. That doesn't mean we can't see each other. You're here now, aren't you?"

"I can't ask you to stop going out. I know you love your nightlife. The booze and jazz and everything."

And Walt would have given it all up in a heartbeat if that was what he had to do to keep Skip.

That was his first thought, anyway, although the longer it sat there, the more he wondered how true it was. Could he give up his life as he'd become accustomed to it? Would leaving the speakeasies and Times Square behind make him resent Skip?

He wasn't convinced that was the real solution, however.

"I do love to go out at night," Walt said. "I will continue to do so. I'm not sure for how long. Maybe a day will come when I'll want to give it up or settle down. But for now, I want to live my life as out in the open as I can. I want to see things and be seen; I want to experience everything the city has to offer." He took a deep breath, feeling like this had gotten a little bit small, that liquor and music were wonderful things, but not essential. What was all that without love, without companionship, without that one person who made you feel complete and alive?

Was that how he felt about Skip?

He wasn't prepared to analyze his feelings that closely. He cared for Skip, but was he willing to make significant changes to his life for the man? He said, "Maybe, just for now, for the next six weeks of the regular baseball season, the two of us only spend time together in private spaces. I don't have to be out in a club or speakeasy to enjoy your company."

Skip scrubbed his face with his hands. "All right. What happens when the season ends? What happens next season?"

Walt was glad Skip wasn't looking at him, because he couldn't keep the surprise off his face. "You think we'll be together that long?"

Skip turned his head, looking at Walt out of the corner of one eye, a little smile on his face. "Well… yes."

Walt's heart seized for a moment. He couldn't begin to guess what was happening here, but he liked it. He smiled back. "So, we take things one day at a time. It's not going to be easy, but there has to be a way."

Skip lunged across the space between them and landed a rough kiss on Walt's lips. Walt put his arms around Skip and held him, though his head still swam with the situation he'd been placed in. There was something about Skip, something Walt wasn't ready to let go of just yet, and he was thrilled that Skip saw them together for the foreseeable future. But this dilemma they'd been pushed into was troubling: Keep their lives as they knew them or choose each other?

He stroked Skip's hair. "I wish you had talked to me sooner. Maybe I could have helped."

"I wanted to work it out for myself." Skip's voice was thick with emotion. "I thought I could figure something out or make a decision. I wanted to decide what was more important before I spoke to you, if it was you or baseball, but I couldn't decide. I'm just so…. I'm too stu—"

Walt put his fingers on Skip's lips. "Don't say stupid. You are not stupid. This is an incredibly difficult decision. I still can't help you make it. All I can do is offer comfort. And that's all I meant. You could have come to me and I would have listened and talked it out with you. That's all."

Skip let out a breath and leaned his head on Walt's shoulder. "I wanted to decide something so you'd think I'm smart."

"I do think you're smart. I told you, you're a goddamn genius."

"What are we going to do, Walt? I don't know what to do."

Walt just held him. "We'll figure it out."

Chapter 9

SKIP didn't think sneaking around was much of a solution.

As September began, baseball season showed no sign of waning. The Giants were still in contention to win the pennant, so there was plenty of media attention on them. But it paled in comparison to the press devoted to the Yankees, who won their one-hundredth game of the season, and Babe Ruth, who was now looking to break the single-season home-run record. The *World* got lips flapping when they declared Lou Gehrig would beat that home-run record before Ruth. Skip was content to let the newspapers hash it out, because at least they weren't talking about him.

Even Walt got bogged down in the baseball happening in the Bronx, writing essays on Ruth and Gehrig instead of sticking with his coverage of the Giants, although he admitted in one of his columns that he was hoping for a Yankees-Giants World Series.

Joe had taken to reading the gossip pages, particularly Walter Winchell's column, which was how Skip knew Walt was still being seen in all the important clubs. Winchell had taken to calling anything Walt said in public "the Dapper Dandy's Discourse" and a fair amount was being implied between the lines. Or so Skip understood, given how the information was filtered through Joe. Skip wasn't sure Joe really understood what Winchell was saying, but Skip had figured out what some of the invented slang Winchell was fond of really meant.

Mickey got it, though. "You were friendly with Selby, weren't you?" he asked over breakfast one morning before a road trip to Philadelphia.

"Yes. But, well. You know. Mr. McGraw thought maybe…."

Mickey nodded knowingly. "Perhaps Selby was sweet on you."

Skip just laughed at that. The statement was so ridiculous, given the truth.

Joe laughed with him. "It's crazy, isn't it? That men can be like that? My brother kept telling me when I moved to New York that I'd run into men like that, but I never did. You, Mickey?"

"Not that I know of."

"But now Skip made friends with this Selby guy."

"Let's talk about something else," Skip said.

Mickey and Joe seemed to interpret the topic change as Skip's discomfort with the idea of a man who was interested sexually in other men. They teased each other about it for a few minutes while Skip ate. By now, they were used to Skip's silences and seemed unfazed by it.

Then Joe said, "I'm asking Estelle to marry me. Day after we get back from Philly, I plan to take her to a swanky restaurant and ask her."

Skip and Mickey congratulated him. It occurred to Skip that this probably meant Joe would be moving out soon.

"Think she'll say yes?" Mickey asked.

Joe chuckled. "She's had wedding bells in her eyes since our third date."

Mickey grinned. "Don't suppose you'll have room for me and Skip in your new house after you get married."

Skip didn't think much of it. Joe would move out and they'd find some other rookie to bunk with them. This very apartment had been lived in by a rotating combination of Giants rookies for the past seven years, and Skip didn't anticipate that changing.

"It's been great rooming with you guys," Joe said. "But if I get married, well, I'll want to spend time with my lady."

"She hasn't said yes yet," Mickey pointed out. "Maybe she's changed her mind. Maybe she's decided Skip is more ideal husband material."

Everyone laughed, though it didn't escape Skip's notice that Joe looked a little worried.

WALT covered the Yankees while the Giants were out of town. The last day of the series, he took a photographer with him, hoping to catch Ruth or Gehrig in action.

It really was a remarkable time to be a baseball fan, Walt couldn't help but reflect. He'd be a Giants fan until his death, but this Yankees team was one of the best baseball teams that had ever existed—even Walt could see that. They were deserving of all the press, as far as he was concerned.

The photographer, a fellow named Lassiter, clicked away as Gehrig went up to bat. Lassiter murmured about the man's beautiful swing. Walt agreed that Gehrig was a pleasure to watch, but he was distracted by all of the personalities in the audience. Among those in attendance at the game that day were Mayor Walker, Governor Smith, and Jack Dempsey. Damon Runyon had wandered in and out of the press box a few times.

Reinhold from the *Times* stumbled in. "How are you, Selby?" he asked.

Walt glanced at Lassiter, who was changing the film in his camera. "I'm all right. Hell of a game, eh?"

"Sure is." Reinhold took a bite out of an apple. With his mouth full, he said, "Heard the Giants won today."

"Not hard," Walt said, watching Tony Lazzeri go up to bat. "Phillies are likely to finish dead last in the National League."

"Your boy Littlefield hit two home runs."

A bit of pride warmed Walt's chest, but he frowned to cover it. "He's not my boy. I just think he's a gifted ballplayer."

"Mmhmm."

Walt assumed Reinhold only thought he knew something, so he shrugged it off and went back to watching the game. Lassiter got back to the business of taking photographs.

Surprising no one, the Yankees won the game. Gehrig, Ruth, and Lazzeri hit a home run each, which the crowd ate up. Walt enjoyed the game, but was feeling a little introspective, missing Skip and wishing they could watch a game like this together. Of course, the issue here was not just the moratorium on their being seen together in public, but also the fact that Skip was currently in Philadelphia. The Giants' travel schedule during the regular season was another factor in the negotiation of this relationship, something that hadn't really occurred to Walt before. He'd gotten so used to seeing Skip daily during the recent home stay—Skip had spent the night at Walt's more often than not—that he felt at loose ends now.

"The rumor," Reinhold said, "is that everyone is headed to the 300 Club tonight."

Walt had only been to Texas Guinan's club on West Fifty-Fourth Street once before. It was almost too high profile, too exclusive, too hard to get noticed, since many of what Guinan called "butter and egg men"—the wealthiest men in the city—were there competing for attention from the laypeople who clamored to get in. "Everyone?"

"Writers, athletes, probably the mayor. So, yes, everyone."

"Do you plan to go?" Walt asked.

"I thought I might go celebrate this victory. I've been trying to get the Babe's autograph for weeks."

"You can't just track him down after a game and ask for an interview?"

Reinhold shrugged. "Or I could get him to write something outlandish while he's zozzled. Which, let's face it, he will be." Reinhold chuckled. "Anytime he complains about a bellyache, I just assume it's because he drank bad moonshine again."

"That's likely."

Reinhold grinned. "Maybe we should tell these rookies that the real secret to hitting fifty home runs in a season is booze and women."

Walt laughed, but his heart wasn't in it.

He and Reinhold shared a cab back to the city. Walt stared out the window most of the drive, thoughts of Skip plaguing him. What had he gotten himself into? This wasn't temporary, the relationship he had with Skip. Once he'd persuaded Skip they could make a go of things in the long term, it was a serious thing. If Skip were a woman, Walt supposed he'd be thinking about proposing by now. Well, maybe not; this was the twenties, after all, and dating didn't work the same way it had when his parents were young.

"You have a girl, Reinhold?" Walt asked.

A funny smile came over Reinhold's face. "Sure. I got married last year, remember?"

Walt did now vaguely recall that Reinhold had taken a few weeks off in the middle of the baseball season last summer. "What's she like?"

"She's a bearcat. Don't get me wrong, I adore her, but she's a bit of a troublemaker. She doesn't like places like the 300 Club, though, because she doesn't like it when she's not the one in the spotlight." Reinhold laughed.

"And you? How do you feel about being the center of attention?"

"Oh, I'm content to let her have the center. I just like watching."

"Which is why you're the only baseball fan in New York who doesn't have Babe Ruth's autograph on something."

Reinhold shrugged. "Yes, well. *You* clearly like it when you get mentioned in the papers, since you seem to put yourself in a place to do it all the time."

"I like to have a good time."

Reinhold smirked. "I'll bet you do."

"I'm content to fade into the background sometimes."

Reinhold crossed his arms over his chest. "You're a lot like my wife. You thrive on the attention. I don't think you'd really be living if you were home leading quiet and domestic life."

Walt understood that Reinhold meant it in jest, but it struck him how true that was. "Well," he said. "Perhaps we do not always get what we want."

"What does that mean?"

"Nothing," Walt said. "Forget it."

"You have a Babe Ruth autograph?"

Walt laughed at the subject change. "He signed a baseball for me when I started covering baseball for the *Times*. In 1923."

"Hooey," said Reinhold.

THE Giants did not win the pennant that year. After Babe Ruth hit his sixtieth home run, breaking the single-season record, the Pittsburgh Pirates won the National League championship.

Once the season was over, Skip found himself with too much time on his hands. He and his roommates went to a couple of the World Series games, cheering for the Pirates out of principle, although Skip secretly wanted to see that Yankees team triumph. How could they not? He was grateful he'd spent his first season in the National League, avoiding playing against an American League team he didn't think the Giants could beat, even in their dreams.

After the Yankees swept the series in Game 4, Skip and Joe ran into Walt in one of the corridors of Yankee Stadium. Skip wasn't even sure if he was allowed to say hello, although Joe did part of the work for him by offering his hand to shake. Walt shot Joe a surprised look but played along. Then he shook hands with Skip, who took a moment to savor the warmth of Walt's hand in his own.

"Hell of a season," Walt said.

"That it was," said Joe, oblivious.

They chatted for a moment. Skip was unable to contribute anything to the conversation, too nervous to speak. Walt eventually bowed out, saying, "It's been a pleasure talking to you fellas, but I have some business in the press box."

Skip hated that they couldn't even pretend to be friends in public, especially not in a baseball stadium, where even if John McGraw wasn't around—which Skip couldn't swear to—whichever of the Giants' spies who had spotted Skip with Walt the first time could be lurking.

On the other hand, once the Yankees secured their victory, the season was over, and technically Skip wasn't beholden to the Giants' management again until he reported for Spring Training in six months.

It made him wonder what he could get away with. As he and Joe descended the stairs to street level, he thought about whether it would be safe to go with Walt to lower-profile clubs and speakeasies, or if it would be better to just spend nights together at Walt's place with no one else knowing.

"Did Mickey tell you he's headed back to Baltimore for the winter?" Joe asked.

"No."

"He said he missed his family. And now that the season's over, I want to take Estelle to spend time with my family in Long Island for a few weeks. So you'll be holding down the fort for a while. Is that okay?"

"It will give me time to find a replacement for you," Skip said. As they walked to the subway, though, it occurred to him that he'd have a lot of time on his hands in an empty apartment. "Maybe I should get a job or something too."

"Do you need the money?"

Skip shrugged. "It wouldn't hurt."

"You're not going back to Ohio?"

Skip had given some thought to that too. It might have been nice to go see his parents, but on the other hand, all his father would do would be to remind him of his failures. No one thought the baseball career would last longer than a season or two. Skip's father still wanted him to come back to work at the repair shop or else get a "real job" that wasn't playing a game. The last time Skip had been home, he'd just felt stupid the whole time.

He hadn't been feeling stupid much lately. He definitely didn't feel stupid when he was with Walt.

"Nah, I probably won't go to Ohio. There isn't really anything there for me anymore. Plus, now I've got time to spend in New York. I know things are less crazy in the winter than they are in the summer, but I'll be able to explore the city without worrying about having to be ready to play the next day."

Joe frowned. "Like you didn't get out to enough nightclubs this summer?"

"Maybe I'll go see the Statue of Liberty."

Joe laughed. "You're right. That sounds pretty great."

"I'll miss you when you get married, you know. It's been a lot of fun, this summer."

"It has." Joe grinned. "I'll see you on the field, though."

"I hope that's true for a very long time."

Chapter 10

THE Giants were all invited to a party at the Penguin to celebrate the end of the season. Skip put on one of the suits Walt had picked out for him and was making sure his hair was slicked into place in the hallway mirror when Mickey whistled.

"You look darb," Mickey said.

"Thanks. You like the suit?"

"Sure, it's pretty swell. Looks like it cost you a pretty penny."

"I got a deal."

Mickey pursed his lips but nodded and led Skip back into the main room.

Joe joined them at the door before they went out. They took the subway downtown. Skip couldn't help but remember the first time he'd been there with Walt, and it made him feel sad and nostalgic. Tonight, Estelle was waiting for them in front of the club, not Walt, and Joe gave her a hug and a brief kiss before they all went inside together. That display made Skip feel even sadder.

Inside the club, everything was chaos. The space was packed with people. The band was raucous, blaring out fast-tempo jazz. Skip had to shout to cut over the sound of dozens of people chattering away. A mixed crowd of men and women was on the dance floor, doing variations on the Charleston. Servers in bow ties zoomed around, handing out cocktails in tall glasses.

"This is intense," Mickey said, echoing Skip's thoughts.

They spent the first half hour or so mingling. Skip mostly shadowed people he knew; he followed Joe and Estelle around for a while, and then he teamed up with Mickey. He danced with a couple of girls he didn't know. He was congratulated by a few members of the press on an outstanding rookie season. It felt like he was trapped in a whirlwind, but he was enjoying the positive attention.

Then he saw Walt.

It was too much temptation, having Walt in the room with him. He wanted to talk to Walt like he wanted to take his next breath, but he knew couldn't, not here, not with John McGraw just over there and that lawyer Thompson talking to Rogers Hornsby. Not with most of the Giants' owners and managers, the very people who wanted to keep Skip and Walt separated, making their way through the crush. And yet Walt had been invited to this party, like the apple on a tree full of serpents.

That was when Skip decided he'd just about had it. This situation was devastatingly unfair. He'd finally found someone who really saw *him*, who thought he was smart and talented, who made him feel like those things were true, but they couldn't even simply talk to each other in public?

Skip was temporarily paralyzed by anger and indecision. Mickey walked over and said, "Hey, whoa, you all right there, fella?"

"I'm all right."

"Good. This is quite a blow. You ever seen anything like it?"

"No. Can't say I have. Will you excuse me?"

He paused for a moment to screw up his courage. He glanced toward the door, wondering if he could make a getaway if he had to. He scoped out the locations of each person who might object to him being seen with Walt. It felt a little like strategizing before an at bat, figuring out where each player was and what his limits might be in terms of visibility, speed, and skill. Then he took a deep breath and walked forward.

Walt was holding a highball glass and speaking with a woman Skip didn't recognize. She was pretty enough, but out of luck if she wanted something more than conversation with her companion, Skip couldn't help but think.

Walt saw Skip coming. When they made eye contact, Walt's expression turned wary. He leaned toward his companion and said something. She smiled and left.

If Skip's calculations were correct, they were pretty well hidden from most of the Giants' leadership, given that one of the grand columns that dominated the room was currently between them and John McGraw. Skip cared less about that as the minutes ticked by, however, so if someone saw them, he would figure out how to deal with the consequences.

"What do you think of this party?" Skip asked.

"It's hopping," said Walt.

"I, ah, just wanted to say thanks. For everything you did this season."

"You're very welcome." Walt sipped his cocktail. "Is this a good-bye?"

"No, not at all. Far as I'm concerned, this is just the beginning."

Walt grinned. Then he darted his gaze around the room. "Are you, ah, sure it's even a good idea to talk to me?"

"Best idea I had all night."

Walt guffawed. "That can't be true. Seems to me you're taking a pretty big risk even saying hello."

Skip nodded. He whispered, "You're worth the risk."

"Your career is not worth risking."

"That's for me to decide."

Walt frowned. "I want to talk about this later." He looked around. "Although, really, I want to get out of here. This party is pretty stuffy, and I get the distinct feeling the press isn't very welcome, despite getting invitations. Or maybe I specifically am not welcome."

Skip shrugged. That was certainly possible.

"So, I think I will head home shortly."

"Me too," said Skip.

Walt nodded. "You're… Thanks, Skip."

"You're welcome."

WALT had been home about half an hour—his heart racing the entire time—when Skip showed up. The first thing Walt did when he opened the door was grab Skip by the front of his shirt, haul him inside, and plant the kiss to end all kisses on him. Skip put his hands up on Walt's shoulders.

"You're crazy," Walt said when he came up for air. "This is crazy. Why did you come talk to me at that party?"

"I had to."

"You did not have to do any such thing. Why would you jeopardize your career like that?"

Skip pulled away and walked across the room with a huff. "Don't you get it, Walt? What I'm telling you?"

"Apparently, I don't."

Skip crossed his arms. "Fine. Then here it is. I have never in my whole life met anyone who makes me feel the way you do. Did you know that? Not once in my whole life has anyone looked at me and seen anything but a worthless, stupid bum. But you look at me and see a genius."

"Everyone else is wrong."

Skip nodded. "Maybe. I don't know. What I do know is that I believe it when I'm with you. You're the first person in my whole life who really sees *me*. You see the whole me, see right through into the center of me, and you see the real me. I've never had that before."

Walt's stomach flopped. It was a goddamned tragedy no one had ever seen the real Skip before. Skip deserved to be seen, to be loved. He was a phenomenal man, a smart and kind man, a man Walt very much wanted to spend more time with.

"I think…." Skip looked at the floor. "I think I love you, Walt. That's what I'm saying. I don't want to give that up."

Walt's heart shattered then. It was like someone had taken a hammer to his chest and made everything break into pieces with one swift pound. He had never expected this man to fall in love with him. He'd never expected to fall in love with this man. And yet that was what had happened, hadn't it? In all the time they'd been spending together, be it in bed or in a speakeasy or just sitting in this very room laughing and talking, Walt had fallen totally, irrevocably in love with this strange man from Ohio.

"I love you too," Walt said.

"You do?"

"I truly do."

"What about all those other men?"

"What other men? There are no other men in the universe. There's just us. Wasn't that obvious?"

Skip tilted his head and narrowed his eyes. "You were with a lot of men before you met me."

"Sure. But I was looking for you the whole time."

Skip winced. "That's a terrible line."

"I know." Walt grinned. "It's true, though."

Skip laughed and put a hand on his forehead. "Well, then, surely you know now what I was thinking. I stood in that club and I thought, that man right there is the best thing in my life, but I can't even talk to him in a room with two hundred other people? That's ridiculous. So, phooey to what McGraw and Thompson say."

Walt didn't like that Skip was likely feeling especially impassioned after an intense night and too much liquor. At the same time, his heart soared to hear Skip talk this way. "You don't mean that," Walt said. "No matter how great that thought feels, no matter how much I love hearing the words, you can't really mean that you'd risk throwing your whole career away just for me. Nor do I want you to. I want to find a way for us to be together that doesn't keep you from playing baseball."

Skip dropped his hand and walked across the room. He slid his hands around Walt's waist. "You're right, of course. But I thought…. I don't know what I thought."

"We'll find a way, Skip. We will."

"But just so you know, if I really had to choose between love and baseball, I'd choose love. It's even better than I thought it could be. You make me feel like a complete person, Walt. Without you, I'm not all there. You make my game better. You make all my nonsense thoughts go away. Without you, I don't think I even *could* play baseball."

Walt kissed Skip, really kissed him, with tongue and teeth. He licked into Skip's mouth and tasted him, and he put his arms around Skip and held him close. He couldn't fathom someone making that kind of sacrifice for him, but he wasn't about to turn it away.

"You are certifiably insane, you know that?" Walt said.

Skip smiled. "Sure. You are too."

KATE MCMURRAY is a savvy New Yorker and voracious reader and writer. Her books have won several Rainbow Awards. She is currently serving as vice president of Rainbow Romance Writers, the LGBT romance chapter of Romance Writers of America. When she's not writing, Kate works as a nonfiction editor. She also reads a lot, plays the violin, knits and crochets, and drools over expensive handbags. She's maybe a tiny bit obsessed with baseball. She lives in Brooklyn, NY, with a pesky cat.

Website: http://www.katemcmurray.com

Twitter: http://www.twitter.com/katemcmwriter

Facebook: https://www.facebook.com/katemcmurraywriter

Home Field Advantage

SHAE CONNOR

Thanks to D.M. Grace for beta, and to my coauthors for sharing baseball and friendship, two of the best things in the world.

"HEY, Toby!"

Toby looked up from where he was picking up another discarded towel, just in time for a wad of athletic tape to bounce off his forehead, thrown by one of the other clubhouse staffers.

"Funny, Charlie." Toby grabbed the tape and dunked it into the trash can next to him with one hand and, with the other hand, dropped the towel into the large rolling laundry basket he'd been pushing around the room. The clubhouse was a wreck, as it usually was after a game, but Toby and the rest of the staff would have it back in shape in no time.

"So, what are you doing over the break, Tobes?"

The question came from Marty Boynton, the assistant team trainer who'd become a mentor of sorts to Toby. Toby grinned. "As little as I can get away with until Tuesday," he said. "And then it's back here for two days of prep work."

Marty shook his head. "Don't know why you do it at all, when you could be sitting in box seats in Phoenix Tuesday night if you wanted."

Toby shuddered. "Who wants to sit in Phoenix heat this time of year? Besides, you know the clubhouse gets an overhaul during the All-Star break. You've been here almost as long as I have."

"Yeah, but I don't share a last name with the team owner."

Toby sighed. "And that's why I'm down here, and you know it."

They'd had this conversation before. Yes, Toby's grandfather was Ray Macmillan, who'd owned the Atlanta Braves for almost thirty years. And yes, Toby himself would soon own 30 percent of the team, left to him in trust when his parents died almost ten years earlier. For Toby, all that meant was he had to work twice as hard to make others believe he wasn't some rich-kid slacker. That was why he worked with the clubhouse crew and the team trainers while in college, and not in some cushy desk job in the front office—or worse, no job at all.

Marty laughed. "You know I'm just giving you a hard time, kid."

Toby snorted and tossed two more towels into his basket. "'Kid'? What are you, all of thirty?"

"Thirty-one, and that's still ten years older than you, kid."

A noise at the door caught their attention before Toby could respond. He looked over to see a (cute, his mind noted) man stick his head inside, blinking blue eyes against the harsh fluorescent lights.

"Um.... Hi," the man said. "I'm Caleb Browning."

Toby blinked. "Oh, hey, we weren't expecting you yet." He dropped another towel into the basket and headed toward the door. "Come on in. I'm Toby. Did you come straight from the airport?"

Caleb nodded as he stepped inside, looking distinctly uncomfortable, his pale skin lightly flushed. "I got the first flight I could out of Jackson." His voice was raspy, making Toby wonder if he'd napped on the plane or if it was always like that. "Kinda hoped I'd get here before the game ended, but I guess not."

Toby smiled. "Nope. But I can give you the buck tour before you head home. Or to a hotel, I guess? Does the front office know you're here?"

Caleb shook his head, that enticing blush still sitting high on his cheekbones. "No. I didn't call anyone. I just.... I guess I was so surprised to get the call that I figured I'd better get here fast before they changed their minds."

Toby had to laugh at that. He might not work in the front office, but he did keep up with the goings-on of the franchise, including the farm clubs, and he knew about Caleb Browning. One of the rare players who'd finished his degree before heading to the minors, he'd spent the past few seasons as a good defensive catcher with too much tendency to strike out at the plate. This was his first cup of coffee in the majors, all the way up from Double-A in Mississippi, and Toby couldn't blame him for finding it hard to believe he'd actually made it.

"We'll take care of you," Toby assured him. "I'll give you a lift over to the Hyatt. We have a team account with them, so unless they're booked up, they'll get you a room without you having to pay an arm and a leg." Taking a half step back, Toby gave Caleb a teasingly appraising look. "You might need those come Thursday."

Well, Toby had intended the look to be teasing. From the flare of heat in Caleb's eyes, he wasn't so sure he'd succeeded. Half expecting Caleb to get the wrong idea (well, technically the right idea) and lash out, Toby took another step back, but Caleb just nodded, gaze locked on Toby's.

"Sounds good" was all he said, and Toby let out a soft sigh of relief. He kept his sexuality under wraps around the ballpark, even with the way things had been loosening up over the past couple of years. If nothing else, his grandfather didn't know, and Toby didn't want to tell him until it became unavoidable. He wasn't looking forward to that conversation one bit.

"Let me get the last of these taken care of"—Toby waved toward the pile of dirty towels in the basket he'd left behind—"and I'll be right with you. Feel free to have a seat." He nodded toward the small grouping of padded leather seats near the doors, set up during the last renovation as a place for quick postgame clubhouse interviews.

"'Kay." Caleb let the duffel bag over his shoulder slide to the floor, next to the rolling suitcase he'd pulled in, and lowered himself to the cushioned seats as Toby went back to work. Toby rolled his eyes as he gathered up the last of the used towels that lay discarded in front of lockers, despite the open basket he'd left sitting near the showers all day. Ballplayers were generally nice guys, but most of them were used to having someone else clean up after them, especially at the ballpark. Which, of course, was part of why Toby and his coworkers were there.

The last few towels corralled, Toby pushed the loaded laundry cart into its usual spot right outside the showers and gave the room one last look. The other crew members had finished up their tasks and were headed out the door one at a time, a few pausing to speak to Caleb or give him a nod of greeting. Toby suppressed an urge to do one last walk-through, as he often did when they had another game the next day. Thanks to the All-Star break, they didn't play again until Thursday, and the whole place would get a thorough cleaning and restocking before them. He could leave with a clear conscience.

Besides, Caleb was waiting for him.

Toby gave himself a mental shake. Caleb was off-limits for many reasons, not least of which that Toby had no clue about his sexuality. Toby could enjoy Caleb's eyes, his body, the shy smile he was giving now as Toby walked back toward him.... But that was all he could enjoy.

"Do you have a car? I mean, obviously not with you, but...."

Caleb nodded as he pushed to his feet and reached for his bags. "I didn't try to drive out because I figured I might not be here long. I left it with my roommate back in Pearl." He named the tiny town outside Jackson where the Braves' Double-A affiliate played.

"Okay, well, if you call the office in the morning, they can probably set you up with something, so you're not spending all your new salary on cabs." Never mind that the major league minimum salary of nearly half a million was probably ten times more than Caleb had made in his entire career to this point. As Caleb noted, he might not stick around long, so he'd better bank all he could while he had the chance.

"Yeah." Caleb slung his duffel over his shoulder and, dragging his roller bag behind him, followed Toby out the door and down the passageway toward the staff parking lot. "I just kind of threw everything into my bags and went when I got the call. Didn't think about what would happen on this end until I was in the air."

"Understandable." Toby waved to the security guard next to the entrance as they stepped outside and then shot Caleb a quick grin. "I keep up with things. I know how long you've been waiting for this."

Caleb gave him an inscrutable look. "Yeah, I guess you'd keep up, since you work here."

It hit Toby that he'd never mentioned his last name, so Caleb likely had no idea who he was. "You could say that," he admitted, leading the way to the parking space that would give him away anyway. When Ray Macmillan was out of town, Toby sometimes used his reserved space. He knew the moment Caleb realized where they were headed, because the man stopped in his tracks.

"Macmill… wait a minute."

Toby turned and gave him a sheepish smile. "Yeah. Toby Macmillan. Grandson. Sorry. Wasn't trying to be all incognito or anything. I just didn't think about it."

The look on Caleb's face sat somewhere between "holy shit" and "oh my God," so Toby leaned in a little closer. "Hey." Caleb slowly focused on Toby's face. "I'm not a spy. I'm not going to report back to the owner on your every move. Maybe if I saw you robbing old ladies on a street corner, but I don't think that's quite your style, is it?"

Caleb relaxed visibly. "Nah. I'm more into card counting. Don't take me to a casino."

Toby laughed as they climbed into his Accord. Once they were buckled in, Toby pulled out and headed toward downtown. "Have you eaten?"

Caleb, who had been absorbed in watching the scenery go by—they'd just passed under the Olympic torch from the 1996 Games, which sat on a corner a few blocks from the ballpark—shook his head. "Not since breakfast. Like I said, I wasn't really thinking about anything but getting here."

"There's a pretty decent restaurant in the hotel, so we can hit that if you want."

Caleb turned his head then, blinking at Toby like he didn't understand. "You want to have dinner together?"

"Sure," Toby said, stopping at a light. "Unless you have a fear of Macmillans, which would be a tough thing, working in this organization. Or maybe you'd just rather be alone to settle in—"

"No!" Toby was surprised by Caleb's vehemence at first, but then he realized he probably didn't know a soul in town and would be happy for a little company. "Dinner's great."

Toby nodded. "Okay." He took the turn onto the interstate and accelerated to highway speed. "There are a couple of ways to get downtown without getting on the interstate, but most of the time, this is fastest. Only a few exits up and a couple of turns to the hotel." He smiled Caleb's way. "With any luck, you'll find a place quickly and not have to do this again anyway."

Caleb sighed and dropped his head back against the seat back. "This is all just…. It's like I'm gonna wake up and be back in a crappy little apartment in Double-A, you know? I haven't been to Atlanta in years. I don't have a clue where to start looking for a place."

Toby maneuvered around a slow-moving, beat-up pickup truck and changed lanes to head for the exit. "Call the front office tomorrow," he urged. "They'll take care of you. They have info on, like, furnished apartments, so you don't even have to worry about that stuff right now."

Caleb chuckled. "Like I said, I barely even took time to pack. Didn't have all that much but clothes with me in Mississippi anyway, but I left a couple boxes for Marvin to ship when I get an address for him to ship 'em to."

"Well, you'll get set up fast." Toby turned left at the end of the ramp and drove toward downtown, the late Sunday afternoon traffic all but nonexistent. "I'll give you my number, too, in case you need any tips. I'm sure it's a big adjustment. Good thing you have a few days to get settled before the team's back in action. And then a home stand too."

He turned right onto Peachtree Street, watching from the corner of his eye as Caleb craned his neck to look up at the giant neon-lit guitar hanging on the front of the Hard Rock Cafe on the corner. He sure gave the impression of country-boy-come-to-town, though if Toby remembered correctly, he'd grown up in the Chicago suburbs of northwestern Indiana. Still, coming on the heels of almost ten years living in rural areas, first in college and then the minor leagues, Toby could understand the culture shock.

Toby pulled into the drive in front of the hotel and stopped. "Hop on out and head inside to check in," he suggested. "Be sure to tell them you're with the team. I'll get the car parked and meet you."

"Okay." Caleb opened the door and unfolded himself from the car, pausing to grab his bags from the backseat before pushing the doors shut and heading inside. Toby elected to climb out there, too, and turned the car over to a valet in exchange for a claim check. He could've parked much cheaper on a surface lot nearby, but sometimes the convenience was worth it.

Walking inside, Toby nodded to the staff members he passed and headed toward the registration desk, where Caleb stood talking to a clerk. Caleb passed over ID and a credit card as Toby arrived, and the clerk, a young woman who looked mildly familiar to Toby, did a double take and then smiled at Toby in recognition before entering information on the keyboard.

"All set?" Toby leaned against the counter.

"Will be in a minute." Caleb shot Toby a quick grin. "Just the smell from the restaurant has me freakin' starving. It's been a long day."

"I bet." Toby turned and tilted his head back to look up at the hotel atrium, rising some twenty stories above their heads. "I love this place. I've been coming here for all kinds of stuff as long as I can remember. Funny how the atrium never seems to get any smaller, even though I was a tiny thing the first time I remember seeing it." He glanced around. "It looks a lot different at this level, though. They just renovated the place again the past couple of years."

"Here you go, Mr. Browning," the clerk said, drawing Toby's attention. "This is your room number, and you're in the Atrium Tower. All elevators go to all floors. Enjoy your stay."

"Thanks so much." Caleb turned, key card in hand, and grinned at Toby. "Let's eat!"

AN HOUR and a half later, stuffed with shrimp, grits, and peach cobbler, Toby set down his fork and leaned back in his seat. “That was....”

“Amazing.” Caleb, still working on his own cobbler, grinned at Toby across the small table. The restaurant was nearly deserted except for them, the only sounds the soft clinking of dishes and the low piped-in music. A jolt went through Toby as he realized how date-like this all was.

Not a date, he told himself. *Just a friendly dinner to welcome the new player to town.*

But as Caleb smiled at him again, Toby saw the glint in his eyes. The way his gaze roamed Toby’s face. The way he leaned in, just a little, as if wanting to be closer.

Toby knew that look. He’d seen it before, dozens of times, and politely ignored most of them.

He just hadn’t expected to see it on someone like Caleb Browning.

He had to be imagining things. *Had* to. He looked away, out into the empty lobby, anywhere but at the gorgeous man across the table, making happy sounds in his throat as he enjoyed the last of his dessert. No way was Caleb interested in Toby. The chances of him liking men at all were miniscule. The likelihood of him risking anyone finding out if he did? Practically nonexistent.

Caleb finally set down his fork and wiped his mouth with the cloth napkin, which he dropped onto the table next to his empty plate. “That was amazing.” He smiled, eyes sparkling with warmth and satisfaction, though the way they drooped at the corners gave away his exhaustion. “If that’s any sample of the way Atlanta feeds you, I may have to step up my workout regimen.”

Toby forced himself to relax and return the (*friendly*, he reminded himself) smile. “Extra warning track runs, for sure,” he agreed. “This place is good, but once you try the local places, the barbecue and the soul food, you’ll be hooked for life.”

Caleb’s gaze softened. “I might be already,” he murmured. He didn’t seem to be talking about food anymore, but Toby couldn’t let himself think that. Instead, he pushed back his chair.

"Let me get this," he said, reaching for his wallet. "A 'welcome to the bigs' present." He nodded to their server as he slid a credit card into the leather-bound portfolio, which was quickly whisked away.

"You don't have to do that," Caleb tried to protest, but Toby just shook his head, his smile more natural.

"No, really, it's on me. Congratulations."

Caleb's reluctance remained clear, but he didn't say anything else as Toby signed off on their dinner. They stood and headed into the lobby in silence, but before they got far, Caleb stopped Toby with a hand on his arm. Toby looked up at Caleb's face and saw the same gleam in his eye that had given Toby pause a few minutes earlier.

"Come up for a drink?"

All the warning bells in Toby's mind went off at once, but none of them were enough to stop him from doing what he did next. He followed Caleb into the elevator, rode up to the sixteenth floor beside him in silence, and then followed him down the hall to his room.

Once inside, Caleb dropped his duffel on the dresser and moved toward the minibar, like he was actually going to make good on his nightcap offer. "Not sure what they have in here, but—"

Toby didn't let him get any further. He took three long steps, reached up to wrap one hand behind Caleb's neck, and kissed the words right out of his mouth.

Caleb's lips were soft and dry, yielding easily to Toby's insistent pressure and soon parting to allow Toby's tongue inside. Caleb tasted like the mint he'd popped as they left the table downstairs, with a hint of sweetness from the tea he'd had with dinner and a deeper flavor of pure Caleb.

Toby wondered if he tasted like that everywhere.

Eager to find out, Toby slid his hands under the hem of Caleb's T-shirt and pushed it up until it bunched under Caleb's arms. Breaking reluctantly away from Caleb's mouth, Toby bent to lick his nipple instead, hearing the hiss from above at the intimate touch. Caleb's skin was saltier here, the remains of a long day of travel clinging to his body, and Toby took another, longer taste, wrapping his lips around the pebbling skin and sucking gently.

"Holy shit, Toby."

Caleb shifted, and Toby saw his T-shirt go flying a second before Caleb grabbed Toby's arms and turned them both, shoved Toby against the wall, and fell against him. Caleb sealed his mouth over Toby's even as he worked his fingers under Toby's shirt and let them roam across his skin. Toby kissed him back desperately, kneading at the strong muscles of Caleb's back, muscles honed from years as an athlete who used his body well. Toby was no slouch, physically speaking, but he relished the few inches and couple dozen pounds Caleb had on him. Toby felt surrounded by Caleb but not overwhelmed, the give and take between them perfectly balanced.

After breaking the kiss, Caleb pushed at Toby's shirt, and Toby raised his arms to let Caleb strip it away like he'd done with his own. Caleb wrapped one arm around Toby's body to pull their chests together and used his free hand to cup Toby's ass so he could grind his pelvis into Toby's. Toby groaned as Caleb licked across his jaw to his ear, where Caleb breathed out, "Jesus *fuck*, you're hot."

Toby let out a strangled sound something like a laugh. "Nothing on you," he managed, turning his head to capture Caleb's mouth with his.

They stumbled toward the bed, kicking off shoes and fighting with buckles and zippers, hands exploring every new inch of skin they exposed. When Toby got his hands into the back of Caleb's jeans and realized he was wearing a jockstrap, he took full advantage, grabbing a double handful of muscular ass and squeezing a moan right out of Caleb's mouth.

Toby pulled away long enough to slide onto the mattress and draw Caleb down on top of him, groaning at the weight pressing him into the mattress. Caleb cupped Toby's face in his big hands and kissed him hard, driving his tongue in deep, and Toby opened his mouth and let Caleb all the way inside.

He opened his legs, too, lifting his knees to bracket Caleb's hips, the shift in position bringing their hard cocks together with just two thin layers of cotton left between them. Toby moaned into Caleb's mouth, the sound echoed back to him as Caleb slid one hand down to cup Toby's leg and pulled it tighter against Caleb's body. Toby took the hint, bringing his other leg up to wrap behind Caleb's thighs and lifting his pelvis to grind up into him.

Toby lost track of how long they stayed like that, kissing and grinding against each other, before Caleb wrenched himself away. "God," Caleb growled. "I want to be inside you, like, yesterday."

Panting, Toby nodded. "You got stuff?"

"Shit. I hope so."

Caleb levered himself away from Toby and off the bed, then dove into his discarded duffel bag. Toby used the break to get rid of his underwear and brought one hand up to stroke his hard-as-nails dick while he watched Caleb's ass and thigh muscles bunch under his smooth, pale skin. With a few moments to look his fill, Toby could see the tan line at Caleb's waist and a lighter one halfway down his thigh, evidence of shirtless workouts and off days in shorts. Central Mississippi was even more hot and humid than Atlanta, so Toby imagined Caleb didn't bother with more clothing than he had to.

Toby had no objections to that idea. At all.

When Caleb turned back around, condoms in one hand and lube in the other, Toby let his gaze roam over his front side, and he liked what he saw. A lot. Caleb had almost no hair on his chest, but a riot of reddish-brown curls sprung to life just below his navel—he had an outie—and surrounded a long, slender cock that curved slightly at the end. Toby's brain did the geometry quickly, and his body clenched at the thought of how that curve would fit inside, the pressure it would exert against his prostate.

He barely had time for a groan before Caleb was back, dropping his jock on the floor and the supplies on the bed before sprawling on top of Toby. "Beautiful," Toby managed, and Caleb smiled for a split second before kissing him again.

Kissing melted into caresses, and in what felt like no time at all, Caleb had Toby prepared and his cock in place, ready to breach his body. Toby lifted his legs to wrap around Caleb's hips again and pulled, encouraging him to move. "C'mon," he murmured. "Get in me."

Caleb was smiling as he eased inside, and Toby had to smile too, even as the stretch and burn made his eyes flutter shut. Oh God, he'd missed this feeling; missed being filled, the weight of a man on top of him, the smell and slick slide of sweat and lube.

Caleb didn't stop moving even when he was in deep, just pulled back and pushed forward again and again and again, each stroke a little longer, with a little more force behind it. By the time he was pulling almost all the way out and slamming back in, Toby was riding a wave of white-hot sensation, skin buzzing all over, cock and balls tight with tension.

Just as Toby suspected, every one of Caleb's thrusts pushed the head of his dick across Toby's gland at exactly the right angle, each pass shooting paroxysms of pleasure through Toby's body. Caleb was going to milk an orgasm right out of Toby without a single touch to his cock, just the sweet pressure from their bodies rubbing together.

"Toby." His name, whispered against his ear in that sexy, raspy voice, shot Toby's desire into the redline. He moaned and reached for Caleb's head with both hands to slam their mouths together in a dirty, messy kiss. It didn't last long, Caleb's thrusts growing suddenly even harder and more erratic, and Toby lasted only a few more seconds before his body and cock jerked hard and he spilled between them.

"Fuck!" The barely coherent word came from Caleb, as Toby could manage no more than a gasp and deep groan of satisfaction as his orgasm ripped through him. As if at a distance, he felt Caleb shudder against him in his own climax.

Caleb collapsed on top of Toby, and even though it made breathing harder, Toby couldn't bring himself to care. Two hundred pounds of warm, sweaty man pressed him into the mattress, and despite feeling completely wrung out, Toby managed to sling arms and legs around him, holding him in place.

"Crushing you," Caleb muttered into the pillow near Toby's ear, and Toby shook his head.

"Like it. Stay," he murmured back.

Caleb did, even as his shrinking cock slipped out of Toby's body and the cum and lube grew cold and sticky on their skin. Eventually, Caleb rolled onto his side, taking Toby with him, and gave him a slow, deep kiss. Toby made a sound of satisfaction deep in his throat, and Caleb pulled away with a smile.

"Let me grab a washcloth or something so we don't—"

"No." Toby tightened his grip around Caleb's body. "Clean up later. Sleep now."

Caleb hesitated, but then he relaxed back against the mattress. They shifted until both were comfortable, bodies tangled together, and Toby drifted toward sleep, satiated and content.

WHEN Toby woke a few hours later, his mind had caught up with his actions, and he was up and off the bed before he even realized he was moving.

"Wha…."

Caleb's groggy voice came from somewhere behind him as Toby pulled on his underwear and reached for his jeans.

"This was a mistake." Even as the words left his mouth, Toby knew they were wrong, but what else could he say? He'd broken every possible rule: sleeping with someone from work was bad enough, but sleeping with a player? If his grandfather found out, he'd hit the roof. Three times over, since said player was also, of course, a man.

"Toby—"

Toby didn't stop dressing, even though his hands wouldn't stop shaking. "I can't do this. I can't…. I just can't. You're a great guy, but this ends now."

He shoved his feet into his sneakers, tied them quickly, and stood, patting his pockets to check for phone and wallet. Only one thing left to do….

He looked up, at Caleb, sitting in the middle of the bed, hair a mess, torso bare, sheets tangled around his lower body. His blue eyes were barely half open, sleep still hanging heavy over him, and Toby's resolve wavered.

No, he ordered himself. *You had your fun. Now get the hell out before you make it worse.*

He gave Caleb one last look, committing that gorgeous view to memory, and then he was out the door.

IT TOOK a good twenty minutes in the shower before Toby could no longer smell Caleb on his skin, though the sense memory remained. His skin raw and his fingers wrinkled, he kept his gaze safely away from the mirror while he dried off.

He walked out of the bathroom as dawn lightened the horizon. The day stretched out endlessly ahead of him. Tomorrow, the clubhouse crew would hit the ground running, spending the rest of the All-Star break getting the place set up for the second half of the season. Today, though, the whole place was getting an intense cleaning from top to bottom.

Athlete's foot in the showers was the least of their worries, what with nastiness like norovirus and MRSA lurking in every crevice.

That left Toby at loose ends. With nothing else to fill his time, he dove into cleaning his own place, pulling out bottles of chemicals and the box of worn-out towels from under the kitchen sink. He scrubbed and wiped until his arms ached, his bathroom and kitchen shone, and his eyes and sinuses burned. After tossing the last bottle and rag into the kitchen sink, he collapsed onto the sofa and closed his eyes.

From somewhere nearby, his phone rang.

Groaning, Toby opened his eyes and looked around, spying the phone lying on the coffee table, just beyond arm's reach. Levering himself up, he stretched for it, not bothering to check the display before he answered.

Mistake. His "yeah?" was answered with a simple "Toby" in Caleb's raspy, sexy voice, and every nerve in Toby's unprepared body shot to high alert. He'd completely forgotten they'd exchanged numbers at dinner the night before.

"Hey." It was all his brain could come up with.

"I heard everything you said this morning," Caleb said. "And I get it. I really do. I just wanted to say, for the record, that I disagree, and I hope you'll change your mind. Because I like you a lot, and the sex was hot as hell, and I would really, really like to do it all again. Soon, and as often as possible."

Toby's mind had checked out entirely right about the point where Caleb mentioned the hot-as-hell sex, and there was absolutely nothing he could say to counter any of that.

"So that's why I called, and I don't expect you to answer, but I do want you to think about it. Think about me. And when you're ready, call me. I'll be waiting."

There was a click, and Toby was left with nothing but dead air.

And a hard cock.

Shit.

THE next three days at work passed in a blur. Toby did his job and helped get everything restocked and shined up and the clubhouse in tip-top shape for the second half of the season. But every time the door opened, Toby tensed, even though he knew there was no way Caleb would come down there. In spite of Caleb's little speech on the phone Monday afternoon, both of them knew exactly what it would mean if their tryst became public knowledge. Yes, the atmosphere surrounding sports had gotten much more open-minded in the past few years, but there still were no openly out active major league ballplayers. A career minor-league catcher who hadn't even played a game in the big leagues yet was not in any position to try to cross that line.

And Toby? He could survive coming out. He planned to, someday. But knowing his grandfather's conservative nature, and considering his precarious position, without even an official piece of the team until his twenty-first birthday in another couple of weeks, Toby wasn't ready to take that kind of risk.

By the time players started to filter into the clubhouse late Thursday afternoon, Toby was strung so tight he thought he'd snap right in two waiting for Caleb to arrive. When the man finally walked in, though, he was talking and laughing with one of the utility infielders. He never even looked Toby's way, and Toby was left simultaneously relieved and disappointed.

He didn't have time to dwell on it, though. With the team back in the house for the first time in four days, Toby and the rest of the crew were kept running. Guys were taking turns in the whirlpool and on the training tables, or stretching on the floor in front of their lockers, and Toby fetched ice packs, heating pads, towels, and drinks while the players worked.

For the first time in the nearly six years that he'd worked in the clubhouse, he resented it all. These guys made millions, were waited on hand and foot, and for what? Hit ball, throw ball, catch ball. Not exactly rocket science, and certainly not anything like saving lives or changing the world.

But then Toby thought of the faces of the kids who would run out on the field before each Sunday home game, picked to stand next to their favorite players while the national anthem was sung. The players would bend to talk to the little boys and girls, and the smiles they'd exchange might not end world hunger or anything lofty like that, but it made the kids happy. Baseball made people happy, and wasn't that just as important as anything else?

Okay, yeah, Toby admitted to himself as he dropped off a stack of fresh towels next to the shower. Probably not a half-million-dollar minimum worth of happy, but careers were short, and players gave back, so it probably came out even in the end, in some convoluted karmic-restitution formula.

The players filtered out of the clubhouse one or two at a time, headed for the dugout, the field, or the bullpen, ready to get things going again. The trainers were the last ones out, leaving Toby and a couple of teenagers behind to straighten up the remnants, as usual.

A whisper in the back of Toby's mind wished Caleb would come back, take advantage of the relative quiet to confront Toby in person, maybe even try to kiss him into compliance. Toby didn't know how he'd react, but he did know how stupid the idea was. Caleb liked him, sure. They'd had great (fucking awesome) sex, sure. But Caleb would not take a risk like that at his first game in the big leagues. Hell, even if Toby had been female, he wouldn't. And either way, Toby wouldn't let him do it.

Forcing himself to not think about Caleb anymore, dammit, Toby gathered the last towels and pushed the cart over to the door for the laundry staff to pick up. He walked back through the room, watching the part-timers finish picking up the trash as he went, and retrieved the vacuum cleaner from the storage closet at one end of the room. Normally, he'd leave that until after the game, or let the custodial staff handle it, but he was perfectly willing to admit—to himself, at least—that he was avoiding heading up to the dugout. He usually spent part of each game watching from the entrance to the ramp that led back toward the clubhouse, occasionally running sweaty towels back or bringing up extra ice packs. And he'd get back to that. He would.

He'd have to face down Caleb at least once first, though.

The game dragged on forever. Toby watched some on the clubhouse monitors, but he spent most of his time wandering the room, looking for things to do. He refolded a stack of towels that was less than perfectly symmetrical, checked the ice machine to make sure it was full, made sure the toilet paper in the stalls was stocked.

He was being stupid and he knew it, but he couldn't bring himself to stop.

By the time the Braves won and the players poured back into the clubhouse, bringing with them the jokes and teasing that always followed a victory, Toby was about ready to jump out of his skin. He realized he'd been so focused on finding excuses to avoid the game that he didn't even know if Caleb had played. A sudden need to find out gripped him, and he almost went looking for Caleb among the crowds to ask. But then the usual postgame madness kicked in, and he was kept busy running for ice and towels, picking up discarded uniform parts to send to the laundry, and then cleaning up the mess the players always left behind.

He never even saw Caleb, much less had a chance to talk to him. Not that he would have known what to say.

ON FRIDAY, fortified by another day of distance, Toby headed to the ballpark determined to talk to Caleb, even if only to say hello. He'd checked the box score and found Caleb hadn't played Thursday night, and Toby had vowed to pay closer attention tonight. He didn't want to miss Caleb's first major league at bat out of a fit of pique.

He kept an eye out as he worked, and when Caleb arrived, gave him time to get to his locker before heading that way.

"Hey, Tobes," Marty called. "Can you help me out here?"

Toby sighed and changed direction. Work first; then he'd corner Caleb for a chat.

After helping Marty with a recalcitrant ice pack, Toby went looking for Caleb again. He picked up towels and trash as he went, but after a complete circuit of the clubhouse, Caleb was nowhere to be found. The showers were empty, and Toby wasn't going to turn stalkery enough to check the toilet stalls, but he couldn't find Caleb—

"Toby."

Toby spun on his heel at the rough, familiar voice, reaching for the wall to steady himself. "Caleb. I was just—"

Caleb gave a crooked smile. "Looking for me, maybe?"

Toby hesitated long enough that he saw the shift in Caleb's eyes as he realized it. "Yes!" Toby forced out. "I just…." He cleared his throat and stood straighter. "I wanted to check on you. I mean, be sure you were settling in okay and all that."

The half smile fell away. "Yeah. Fine. Thanks."

Caleb stepped back, but before he could leave, Toby reached out to grab his arm. "Caleb," he said, keeping his voice low. He could hear the pleading note in his voice. "I'm sorry. I am. I'd like to be friends, at least."

Caleb looked at him, looked down at his hand, and then moved away, leaving Toby's hand hanging in midair. "I don't know if I can do that." He gave Toby one long, heated stare, making it very clear what he wanted to do, and then he was gone, leaving Toby alone with his insecurities.

Toby closed his eyes and leaned his head back against the wall. *Well*, he thought, *that went well.*

"Trouble in paradise, Macmillan?"

And that's just the capper to this week, Toby thought.

Grimacing, he opened his eyes and turned his head to meet the gaze of one Barry Knight, the new intern backing up the Braves' regular beat reporter. Matt Sussman had been covering the team for well over a decade and was well liked by everyone, but as Toby knew from experience, Barry Knight wasn't half the man Matt was.

"What do you want, Barry?" Toby didn't even try to make it sound friendly. He wasn't anything officially but a clubhouse peon, and if Barry tried to make it sound like Toby was speaking for the team, he'd get laughed out of the newsroom. Toby and Barry had gone to high school together and had been friends for about five minutes, five years ago, when Toby'd been a starry-eyed sophomore harboring a secret crush on the senior Big Man On Campus Barry had tried to be. Toby had been crushed when he'd figured out Barry's only interest had been in Toby's family connections, not Toby himself.

Barry snorted. "Just cleaning up after the losers," he snarked. "I was gonna talk to the new guy, see if there's some dirt to dig there, but looks like you beat me to that."

Toby rolled his eyes. "You wouldn't know a good story if it bit you on the ass." It was true, too; Barry had ego and ambition to spare, but not half the talent or drive he needed to make it as a big-league reporter. Toby shoved off the wall before Barry could wind up for a retort. "Now, if you'll excuse me, some of us around here have actual work to do."

Spinning on his heel, he headed off to do it.

WITH the Los Angeles Dodgers in town and the game picked up for television, the Braves had been moved to an unusual 4:20 p.m. game start time on Saturday. Toby hated that crap. Games should be at seven thirty, except Sunday afternoons and occasionally a "businessfans' special" during the week. He knew purists would scoff at him; baseball was made to be played in the sun. But it wasn't baseball tradition that drove him. He just wanted things to be consistent.

Totally off his game, so to speak, Toby got to the clubhouse fifteen minutes later than usual, though still a good five minutes before he actually needed to be there. A handful of players were already in the clubhouse, but Toby would bet one or two would arrive late because they'd forgotten about the time change.

Toby dove into his usual pregame routine, pausing a few times to exchange pleasantries with players—in the form of insults and teasing, as in most locker rooms. He thought about that while he was tossing some trash away and realized that, over the six years he'd been working here, the flavor of the clubhouse talk had shifted. Sex was less of a focus in general, and in particular, comments about players' sexuality had become much more rare. The team had done an anti-bullying video during Spring Training for the It Gets Better project, so maybe that had contributed.

But things had been changing long before that. The world was changing. Maybe it wouldn't be such a big deal if the players knew he was gay. Or even for Caleb. Players had come out after retirement in several of the big professional sports, and now there was Jason Collins in the NBA. Gay players were no longer big news in other sports. Maybe Major League Baseball was ready for its gay members, on and off the field, to stand up and be counted.

Toby just didn't know if he was ready to become number one on that list.

Toby heard the door clink open and looked in that direction automatically. He frowned at the sinking sensation in his stomach when he saw it was just the pitching coach, Carl Zambronsky, but then a hand caught the door before it shut completely, and Toby's heart lifted when he saw it was Caleb.

And then his heart dropped right back down when Caleb's gaze skimmed over Toby as if he wasn't even there.

Toby sank back against the wall as Caleb moved toward the locker he'd been assigned. Well, that was apparently that. Caleb didn't want to be friends, and Toby couldn't be more. So they'd be nothing at all.

Resigned, Toby pushed away from the wall again and got back to work.

THE atmosphere in the clubhouse after the loss was completely different from the previous two nights. Sure, it was just a game, but these were people who lived and breathed baseball. A dark cloud hung over the clubhouse. Players sat slumped in front of their lockers in the quiet or plodded silently to the showers. The manager stood in the corner by the door talking to the press, taking the loss on his shoulders to keep that weight off his players.

On his usual task of gathering up used towels and bits of tape that seemed to land everywhere except the trash cans, Toby jumped when he turned and Caleb was standing right behind him. "Um…. Hi." *Articulate*, Toby thought, but it was all he could get out.

"Hi. Um…. Can we talk?" Caleb looked uncomfortable, eyes darting around as if they were being watched, which might well be the case, for all Toby knew. But if they were going to be in the same place at the same time for a while, as it seemed they would be, then they should probably figure out how not to be this completely uncomfortable around each other.

"Yeah." Toby nodded. "Probably should. When we're done here?"

Caleb bit his lip, and all Toby could think was how that felt when he'd been the one doing the biting. "Meet you outside?"

Taking in a shaky breath, Toby nodded again, and Caleb wandered away. He looked a little lost, and Toby couldn't blame him. Caleb had gotten his first big-league hit tonight, but he wasn't able to celebrate the way he wanted because the team had lost.

Maybe Toby could help. He could buy Caleb a drink, or a more appropriate cup of coffee. A combination peace offering and reward for his milestone.

By the time the clubhouse had emptied out and Toby finished up with the never-ending dirty towels, he'd settled into the idea of being friends with Caleb. Sure, he was still going to be attracted to the man, but he'd had plenty of friends he found attractive, even a couple he'd messed around with. He could do the same this time.

Toby pushed the cart full of towels toward the door, where Caleb sat waiting for him. Toby smiled. "All done," he said, bringing the cart to a stop. "Let me grab my keys and stuff, and we can head out."

Caleb didn't say anything as they walked to the staff lot. Toby's grandfather had been at the game this time, so Toby had parked in his usual place, which was farther away, of course. The night air was steamy, thick with humidity from the day's heat, and by the time they got to his car, a light sheen of sweat covered Toby's skin.

"Hop in and I'll get the AC going." He popped the locks and slid into the driver's seat as Caleb did the same on the other side, and within a few moments, the car's engine hummed to life and cool air began pouring from the vents.

"I swear, July in Georgia is why air-conditioning was invented." Toby threw a grin in Caleb's direction, but Caleb simply stared straight ahead, brow creased as if deep in thought. Toby cleared his throat and tried again. "Any place in particular you'd like to talk?"

Caleb lifted one shoulder. "Whatever. In the car is fine." He turned his head, and Toby almost recoiled at his furious expression. "You fucking used me," Caleb spat out. "You got your rocks off and ran for the hills because you were too spineless to be honest."

Toby opened his mouth, but Caleb cut him off before he could even try to respond. "I get what it means to be gay and have to hide it. God knows I've gotten to be an expert at it. But hiding it and running from it are two different things." Caleb paused and blew out a breath. "Shit. I told myself I wasn't going to attack you over this. Because I do get it. But dammit, Toby, I'm not a sex toy. I'm a person. And I deserve to be treated like one."

Toby's face flushed and his stomach turned over. "I'm sorry," he whispered. "I know it's not enough to apologize, but you're right. I treated you like crap, and I'm sorry." He slumped against the seat. "I've known I was gay since I was fifteen. Hell, I started fooling around with one of my classmates before that. But I've lived and breathed this game since I can remember, and after my parents died.... I have to have baseball. I can't live without it."

Caleb reached out, and Toby let him cover his hand where it lay on his thigh. "I get that. My parents know about me, but they've never been happy about it. I'm probably lucky they haven't cut me off. They're pretty conservative."

Toby's laugh was hollow. "My grandfather is about as conservative as it gets. And he owns 60 percent of the team. I mean, my father left his share in trust, and I'll inherit that when I turn twenty-one, but that's only 30 percent. Ray has twice that. He could cut me off so easily."

Caleb squeezed his hand. "I won't blow smoke and tell you he wouldn't do that. But with your parents gone, maybe he'd at least think twice."

"I wish I could be so sure." He slid his hand away from Caleb's and shifted into reverse. "Let's get you home. Day game tomorrow, and then you're on the road." He managed a small smile in Caleb's direction. "You'll have to tell me where I'm going."

Caleb studied him for a long moment, and while he didn't return the smile, it did seem he'd burned off the anger. He started giving directions, and Toby felt himself relaxing. Maybe they could be friends after all. He'd like that.

He'd like more, but that just didn't seem to be in the cards.

SUNDAY was…. Well. After it was over, Toby felt like he'd been through a war. Three hit by pitches, one on-field brawl, six ejections, and on top of it all, the Braves lost. Good thing it was a getaway day and the team headed for the airport almost as soon as it was over. Toby had seen the aftermath in the clubhouse from a game like that, and it wasn't pretty.

As it was, the mess the disgruntled players left in their wake took a good half hour longer than usual to clean up. If they hadn't had a ten-day road trip ahead of them, it would've been even worse. Thank the baseball gods that the clubhouse staff had plenty of time to restock and reset for the team's return, so Toby just made his usual towel-and-trash rounds and headed home.

He found a note stuck under the windshield wiper of his car. Frowning, Toby pulled it free and slid inside before opening it.

Toby—

Hotel rooms on the road are bad enough with a roommate. Looks like I'll be on my own for this trip, so I could use a friendly voice to talk to. Give me a call if you want.

Caleb

Underneath Caleb's name was his number, though Toby already had it from Caleb's call earlier in the week. Toby smiled. Maybe this friendship thing could work out after all.

Instead of calling, he pulled out his phone and sent Caleb a text message: *Got your note. Call or text anytime. My schedule's light with school out and the team on the road.*

His phone buzzed before he got out of the parking lot. He glanced down to read it before he pulled out onto the street.

Will do. Plane's about to take off. See you when we're back.

Toby smiled again and drove off into the dusk.

"A HUNDRED and twenty-four on the field. I don't care how dry it supposedly is. That should be illegal."

Toby laughed and picked up another towel to fold. His phone sat beside him on a sofa cushion, speaker on, as he and Caleb talked. It was late on Wednesday night, three days into the road trip, and spending those three days in the Arizona heat had apparently been more than Caleb could stand. Even the trip on to Denver for the next series hadn't stopped his grumbling. Toby had heard all about it during the phone calls each of the previous two nights too.

"Just wait until you get back to Atlanta," Toby warned. "It won't hit 124, but it'll feel like it when the humidity kicks into full gear. Hard to breathe in that kind of sludge."

"Ugh." Caleb blew out a breath. "I took three cold showers a day while we were there, and I still felt like the top of my head was gonna blow off." He fell silent for a few seconds before letting out a snicker. "Okay, that sounded way less dirty in my head than it did out loud."

Toby felt his cheeks warm. That first call late Monday night—early Tuesday morning, really—had started out stilted, both of them treading carefully to keep things light and avoid the subject of the night they'd spent together. By the time sleep had demanded they hang up an hour later, Toby had been smiling. Call number two had been better, and tonight, he'd been looking forward to talking with a friend. Just one little innuendo, though, and suddenly all Toby could think of was spreading Caleb out on a bed and riding him hard and fast.

Shit. Toby shook his head. “Dirty mind,” he replied, after too long a pause. He tried to keep his voice light. “At least you’re out of the desert. Well, out of one type of desert and into another, I guess. How’s Denver?”

“Dark.” Caleb snickered. “But at least it’s cooler. Pretty, what I could see of it on the way in from the airport. We’ve got all day tomorrow, though, so maybe I’ll look around some before we have to head to the ballpark.”

“It’s a nice city.” Toby set aside another folded towel. “High sky. Watch out for pop flies behind the plate, and be glad you’re not playing outfield. Easy to lose a ball in all that bright blue.”

Caleb made a sound of agreement in his throat. “Gotta admit, I’m hoping to get a chance to launch one in the thin air. It’d be nice to get at least one long ball while I’m with the big club.”

Toby rolled his eyes and reached for another towel. “Seriously, you’re not going anywhere anytime soon. You’re doing great, and the team recognizes that. You started yesterday, didn’t you?”

“Only because it was a day game after a night game and Berrymann always gets those off.” Partly true, Toby knew. Catchers rarely started two games that close together. All that squatting was damn hard on the knees. But it was more than that.

“And you’ve pinch-hit in almost every game,” Toby pointed out. “Diamont’s been hurt almost more than he’s been able to play the past two seasons. Stay healthy and you’ve probably got the backup catcher job wrapped up for a good long while.”

Caleb blew out a break. “From your mouth to management’s ears.” He barked out a laugh. “Oh wait. You *are* management.”

Toby couldn’t help the grin. “Am not. I have another couple of weeks before I even get my share of the team, and that just makes me a stockholder, not management.” His grin turned as evil as his thoughts. “But you’d better behave yourself if you want to stay on my good side.”

“Oh, I can be very, very good.” Caleb practically purred his reply, and a white-hot flash of desire shot through Toby at the sound. He cleared his throat and heard Caleb chuckle.

“Stop that.” Toby managed to make it sound chiding and only a little shaky.

"But you make it so easy," Caleb shot back, his voice back to normal and infused with more than a little humor. "You know I'm just giving you a hard time."

It was Toby's turn to laugh. "Oh, now that was a fastball right over the center of the plate if ever I heard one."

"Yeah, yeah," Caleb groused. "Taste of my own medicine, go ahead. I deserve it."

"Nah, too easy." Toby flipped the last neatly folded washcloth on top of his stack. "Much as I'd love to harass you some more, it's late, and some of us have to work in the morning."

"Oh, wow, I didn't realize it was after midnight already." After 2:00 a.m. for Toby, actually, but Caleb was off in Mountain Time. "You have to go in even when the team is on the road?"

Toby rolled his tight shoulders and leaned back against the cushions, stretching out his legs. "Not all the time, but we have a staff meeting tomorrow and a couple of shipments to get put away. I'll have the weekend off for a change, though. Maybe I'll go to the movies or something."

A sound in his ear confused him for a second until his realized it was Caleb yawning. Naturally, his body immediately responded to the cue. Once his own jaw-cracker ended, he huffed out a laugh. "I think our bodies are trying to tell us something. No, wait!" He interrupted whatever Caleb was about to say. "Forget I even said that. Except for the part that means it's time for us to go to bed. Oh, for crying out…."

Caleb was laughing at him openly by then, and all Toby could do was join in. "Get some sleep, and have fun tomorrow."

"Will do." Caleb's words were interrupted by another yawn. "Talk to you tomorrow."

Caleb had ended the call before Toby could respond. He stared at his phone, wondering whether this whole let's-be-friends thing was such a good idea. Because his first reaction to the idea of Caleb calling him again tomorrow was how long it would take for him to have Caleb naked and moaning in his ear.

Shit. He stared down at his crotch, where his dick had decided it liked that idea way too much. Sighing, he pushed himself up, grabbed his phone, and shoved it into the pocket of his gym shorts before gathering up his folded towels. *Get these put away and go to bed—to sleep*, he ordered himself. *No fantasizing about what you can't have*.

He doubted any part of him would listen, but he could earn that A for effort, right?

"UNTIL this week, I honestly can't remember the last time I had a hotel room to myself. Hell, in the low minors, we were stuck three or four to a room in some towns. And you try shoving four grown men into a room with two doubles and see how that works out for you."

"Ouch." Toby winced at the thought and switched his phone to the other ear. "Never really thought about it, I guess. I mean, I've been around the big ball club all my life, and I keep up with the talent on the farm teams, but I've never spent much time actually around the minors."

He lounged against the headboard of his bed, where he'd been listening to Caleb's low, near-exhaustion voice for almost an hour now. Not the worst Saturday night he'd ever had, he admitted to himself.

Caleb had started tonight's call by noting that housekeeping kept replacing the "ungodly" number of pillows on his bed every day in Denver, even though he'd stacked them neatly on the side chair, obviously unused. The conversation had wandered from there, but they'd circled back around to hotel rooms again.

"That could be something to look into." Toby heard rustling as Caleb shifted on the other end of the phone. "I'm not complaining, not really, but it's hard to get by. Most players have off-season jobs, but those are tough to keep when you're playing ball from April through September. I've already made more the last two weeks than I did all of last season."

Toby blinked. "Holy crap. I knew the pay was lousy, but that's worse than I thought. They should do something about that."

A low chuckle came through the phone, sending shivers down Toby's spine. "'They'? Didn't you say you'd own part of the team in another couple weeks?"

Toby smiled slowly. "Not a majority, or anywhere close to it."

"But enough to give you a voice."

And not just about pay for minor league players, Toby thought, though he kept that to himself. While he knew Caleb was comfortable with his sexuality, they hadn't talked about what it might mean for him to come out. Hell, they hadn't talked about what it might mean for Toby to come out, and he wasn't the one who then had to go out on the field and face not only opponents and fans who could be hostile for any of a number of reasons but also the potential for backlash from the people with whom he shared a uniform. And, maybe more important, a clubhouse.

Toby shook off that train of thought. It didn't matter now, not when there wasn't anything to tell. Knowing Caleb would see right through him, he changed the subject anyway. "Did you hear O'Malley got suspended? You'd think these guys would figure out the steroids aren't worth the trade-off for fifty days out of uniform."

After a long pause, Caleb finally spoke. "Yeah, I don't get it. Not so much of a problem with the guys who did it back before they changed the rules. I mean, it was stupid then, but it didn't mean losing a third of a season."

Caleb went on, but Toby only half heard him, listening more to the warm, deep cadence than to his words. It should freak him out, the contentment that came just from hearing Caleb's voice, but instead, it soothed him. He relaxed and let the sound wash over him.

He wasn't sure when he fell asleep, but he woke up in the wee hours with his phone still in his hand and a text from Caleb waiting for him.

Sleep tight. Don't let the bedbugs bite.

Smiling, he set his phone on the nightstand, turned off the lamp, and rolled over to hug a pillow, trying not to think about what—who—he'd rather have his arms around.

"SO DAMON'S cutting up and waving the bat around, and he misses taking out the Polish sausage by, like, two inches. I don't think the guy ever even saw it, but I'm betting ESPN will have it on a highlight reel."

The silly-fun, between-inning races between four people wearing different sausage-based costumes in Milwaukee had been the highlights of the week for the Braves, who'd dropped three so far to the Brewers. They had a day game up next, and Caleb was set to start, so he should have been going to sleep—shouldn't have called at all, really—but Toby couldn't bring himself to hang up. They'd talked for nine of ten nights now, only missing Monday night, when the game went fourteen innings and didn't end until nearly 2:00 a.m. Toby had still been awake, even though it had been an hour later in Atlanta, and when he'd finally dropped off around four, he'd slept only intermittently.

Once again he'd woken up the following morning to find a text from Caleb waiting: *Did you get the number of the beer truck that hit me? Damn, I'm glad the day game isn't until Thursday.*

Now here it was, Wednesday night, and they were up late again anyway, though Caleb's voice sounded like it was starting to slide off toward dreamland. Toby's mind was headed the same direction, his thoughts starting to drift away.

"Toby?"

Caleb saying his name drew Toby's attention back. "Hmmm?" he murmured.

"Can I ask you something?"

The change in the timbre of Caleb's voice told Toby that, unlike much of their conversations had been, this was no idle question. Toby was suddenly more awake, and he swallowed, his mouth dry. "Sure."

"When we get in tomorrow night… can I come over?"

Toby knew he should say no. He knew even thinking about anything but friendship with Caleb was playing with fire. But the only thing their conversations had done, rather than cementing a friendship, was make him want Caleb more. Toby's heart took over, and there was only one thing he could say.

"Yes."

I NEED a longer hallway.

The absurd thought almost made Toby laugh. He paced back and forth, spinning on his heel after far too few steps, wishing for another twenty feet or two hundred yards or two miles to walk. Maybe that would have half a chance at calming his nerves.

Caleb would arrive any minute, and Toby had no idea what to do about it. His body and his heart warred with his mind. Any kind of relationship with Caleb beyond friendship had the potential for so much damage, and Toby had no illusions that Caleb was planning just a friendly visit.

But he'd never felt a connection like he had with Caleb, and not just the explosive sexual chemistry of that first night. He'd looked forward to their nightly chats and spent more time thinking about those than he had the feel of Caleb's warm, smooth skin under his hands.

His skin tingled at the sense memory. Okay, yeah, he'd thought about that too. Quite a bit, and he had the dirty sheets to prove it.

Well, formerly dirty. They were clean now.

Despite all his qualms, he had high hopes they wouldn't stay that way long.

Predictably, the knock at his door nearly made him jump out of his skin. So calm, cool, and collected, he was. Laughing at himself, Toby walked to the door, took a deep breath, and opened it.

"Hi." Caleb smiled at him, looking better than should be legal after playing nine innings and sitting through a three-hour flight. Toby's last rational thought threw up its tiny hands and slunk away in defeat.

"Hi," Toby murmured in reply, even as he grabbed the front of Caleb's shirt with his left hand and dragged him inside. He slammed and locked the door with his right hand, but Caleb was already kissing him by then, and Toby couldn't spare another thought for such silly considerations as home safety.

Toby wound his arm around Caleb's neck, digging his fingers into his hair, and they stumbled across the room in the general direction of the sofa. Toby almost fell over backward when he bumped into it, and he managed to tear himself away from the feast that was Caleb's mouth.

"Bedroom," he said, and he redirected them down the hallway that suddenly seemed about ten times too long.

It took them about ten times too long to make it to the bed too. They kept stopping to press each other against walls, doorframes, furniture, whatever they could find that would allow them to brace and kiss deeper, rub against each other harder. Buttons and zippers were navigated with shaking hands between grasps and moans, but when the backs of Toby's legs hit the side of the mattress, he still had on his jeans, though they were open and sagging toward his knees. Caleb had a hand shoved down the front of Toby's boxer briefs, working his cock toward full hardness, so Toby just kept kissing him, heedless of anything but the feel of Caleb's touch.

He snapped out of it about the time he bounced on the mattress, thanks to a hard shove from Caleb. Toby glared up at him, but Caleb just grinned back, lifting his eyebrows, and stripped Toby's jeans and boxers out of the way.

"There." Caleb crawled onto the bed to hover on hands and knees over Toby. "This would've been easier if you'd just been naked when I got here."

Toby laughed, playfully dodging Caleb's mouth as it tried to recapture his. "I would have, but I had this silly idea we might actually talk or something crazy like that."

Caleb growled and raised one hand to grasp Toby's jaw, holding him in place. "I think we've done enough talking, don't you?"

He kissed Toby hard, tongue driving deep, stealing the breath from Toby's lungs and every thought from his head. Toby groaned low in his chest and wrapped his legs around the backs of Caleb's thighs, pulling himself closer to Caleb so their cocks bumped and brushed between them. The kiss went on and on as they serenaded each other with the sounds of their moans and the harsh pulls of air they managed through their noses, unwilling to break apart even for breath.

Toby wrapped his fingers around Caleb's asscheeks, intending to pull him closer, when a stray thought escaped the cloud of lust, making him smile into their seemingly endless kiss. Instead of yanking, he lifted one hand and brought it down sharply, the sound of the slap echoing loud in the room. Caleb gasped, finally jerking his mouth from Toby's, and Toby just giggled and did it again.

"What the hell?" Caleb flailed a hand back to grab Toby's, but Toby just let him have it with the other hand. He kept up a rain of smacks, none of them particularly hard, just playful. He broke into full-out laughter as Caleb twisted and jerked above him.

When they finally came back to rest, Caleb had his hands wrapped around Toby's wrists, pinning them to the mattress on either side of his body, and his legs pressed against either side of Toby's, holding them in place. Toby still shook with laughter, and Caleb was grinning like a loon, but when Caleb narrowed his eyes and said, "You're gonna get it for that," Toby had all of a second to brace himself before Caleb's mouth descended onto Toby's right nipple.

Toby lost track of time while Caleb tortured him, sucking and nipping and licking at his nipples until both were red and throbbing, then biting his way down Toby's abdomen to tug at Toby's pubic hair with his teeth. Each little zing of sensation sent Toby's arousal higher, and he writhed under Caleb's assault, as much as he could with Caleb holding him down. And that? Only made it all hotter.

When Caleb finally responded to the pleas that poured from Toby's mouth and wrapped his lips around the tip of Toby's cock, it took every ounce of willpower in Toby's body not to come on the spot. He strained against Caleb's grip on his wrists, but he didn't really fight to free himself, or ask Caleb to let go. He liked it. Not in a way that meant he wanted to do it all the time, but right now, with Caleb holding him while he sucked his brains out through his dick, it was perfect.

And then Caleb's mouth and hands disappeared, and Toby actually heard himself whimper.

He pried his eyes open, not even sure when he'd closed them, and what he saw when his eyes focused had him scrabbling for self-control again. Caleb had leaned back on his heels, and both hands were working as he rolled a condom down his own cock. When he finished, he looked up, and Toby caught his heated gaze.

"Roll over," Caleb rasped, and Toby didn't hesitate to comply.

Once he hit hands and knees, Caleb gave him a cursory few strokes with slicked fingers to lube him up before setting his cock against Toby's hole and pushing inside. Toby pushed back, letting his head hang loose as he concentrated on relaxing everything so he could get Caleb all the way inside him as soon as possible. It burned like hell, but he didn't care. He knew how good it would feel in a few minutes.

Caleb's hips soon rested fully against Toby's ass, and Caleb paused there while Toby breathed through the residual pain. It didn't last long, and soon Toby rocked his hips back, letting Caleb know without words he could move.

And move he did. Caleb drew back and then slammed home. A surprised yell burst out of Toby as he scrabbled with his hands to brace himself more firmly, and Caleb didn't let up, fucking Toby fast and hard, like he'd been holding back the tide and the dam had finally burst. Maybe it had, their phone conversations over the past week and a half building up between them until something had to give. Apparently it was Caleb's control.

Not that Toby had any complaints, except that this was going to be over a lot faster than he would have liked. He couldn't spare a hand to jerk himself off, but that might not even matter, at the rate Caleb was going. And even if Caleb came first, it wouldn't take more than a few strokes for him to follow.

Caleb shifted his hips then, and Toby lost his train of thought as the new angle hit just the right spot deep inside. Oh hell, maybe he wouldn't need a hand at all. He threw his head back on a moan, arching his back, feeling Caleb dig his fingers into his hips. One corner of the sheet popped off the bed, dragged loose by Toby's grasping hands, and just when he thought he couldn't take it another second, Caleb moved again, reaching around to grab Toby's desperate cock.

Three more seconds stretched into forever and then Toby was finally there, making an incoherent sound as his body seized in pleasure. He jerked and shot over Caleb's hand and onto the mattress, and before he'd finished, Caleb slammed deep into him and groaned out his own release.

Panting as if they'd run a marathon, they slumped sideways onto the mattress in a tangle of sweaty limbs. Toby throbbed pleasantly from head to toe, and while he had a fleeting thought of getting cleaned up, his brain decided it liked the idea of sleep better.

HALFWAY through the next day—after three more rounds of sex, breakfast in bed consisting of Pop-Tarts and coffee, and a thrown-together lunch of whatever leftovers in Toby's fridge weren't too old for consumption—Toby decided he kind of liked this sleepover thing. He'd rarely spent an overnight with the few men he'd been with before Caleb, and even then, one of them always ended up doing the Walk of Shame the next morning. The actual sleeping part of sleeping with Caleb wasn't so easy, other than a couple of postcoital naps. He kept waking himself up just as he started to doze, afraid he'd snore or drool or do something embarrassing that would scare off his bedmate.

Caleb didn't seem inclined to go anywhere, though. After they'd cleaned up from their lunch, Caleb had trailed him over to the sofa and then settled in close while Toby turned on the MLB Network to find out who was playing that afternoon. With the Orioles and Rays in a pitcher's duel at Camden Yards for background noise, they talked.

"Believe it or not, the main thing I remember about my dad isn't him taking me to baseball games." Toby slid his hand along Caleb's forearm where it had ended up lying across his hips. "It's not baseball at all. It's sitting on the front porch on the swing and watching him shuck corn. Helping when I got a little older, though it probably took him a lot longer with me 'helping.' Corn on the cob was his favorite thing in the whole world, and he'd buy it by the bushel in high season and freeze it so he'd have it all year-round."

Caleb laughed. "There's a lot of corn in Indiana," he said, voice wry. "We ate it almost every meal in the summer. I boycotted once. Preteen rebellion. I loved the stuff, still do, but for some hormonal reason I thought, 'I'll show them.' Cut off my nose to spite my face, but Mom never flinched. Never even mentioned it. I lasted about a week."

Toby shifted closer to Caleb's long, warm body. "Guess I skipped the rebellious stage. Unless this counts." He ran a hand down Caleb's stomach to brush over his crotch, and Caleb gave a soft moan.

"Better late than never," he murmured, bringing his own hand over to press on top of Toby's. Toby felt the flesh under his palm firm and grow, and his own body responded in kind. He shifted again, pulling himself up to lie half on top of Caleb so he could look down into the other man's deep-blue eyes.

"*Viva la revolución*," he said just before he kissed Caleb's full lips.

ANOTHER freakin' weird start time.

Toby grimaced as he pulled himself out of his car much too early on Saturday afternoon and headed toward the clubhouse. He couldn't believe they'd gotten hit with two late-afternoon games two weeks apart. The gods of baseball broadcasting must hate him.

At least he knew Caleb would be on time. Toby'd stood over him while he programmed a reminder into his phone before Toby left that morning. Toby had rewarded him with a deep, lingering kiss and then headed home to shower and change. He would've taken a bag with him to Caleb's, but even after they'd spent almost two days together at Toby's place—most of them in bed—he hadn't thought when he went to the ballpark the evening before that a few hours later he'd be laid out on Caleb's bed, getting fucked to within an inch of his sanity.

Toby forced his mind away from that train of thought, which led to nowhere he needed or wanted to go in public. He focused on his pregame prep, which went smoothly, and sure enough, Caleb showed up on time, pausing just long enough to shoot Toby a heated glance and a big smile before heading to his locker to dress for the game. Even the stragglers arrived with enough time to hurry into their uniforms before batting practice, and game time came and went with no major glitches. Toby breathed a little easier then.

By the third inning, shadows were creeping across the field, and Toby knew the batters would have a hell of a time for the next hour, until the sun fell completely behind the stands. Twilight games weren't just a bitch for the off-the-field staff to deal with. They didn't have to try to track a 95-mile-per-hour fastball from the bright sunlight streaming on the pitcher's mound to the darkness enveloping the plate. As if those pitches weren't hard enough to follow under perfect conditions.

Toby didn't see the play when it happened. The Braves were leading after four and a half innings, and even in the typical July heat, the contrast between sun and shade was enough that the starting pitcher asked for his jacket to keep his arm warm while the Braves were at bat. Toby jogged down to the clubhouse to get it and was on his way back up the ramp to the dugout when he heard the crack, followed instantly by a collective gasp from the crowd.

He ran the last few steps until he could see the field, and then it took him a few minutes to figure out who was lying on the ground next to home plate, his helmet spinning slowly in the dirt a few feet away.

Holy shit.

It was Caleb.

Toby had to grab hold of the railing next to him to keep from following the manager and trainers, who'd sprinted out onto the field. Caleb wasn't moving, and that, combined with the sickening sound of what Toby now knew was ball hitting skull that still echoed in his head, did not bode well. The last time Toby had seen a player down this long, he'd never stepped foot on a baseball field again.

Toby watched, leg bouncing impatiently, as Marty and Joe, the head trainer, checked Caleb over. Somebody took the jacket Toby still held, but he barely noticed. At one point, Marty shifted enough that Toby could see Caleb's mouth moving, so at least he was conscious, which gave Toby a few seconds of relief. Unfortunately, the next thing he saw was blood, and that sent him right back over the edge into sheer terror.

At almost the same moment, the home plate umpire and Lou, the manager, motioned toward the outfield. Toby's heart sank further. They were calling in the cart to take Caleb off the field, which meant his injury was bad enough, or risky enough, that either he couldn't walk off under his own power or the trainers wouldn't let him. Toby heard the murmurs from the crowd and the low chatter of the players around him, but it was only so much white noise. His mind was racing, trying to figure out if he could follow Caleb to the hospital or if he'd need to hang around until after the game before heading over.

The next second, he discarded the question. If Caleb was going to the hospital, then Toby was going too, and damn the consequences.

Mind made up, Toby took the last few steps to the field and jogged over to home plate, trying to make his choice look casual. "Hey, guys, need a hand?"

Marty glanced up at him. "Yeah, great, Toby. Can you steady his legs while we get him on the backboard? We don't think his neck is injured, but we gotta take precautions."

"Sure." Toby moved down to grip Caleb's ankles, happy to be able to touch him somewhere, at least. Joe held Caleb's head still while Marty and the two medics that came in with the cart rolled him to one side and slid the backboard in place. Toby didn't move until Marty had the straps buckled across Caleb's body, and then he moved down to grip the bottom of the board instead, helping lift it up and onto the back of the cart.

Toby stepped away then, but just long enough to catch Marty's eye. "I'm going with him."

Marty grunted as he tightened down a strap. "I know you guys are friends, Tobes, but…."

"I'm going. No buts. If there's no room for me in the ambulance, I'll drive."

Marty looked at Toby again and then nodded. "Okay. I'm riding with him. Joe's gotta stay with the team. You can meet us at the ER. It'll help having someone else there."

Toby nodded and turned away without another word, heading straight for the dugout and down the ramp to the clubhouse. He darted inside just long enough to grab his phone and keys from the lockbox near the door, and then he was on his way to his car.

THE hospital was too damn far from the ballpark. Toby felt like he'd been driving for hours by the time he finally turned off Peachtree and into the parking lot. He found an empty space and jumped out of his car, hitting the key fob to lock it behind him as he took off at jog toward the emergency room's walk-in entrance. He'd been to the hospital only a handful of times, but he knew where to go to find Caleb.

Inside, he ignored the check-in desk and looked around until he saw Marty standing off to one side. He hurried over. "How is he?"

"Still awake." Marty nodded toward the curtain a few feet away. "Not entirely coherent, and his eye looks like he got hit with an anvil. But he was talking on the ride in, and I don't think he passed out. They're checking him over, and he'll be going to X-ray soon."

Toby bounced on his toes, overflowing with nervous energy. "When can I see him?"

Marty gave him a long look. "They'll probably let us in when he gets back from X-ray. Don't know how long it'll take for them to get him into a room." Marty paused. "You seem awfully anxious about all this. He's only been here a couple of weeks. When did you find time to get to be such good friends?"

Toby nodded, gaze glued on the curtain hiding Caleb from him, hoping for a glance. "We, um, yeah." He caught himself and shot Marty what hoped was a casual smile. "We had dinner the night he got here and again the other night. We've talked some. Nice guy."

Marty didn't say anything else, though Toby could tell he wanted to. Marty knew Toby better than anyone else involved with the team, his grandfather included, but even he didn't know Toby's biggest secret. Toby had almost blurted it out more than once, but now he was glad he hadn't. Not for his own sake, but because if Marty knew Toby was gay, he'd be more likely to draw conclusions about Caleb, and the last thing Toby would want to do would be out Caleb to anyone. That had to be Caleb's choice.

Before either of them said anything else, the curtain moved and a nurse stepped out. She gave Marty a nod and a quick smile.

"Hey, Carla," Marty said. One side effect of being a trainer for a Major League Baseball team was being on a first-name basis with a lot of medical staff. "How's our boy?"

"Stable," she replied. "They're prepping him to move to X-ray now. Looks like a broken cheekbone, but the nosebleed stopped, and his eyes are responding well, so we're hopeful that's all we're dealing with."

Marty nodded. "Any idea how long they'll keep him?"

"Probably a couple of days, if he doesn't need surgery." Carla glanced at Toby but turned her attention back to Marty. "They'll want to keep an eye on the swelling and make sure there's nothing else. He'll probably get a room in an hour or two. We've got some empty beds today."

"Sounds good." Marty turned to Toby as Carla walked away. "You hungry?" Surprised by the question, Toby shook his head. "Well, I am," Marty said. "Missing the postgame feast. Let's hit the cafeteria before it shuts down."

Toby opened his mouth to argue that they should wait there, but Marty had already headed down the hall, so Toby jogged to catch up. "Marty, I really think I should—"

"—get something to eat while you can. We don't know how long we'll be here, and trust me, you don't want to be stuck with nothing but vending machines when you're starving in the middle of the night." He glanced at Toby. "Eat now. Worry later."

"Yeah, right," Toby muttered. As if he'd stop worrying. But he shut up and kept walking.

Marty led him to the cafeteria, through the line, and to a table. Toby had no idea what they were ordering; he just followed Marty's lead and ended up with meatloaf and mashed potatoes covered with brown gravy, a small pile of green beans, and a glass of sweet tea.

"Dig in," Marty instructed once they sat down, and Toby began eating on autopilot. Some part of his brain noted that the food was actually pretty good, for a hospital cafeteria, but most of his mind was still back in the ER, focused on Caleb.

Halfway through his meal, Toby stopped eating. He set down his fork. He looked at Marty, and he said the one thing he knew he shouldn't: "I'm gay."

Marty stopped chewing for a few seconds and then started back up again. He swallowed, took a sip of his tea, swallowed again, and looked Toby straight in the eye.

"I know."

Toby's jaw dropped, but Marty wasn't done. "I've known for years, Toby. All the time we've spent together? I'd have to be pretty clueless not to figure it out. And no, before you even ask, you don't give off a vibe or 'act gay,' whatever that even means. I couldn't even point to one thing that made me say, 'oh, okay.' It's just.... I know you. Okay?"

Toby sat back, stunned. He'd had no.... "I had no idea. You could have said something."

Marty snorted and forked up another bite of meatloaf. "Yeah, and if I happened to be wrong, you might've bit my head off about it. I figured you'd tell me when you were ready."

He popped the bite into his mouth, and Toby watched him chew, his own jaw working from side to side as he considered what Marty had said. "And it doesn't.... You don't care?"

Marty stopped chewing again, and then swallowed. "Well, yeah, I care." He leaned forward, resting his forearms on the edge of the table. "I care that you're happy, and that you're not dating some asshole who beats you up or something. But whether that's a guy or a girl or whatever?" He waved a hand dismissively. "I couldn't give a rip about that."

Toby sighed and picked up his fork to poke at the remains of his mashed potatoes. "What if it was a ballplayer?"

Marty stayed silent long enough that Toby looked up to find out what he was thinking. Marty's brow was furrowed. "Is that why you're here? Is it...?"

Toby lifted one shoulder and let it drop. "We kind of hit it off, you could say. And I kind of freaked out about it." He returned his attention to his plate, though he'd lost interest in eating. "Not just because of the gay thing. It's, well...." He laid down his fork and sat back, meeting Marty's steady gaze. "I'm almost his boss, you know? And even if I wasn't, we work in the same place, and that's never a good idea."

Marty nodded. "It can be a problem, yeah. But it doesn't have to be. I mean, maybe it's too much when you put it all together like that. The gay thing, the boss thing, the work thing. Three strikes?" He copied Toby's one-sided shrug. "Maybe. Maybe not. That's up to you to decide."

Marty reached for his tea glass and drained it. After setting it down, he pushed back his chair. "Now. We have food in our bellies and a patient to see about. All the rest can wait."

Toby couldn't agree more. He followed Marty's lead again, thankful Marty didn't mention his still half-full plate as they dropped off their trays and headed back down the hall.

"Ow."

It wasn't exactly what Toby expected would be the first thing out of Caleb's mouth, but he'd take it. He laughed, knowing the sound had an edge of hysteria to it.

"Yeah, pain kind of comes with the territory when you take a fastball to the face." Marty's voice might have been dry, but Toby could see the relief in his eyes.

They stood on either side of Caleb's bed in the ER, where he'd just been wheeled back from X-ray. Caleb had an IV line in the back of one hand, his eyes were taped shut, and the left side of his face looked like someone had injected grape juice just underneath the skin. The color was particularly vivid considering that the rest of his skin was several shades paler than his usual light tan.

"You're gonna have quite a shiner, son." Marty reached out to tap two long fingers on Caleb's forearm. "Gotta learn to duck faster."

Caleb's face moved in what probably started out to be a smile but ended up in a wince. "You should see the other guy," he murmured.

Toby snorted. "The other guy is a five-ounce ball made of cork, yarn, and leather."

"Yeah, and he was speeding." Caleb turned his head in Toby's direction. His lips quirked, like he'd thought of trying to smile again but reconsidered. "Hope you saved it. Need that one for the trophy case. Maybe a T-shirt. 'I Survived A Beanball.'"

He reached out a hand, and Toby took it, lacing their fingers together. Caleb relaxed for a moment but then jerked, tugging a little. "Is Marty still—?"

"Right here, Caleb," Marty cut in. "Not a problem. Already had a little talk with Toby."

Caleb didn't relax, though. "It's just…."

Toby stepped forward and wrapped his free hand around both of theirs. "Caleb. Shut up. It's fine, okay?"

Toby swore Caleb rolled his eyes behind his closed eyelids. "'Shut up'? Really? This is how you treat a man who's been hit in the head with a fastball and lived to tell the tale?"

"So far, he has," Marty intoned. "Watch yourself, or we might start thinking of ways to change that."

The clips holding the curtain behind Marty to the ceiling squeaked, and Toby released Caleb's hand instinctively. The cloth moved to admit a tiny young woman who didn't look a day over fifteen but wore a white coat with a badge proclaiming her to be Madeline Grace, MD. "All right, Mr. Browning," she said, stepping adroitly around Marty to stand next to the bed. "The X-ray showed only a hairline fracture, so surgery won't be needed. We'll be admitting you overnight to monitor the swelling in your brain—"

"Hold up a second," Caleb cut in, lifting one hand. "Can you back that up and slow it down a little? I just woke up, and…. Did you say swelling in my brain?"

Dr. Grace glanced at Toby and Marty, who'd moved to the far side of the bed. "You're the family?"

"Marty Boynton, assistant team trainer." He tilted his head to the side. "Toby Macmillan, grandson of team owner. This is official business, of a sort."

Dr. Grace narrowed her eyes for a second but then turned her attention back to Caleb. "Mr. Browning, is it acceptable to you for me to discuss the details of your condition in front of Mr. Boynton and Mr. Macmillan?"

Caleb nodded. "Yeah. Saves me from having to tell them later. Not sure I could do that all that clearly with this headache."

Dr. Grace nodded. "Mr. Browning, you've suffered a rather serious blow to the head that's caused some degree of swelling and at least a mild concussion. As I said, the X-ray showed only a hairline fracture of your cheekbone, so you will not need reparative surgery. You have extensive bruising and some swelling around the impact point, as well as the blurry vision you described earlier. None of this is particularly serious, but we do need to monitor you in case you develop bleeding in or around your brain. A subdural hematoma is always a risk after an injury such as yours."

Toby couldn't be sure how much of that Caleb got, all things considered. "So he'll be here overnight, and if everything looks okay tomorrow, he'll be able to go home?"

"Or the day after." Dr. Grace turned to the computer sitting in the corner of the cubicle and signed in, then pulled up a screen with row after row of data, none of which Toby could read from where he was. Dr. Grace clicked and typed for a couple of minutes, pulled up another screen showing an image that had to be Caleb's X-ray, and then typed a few more notes before clicking out and, apparently, logging off.

She turned to face Toby and Marty. "He'll need to be monitored pretty closely even after he goes home," she told them. "Head injuries can be tricky."

Names flashed through Toby's head, players who'd lost seasons, careers, even their lives to nasty beanballs. He shuddered and resisted, barely, reaching out to take Caleb's hand again.

"We've been through this a time or two," Marty said. "We'll have the team doctor in to check him out while he's here, too. He'll be the one handling the follow-up."

"Good." Dr. Grace held out a hand, and Marty and Toby each took a turn shaking it. She turned back to the bed. "We'll get you in a room and settled soon, Mr. Browning."

"Thanks." Caleb almost got a real smile out this time, though he favored the injured left side. Dr. Grace stepped back out and pulled the curtain back into place, and Toby let himself grab Caleb's hand again once she was gone.

Marty cleared his throat. "Look, guys, I need to head back to the ballpark, let everyone know what's up. The guys'll be asking. I doubt any of them will try to come up tonight, but you might get some company tomorrow."

Toby heard the unspoken warning: play it safe if you don't want the world to know about this. He gave Marty a half smile. "Thanks," he said. "For, well, everything."

Marty clapped a hand on his shoulder and gave it a shake. "No problem, kiddo."

He stepped around the curtain, and Toby heard his footfalls fading as he walked away. He moved closer to the bed and lifted his free hand to brush Caleb's uninjured cheek.

"You're gonna be just fine," he murmured, and Caleb turned his head into the gentle touch.

"Stay?" Caleb's voice was low, like he was a step away from sleep, and Toby couldn't have denied him even if he'd wanted to.

"Not going anywhere," he promised.

"JESUS CHRIST, this headache won't quit."

Caleb had been griping most of the day, first about how he couldn't get a decent night's sleep with nurses waking him up every couple of hours to check on him, and then how they gave him bland food because he kept having bouts of nausea from the concussion. Toby had let him rant, knowing he was in pain and feeling rotten, but now the pain itself had become the focus of Caleb's dissatisfaction.

"Jesus Christ, Caleb." Toby gave up standing next to Caleb's bed, trying to soothe him, and threw himself down into the relatively comfortable recliner he'd mostly not slept in the night before. "You got hit in the head with a goddamn baseball. Of course you have a fucking headache!"

The glare Caleb gave him would have been more effective had the left side of his face not been swollen and spattered with a rainbow of colors. At least his eyes were open, which was an improvement, and he'd shown no signs of bleeding on his brain. But his vision was still blurry, especially in his left eye, so he was scheduled for another scan to make sure nothing major was going on, and he'd be stuck in the hospital another night or two.

Toby glared right back. "Look, I know you're in pain and frustrated and all that. I get it. But could you ease up a little on the throttle? You're giving *me* a headache, and that won't help anyone."

Caleb rolled his good eye. "Oh, poor you, stuck here babysitting instead of out having a high old time. Why don't you—"

That was it. Toby jumped to his feet, took the two steps to the side of the bed, and leaned over to kiss Caleb, hard. He didn't even care if it hurt. Maybe that would snap Caleb out of his little self-pity party.

Caleb made a muffled sound, but after a moment, he kissed Toby back, bringing up one hand to slide into Toby's hair. Toby held the kiss and then broke away to catch Caleb's gaze.

"I'm here because I want to be, idiot," Toby said. "And because I know you want me here. So save the drama for yo' mama. Got it?"

Caleb stared at him for a long moment before giving a slow, lopsided smile. Toby met it with one of his own before leaning in to kiss him again.

The kiss was slow, deepening gradually until their tongues twined together and Toby's pulse pounded and his cock got really, really interested in where things were going. He'd just realized they were in a hospital and he should probably ease up on the guy with the concussion when a noise at the door made them pull apart. Toby turned to see two people standing in the doorway, both of them wide-eyed. One was a nurse, and through the sudden panic, Toby was pretty sure she'd keep her mouth shut, or risk losing her job.

The man standing next to her was a bigger problem: Barry Knight.

Oh, fuck, Toby thought. No way in hell Barry wouldn't go public with what he'd just seen. Toby wouldn't have been surprised to see him pull out his phone and put it out on Twitter before he even left the room.

The nurse had slipped away by the time Toby managed to say anything. "Barry, I don't know what—"

Barry waved a hand. "Do you have an official comment?" He flicked his gaze over to Caleb. "Either of you?"

Caleb sat up straighter. "Don't do this, man," he warned, though all three of them knew it was an empty threat. Random, stupid, blind luck—good for him, bad for them—and Barry was about to write his ticket as a sports reporter.

Barry nodded. "No comment. Got it. See you guys in the papers."

He was gone before Toby or Caleb could say another word.

"I HADN'T planned for it to come out like this."

Caleb's voice was flat. After Barry's visit, all the fight had gone out of him. As much as Toby had wanted him to be calmer, this wasn't what he'd had in mind.

"I told my parents senior year of high school." Caleb fiddled with a loose thread on the blanket that covered him from the waist down. "They were pretty upset, but the main thing Dad said was that if I wanted to play baseball, I had to keep it quiet." Caleb shrugged. "He was right."

Toby had pulled his chair close to the side of the bed, and at that, he reached out to cover Caleb's restless hand with his own. "He might have been right back then," he said. "But things change. Times change. Coming out isn't as big a deal now. Look at Jason Collins. Basketball seems to be surviving that."

Caleb gave Toby a look. "Except that he still hasn't signed on with a team for this season."

"He's also thirty-four years old and was never a superstar," Toby replied. "He might not have been signed anyway."

Caleb let his head fall back against the pillows. "And I'm barely even a major leaguer," he muttered. "No way I'm gonna stick after this."

Toby wished he could reassure Caleb, but anything he said would be false hope, and they both knew it. The chances of the team doing anything immediately were slim, simply because it would be a public relations nightmare in the current climate to dump a player who'd just come out. But the long run was another story. And even with a voice that counted, which Toby would officially have in another few days, he couldn't guarantee anything.

A knock sounded at the door, and an older black man stuck his head in. Toby recognized him after a moment as the orderly who'd brought Caleb's bed upstairs the night before. "Hey, guys," the man said. "Mandy sent me down to see if everything's okay. Said some guy might've been giving you trouble?"

He flicked his gaze down to the bed, and Toby realized then that he still had his hand over Caleb's. He didn't guess it mattered all that much anymore.

"Just some asshole looking to write his ticket." Caleb leaned forward. "You got anything you'd like to add?"

The man stepped fully into the room and shut the door behind him. He leaned against it, crossing his arms behind his back and one ankle over the other. "My youngest brother got kicked out when he was sixteen." His tone was as casual as his stance. "Our mama found out he was kissin' on the boy across the way. He was on the street for a year before I found him and took him home with me. Took almost another year before he trusted I wasn't gonna yank the rug back out from under him." He let his gaze flick between them. "You got nothin' to worry about from me."

Tension drained out of Toby, and he gave the man a smile. "I'm Toby Macmillan, and this is Caleb Browning," he said, tilting his head in Caleb's direction. "If you ever need anything for you or your brother, you just call the Braves' office and ask for me. I'll do what I can."

The man smiled. "Otis Washington," he said. "And if you boys need any help around here, keepin' the sleazeballs away or whatever, you just let me know."

"We will." Caleb squeezed Toby's hand, and Otis flashed them a quick, bright grin before he slipped back into the hall.

TOBY got the phone call just after midnight, not twenty minutes after he'd gotten home from the hospital. Caleb had finally convinced him to go get some decent sleep so one of them would be rested when Caleb got released, which looked like it would be Tuesday. Toby had stripped to his boxers and flopped down on the bed when his cell phone rang, and he picked it up to see the Braves' main switchboard number on the caller ID.

"Fuck." He blew out a breath, debated ignoring it, then decided he might as well get it over with.

"Hello?"

"Please hold for Mr. Macmillan." Toby didn't recognize the voice, but he supposed it was one of the backup admins, since his grandfather's executive assistant worked a normal weekday schedule. While he waited—once again considering hanging up and trying to ignore it all—he tried to figure out what Ray's reaction would be. Breaking a story like this at midseason broke all the rules, and leaving the public relations department out of it only made things worse. It wouldn't matter much that they hadn't been given a choice about it. The team was still going to have to deal with a mess.

"Toby!" his grandfather practically bellowed into Toby's ear, and Toby jerked the phone back instinctively. "What in the goddamn hell are you playin' at, boy?"

The good old boy in Ray Macmillan rarely made an appearance anymore, unless he was playing up to the public. But apparently anger brought it out in him.

"I'm not playing at anything, Granddad." Toby fought to keep his voice steady. "I didn't plan for this to happen."

"And you're gonna goddamn fix it," Ray growled. "You be in my office at nine o'clock in the morning, you hear me?"

Toby's headache was starting to rival Caleb's. "What for?"

A sharp noise rang through the phone, and Toby realized Ray must've slammed a fist down on his desk. "You just do what you're told and get your ass down here. And you damn well better not be late."

Another noise, and the line went dead. Ray had hung up on him. Toby couldn't bring himself to be surprised, or to care all that much about what might happen in less than nine hours. The only thing he wanted to know was that Caleb would be fine, and they'd be together.

Rolling to the side, Toby crawled under the covers. He paused to set his alarm for way too early, to give himself time to call and check up on Caleb before heading to the ballpark, then curled a pillow close to his chest to try to sleep.

"THIS ends right here. Right now."

Ray Macmillan glared at Toby across the expanse of his shining mahogany desk. Impressively large even in the expansive office, the desk was older than Toby. He remembered crawling under it when he was a toddler and sticking his head out the opening in the front, just like the famous picture of JFK Jr. under his father's Oval Office desk.

Toby had sat in the chair across this desk from his grandfather more times than he could count, even sometimes for a dressing-down. But never had his grandfather looked at him with this kind of venom in his eyes.

"What ends?" Toby knew the answers. He just wanted to force Ray to say them.

"This whole… thing with you."

Toby's laugh was hollow. "You mean the thing where I'm gay? Or the thing where I'm falling for one of the ballplayers?"

"All of it!" Ray roared, his face going even redder, so much so that Toby almost feared for his heart. "You are not some sick, perverted—"

"I'm gay, Granddad." Toby was on his feet by then. His sleep had been fitful, and he'd had no breakfast and only half a cup of coffee. But he felt more energized in that moment than he had in days. "I've always been gay. I'll always be gay. You can be upset about me dating a ballplayer. I can accept that. But you do not get to sit there and call me names for being who I am."

Ray's scowl deepened. "I'm glad your father isn't here to see this."

"I couldn't agree more." Toby leaned forward, hands on the desk. "I'd hate to see him figure out exactly how much of a bigot his father is."

Ray jumped to his feet. "Now you listen here," he growled. "I set up a press conference tomorrow at one. You will give a prepared statement denying everything you've been accused of, and then you'll sign a nondisclosure agreement about all of this. If you don't, I'll write you out of my will. I will get your trust fund overturned. I already have my lawyers working on it. I swear, you will never own a single piece of this ball club if I have anything to say about it."

Toby leaned back, stunned that his own grandfather would seriously try to cut him out so completely. His father had brought him up with baseball, had woven the ball club so completely into his genes that Toby wasn't at all sure he'd know what to do with himself without it. He didn't have a clue if Ray could actually do anything about the portion of the team he was slated to own in a few more days, but the idea that his grandfather could be so vindictive as to take that away from him? A baseball to the head might have been less painful.

"Some grandfather you are," he spat. "Hating your own grandson so much that you'd take away the one thing that's always been a part of his life. Well, good luck with that." He nodded and rapped his knuckles on the gleaming wood surface between them. "I'm sure this desk will take care of you when you're too old to do it for yourself."

He spun on his heel, ignoring his grandfather's attempts to call him back. Let him think what he wanted. Toby had plans of his own.

THE pressroom hummed with conversation, but Toby tried to ignore the noise. Dexter, the team's PR director, stood next to him behind the curtain that hung at the back of the podium where players and coaches sat for organized press conferences. Toby'd never had a turn there, but he was about to find out how it felt.

Toby hadn't slept much more the night before than he had Sunday night. After his disastrous meeting with his grandfather, he'd visited Caleb, who'd gotten the full story out of him and then urged him to go see his own lawyer, who'd been managing his parents' estate and his trust for nearly ten years, before he did anything rash. Toby had managed to get an appointment early that morning, and between that and the hours of conversation with Caleb the day before, he knew exactly what he was going to do.

Steeling himself, Toby nodded when Dexter's assistant asked if they were ready, and he followed Dexter out to the table. He sat down behind the microphone and looked up, finding his grandfather where he sat on the front row, looking dire. Just behind him sat Matt Sussman, though, and he gave Toby a smile.

"Thank you for coming, ladies and gentlemen," Dexter began. "Toby Macmillan is here to read a statement."

It wasn't precisely true, and Toby had warned Dexter of that, though he hadn't given him details. When Dexter turned his head toward Toby, Toby took a deep breath and started.

"Good afternoon," he said. "I have a prepared statement here—that I'm not going to read."

Ray Macmillan's eyes widened, but before he could react further, Toby went on. "My name is Toby Macmillan, and I am a gay man."

The murmurs he expected started among the crowd, but he ignored them, continuing to stare down his grandfather. "I'm making this announcement not because I think it matters, but because it shouldn't. My private life should stay private, but it doesn't always work that way. Coming out is a personal, private decision, but making an announcement in public like this isn't something you do for yourself. It's something you do for others."

He finally broke eye contact with his grandfather and looked around at the other faces in the room. "I want to be clear. This changes nothing about me or who I am. I've been working with this team since I was fifteen, and the only thing different now is that I'm almost twenty-one."

He saw Barry then, standing near the back wall, his face reddening, though Toby had no idea if he was embarrassed, angry, or what. He also didn't care. "It's important to note," Toby said, holding Barry's gaze, "that Major League Baseball, and the Atlanta Braves specifically, have policies against discrimination on any basis, including sexual orientation. These policies apply not only to the front office but on every level of the organization, top to bottom. And that includes the ballplayers."

Toby looked down at his hands and unfolded the piece of paper he still held. "On that note, I do have a prepared statement to read. This is on behalf of Caleb Browning."

He knew what the statement said, but he kept his eyes on the paper as he read it anyway. “Caleb says: ‘In 1947, Jackie Robinson broke baseball’s color line when he debuted with the Brooklyn Dodgers of the National League. I know I’m not the first gay man to play in the majors, and I certainly have no illusions that I am, or ever could be, a fraction of the player that Robinson was. But if by breaking this barrier, if by coming out openly, I can help other players like me even a fraction as much as he did, then it’s worth whatever consequences I might face.’”

Toby paused for a long moment and then looked up at the crowd in front of him. “Caleb Browning has spent his entire professional baseball career with the Atlanta ball club. He was thrilled to finally join the Braves at the All-Star break. A few days ago, he suffered what could easily have been a career-ending injury on the field. It would be shameful for his career to suffer because of his choice to be honest about his sexuality.”

Toby leaned forward, speaking directly into the microphone. “In closing, let me be very clear. If I have anything to say about it, this ball club will not tolerate discrimination of any kind. Any employee who has a problem with that is free to seek employment elsewhere.” He met his grandfather’s gaze and, to his surprise, saw a glimmer of respect there, among the expected shock and anger.

Toby looked around the room again. “I will not be taking questions at this time. Assistant team trainer Marty Boynton will be available shortly for questions about Caleb’s injuries and projected recovery. Thank you for your attention.”

Toby pushed to his feet, ignored the shouted questions, and walked away from the table and out the door, for once in his life feeling completely at ease in his skin.

No matter what happened next, he knew he’d done the right thing.

TOBY knocked on the side door to the hospital Otis had tipped him off about and smiled at Otis when he opened it a few second later. “Thanks, man.”

Otis grinned and held up one fist for Toby to bump. “No prob. Saw the press thing. You did good.”

Toby shrugged and bumped Otis’s fist. “Did what I needed to do.”

Otis nodded. “Now go see about your boy.”

CALEB was dressed and ready to go when Toby gave a knock out of deference and pushed into his room. "Oh, thank God," Caleb said the second he saw Toby. "Come over here and let me give you the biggest hug and kiss ever, and then get me the hell out of here!"

Toby had to laugh even as he obeyed. Caleb pulled him in tight, cupping the back of his neck with one hand and sliding the other around his waist, and kissed him, his mouth minty fresh. Caleb smelled clean and right, even through the antiseptic scent that lingered after any hospital stay, and Toby would have been content to stay right there.

But Caleb was finally going home, and the sooner Toby could get him there, the better.

Full of reluctance, Toby drew away. "Are you all checked out?"

"Yep." Caleb pushed to his feet, and Toby reached for his hand without even thinking about it. Caleb meshed his long fingers with Toby's immediately, as if they'd been holding hands for years instead of for the first time, and that little something in Toby's chest turned over again.

God, I am *falling in love with him.* Even though it had been only a couple of weeks, the feeling hit him hard, and he didn't allow himself to fight it. He squeezed Caleb's hand and reached over to pick up the duffel bag sitting on the bed.

"Let's get you home."

OTIS pushed Caleb downstairs in the hospital-required wheelchair, but he'd scouted things out in advance and knew a couple of news teams waited outside to pounce when they emerged, so he let them out the same side door as before. Even with the subterfuge, Toby breathed easier once they were in his car and headed out of the parking lot. He had no idea whether they'd encounter media at Caleb's apartment, but he guessed that would probably be a safer bet than his own place. Caleb hadn't been living there long, so maybe the press hadn't found it yet.

Things looked promising when they pulled up to the gates—nothing resembling a news van in sight—and soon they were climbing the flight of stairs to Caleb's place. Toby kept his hands off Caleb, not because he was worried about being seen but because he didn't want to give the impression that he thought Caleb couldn't make it on his own. Caleb had been checked, rechecked, and given every all clear in the books, with just fading bruises and prescription painkillers to show for his troubles. He'd be off the field for a little while yet, but daily life he could handle just fine.

Toby still carried his bag for him, though. And Caleb, he noted, hadn't protested.

Caleb unlocked the door and pushed it open. He shot Toby a wry grin. "I guess it's not going to feel much like home," he noted, "considering I've only spent about a half-dozen nights here."

Toby laughed. "Well, it's a definite improvement over a hospital room, that's for sure."

Caleb chuckled in agreement and walked inside. Toby followed closely behind and shut the door behind them. Caleb dropped his keys on the breakfast bar, kicked off his sneakers, and kept walking, straight into the bedroom. Toby hung back, unsure whether he should follow, but in another few moments, Caleb stuck his head back out.

"I'm going to scrub the hospital off me." He let his gaze wander Toby's body, so much like a caress that Toby almost felt it. "Want to wash my back?"

Toby's mouth stretched into a grin, even as he dropped the duffel bag and went after his boyfriend. When he got to the bathroom, Caleb had his shirt and shorts unbuttoned and was bent over, turning on the water. Not about to miss that opportunity, Toby walked up right behind him, cupped Caleb's hips with his hands, and pressed his crotch, and his rapidly hardening cock, into the valley between Caleb's cheeks.

"Shit!" Caleb jumped and then moaned as Toby rubbed harder against him. "Fuck. Toby."

Toby bent over Caleb's back so he could lick his way up his neck to bite his earlobe. "Missed you," he murmured. The shiver that ran through Caleb's body sent Toby's heart rate galloping.

Caleb groaned. "I want this"—he rubbed his ass against Toby's crotch—"so fucking much." He turned his head and kissed Toby's cheek, his lips soft and warm. "But let me wash the antiseptic smell off first? I don't want us both to stink of it."

"You smell like heaven," Toby replied. He took a step back and away and attacked his clothes. "But I get it. Get your clothes off, and we'll take care of that fast."

Clothes discarded and water temperature adjusted, they stepped into the tub, and Caleb moved immediately under the spray. Toby followed, reaching for the tiny bar of soap sitting on the corner shelf. He laughed as he reached forward to wet it in the water and started working up a lather. "Did you steal the soap from the Hyatt?"

Caleb turned his head, and Toby saw he was blushing. "I haven't exactly had much time to shop since I got here, and I left mine in Pearl."

Toby moved in even closer and ran both hands across Caleb's chest, rubbing the soap across his skin. "You know I'm just teasing you. I like this stuff, though. Smells like you."

Toby felt Caleb's chuckle under his fingers. "I smell like it," he pointed out. "Especially with you rubbing it all over me."

Toby grinned against Caleb's shoulder. "Not all over. Not yet, anyway." He let one hand drift lower, working suds into the hair below Caleb's navel, and Caleb shivered again and leaned back into Toby's body. Toby stopped any pretense of washing him and just held him there, turning his face into the side of Caleb's neck.

"You scared me," he whispered. "Don't scare me like that again."

Caleb pushed away, making Toby's heart jerk in his chest, but he only turned around and cupped Toby's face in both hands. "I'm fine." His voice was low but strong. "I'm not going anywhere, okay?"

Toby ran his fingers oh so lightly over the side of Caleb's beautiful face, now marred with bruises. "You better not," he said. "I'm kind of getting used to having you around."

Caleb smiled. "It's not like I haven't been hit by pitches before. Hell, from behind the plate more than at it. They don't call catcher's gear the 'tools of ignorance' for nothing. We're sitting ducks."

"But a batter doesn't have a catcher's mask."

"Kind of hard to see the pitcher that way."

Before Toby could reply, Caleb bent to kiss him, and Toby could only open his mouth and slide his tongue out to tangle with Caleb's. The risks came with the game, he knew. What had happened to Caleb was a one in a million shot, and odds were extremely low that it would ever happen again.

Didn't mean Toby would stop worrying, but he'd have to learn to live with that.

Caleb's lips moved away, sliding across Toby's cheek to his ear. "Let's get showered," he rasped. "Because I think we're gonna need to be lying down for me to do what I want to do to you."

Toby's whole body tightened at Caleb's words, and he groaned, the low sound reverberating off the tile. He forced himself to take a step away from Caleb's warm, wet body, reached for the sliver of soap again, and worked up new lather. He tried to keep his touch impersonal, efficient, but he failed miserably. Caleb's skin just felt too good under his fingertips, and he lingered much too long on some of his favorite spots.

By the time they were both washed and rinsed off, they could barely move without bumping into each other's hard cocks. Caleb grinned down at Toby and shifted his hips back and forth, letting their dicks bounce across each other as if jousting. Toby laughed and grabbed Caleb's shaft to give it a squeeze. "Trying to start a fire?"

Caleb hissed and blinked. "Think we already have."

Toby brushed a quick kiss over Caleb's mouth but didn't release his grip, even as he bent forward to turn off the water and then pushed the shower curtain aside. Caleb followed him out of the tub and reached to snag the towel off the bar, then used it to dry off the worst of the wetness while Toby continued to tease his cock. Toby leaned forward to suck droplets off Caleb's nipples, and Caleb let out a sound between a whimper and a whine.

"You're killin' me," he said, and Toby looked up at him from under his lashes as he closed his lips around Caleb's right nipple. Caleb jerked all over. "Jesus," he rasped out. "Bed. Now. Please."

Toby pulled his mouth away but not his hand, using it to pull Caleb toward the bedroom. Caleb laughed roughly. "Leading me around by my dick?"

Toby ran his tongue all the way around his own lips before he answered. "It's working, isn't it?"

Caleb grunted, and then he pounced. He grabbed Toby with both arms, trapping Toby's hand right where it was, and fell onto the bed, dragging Toby down and under him. He came up breathing hard but lying full-length on top, and Toby had absolutely no complaints about his position.

Caleb brought his hand up to push the still wet hair back from Toby's forehead. "Want you," he said, and then he kissed Toby so tenderly and deeply that it simultaneously melted Toby's heart and stiffened his dick. God, Caleb could kiss. Toby could stay right there and just kiss Caleb forever and be satisfied.

But there was so much more they could be doing.

Toby wrapped his legs around Caleb's and used the leverage to push his pelvis against Caleb's, rubbing their cocks together between their bodies. Caleb groaned into their kiss and pushed back, setting up a give-and-take movement that rocked them closer and closer to orgasm. Toby raked his fingernails down Caleb's back, probably leaving red marks behind, but he didn't care. He just wanted more of Caleb against him, around him. Inside him.

"Can't wait." Caleb murmured the words against Toby's mouth and dove back into their kiss, even as he maneuvered them to the side so he could work a hand in between them. He caught their cocks together, the warmth and pressure of his fingers perfect, and Toby gasped against Caleb's mouth.

"Fuck," he breathed out. "Caleb."

Caleb made a sound in his throat and plunged his tongue into Toby's mouth, and Toby opened wide to let him in. He got a handful of Caleb's hair and a handful of his ass and rode it out, letting Caleb carry them to the edge and then throw them right over.

They came down together, panting, skin flushed and sweaty, their mixed cum pooled on Toby's stomach. Toby floated on a wave of sensation, residual shockwaves zapping through him, feeling the warmth of Caleb's breath against the side of his face. Caleb tightened his arm around him where he still held him close, and Toby's heart did that little flip again.

I am so far gone it's not even funny. Ironically, the thought made him snicker

"What's funny?"

"Nothing." Toby pressed a kiss against Caleb's temple, the closest part of him he could reach. "Just rest. We'll get cleaned up in a bit."

GOD, I hate this.

Toby stopped outside his grandfather's office and gave a cursory knock on the frame before stepping into the open doorway. "You asked to see me?"

"I did." Ray Macmillan sat behind the desk, just as he had two days earlier, but the look on his face was about a millions shades less dire. He lifted his chin in the direction of the chair nearest Toby. "Have a seat."

Toby did, noticing as he moved closer that a folder lay open on his desk with what looked like legal paperwork spread out from it. He tensed, waiting for his grandfather to bring the hammer down on him.

"These documents," Ray began, "are the ones my lawyer started drawing up for me on Monday. They include a revised version of my will and paperwork related to the ownership of this team." He looked up, pinning Toby with his piercing gaze. "Every one of them is written to exclude you from ever inheriting or otherwise acquiring any portion of the 60-percent stake I hold in this ball club."

Toby nodded. He'd expected as much when he'd defied his grandfather. After talking with his lawyer, Toby knew there was no risk of him losing the share his father had left him, the 30 percent he'd gotten on his own twenty-first birthday. But it didn't surprise Toby that his grandfather would make sure Toby would never have any more.

Ray held his gaze for a few long moments, and then he picked up several of the sheets and slowly, deliberately, tore them in half from top to bottom. Toby sat up straighter, and Ray picked up another set and repeated the motion.

He pushed the ruined paperwork aside, along with the folder they'd been inside, revealing a second folder. He opened this one and pulled out a single sheet of paper.

"This is the document I had written after I told my lawyer to dispose of those." He nodded toward the ruined paperwork. "It is a press statement confirming that I am aware of your sexual orientation, and that of Caleb Browning. Further, it states that it is the policy of the Atlanta Braves not to discriminate against its employees on the grounds of sexual orientation, and that the team will not tolerate any such actions by any of its staff." He looked away from Toby finally. "It's being released to the press as we speak. It is all I will have to say on the matter."

Toby waited, wondering if his grandfather would have something a little more personal to say. When Ray didn't continue speaking, Toby leaned forward. "So…. What? You're not going to cut me out of the team because it would be a bad PR move? What about the fact that I'm your grandson and you're supposed to actually, oh, I don't know, care about me?"

Ray lifted his head, and Toby was taken aback by the weariness on his face. Suddenly, Ray Macmillan looked every one of his sixty-four years. "I don't…. This is what I can do. I can't…."

He trailed off, and despite himself, Toby felt a pang of sympathy. His grandfather was from a different generation, raised under different belief systems and societal structures. Just the fact that he was willing to overcome those learned prejudices enough not to cut Toby out of his life was a huge step.

Toby decided he could live with that, for now.

"I…. Thank you," he finally said. He pushed to his feet. "I'll see you—well. I'll see you."

He turned and walked out of the office, his heart aching, but not broken.

"HAPPY birthday, dear Tooooo-byyyyyy! Happy birthday to you!"

Toby leaned forward and blew out the candles, to a chorus of cheers. His face hurt from grinning so wide, but he couldn't help himself. He stood in the middle of the Braves clubhouse after Friday night's game, surrounding by the team and staff, a huge sheet cake decorated with an elaborate depiction of a baseball game sitting in front of him. He'd expected to get birthday wishes—he did every year—but the clubhouse staff had outdone themselves this time. Even the postgame meal was Toby's favorite—pulled pork sandwiches with all the fixings.

Best of all was Caleb, standing next to him and smiling almost as much as Toby. Tonight was his first night back with the team, though he'd stay on the disabled list for at least another ten days, and they'd both been heartened by the many supportive greetings he'd received when they arrived. A few players avoided him, though because they disapproved or didn't know what to say, Toby didn't know. Heck, for all he knew, they might have their own secrets they weren't ready to share.

"Speech! Speech! Speech!" Toby didn't know who'd started the chant, but he suspected Marty, from the smirk on his face. Toby waved a hand until everyone quieted down a little.

"I think I'm kind of speeched out this week," he said, to several hoots and even a couple of "go, boys." "So I'll just say thank you, for the cake and, well, just for being good guys and standing by me. Us."

He reached for Caleb's hand, giving it a quick squeeze. "Now," he said, reaching for the cake server sitting on the table. "Who wants the first slice?"

With his friends and coworkers clamoring for first dibs, Toby felt Caleb step up beside him, close enough that Toby could feel his body heat. He didn't have to look. He knew Caleb would be right there, and that was enough for him.

SHAE CONNOR lives in Atlanta, where she works for the government by day and reads and writes about pretty boys falling in love by night. She's been making up stories for as long as she can remember, but it took her a long time to figure out that maybe she should start writing them down. Now, she usually has far too many stories in progress, but when she does manage to tear herself away from her laptop, she enjoys running, hiking, cooking, and traveling, not necessarily in that order.

Shae posts snippets, updates, and thoughts on writing and editing at her website, http://shaeconnorwrites.com. You can contact her at shaeconnorwrites@gmail.com.

One Last Road Trip

KERRY FREEMAN

In memory of Glenn Burke (1952-1995)

Acknowledgments:

Thank you to Shae Connor for inviting me to contribute to this anthology (GO BRAVES!), to Kate McMurray and Marguerite Labbe for sharing the love of baseball, to Trinity Stanley for being the best alpha reader a writer could have, and to my wonderful husband for buying takeout dinners and covering for me at family functions so I could finish my manuscript.

Prologue: San Diego

THE clubhouse was finally quiet. Jake had had enough microphones and cameras shoved in his face for one day. As he sank down into a big brown leather recliner, he smiled at the realization he would never have to do another postgame interview again.

Sure, he was bummed that they'd missed the wild card by a half game, but he was secretly a little relieved. He was ready to hit the road. He wanted to see his kids, and he wanted to get back home. It'd been years since he'd been in Georgia for more than a three-game stand in Atlanta, and he missed it. He missed everything—and everyone—he'd left behind there.

"Hey, Jake," the clubhouse manager called from the doorway. "Did you already clean out your locker?"

Jake smiled. He remembered the old metal lockers from high school. The fancy wooden shelving he had here was as far from that as he could get. "Yep, everything's in my car."

The manager walked to Jake's locker and looked up. "Not everything." He gingerly climbed onto a wheeled chair and pulled down Jake's nameplate. He hopped down and tossed the plate to Jake. "Here you go."

Jake caught the plate and took a long look at it. "I guess that makes it official."

"What are you going to do now?"

"I'm going on a road trip back home to Georgia. Gonna stop and see the ex and the kids on the way."

The manager shook his head and laughed. "You'd think you'd have gotten your fill of road trips as long as you've been playing."

"Yeah, well, this is my last one."

"We're gonna miss you around here. I know the team will miss you on second base."

That was a polite lie. Maybe if he'd retired last year, but this year he'd been hobbled by knee pain more often than not. "Thanks. I'm sure I'll be wishing I was here when next season starts."

"Well, you just make sure you've got someone to keep your mind off baseball by then," the manager said with a wink.

Jake smacked the nameplate against his leg. "I just might do that."

Chapter 1: Albuquerque

JAKE was pretty sure he'd never get over being amazed that every possession that meant anything to him would fit in a five-by-eight trailer. But there he was, trailer behind him, driving out of San Diego before most people were awake.

At first, Jake enjoyed the time alone. The skies were crystal clear and the weather warm. He rolled down the SUV's windows once he hit I-8 and let the fresh air flow around him. He admired the passing scenery. He cranked up the music and sang along as loudly as he could.

Several hours and several turns later, Jake hit the beginning of a 233-mile stretch of I-40, and he was ready for the damn day to be over with. Why had he thought a twelve-hour driving day was a good idea? He was too damn old for this shit, and his knee was beginning to really hurt. All he wanted was a nice long shower and some food. A soft bed would be nice too.

He grumbled as he pulled into the drive of his ex-wife's modern adobe house. Marcy waved, and next to her stood a fit young Native American man who couldn't have been more than twenty-two years old.

"Oh Lord, is that the boyfriend?" Jake shook his head.

Jake climbed out of the SUV and gave his knee a few experimental bends before placing his full weight on his leg. He pulled his duffel bag out of the backseat and slung it over his shoulder.

Marcy ran up to Jake and planted a swift, friendly kiss on his lips. No matter how much he reminded her that divorced couples should not kiss that way, she persisted in doing it. He only hoped the approaching probable boyfriend wasn't the jealous type.

"Oh, Jake, I'm so glad you finally got here," Marcy exclaimed. "I was starting to get worried. Eddie said I was being silly, but you know how I am."

Jake gave her a hug and kept one arm around her shoulders when he finished. "Yep, I do. You always fretted over my road trips."

"I can't help it. People are killed all the time by a rock or a log or a tire just flying up from the road and crashing through their windshield."

The young man—Jake assumed it was the aforementioned Eddie—held out his hand and firmly shook the one Jake offered in return. "I'm Eddie. Nice to meet you, sir. I'm a huge baseball fan. Let me take your bag to the guest room."

Jake, shocked by the greeting as well as Eddie's rapid-fire delivery, handed over his duffel. Eddie took it and dashed through the front door.

"Did your boyfriend just call me *sir*?"

"I'm afraid he did," Marcy said with a laugh. "You'll have to forgive him. He's been so nervous about meeting you. I think he'll calm down once he realizes you won't smother him in his sleep."

"He's safe. Well, as long as I don't find out he's a Yankees fan."

Marcy softly punched his gut. "Give me a little credit. Like I'd ever get involved with a Yankees fan." She pulled away and grabbed Jake's hand. "Let's get inside. Eddie has been working on dinner all afternoon, and I think you'll really like it."

Every time Jake visited Marcy, he was impressed with the warmth of her home. From the beautiful, plush rugs to the oversized couches and chairs, everything was designed for comfort. She'd done the same in their home together. He'd tried his best to make his apartment in San Diego feel the same, but he'd never been very successful. He was determined the new house in Georgia would feel more like a home, even if he had to fly Marcy out there to do it for him.

Marcy led him to the kitchen, which was full of the delicious smell of fresh fry bread. The kitchen table, which was framed on three sides by huge picture windows overlooking the Sandia Mountains, was teeming with all sorts of toppings for fry bread tacos: fresh vegetables, shredded beef, homemade salsa. Eddie stood at the stove, flipping fry bread in a pan of sizzling oil.

Jake sat facing the largest window. "Wow, y'all really know how to feed a guy. Everything looks great."

Eddie grinned. "Marcy doesn't let me feed her this stuff very often. Thinks she has to watch her figure. But she gave in since we had a guest."

Marcy brought a bowl of chopped cilantro to the table and sat down. "If he fed me this way every day, I'd weigh five hundred pounds."

"Hell, I'll eat whatever you don't," Jake said. "Nobody cares how much I weigh anymore."

Eddie carried a plate piled high with pieces of fry bread separated by paper towels and joined them at the table. After he sat down, he leaned over and gave Marcy a brief kiss. Jake was surprised by the small stab of jealousy he felt. He wasn't jealous that someone was kissing his ex-wife. He was jealous that he didn't have anyone to kiss himself.

As he set to making his first taco, Jake cleared his throat. "So, how's the shop doing?"

"It's doing really well," Marcy answered. "We get tons of business now that we're in Old Town, what with all the tourists. Eddie's fetishes just fly out of the store. People buy them almost as fast as he can carve them."

"Still selling those rugs?"

"Absolutely. I have an exclusive agreement with an older Navajo artist, and her rugs are just stunning."

Jake took a big bite of his taco, and the flavors were bold and explosive. "If the fetish market ever crashes, Eddie should think of opening a restaurant. This is amazing."

"Thank you," Eddie said, a huge smile on his face.

Marcy rolled her eyes. "He's going to be impossible to live with now."

Jake shrugged. "Just being honest. But about those rugs, I was wondering if you could pick out two for my new place and send them to me. One for the bedroom and one for the living room."

"What size do you need?" Marcy asked.

"Hell if I know. Big?"

"Oh, that's helpful. Send me the dimensions you want once you get moved in, okay?"

"Will do." It was time to take the boyfriend on. "So, Eddie, how old are you, anyway?" Jake ignored the choking sound Marcy made.

Eddie's eyes went wide. "Um, me? I'm twenty-five."

"Well, that's three years older than I thought. Anyway, technically, you're young enough to be Marcy's son." Jake was almost positive he saw Marcy spit out her tea in his peripheral vision.

Eddie sat up straight and squinted at Jake. "Technically, it's really none of your business anymore, is it?"

Jake liked that Eddie stood his ground. He'd need that determination to be with Marcy… and to survive the kids. "You may have a point there. Actually, you do have a point. But the kids seem to think it's their business."

Marcy burst into laughter, making both Jake and Eddie jump in their seats. "The kids? *The kids*? The kids are now adults, and they don't even live here anymore. I can't believe they put you up to this."

"They're worried. But, for the record, I did tell them you were a big girl and not likely someone to be taken advantage of."

"So why the interrogation?" Marcy paused then pointed at Jake. "Erin used her oh-Daddy-please voice on you, didn't she?"

"You know I can't deny her anything when she uses The Voice," Jake whined.

"At least I don't have to worry about that," Eddie interjected.

"Don't be so sure. Erin always finds a way to get men to do exactly what she wants, just like her mother." Jake patted Marcy's hand. "I feel sorry for any man Erin settles on. He'll have to get used to her having her way. I'm pretty sure you know what I mean."

Eddie laughed and took Marcy's other hand. "I like letting her have her way."

"Thank you, sweetie," Marcy said as she squeezed Eddie's hand.

Jake scooped shredded beef onto another fry bread. "Don't worry. I'll tell the kids exactly what I figured out right away: you two are good together. And to quit acting like their mother is some poor senile woman."

"They'll forget all about me once you tell them your news," Marcy said.

Jake glared and hissed at her.

Marcy waved him off. "Oh, please. Eddie knows all about it. You can't have already forgotten my rule. Tell me something, know I'll tell my partner."

Jake hadn't realized Marcy and Eddie were that serious. "I didn't know that was the situation."

Eddie nodded. "I moved in two months ago."

"Okay. Do the kids know?"

"No, not yet," Marcy said. "I'm going to tell them when they come home for Thanksgiving. You are coming for Thanksgiving, aren't you?"

"Are you kidding? I wouldn't miss that revelation for anything."

"Maybe you'll have someone to bring with you by then."

Jake sighed. “Marcy.”

“I think that’s my cue to excuse myself.” Eddie pulled away from the table and stood.

Jake shook his head. “Really, you don’t have to do that.”

Eddie leaned over and gave Marcy another quick kiss. “I think you two need some time to talk, and I’ve got a sculpture waiting for me in the studio. We’ll see each other in the morning, okay?” He waved at Jake before leaving the room.

Marcy left the table and retrieved a large pitcher from the refrigerator. “I think this conversation calls for alcohol. Margaritas okay with you?”

“Sure.”

As Marcy returned with the pitcher and went off again to get glasses, Jake took a good long look at her. Her brown hair, now streaked with gray, flowed around her face and down her back. Her skin was darker now, probably from all the New Mexico sunshine she was getting. When she sat back down, Jake noticed she wasn’t wearing any makeup, something she never would have done in San Diego. Not that she’d ever needed it. Still, she looked healthy, young, and happy. Albuquerque—and Eddie—definitely agreed with her.

Jake took the drink Marcy offered him. “You look really great, Marcy. I can tell you’re really happy here. The kids, they’ll understand once they’re home. You’ll see.”

Marcy took a sip of her drink, thought about it, and then took a large gulp. “I know. The kids are just worried about me. I am worried about you.”

“Me?”

“When we got divorced and I moved away, you promised me you wouldn’t be that guy sitting alone in his apartment and eating takeout every night.”

Jake would have to drink faster if they were going to have this conversation. “I know I did. But I’ve been busy with the team—”

“You’ve had four years of off-seasons to get out, meet somebody. Did you even hook up? Take anybody home?”

“Of course I did.”

“Women or men?”

Jake drained his glass and refilled it. “Both.”

Marcy sighed. "Well, at least there's that. And you never met anyone you wanted more from?"

"There were only two times in my life I ever wanted more from someone," Jake snapped. "You know how those both ended."

"I know how we ended. But the other… maybe you haven't reached the end yet."

All Jake knew was that "the other" was all he thought about anymore. During his marriage, he'd tried to put those thoughts away, but he'd completely given in to them since the divorce. He loved Marcy. He loved his children. But, God forgive him, sometimes he'd dreamed of what his life would have been like had he never made the choice that led him to them. He was crushed by guilt when he woke up.

"I can't afford to think that way." Jake scratched under his short beard. "I can't get my hopes up like that."

Marcy refilled her glass and topped off Jake's. "Does he know you're coming?"

"Yeah, but he doesn't know why."

"But he's seriously dating again, right?"

Jake wanted to growl. He didn't like thinking about Mikko seriously dating again. "Yes."

Marcy took his hand. "Then all you can do is try. Maybe he'll see that you've grown up, changed. You're not a scared little boy anymore."

"I might not be a little boy, but I'm terrified."

"It'll all work out like it's supposed to."

Like it's supposed to. Jake hated that saying. He wanted it to work out like he wanted, damn it!

They sat at the table for a while, holding hands and drinking margaritas. The sun had gone down, and Jake stared at the moon shining down on the desert. As beautiful as it all was, he was ready to go home to hills and grass and trees.

Jake's head was spinning a little, but he needed to know one more thing. "Us. We were good together for a while, weren't we?"

"We were really good for a while," Marcy said while she swayed in her chair. "You were an awesome husband, and you're an awesome friend. I'm sorry we just weren't awesome being married anymore."

Jake lifted Marcy's hand and kissed it. "I know. But you know what? We have two great kids. And we still like each other. How many couples who've known each other twentysomething years can say that?"

"Not a lot." Marcy picked up the pitcher and sloshed the remaining contents around. "You wanna help me finish this off?"

Jake lifted his glass. "Absolutely."

Chapter 2: 1986

IT HAD been a lonely few months in Atlanta. Jake had gone from being a high school baseball star to just another hick jock. It didn't matter that his test scores and grades would have gotten him into Georgia Tech regardless of the baseball scholarship. The smart kids looked down their noses at him. And the other jocks? Until Jake played a game and played it well, he was only a wannabe freshman.

The first day of preseason training, it all started to turn around for him. He and the other freshman bonded over their mutual desire to prove they were worthy to wear the gold-and-white. They worked hard and cheered each other on. They quickly became favorites of the handful of regular practice spectators, who all seemed to have a soft spot for the awkward newcomers.

One spectator stood out. Jake tried not to stare, but he couldn't stop his surreptitious glances at the man. Jake had known since forever that he could be turned on by men as well as women, but this was different. The man's square jaw and tight swimmer's body made Jake have evil, evil thoughts, thoughts of things way beyond the frenzied hand and blow jobs he'd experienced with other equally frightened high school boys.

Jake also had more tender thoughts, which he found slightly frightening. Every time the man brushed his hair from his eyes, Jake wondered if the hair was soft, how it would feel if he ran his fingers through it. He snuck enough glances to determine that the man's almond-shaped eyes were a beautiful hazel, and, more often than not, those eyes were trained on Jake. Worst of all, Jake wanted to pull the man's full bottom lip between his and find out how the man tasted. He had never kissed a man, but God, he wanted to kiss this one.

After a few weeks of torture, Jake decided he'd had enough. He might make a fool of himself. He might even get his ass kicked. But he was going to talk to the man who'd been starring in his dreams.

When practice was over, Jake hung back on the field, waiting for the other players to head toward the locker room and hopefully out of earshot. He'd noticed days before that the man would not leave right away; he'd linger, reading a book or relaxing on the bleachers. It was almost as if he were waiting for someone. Then again, Jake thought, that could be his own wishful thinking.

As he walked, Jake brushed off his pants and straightened his cap. When the man looked up from his book to see Jake heading his way, his smile was unmistakable. Jake was sure he'd never seen a clearer invitation to come closer, and he struggled to keep his feet from speeding up. He needed to play this cool, keep his intentions a secret until he was sure they were welcome.

"Hey." Jake shoved his glove under his arm. "What you reading?"

The man waved the small paperback. "Oh, this? *To Kill A Mockingbird.* I have been told it is a classic American novel. I like it so far."

Oh holy fuck, Jake thought. *He has an accent on top of everything else*. The man's voice was cool and smooth, like a window in an air-conditioned room. It sent frissons cascading over Jake's sweat-damp skin. Each word was clearly enunciated, crisp.

Jake sat down, leaving a respectable distance between them. "It is. I read it in high school, and it's pretty good."

The man folded the corner of a page and closed the book. "We read a few American novels in school in Finland, but not this one. I think I may recommend it to my teacher back home."

"Finland? How did you end up here?"

"I wanted more sunshine and warmth. My family visited friends in Savannah once, and I fell in love with Georgia."

"Well, you definitely came to the right place for sunshine." Jake was positive if he heard much more of the man's accent, he would melt on the spot. "I'm Jake Wilson," he said, holding out his hand.

The man stared at Jake's hand before finally shaking it. "I know," he said. "I read about you in the student paper. My name is Mikko Niemi."

Mikko. Jake liked the name. Solid. Exotic. *Easy to say when you're breathless and eager.* "So, you a baseball fan, then?"

Mikko nodded. "Yes. I loved playing baseball in Finland, but our version—pesäpallo—is a bit faster."

"Really?"

"The ball is pitched over the batter's head." Talking about baseball animated Mikko, and he gestured with large, long-fingered hands. "It results in quite a lively game. But I like the American version as well. It gives you more time to become acquainted with the players." Mikko's smile was gentle and friendly, but the look in his eyes was something more.

Jake was more than happy to let Mikko become as acquainted with him as possible. "Say, I reek, and I really need a shower. But you want to wait for me and have some dinner? I'd really like to hear more about Finnish baseball." *Or anything else that happens to come out of that gorgeous mouth.*

"That would be great. Should I wait here?"

Jake hopped up, ready to run to the showers and then get back to Mikko. "Sure. Shouldn't take me more than thirty minutes."

Mikko nodded and returned to his book. "No need to hurry. I won't go anywhere."

Jake wasn't taking any chances. He sprinted to the locker room, threw off his practice uniform, and ran into the shower. He cleaned himself up as quickly as he could without basically just rinsing off, but he took a little more time getting ready. He dressed in the jeans and Guns N' Roses T-shirt he'd left in his locker. He fussed over his hair, which he'd never had any luck taming.

By the time he got back to the bleachers, he was sure Mikko would be gone. As he took the last turn to the field, he was thrilled to see Mikko sitting there, still reading that book. When he reached the bottom bleacher row, Mikko smiled and climbed down to meet him.

"I have a place I think you'd like," Jake said.

"Lead the way."

As they walked, they talked about school. Turned out Mikko had also had a lonely first few months of his freshman year, and he hadn't gone out exploring Atlanta much. He mentioned liking the food in Savannah, though, so Jake was sure dinner at his favorite meat-and-three would be perfect. When they arrived, they sat in a booth facing each other and read over the daily menu. Jake felt the occasion called for the fried chicken, while Mikko went for the cubed steak smothered in gravy.

Mikko talked about baseball, about how there were teams in Finland that also played the American version. He could have talked about belly-button lint and farts, and Jake wouldn't have cared. All he wanted to do was listen to the man speak. It wasn't just Mikko's accent that drove Jake mad. It was also the passion with which he spoke, as if he was grateful to have Jake's attention and wanted to keep it. Little did he know he didn't have to work so hard.

"I think I am monopolizing the conversation. Tell me about yourself, Jake."

Jake shrugged. "Not a lot to tell. I grew up in Georgia. In Waynesboro, the Bird Dog Capital of the World."

"Bird Dog Capital?" Mikko laughed. "How does a town become the Bird Dog Capital of the World?"

"They just say so, I reckon. I've never really been anywhere else, except for a few schools I visited before deciding on Georgia Tech."

Mikko took another bite of his steak and hummed. "This place is really good. You must bring me here again. Well, wasn't that very demanding of me?" Mikko laughed. "We should come here again."

"Oh, I don't have a problem with demanding guys." Jake blushed when he realized how that might sound.

"Good to know." Mikko winked.

Jake took a deep breath and tried to calm down. "Okay. How 'bout some dessert?"

"Aren't you on a training diet?"

"Not tonight I'm not. You can't eat a good Southern meal unless you're willing to take in a few extra calories. I'll just run an extra mile tomorrow morning." Jake looked down at the dessert menu. "Would you be interested in running with me?"

Mikko patted his stomach. "Are you trying to say I need to exercise?"

Jake waved over the waitress. "Nope. Just like your company." When the waitress arrived, Jake ordered a slice of chess pie. "Mind if I suggest something for you?"

"Not at all."

"If you've never had Coca-Cola cake, you really should give it a try."

"Well, Coca-Cola cake it is, then."

The waitress gave the guys a nod and walked off. Just as Jake and Mikko finished up their meal, their desserts arrived.

"I'm not sure what I thought Coca-Cola cake would be," Mikko said as he took his second bite. "But this is incredible."

"It's a little slice of chocolate heaven is what it is. My mom makes the best cake ever. This is probably a close second."

"My father is the chef in our family. He owns a restaurant, and he makes a cloudberry mousse that is just incredible."

Jake wasn't sure he'd ever met anyone whose father was the family cook. "What's a cloudberry?"

"They are shaped a bit like raspberries, and they have a really nice tart flavor."

"Think you inherited your dad's cooking skills?"

"Maybe a little." Mikko pointed at the cake. "I would like to know how to make this."

"I'll get my mom to send me the recipe."

This simple statement made Mikko smile more than anything else had that night. "That would be nice."

When the check came to the table, Jake declared that it was his treat since, after all, he'd suggested the place. Mikko argued, but when it became clear that Jake wouldn't budge, he left the tip instead. As they walked, there was no mention of where they were headed or what they'd do once they got there. Jake just wanted to follow Mikko, so that's what he did.

Mikko led Jake to a small off-campus apartment, and he held the door open for Jake to enter. Unlike Jake's dorm room, Mikko's apartment had a small living room and kitchen. It also appeared that Mikko didn't have a roommate.

Mikko sat on the small sofa and motioned Jake to join him. It was something Jake would do on a date with a girl. Was this a date? Jake certainly hoped so.

After a few moments of awkward silence, Jake finally locked eyes with Mikko. "You seem like a nice guy, like someone who wouldn't kick someone's ass over a misunderstanding."

Mikko frowned. "No, I wouldn't."

Jake nodded and looked down at the floor. "Do you like guys?"

"Like? Are you asking if I'm gay?"

"Yes." Jake could feel the embarrassed blush bloom on his cheeks.

"I am. Does that offend you?"

"No, no." Jake finally looked up with a smile, which Mikko returned. "I like guys too. I mean, I like girls and guys."

Mikko slowly scooted closer. "I'm very happy to hear that."

"Oh, good." Jake scooted too, closing the distance between them. "I haven't done much, though."

"We don't have to do much now."

"Okay." Jake let his head fall onto the back of the couch. "You are absolutely gorgeous, you know that?"

Mikko wrapped his arms around Jake's waist. "I didn't think you'd noticed me."

"I noticed. I absolutely noticed. Those hazel eyes always watching me. How could I not?"

"I'm going to kiss you."

"Okay, "Jake whispered.

Jake resisted the impulse to close his eyes. He wanted to see Mikko move closer, and Mikko did, until Jake could feel Mikko's breath on his face. When their lips finally touched, it was a soft kiss followed by another. Mikko pulled away, his brow furrowed and breath quickening. He returned to Jake's mouth, and Jake felt the difference. The new kiss was hard, and his mouth was urged open by Mikko's exploring tongue.

A girl's kiss had never had this force behind it. Jake loved it, and he let Mikko take the kiss as fast and deep as he wanted. The scraping of stubble against his face made Jake hard, and he threaded his fingers through Mikko's hair—oh, it *was* soft—and encouraged him by applying gentle pressure to the back of his head.

Mikko pushed Jake back until they were lying on the couch, their legs interlocked, so they both had the other's thigh to grind against. And they grinded for all they were worth, chasing the release that could only come from orgasm. Mikko was hard as a rock against Jake's leg, and Jake hoped one day he'd get to see all of Mikko.

"I'm almost there," Mikko said against Jake's lips.

"Holy fuck, me too."

Mikko attacked Jake's mouth again and refused to surrender it even as Jake came with deep moans. Jake's entire body was a mass of overstimulated nerves throbbing in unison. Everything in the world had narrowed down to that couch and the man writhing above him. When Mikko buried his head into the crook of Jake's neck and cried out, Jake held him and kissed his cheek until he came down.

Mikko raised his head and looked down at Jake. "I'm so glad you like guys."

Jake smiled and kissed Mikko. In that moment, Jake was glad too.

Chapter 3: Norman

JAKE barely made it through breakfast. His head was pounding, and his stomach was rioting. The smell of frying bacon almost made him vomit. He was never fucking drinking margaritas again.

He was grateful for the sunglasses Marcy had found for him. On the passenger seat next to him sat the small buffalo fetish Eddie had given him. The buffalo fetish was about great emotional courage, and Eddie had told Jake he had enough courage for everyone. Unsure of that but touched all the same, Jake had given Eddie a hug.

The drive from New Mexico through the Texas Panhandle to Oklahoma was straightforward, I-40 most of the way. Jake played calming music and stopped several times to buy large bottles of water and aspirin. His headache was gone by the time he drove onto the campus of the University of Oklahoma. He'd timed the trip perfectly. As he pulled up in front of Mitchell Park, his son walked out of the building.

"Dad!" Johnnie ran up to the SUV and jumped inside. His hair was much shorter than Jake remembered, but sometimes players cut a bunch off at the beginning of the season.

Jake clapped his son's shoulder. "Hey there, Sport. How did practice go?"

"Great. I think I might get a good bit of pitching time during the season. Probably not starting, but definitely relief."

"You've got time to be a starter. If you play well this season, I bet they'll start you next season."

Johnnie took off his cap and ran his fingers through his wet hair, which was dark blond like his father's. "That's what the sophomore pitchers said. Sometimes, though, it's hard to tell when they're being straight and when they're yanking a freshman's chain, ya know?"

"Yeah, I remember being a freshman. They're not hazing you, are they?"

Johnnie laughed. "Nothing bad. We'll have to wear something stupid to the first game. Probably pink tutus or something."

If that was the worst of it, Jake probably wouldn't have to kill anyone. "So, where you want to go?"

"There's a great sushi place over on East Main if you're up to it."

Jake wasn't, really, but he thought he could possibly keep it down. "Sure. Just tell me how to get there."

The conversation died as Johnnie gave turn-by-turn directions. Jake pulled into a spot in front of a nondescript brick storefront next to a tattoo parlor. His stomach growled, but he wasn't sure if it was in hunger or protest.

Once in the restaurant, Jake found some mild things to order: miso soup, steamed rice, tempura, and tea. Johnnie ordered four sushi rolls and a diet soda. After the waiter left the table, Johnnie began to once again converse.

"How was the drive?"

"It was good," Jake said. "I thought the drive to Albuquerque would never end, and the drive here went by fast in comparison."

"Did you meet Mom's boyfriend?" There was obvious venom in the word.

Jake frowned. "Yes, I met Eddie. He's actually a pretty nice guy."

"Whatever."

"Jesus, I hate that word. Don't 'whatever' me. Do you have a problem with Eddie as a person, or are you just pissed off that your mother has gone on with her life?"

Johnnie crossed his arms over his chest. "Well, he's only seven years older than me."

"So?"

"Don't you find that a little… odd?"

Kid, you ain't heard nothin' yet. Jake paused as the waiter dropped off their drinks and his soup. "Sure, it's not the norm."

"And you're okay with that?"

Jake knew where this was going. "Why wouldn't I be? Your mother and I aren't married anymore. I want her to be happy. Don't you?"

"Sure I do," Johnnie admitted. "I guess I just had that stupid fantasy you'd two would get back together."

"I love your mother, but not that way anymore. We're better friends."

Johnnie dropped his arms and sunk back into his chair. "Yeah, Mom says that too."

"Well, she's a smart woman. Now sit up and tell me about school so I can eat my soup."

Just like Jake at his age, Johnnie had to be prompted to talk about his classes. He rattled off his schedule, spending little to no time discussing what he'd actually learned. The only class he admitted any affinity for was sociology, and Jake encouraged him to consider majoring in it.

Their food arrived, and Jake was surprisingly hungry. "You need to make sure you have something to fall back on in case baseball doesn't pan out. And you—"

"Need to graduate. I know, Dad. No early draft for me." Johnnie popped a piece of sushi into his mouth.

"Right. I've always regretted not getting my degree. I'm just lucky I didn't need anything to fall back on."

"So what are you going to do now?"

Jake shrugged. "Don't know. I really don't have to make that decision anytime soon."

"Have you thought about commentating?" Johnnie asked.

"Not unless a major league team moves to Waynesboro. I'm not interested in moving for a team again."

Johnnie scrunched his nose like he smelled bad fish. "I can't believe you're moving there."

"You didn't grow up in the South. You don't get the pull it has on someone who did." Jake put his fork down. "I just want to go home."

"Was San Diego ever home?"

"Not since everyone left."

Jake and Johnnie fell silent, and Jake felt the discomfort crawling over his skin. He didn't want his son to pity him. He just wanted Johnnie to understand. Or at least accept that it was Jake's life to do with as he wished.

They finished their meals while exchanging pleasant chatter. When Johnnie put his chopsticks down, Jake took a deep breath and jumped into the conversation they really needed to have.

"Johnnie, I need to talk to you about something."

Johnnie leaned toward his father. "Sure, Dad. What's up?"

"There's something I've always… known about myself. Your mother knows too. Always has. But I didn't tell you or Erin because… well, because it didn't seem to matter until now. But it does matter, and I need you to listen and remember that I'm your father and I love you."

"I know. I love you too."

Jake smiled, even though it was a little sad. "Thank you. Johnnie, I'm…. I'm bisexual."

Johnnie jumped back, and his chair screeched horribly. "What?"

"I said I'm—"

"No, no, stop. I heard you. Why are you telling me this now? Do you have a… a boyfriend?" If Johnnie had used venom when applying the word to his mother, he used deadly poison now.

"No, not right now, but I'm going to come out publicly."

"Yeah, great." Johnnie stood up. "I'm gonna walk back to the dorm. I need some air."

Jake deflated. "Yeah, I understand. I can get a hotel room if—"

"No, it's okay. You can still come to the dorm." Johnnie threw a key onto the table. "I'll meet you there later."

Jake watched Johnnie leave without so much as a wave. The kid was obviously in shock, but Jake was afraid it was more than that. Maybe Johnnie was disgusted. Maybe Johnnie hated him now.

Jake paid the check, slunk back to the SUV, and called Marcy. She had a way of calming him, which worked now as it always had. By the time he finished the call and followed the GPS directions to Johnnie's dorm, Jake could breathe, and his heart had stopped pounding. When he found the dorm room empty, he lay on one of the beds and took big breaths in and big breaths out.

The room wasn't much different than the one he'd had at Georgia Tech. He smiled, remembering all the girls he'd snuck into his room. He'd never had to sneak Mikko in. Mikko's parents had known what it could be like for a gay man in the U.S. in the eighties, and they'd made sure Mikko had his own apartment, a safe place to be himself.

It had also been a safe place for Jake to be himself. There with Mikko, Jake had allowed himself to experience all the things he'd wondered about. Mikko had been a generous teacher, and Jake had soaked in all the knowledge Mikko would give. He'd wanted nothing more than the freedom to spend every moment under Mikko's tutelage.

But freedom was something he'd never had.

Two hours later, Jake was awakened by the closing door. Johnnie smiled and pulled up a chair to sit next to the bed.

Jake rubbed his eyes. "Hey, sport. Where ya' been?"

"I went to talk to my girlfriend."

That was news. "I didn't know you had a girlfriend."

"You're the first person I've told," Johnnie said. "Mom doesn't even know yet."

"She's a nice girl, I hope."

"Very nice. Except when she's telling me I'm being a selfish dick."

Jake laughed. "Did she use those words?"

"Those exact words. She always calls me on my bullshit." Johnnie took off his cap and threw it onto his desk. "Look, Dad, I am so sorry about the way I reacted. I was just not expecting that. And, like I said, I'm still this stupid kid who wants his parents back together. It never occurred to me that marrying Mom had been so hard on you."

"Whoa there, fella," Jake said as he made the time-out signal. "I loved your mother. Hell, I was crazy about her. I had to beg the woman to marry me."

"But you said—"

"That I'm bisexual. I'm attracted to men and women. And I was most definitely attracted to your mom from the second I met her."

Johnnie frowned. "Then why did you get divorced?"

"We were kids when we got married, and then we spent lots of time apart while we were growing up. We just looked at each other one day and knew that the love two partners should have wasn't there anymore."

"I guess I can understand that. Do you have someone you love that way now?"

"Yes."

"Oh," Johnnie whispered. "Does he love you?"

Jake tapped his nose. "That is the million-dollar question. I don't know the answer. I'll be sure to tell you when I do."

"Anything else I need to know?"

"I'm going to issue a press release once I get to Georgia. Not sure anyone will care now that I'm retired, but I want it out there on my terms." Jake remembered Marcy's secret roommate. "By the way, I think you should bring your girlfriend to Thanksgiving dinner at your mother's house."

"I've been thinking about it." Johnnie blushed. "Think Mom will make us sleep in separate rooms?"

"I seriously doubt it."

Chapter 4: 1987

EVERYTHING was different sophomore year. During his freshman season, Jake rocked second base, and it wasn't long before he was starting every game. It earned him the respect of the other players and the attention of quite a few college girls.

He was more than willing to take advantage of his new popularity. He partied with the team almost every weekend, and after every party he hooked up with a different girl. There was plenty of alcohol to make everything go smoothly. He made the girls no promises, and they had no expectations. It was the perfect situation.

Then there was Mikko.

At least once a week, Jake and Mikko had dinner, maybe watched a movie, and then ended the evening wrapped around each other, their jeans ripped open and yanked down around their knees. When he wasn't with Mikko, Jake often rubbed one out while thinking about Mikko's cock in his mouth. It wasn't long before Jake realized that his best days were those he spent with Mikko.

They didn't often cross paths on campus outside Mikko's consistent presence at Georgia Tech baseball home games. Mikko wasn't the party type, and they were never in the same class. Jake ignored the deep urges he had just to see Mikko for nothing more than a few minutes of company. After all, just like his encounters with the party girls, Jake made no promises, and Mikko had no expectations.

THE frat party for homecoming was in full swing by the time Jake and his date finally arrived. She was some girl on the volleyball team, and Jake had had too many beers to even remember her name. His date led him to a dark hallway on the remote end of the third floor. Alone above the party, they exchanged sloppy kisses and practically fucked each other through their clothes. She tasted like tequila and salt. Jake slumped back against the wall when she fell to her knees and pulled his half-hard cock out of his jeans.

Jake was having trouble getting it up until he heard someone cry out from the room at the end of the hall. It was a man's voice, deep and strained. Jake gasped when he heard another man respond, "Hush, baby, or we'll have to stop."

"Just fuck me." The command was plain, and the desperation with which it was given was thick.

Jake closed his eyes and imagined what it might feel like to be the desperate one, begging Mikko to fuck him, to do anything as long as they were joined. What would Mikko say? Would he be gentle, knowing Jake had no experience? Or would he be rough, too turned on by Jake's supplication to take him slowly?

"Oh, yeah." The girl at Jake's feet hummed. "I was starting to think you didn't like me."

Jake looked down at blonde hair, blue eyes, and enough makeup for two people. This wasn't what he wanted. He wanted chestnut hair, hazel eyes, and scratchy stubble.

Jake pushed the girl away and stuffed himself back into his pants. "Sorry."

"What's wrong?" She wobbled as she stood.

"Don't feel good. Too much to drink." He watched his date try to straighten her hair and clothes. "Maybe I should take you back to the dorm."

"Naw, it's fine." She waved toward the room to their left. "This is my cousin's room. I'll just crash here."

"You sure?"

"Yeah, he lets me sleep it off here all the time."

Before Jake could protest, his date pulled out a key and unlocked the door. "Feel better."

Staring at a closed door, Jake wondered what was wrong with him. She'd been a sure thing. But he didn't want a sure thing whose name he couldn't remember.

He wanted Mikko.

Jake walked across campus. The cool autumn breeze and the exertion began to burn off the cheap beer flowing though his body. By the time he reached Mikko's darkened apartment, Jake was sweaty, and his buzz was almost gone. He hesitated only a second—what if Mikko had someone with him?—before leaning on the doorbell.

Mikko yanked the door open and glared at Jake. Mikko's hair was everywhere, his eyes glassy, and he was definitely angry. "I told you not to come here drunk."

Jake swayed, his rubbery legs betraying him. "I'm not drunk, at least not anymore."

"Get inside before you wake my neighbors."

Jake was pretty sure all Mikko's neighbors were on campus at the homecoming parties, but he wasn't going to argue with anything that got him closer to Mikko's bed. Mikko directed Jake to the couch and went to the kitchen. He returned with a tall glass of water.

"Drink this." Mikko flopped down on the couch. "You look awful."

"Thanks." Jake gulped down the water and placed the glass on the coffee table when he was finished. "You look like I dragged you out of bed."

"You did."

"Are you still mad?"

Mikko rolled his eyes. "Irritated, but that's not the same as angry." Mikko waved Jake over until they were snuggled close. "Rough night?"

"No." Jake leaned into Mikko until he felt Mikko drape his arm around his shoulders. "Just wanted to see you."

Jake let his head fall back and waited. Mikko's kiss was soft, and he didn't try to deepen it. It was easy and familiar and so good.

"I want you to fuck me," Jake whispered.

Mikko jerked back and glared down at Jake. "Now I know you're drunk."

It took a few seconds for Jake's gears to shift. "What? No, no I'm not."

"Just go home. I'll see you later this week." Mikko stood up and began to walk away.

Jake grabbed Mikko's hand and pulled him back. "I don't want to. I want to stay here with you tonight."

"Fine, but I'm going to bed. To sleep. You can have the couch."

This was not going the way Jake had imagined. "Can't I sleep with you?"

"Why?"

"I just want to be with you. I promise I'll sleep."

Mikko shrugged and walked away. “Have it your way.”

Jake scrambled to follow Mikko down the hall. Once they reached the bedroom, Jake realized that in all the months they’d been getting each other off, he’d never seen Mikko’s bedroom. It was so much better than the plain dorm rooms. A large bed, covered with rumpled green sheets, occupied the center of the room. The only light was that streaming through the window from the streetlight outside… or maybe it was the moon. Mikko’s walls displayed framed pictures and paintings, not the rock or pinup girl posters you’d see in a dorm room. To the side was a sleek, modern desk, piled with textbooks and strewn with graph paper. The room felt permanent, unlike the dorms, which seemed like shantytowns in comparison.

Mikko peeled off his T-shirt, leaving his orange-striped boxers on. It was the most naked Jake had ever seen him. As Mikko climbed into bed, Jake rushed to strip off his shoes and clothes. Once he was down to his plain white briefs, he eased into the bed next to Mikko.

He didn’t reach out for Mikko, nor did he really expect Mikko to reach out to him. They lay there, side by side, an invisible line partitioning the bed into halves. Jake so wanted to cross that line, but he didn’t feel like starting World War III. He decided to just enjoy the fact that he was this much closer to letting Mikko have him.

As Mikko’s breathing evened out, Jake continued to stare up at the ceiling. What was he doing here? Mikko seemed to want him well enough when they were sucking each other off, but he didn’t want to take things further. Sure, Jake was inexperienced with men, but he didn’t think it was a top/bottom issue. After all, Mikko had silently asserted his dominance every time they fooled around, and Jake had been happy to let him. Sure, every once in a while Jake imagined being the aggressor, but usually he was the one being plundered.

After an hour or so, Mikko turned toward Jake. “I can hear your brain working. What are you thinking about so intently?”

Jake’s mouth was dry. “Do you not want to fuck me?”

Mikko chuckled and crossed the invisible divider to stroke Jake’s cheek. “Of course I do. But why do you want me to, after all this time?”

“I’ve wanted you to for a while. I was just too afraid to ask.”

“And the alcohol gave you the courage?” Mikko asked with a frown.

Jake rolled toward Mikko. "I don't use alcohol to come here. I use alcohol to keep me away."

"You never have to stay away."

Mikko grabbed Jake and kissed him, instantly thrusting his tongue between Jake's lips. Jake opened up, letting Mikko have anything he wanted. Mikko grabbed Jake and pulled him close, pressing their bodies together. They kissed, they stroked, they tasted each other's skin. What little fabric separated them was quickly gone. Finally, Jake was exactly where he wanted to be: on his back, with Mikko nestled between his legs.

Mikko reached out to his nightstand and found lube and a condom. He poured a generous amount into his hand, and he began to massage Jake's hole with his fingers. Jake jumped at the first cold touch, but as the liquid warmed and Mikko's touch firmed, Jake hummed.

"God, that feels so good." Jake raised his legs to bare more of his ass and flinched when he felt Mikko push a finger inside him.

"Just relax and take it. I won't go too fast. I promise."

Jake took deep breaths and watched Mikko concentrate on opening him up. As soon as Jake began to enjoy a single finger, Mikko added another. Mikko worried his bottom lip as he worked, and Jake pulled Mikko down for a kiss.

"It's okay. I'm okay," Jake whispered. "You're so good to me."

"I just want it to be good for you."

"It will be."

Mikko sat back on his knees and ripped the condom open with his teeth.

"Do we really need that?" Jake wanted to feel everything.

Mikko frowned. "This is your first time, yes?"

Jake nodded.

"It's not safe to do this without it, even if you think someone is okay." Mikko rolled the condom down over his thick cock. "Promise me you'll always use them. Top or bottom."

Jake had heard of the deadly virus, seen the awful things people did to those who had it. "I promise."

Mikko leaned down and hooked Jake's legs over his outstretched arms. "Good."

Jake closed his eyes and tried to force his body to stay pliant when Mikko stroked the head of his cock between Jake's cheeks. Jake reminded himself that he wanted this, that whatever pain he'd feel would pass if he just gave it time.

"Take a deep breath," Mikko said, "then let it go slowly."

When Jake filled his lungs with cool air, Mikko pushed. The pain of the stretch was intense, and Jake struggled to exhale through it. With each deeper thrust, Jake controlled his breathing, convinced his body to accept what was happening. Mikko took his time, thrusting just a little deeper each time. When he was fully inside Jake, Mikko stayed there, unmoving.

Closing his eyes, Jake concentrated on the fullness, on the ache of allowing Mikko inside him. Mikko peppered Jake's face with slow, soft kisses. When he opened his eyes, Jake finally saw the hazel he'd wanted all along.

Mikko smiled as if he understood Jake's every thought, and he pulled out in millimeters until he was barely there. He returned with strength and speed that left Jake panting.

"Again," Jake commanded.

Mikko pulled out and thrust deep and hard.

Jake could hardly breathe. "Again."

Another pounding thrust.

"Again."

Jake's entire body shook with the force of Mikko's movements. Mikko let Jake's legs down and wrapped his arms around Jake. Jake in turn wrapped his legs around Mikko's waist. The only word he could say turned into a plea.

"Again. Again. Again."

Mikko's pistoning hips never let up, never gave Jake a chance to catch his breath. They were powering toward release, and nothing was going to stop them. Mikko captured Jake's lips, and his tongue was the only thing that kept Jake from continuing to beg for more.

Jake buried his fingers in Mikko's hair and pulled back, baring Mikko's neck. He licked and sucked and bit, never hard enough to leave a mark, even though he desperately wanted to.

"Do it. Just once. Please," Mikko whispered.

Jake licked a spot over Mikko's carotid artery and latched on, sucking a deep purple spot onto Mikko's fair skin. Let them think a girl did it. It didn't matter. He and Mikko would know how it really happened.

"Yes," Mikko hissed. "Close now." He wrapped his long fingers around Jake's cock and stroked it. "Need you to be there with me."

They looked at each other. No words. Just looked at each other.

As Jake tensed in anticipation, Mikko nodded and stroked Jake's cock faster. Jake felt it bubbling inside him, felt his flesh burning. Then he came, his glowing glass body shattering into a billion flying pieces.

He was still flying apart when he felt Mikko stutter above him, his steady tempo becoming erratic. Jake watched as Mikko arched his back and cried out, his mouth a perfect, beautiful circle.

When it was over, they lay together, Mikko resting on Jake's chest. Mikko didn't ask Jake to stay, and Jake didn't offer to leave. They simply wrapped around each other and drifted off to sleep.

Chapter 5: Nashville

DRIVING into Nashville was a relief. Jake was beginning to wonder why he ever thought driving across country by himself was a good idea. He was too old and too soft for this shit. It had been years since he'd traveled less than first class on a road trip.

Although he wasn't exactly by himself. In addition to his buffalo fetish, two new friends occupied the passenger seat: Boomer and Sooner, stuffed toys Johnnie and his girlfriend had bought at the on-campus bookstore. Johnnie mentioned that his girlfriend thought it would be romantic if Jake gave one of the stuffed UO mascots to Mikko. Johnnie, however, thought that sounded more than a little goofy.

It had been more than a year since Jake had been to his daughter's condo. Erin had balked at Jake buying it for her, but he and Marcy had insisted. Jake knew Erin was never going to get rich working for a hockey team, and he at least wanted to know she didn't have to worry about rent.

A hockey team! Jake still couldn't understand it. Erin had grown up surrounded by baseball players. She'd gone to games her entire life. But from the moment she could play a sport herself, his tomboy had wanted to play hockey. He wasn't even sure how she'd learned about the game, but it was all she'd ever talked about. After college, Erin had immediately been hired by the Nashville professional team, and Jake was happy she'd found her dream job… even if it was with a *hockey* team. At least it was in the South.

Jake rang the doorbell and was surprised when a man answered.

"Hello, Mr. Wilson!" The man was extremely cheerful. He was at least six feet tall, and he was built like a brick shithouse. And he had an accent Jake couldn't place.

Jake squinted. "And you are?"

"I'm Patrick," the man said as he held out his hand. "I've heard so much about you, and I'm glad to finally meet you."

Jake warily shook Patrick's hand. Just as he let go, he heard Erin call from inside the condo.

"Patrick, is that Dad? Bring him on in. I'm sure he's tired."

Ah, that was his girl. Thinking about her poor, broken-down father and wanting to offer him some comfort. Unlike Patrick, whoever he was.

When he entered the living room, Jake was greeted with a bouncing bundle of auburn-haired energy. Erin jumped into his arms, and he gave her a tight hug.

"Well, hello, little girl!" Jake swung her around, which wasn't as easy now that she was in her twenties. "So good to see you."

Erin bounced back a step and brushed her long locks of hair from her face. "I'm so glad you're here! We've cooked up such an awesome dinner for you. We're going to spoil you rotten."

We. Jake tried not to frown at his grinning daughter. Something was up, and Erin's use of the plural pronoun only confirmed it.

"Do you want to change or wash up before dinner? Patrick can get your bag and take it to the guest room."

"That would be great, sweetheart. My bag is right outside the door."

Patrick dashed and retrieved the bag. He led Jake to the guest room, and Jake was glad for the privacy. He stripped off his sweaty driving clothes and changed into a comfortable pair of jeans and an old road jersey. Looking around the room, he saw several pictures of his family over the years. The first one, in a frame on the nightstand, had been taken when Erin was five and Johnnie was barely walking. It had been a supreme act of patience to get the children to sit long enough to take one good picture.

He and Marcy were so young in the picture. He'd almost forgotten ever being that young. In his mind, young was forever associated with Mikko, and Jake felt so much older after him. He'd grown up, learned not to take a good thing for granted. And then he met Marcy, who had been the absolute right person at the absolute right time. They hadn't made it in the end, but he'd never regret a second with her and his children. He loved them more than he could ever put into words.

He walked into the kitchen and found Erin and Patrick, their heads bent over a pot of something that smelled delicious, Patrick resting his hand on the small of Erin's back. Jake was busted as soon as his stomach growled loud enough to be heard three streets over.

Erin laughed. "There you are. Sounds like you're ready for dinner."

"Absolutely. It smells great."

Patrick put on a pair of thick oven mitts and picked up the pot. "Hey, babe, can you get the trivet?"

Erin grabbed the trivet, and they all headed for the dining room. The table was small enough that everyone could reach the pot Patrick placed in the center, but Erin insisted on serving. She gave Jake the first bowl, and it was a thick beef stew, Jake's favorite.

Jake grabbed a crusty roll from the basket and tore it in half. "So, Patrick, where are you from?"

Patrick settled over his own bowl of stew. "Edmonton, sir."

Jake's stomach sank. Patrick was huge, and he was Canadian. *Please don't let him be a player. Please don't let him be a player.* Jake wouldn't wish a relationship with a professional athlete on his worst enemy, and he might just forbid it when it came to his own daughter.

Erin patted Jake's hand. "He's a team doctor, Dad."

Patrick nodded. "Yep. I blew out my knee early in college, but I still wanted to be close to the game. I decided the best way to do that was to become an orthopedist."

"Oh, a doctor," Jake said with a smile. "You should have led with that."

"Come on, Dad, you didn't think I'd date a *player*, did you?"

Patrick reached out for Erin, and she took his hand. "Good thing I have a bum knee, then."

That was when Jake saw it: a big, sparkling diamond ring on his little girl's finger.

"Is there something you two need to tell me?"

Erin looked at her father then followed his gaze down to her left hand, which she immediately jerked back. "Oh, shit, I forgot to take it off. We were getting to that."

"Well, get to it now."

Patrick swallowed hard. "Sir—"

Jake grimaced. "Quit calling me sir. It makes me feel old. Call me Mr. Wilson."

"Dad!" Erin glared at him.

"Okay, fine," Jake said with an eye roll. "Jake, then. You happy?"

"Jake," Patrick warbled as he began again, "your daughter and I have been together for six months—"

"Then why have I never heard of you before now?"

Erin huffed. "Because telling you anything during baseball season is useless."

Jake had to give her that, and it made him feel like shit. "Go on."

Patrick sat up straighter, as if he'd gotten a second wind. "Here's the long and short of it. I love Erin. Erin loves me. We make each other happy, and I can make sure she stays that way. We're getting married after next hockey season."

"Well, when you say it like that…." Jake held out his hand. "Welcome to our crazy family."

Patrick's face lit up, and he shook Jake's hand. "Thank you, s…. Jake. Thank you so much."

Erin beamed at her father. "Dad, thanks."

"Of course, sweetie."

"Now let's eat this stew before it gets cold. I used Mom's recipe."

Jake spooned a bite into his mouth and chewed slowly. The taste always took him back to college and his different life there. "It was a recipe I got from a college friend a long time ago. I think you make it the best, though."

"Thank you, Dad. I'm so glad you like it."

After dinner, they spent the evening watching the baseball playoffs on TV and going back for more stew several times. It really was the best version of that recipe Jake had ever had, and he hadn't even known Erin could cook. It seemed Erin and Johnnie had lives that didn't necessarily involve their parents. It was hard to accept that his kids had grown up, but Jake was glad to see them finding happiness of their own.

JAKE woke up bright and early the next morning, and padded into the kitchen. He was sad to see that someone had finished off the stew overnight. He didn't think he'd ever eaten so much in his life, and he felt heavy. But it was a good kind of heavy.

He made a pot of coffee. He couldn't cook, but he could manage that. He liked having a little time to himself before the last leg of the trip. He'd thought he'd be nervous, but he was very calm. Even if things didn't go entirely his way in Savannah, at least he'd have made his wishes known.

"Hey, Dad," Erin whispered. Her hair stood up in twenty different directions, and she wore an oversized Nashville jersey. "Oh, coffee. Awesome."

She grabbed a mug and filled it. She added nothing, just like her father, and sat on the stool at the kitchen bar. Jake found the ingredients for the only other thing he was good at making—pancakes—and got to work.

Erin took a sip of her coffee. "Johnnie says there's something you want to talk to me about."

Jake whisked the batter a little more forcefully than necessary. "What else did he tell you?"

"I made sure you weren't dying and didn't have some mystery love child somewhere, but he didn't tell me anything else. I figure I'm good otherwise."

Jake smiled. If Erin had gotten anything from her mother, it was her laid-back attitude. "Well, that's good to know."

"Come on, Dad. I know we caught you off guard with our news last night. But Patrick's still asleep, and you and I have time to talk. Just the two of us."

Jake poured batter into a large skillet. "When your mother and I met, we fell very much in love very quickly. I told her everything there was to tell about me, and she accepted me."

"I'm glad," Erin whispered.

"Thank you, sweetheart." Jake watched the batter begin to bubble over the heat. "One of the things I told her, I've never told you because there wasn't a reason to."

"But now there is."

Jake nodded. "Yes, now there is. I'm bisexual."

"I know."

Jake looked up at Erin, who was taking another sip of coffee. "Johnnie did tell you."

"No, he didn't. I just noticed things when I was a teenager." Erin shrugged. "I figured that maybe you didn't understand it yourself."

Jake flipped over the pancake, which was just starting to burn. "What things?"

"You seemed to get little crushes on some of the other players." Erin waved her hand when Jake opened his mouth to reply. "Now, I'm not saying you were fanboying over them or anything, but it was like you felt the same way that I felt about a few guys I crushed on back then."

"Holy shit," Jake said. "I didn't think anyone knew, especially not you."

"I thought maybe that's why you and Mom got divorced. But you are really good friends now, so I figured maybe it was another reason."

"No, it was because we grew apart. I know that sounds lame."

Erin shook her head. "It doesn't. Now that I'm older, I've seen it happen to people."

Jake plated the pancake and handed it and some syrup to his daughter. "Are you okay with this?"

"I think so, yes. I'm worried about what will happen when you come out, but I want you to be happy."

Jake watched her eat and reminded himself that this wasn't the four-year-old who begged him for ice skating lessons. This was a very mature young woman, and he was just learning who she was. "I'm coming out soon."

"Good."

"Yeah?"

"Yeah."

"I need to tell you something else."

Erin popped a slice of pancake into her mouth. "Okay."

"There's a man, in Savannah. We dated in college, and I'm going to see if there's still anything there."

"Sounds like there's obviously something there on your side. How 'bout his?"

Jake shrugged and walked to the stove to start another pancake. "We've talked some on Facebook and in e-mail. Nothing romantic, though. His partner died last year, and he's just started dating again."

"Ah, so now you have competition, and you need to go stake your claim."

"Something like that."

Erin laughed. "Good to see you haven't lost your old competitive spirit in your retirement."

Jake stuck his tongue out at her. "I'm not dead yet, missy."

"So why did you two stop dating? Don't get me wrong. I'm glad you did or I wouldn't be here. But how did you end things in college?"

"I was a selfish dick."

"Dad," Marcy whispered. "You were a kid, and it was the eighties. It wasn't easy back then, I'm sure."

"No, it wasn't. What little gains queer people had made by then were pretty much wiped out by the fear of AIDS. People are ignorant and bigoted now, but there were lots more of them back then, it seemed. Still doesn't excuse me."

Marcy stuck her plate out for the new pancake. "You might be surprised. He may have forgiven you by now."

"Maybe," Jake said with a shrug. "At least I hope so."

Chapter 6: 1989

THE first season of AA ball sucked. When Jake was drafted after his junior year, he thought he'd light up the minors and be called up to the show in no time. Instead, he found the change from aluminum to wooden bats killed his batting average, and the long season as well as night games played havoc with his stamina. The packed schedule left little room to rest up for the next game.

He also hated not seeing Mikko for weeks at a time. He'd gotten used to seeing him almost every day and waking up with him a few times a week. In this new world, he was lucky to *phone* Mikko once a week. Mikko said he understood, and they more than made up for it when Jake could make quick trips back to Atlanta.

During the long stretches between visits, there were two things guaranteed to keep him occupied: alcohol and baseball groupies. He drank to forget how lonely he was, and he fucked all the groupies because… well, because they let him. They were just like the girls in college. They had no expectations. They just wanted to see how many players they could hook up with. It increased the chances of them one day saying, "Yeah, I fucked the MVP when he was in AA."

Every once in a while, Jake had the opportunity to have sex with another man. Jake wouldn't fuck them or let them fuck him. He would exchange hand jobs or blow jobs, just like he did in high school. He would close his eyes and thrust into some stranger's mouth and imagine it was Mikko at his feet.

After a particularly brutal road trip, Jake was looking forward to a few days off and a chance to see Mikko. It had been too long since they'd touched, and he was dying for it. He was shocked to unlock Mikko's door and find most of the apartment packed into boxes. He called Mikko's name, and Mikko came down the hall carrying a box.

Jake walked around the living room and kitchen. Everything was gone. "What the hell is going on here?"

Mikko dropped the box next to the front door. It was labeled "Jake." "What does it look like? I'm moving."

"What? Where? Why didn't you tell me?"

Mikko sat on the far end of the couch. "Why would I tell you? I haven't heard from you in more than a month."

Jake knew from Mikko's body language not to approach him, so he sat on the opposite end of the couch. "I've had a rough schedule. I didn't have a lot of time."

"You had enough time to fuck… what's her name? Oh yes, Lindsey. She and I had the most interesting conversation when I called."

Jake froze. He didn't remember a Lindsey, but then again, he didn't remember the names of most of his hookups. He certainly didn't remember one talking to Mikko. He wouldn't have allowed it unless he was—

"I must have been drunk. I don't remember any Lindsey, and I certainly don't know her well enough for her to tell you anything."

"Oh, but she knew you." Mikko's voice was sad instead of angry. "You're the new player who likes to party and fuck whatever moves. She said her friend had been with you and told her to make sure to try you out. That most of the girls had."

Jake winced. It hurt to know he'd been talked about behind his back. "Look, Mikko—"

"What are we?"

"Huh?"

"I've never asked you for monogamy, and God knows you've never offered it. I don't expect it. But I do expect some kind of acknowledgment that I'm more than those girls and any other man you've fucked on the road."

"I don't fuck other guys," Jake said with a growl.

"Fine, you don't fuck other guys." Mikko didn't sound convinced. "So what are we?"

"We're friends," Jake whispered.

"Friends. With benefits?"

Jake stared down at his feet.

"Fuck buddies? Isn't that what Americans call it? A friend you can fuck whenever you feel like it?"

"What do you want from me?" Jake cried. "Do you want me to come out? 'Cause I can't do that, and you know it!"

Mikko slid across the couch and grabbed Jake's hand. "I know, and I'm not asking you to. But I need us to be something more than this. I need to be someone more than just a guy you let fuck you when you're home from the road."

"You are."

"Then tell me what I am," Mikko begged.

Jake knew what Mikko wanted. He wanted to be the boyfriend. He wanted a formal name for the feelings they had for each other. But Jake couldn't do that. He couldn't.

Mikko pulled away. "You can't say it, can you? It's such a simple goddamned word, and you can't say it." He walked to the door and opened it. "I need you to leave."

"Mikko, don't."

"Now," Mikko commanded.

There was nothing else to be done tonight. Jake would try again in the morning, when Mikko had had time to cool off.

As Jake walked through the door, Mikko stopped him.

"Don't forget your box."

With those words, Jake knew no cooling-off period would make this better. Mikko was done with him.

The box sat in the backseat of Jake's rental car outside the first bar Jake could find. He drank until he felt no pain and went home with the first girl who offered. He woke up the next morning lying naked in bed, a little boy staring down at him. He didn't know how he got there, and he wasn't even sure if he'd used protection. He certainly didn't remember the girl's name or her mentioning having a kid at home.

As soon as he got dressed, he snuck out and headed straight to Waynesboro. At his parents' house, he had a long shower and a good meal. And he had time to think about how he wanted to live his life. Maybe if he stopped drinking so much and whoring around, he could get Mikko to give him another chance after the season was over.

Three months later, he met Marcy.

Chapter 7: Savannah

"OKAY, guys, here we are."

Jake looked down at his passenger seat menagerie. Erin had given him a plush version of Nashville's saber-toothed tiger mascot, which joined the buffalo from Albuquerque and the horses from Oklahoma. Somewhere around the Georgia state line, he'd begun talking to them.

"Should I go knock?"

The menagerie stared back.

"You guys are no help."

Jake counted to twenty, then one hundred. He meditated. He tried deep breathing. Nothing calmed his racing heart, and he eventually gave up and got out of the SUV.

Mikko's house was in a good neighborhood. It looked cozy, and the yard was beautifully landscaped. The brick sidewalk had been perfectly laid, and the porch swing was the crowning touch. It was a home that had obviously been loved for a long time.

Jake knocked on the door and waited. He could hear footsteps moving through the house. The door cracked open then swung wide.

The pictures on Facebook hadn't done Mikko justice. His hazel eyes were clear and wide, and only the small lines at their corners indicated the passage of time. His hair was a little longer and highlighted in spots by streaks of gray, which was also present in the very short beard he'd grown.

"Jake, you made it!" Mikko stepped back and waved Jake inside. "Please, come in."

After Jake entered, Mikko led him to the living room, and Jake took the opportunity to ogle. Mikko was still tall, tight, and lean, and his arms looked even stronger. The years had been good to him.

Mikko motioned Jake to a leather couch and disappeared. Jake took some time to get comfortable and scan the room. Just like the outside, this room was well kept. The couch and two recliners circled a glass coffee table, while a second couch behind him faced a flat-screen TV mounted on the wall. There were pictures everywhere of Mikko and his late partner. From the looks of it, they'd been very much in love.

When Mikko returned, he carried a tray with two steaming mugs of black coffee and a plate of shortbread cookies. He placed the tray on the table and took a mug for himself before sitting in a recliner.

"Well, Jake. You have certainly aged well, my friend. You look nothing like the washed-up, has-been ball player you said you were."

Jake took a cookie and smiled. "You don't look so bad yourself. Are you a vampire or something?"

"No, it's just my high-quality Finnish blood. We don't age like Americans do."

"Is that so?" Jake bit off a piece of the cookie. "This is great. Just like the ones your dad used to send."

"Thanks. I use his recipe." He smiled. "He treats it as a state secret, so I feel very honored."

"How are your folks?"

"Good, good. My father is like a horse, and my mother just tries to keep up. She's had a bit of a time with her arthritis, and the cold weather in Finland doesn't help. They're thinking of moving to Spain."

"My parents retired last year to the Gulf Coast. They both love the beach and love to fish, and they figured why not live near both."

"It's a beautiful area," Mikko said. "We went there a few times. The sand was like sugar, and your feet just sunk into it. It was wonderful."

"I was really sorry to hear about your partner," Jake whispered.

Mikko nodded. "Thank you. It was a very difficult time. We'd been together fifteen years, and we fully expected it to be another thirty. Cancer is evil that way. Just comes in and changes everything. At least we had that last year. I can't imagine just sending Seth out expecting him to come home and never seeing him again. At least we had a chance to say good-bye."

Jake found himself glad Mikko had that time with Seth, glad they'd had such a good life together. "I can't imagine that either. And if something happened to one of my kids…."

"How are they?" Mikko asked. "You have a boy and a girl, right?"

"Well, I've recently found out I have a young man and a young woman." Jake laughed. "They grew up when I wasn't looking."

"Kids tend to do that. My nieces and nephews are doing the same. They're still kids for a little while yet."

Jake took a big gulp of coffee, and it helped perk him up. "Driving across the country was not the smartest idea I've ever had. I'm glad I'm almost home."

"You're moving into your parents' house?"

"Yep, until I decide what I'm going to do now that I'm jobless. I know I want to stay in the South, but that's as far as my plans have gotten."

Mikko's eyes widened. "You do? I thought you'd stay in California. Take a job with the team."

"Oh no. I'm ready to be back in Georgia. I never got used to the big cities out West. Atlanta is probably all I could handle now, and I'm not even sure about that."

"What does your family think about that?"

Jake shrugged. "Well, to be honest, they kind of all left me behind in California. Marcy and Johnnie moved to Albuquerque after the divorce, but now Johnnie's at school in Oklahoma. Erin, my oldest, was already in college when Marcy moved, and she's in Nashville now working for a *hockey* team and getting ready to get married. As soon as I decided to retire, I sold the house, divvied up the money among the ex and kids, and made plans to come home."

"And what was waiting for you here besides your parents' empty house?"

Jake set his mug of coffee down. "You."

Mikko gasped. "What?"

"I came back to Georgia because you are here."

Mikko jumped up, piled the mugs back onto the tray, and headed out of the room. "That is crazy. You are crazy."

Jake followed, and he found Mikko standing over the kitchen sink, facing out the window. Jake hadn't meant to blurt it out like that, but lack of sleep combined with sugar and caffeine had made him less patient or subtle. He stayed back, not wanting to freak Mikko out any more than he already had.

Mikko sighed. "If you need a fuck buddy—"

"That's not what this is about."

"—I suggest you find one in Atlanta. There's lots of gay clubs there now, you know."

Jake knew. He'd been to them on his last road trip. "That's not what I want."

"What do you want, Jake? I'm not a closeted college boy anymore, and I refuse to be a closeted middle-aged man. And I know what it's like to have someone love me and only me. I won't settle for anything less."

So much pain, and Jake had never known. He knew he'd hurt Mikko, but until now he hadn't been aware of just how much. "I don't want you to. I'm only asking for a chance to get to know each other again. To see if we still might want to be together."

Mikko turned around. "And what will you tell your children? Are you going to come out?"

"My kids already know, and, yes, I'm going to come out. To everyone."

"Why now? Because baseball is finally over?"

Jake slowly walked toward Mikko and stopped when Mikko held up his hand. "I'd be lying if I said I would come out if I was still playing. I don't know. I just know that I was in love and married, and then I wasn't. But I learned how to be faithful. I learned how to understand myself and not try to drown out my desires with alcohol. And ever since I've been on my own, I've wondered what it would be like to be this person with you."

"And when you found me on Facebook, I had just lost Seth."

"Right. I just wanted to be your friend again and offer my condolences. I wanted to be there if you needed to talk about how much life sucked or how guilty you felt the first time you laughed after Seth died."

A tear ran down Mikko's cheek. "And you were."

"I was. After a few months, I knew for sure I wanted to be with you. I didn't want to push. I would wait however long it took to tell you."

"I just started dating."

"Yes, you did."

"You want to date me?"

"I want to be in your life any way you'll have me. If that's only as a friend, that's what I'll be." Jake took one step and placed his hand over Mikko's clenched fist.

Mikko looked down, his hazel eyes red and watery. "I need time to think about this."

"I understand. I'll e-mail you went I get to Waynesboro and send you my contact info. For when you're ready to talk."

Mikko nodded. Jake took a step back, then another, and then he left. When he climbed into the SUV, he addressed the menagerie again.

"Well, it could have been worse."

THE rugs arrived from Albuquerque a week after Jake moved into the house. He was glad he was rich, because Marcy sent him only the best rugs she could find. One was under the dining table, another was in the center of the living room, and a third was under his bed. He'd just finished laying down the hall runner when the doorbell rang.

On his doorstep stood Mikko, dressed in tight jeans and a tighter T-shirt. When he looked into Mikko's eyes, Jake shivered.

"I've thought about it," Mikko said.

"Yeah?"

"Yeah."

Before Jake could ask him for his decision, Mikko pushed Jake back against the foyer wall. Mikko slammed the door closed and descended. It took Jake a few seconds to catch up, but when he did, he thought he was dreaming.

Mikko kissed Jake without pretense and forced his tongue into Jake's mouth. Jake opened for Mikko as he always did, but this time he knew it meant something. Mikko stripped their shirts off over their heads and locked his lips around Jake's nipple. He alternated tongue swipes with sharp nips, and it drove Jake crazy. He yanked Mikko back by his hair and pushed him to his knees.

Mikko unzipped Jake's jeans and pushed them and his boxers down around his feet. Jake was already rock hard, and Mikko took Jake's cock down his throat as easily has he'd ever done. Jake reached down and cupped his hand over Mikko's throat to feel the bulge his cock made as Mikko deep-throated it. Jake reached the edge several times before Mikko pulled away and stood up.

"Get those pants off and take me to your bed."

As they walked to the bedroom, Jake remembered the nights Mikko was this wired, this ready to be inside. They'd fuck until dawn and wake up sore but happy. They might not make it to dawn anymore, but he was sure he would still wake up sore and happy.

Already naked, Jake set to removing Mikko's clothes. Mikko was still so lean, and his skin was pale and soft. If there were signs that Mikko was now in his forties, Jake didn't notice them. He hoped Mikko was as pleased with him.

When Jake knelt to help Mikko take off his shoes, Mikko stroked Jake's head. "I never forgot how good you felt. I can't believe we're doing this again."

"I never forgot either." Jake unbuttoned Mikko's jeans and licked the head of Mikko's uncovered cock. "I want to take our time later, but right now I just need to feel you inside me."

Mikko answered by pulling Jake to his feet and pushing him onto the bed. As he finished undressing, Mikko gazed up and down Jake's body. "You are still so beautiful. More than I remember." Mikko kissed Jake softly. "Turn over."

Jake held his breath as Mikko climbed onto the bed and between Jake's legs. Jake felt Mikko pull the cheeks of his ass apart, and then he felt Mikko swipe his warm, wet tongue over his hole.

"Oh, God, do that again."

Mikko licked back and forth, up and down, around one way then the other until Jake began to open up. Mikko fucked Jake with sharp jabs of his tongue and, once he scrambled and found the lube and condoms, deep thrusts of his fingers. Jake moved to take more, and Mikko gave him everything.

Jake cried out when Mikko entered him. Mikko lay over Jake and wrapped his arms around Jake's chest. They moved in concert, Jake lifting his hips to meet Mikko's thrusts. For all his eagerness to get to bed, Mikko was now slow and gentle, and Jake could feel every inch of Mikko fill him and leave him.

Mikko kissed Jake's shoulder and then sucked his earlobe. "Is this good?"

Jake could barely speak. "So good."

"God, Jake, I love you."

Jake turned his head and found Mikko's lips. "I love you too."

Mikko groaned and increased the speed of his thrusts. Jake couldn't keep up, and he let Mikko do what he wanted.

"That's it, baby. Just let me have you."

Jake remembered their first night, how he'd felt like shattering glass when he came. This time was different. Mikko made Jake feel whole again, made him soar like he'd never come down. Without even touching himself, Jake was coming, and the hot liquid pooled under his body. He delighted in the contractions of his body around Mikko's cock.

"Jake. Jake. Jake."

His head snug in the crook of Jake's neck, Mikko let go. He buried himself inside Jake and groaned through his orgasm. Jake loved the sound and wanted to hear it again. He wanted to hear it many, many more times.

After Mikko pulled out, Jake turned over, and they took each other into their arms. Neither spoke. They could hardly breathe. It was a long while before Jake could have a coherent thought or form a sentence. But once he did, there was only one thing he could think to say.

"I'm in the wet spot."

Mikko laughed. "Sorry. We'll get up soon."

"What will we do once we get up?"

"I don't know. Take a shower. Order a pizza. Watch a movie."

Jake scratched the center of Mikko's chest, and Mikko practically purred. "Will you stay tonight?"

"If you want me to."

"I do."

Mikko kissed Jake's forehead. "One of these days, we're going to have to talk about what all this means."

"I know," Jake said. "Not tonight. But very soon."

"Okay."

Jake nodded. "Okay."

"Can we order that pizza now?"

Epilogue: San Diego

Wilson Returns to Throw First Pitch

SAN DIEGO—Jake Wilson, former San Diego second baseman, looked over the field. He hadn't been there since he retired last year, and he's proud he's been asked back to throw the first pitch of the first home game of the season.

His son Johnnie, a baseball standout at the University of Oklahoma, and his daughter Erin, a member of the Nashville Predators front office, were back in the clubhouse catching up with the players and their children. But Wilson wasn't on the field alone.

With him was his fiancé, Mikko Niemi.

Three weeks after retiring, Wilson stunned the baseball world with his decision to announce his bisexuality. Two months later, he attended his first public event with Niemi, a chemical engineer from Savannah, Ga.

Not all the reaction was pleasant or even polite, but Wilson and Niemi felt safe enough at the stadium to hold hands.

"I used to watch Jake play when we were in college," Niemi said as he tells their story.

"And I used to watch Mikko sitting in the stands," Wilson added.

It's the classic story of reuniting with a first love, with a little baseball and marriage equality thrown in.

"We could get married while we're here, but we're hoping we'll someday be able to marry at home in Georgia," Wilson explained. "It's going to happen. I believe it."

Players from both teams came up to Wilson and Niemi, eager to shake their hands and offer support. A few players obviously avoided them.

"Will an active player come out? I hope so," Niemi said. "It would be better if people could feel free to be who they really are."

Wilson agreed. "I hope that someday no one has to feel like I did before I came out. That no one feels like they have to make a decision between love and baseball."

KERRY FREEMAN was born and raised in Alabama and she grew up swearing she was going to get the hell out of Dodge the instant she could. Turns out Dodge ain't so bad, and she never left. Alabama's version of a city girl, she married a country boy, and the couple lives in a small town with their two socially awkward dogs.

Kerry loves to write about love, and it turns out most of the voices in her head are men. She also loves to write about the South, so most of her stories end up there, one way or another.

A tomboy and a geek from way back, Kerry has a day job but dreams she will one day write full time. She has a weakness for yaoi, Japanese stationery, YA, and ginger-haired singers from Britain. She owns an impressive t-shirt collection. Nowaki & Hiroki are her homeboys.

Website: http://kerryfreeman.com/
Twitter: https://twitter.com/kfwritesbooks
Facebook: https://www.facebook.com/authorkerryfreeman

Wild Pitch

MARGUERITE LABBE

To my son Christian and his constant companions Moosie and Angie.
You taught me what unconditional love truly means.

Chapter 1

"WHY'RE you here today?" Alan Hartner asked as he came into the batting cage lobby, toting a large equipment bag. "I thought you wanted to get the kids' rooms ready."

A sick flash of acute disappointment and hurt went through Ruben Martell like a barbed spear. He saved his file on the laptop, shut the lid, and forced a smile. "It can wait. How was practice?"

"The kids were on fire today. It took a while to get them settled and focused." Alan gestured to one of the occupied cages and the kid swinging at the machine pitched balls with fierce determination. "I see Tyler beat me here."

"Yeah, he knows he barely made the cut, so he's trying to get in extra practice whenever he can."

Alan opened the equipment locker, set the bag down by the bench, and began to put everything away. Ruben watched him, sweaty from being out in the sun for a couple hours, his skin flushed red. A wave of intense longing washed over him. He wanted to go to him and pour his heart out. He knew Alan would listen, be supportive. He knew Alan would understand exactly why he was hurting and how much. He was also afraid he'd end up telling Alan everything that was eating at him and he wasn't sure Alan could deal with that.

"So, I've been thinking," Alan said, checking over the spare bats as he drew them out of the bag. "We've done pretty well for ourselves in the past year. Now that I have you with me full time, maybe we should consider expanding."

Ruben's gaze drifted over the batting cage with its concrete walls that kept it cool in the summer and chilly in the winter. Three separate cages lined the back wall and all were occupied. There was a small arcade and vending area off to the left, and a room for parties on the right next to the tiny office they shared. Ruben stood at the glassed-in counter that held baseball cards, Todd McFarlane action figures of baseball players, and even a few signed balls they'd gotten from the last game they went to.

"Did you have any specific plans?" Ruben could think of several options, from adding a couple more cages to expanding the arcade.

"Well, Sylvia is thinking of retiring and selling the salon. We could take over the space, knock out the wall, and put extra cages there."

"I don't think she's going to sell in the next year." Expanding would mean investing even more into this enterprise he'd fallen into. He couldn't deny they were successful or that he enjoyed his new career. He just wasn't sure it was enough anymore.

Alan studied him with a thoughtful expression, and Ruben's masochist heart skipped a beat. "Maybe not, but we could still consider the possibility. What would you like to do with the space, if we had it?"

"Honestly?"

"Since when have we been anything but honest with each other?"

"I'd move the arcade into the new spot, add a cage, then open up that side and put in a practice pitching area."

"Huh," Alan said thoughtfully, turning to look around as if he were trying to picture it. "That's a possibility."

Ruben opened his laptop again as Alan returned to dealing with the equipment. He needed something to occupy his attention to pull him out of his brooding thoughts and to keep him from watching Alan like a lovesick teenager.

CRACK. The sound of a bat connecting just right with a ball filled Ruben's ears, followed by the *chink* when the ball struck the chain-link fence of the batting cage. He glanced toward Tyler and noted how the kid had his hands positioned on the bat with a sense of satisfaction. About time he listened.

"Good one, Tyler, keep it up," Alan encouraged as he finished wiping down one helmet before setting it away with the others. It might've taken Ruben and Alan a couple of months to get Tyler to loosen his death grip on the bat, but it had paid off. "See what happens when you don't overthink it?"

Ruben's gaze lingered on Alan as his friend turned his attention back to the task in front of him. The familiar sounds of practice were a comfort, though none of them as much as Alan's voice. Ruben could pick it out anywhere, whether they were in a crowded locker room, or hanging out after the game in a bar, or even now amongst the clamor of a dozen kids scrambling to get extra practice in as the Little League All-Star season started.

Alan's voice stood out amongst all that not because he was loud or obnoxious, but because over the past fifteen years, he had been just about everything to Ruben: Teammate. Best friend. Rival. And now business partner. And despite all that, Ruben couldn't stop himself from wanting more.

He was staring at Alan again, just as he had all those years ago when they'd played for the Red Sox. Alan's fire had mellowed some since then. The drive to be the best batter and outfielder in the American League had transformed into the drive to be the single parent of four young sons and coach of one of the local Little League teams. He had a few new lines around his blue eyes and the hair on the back of his head had started to thin, but he was still damn beautiful.

A car horn blared and Ruben peered out the window at the familiar sedan that had pulled up in front of the batting cage. Mrs. Netty waved at him and he lifted his hand in return. "Tyler, your mom's here."

"Okay!" Tyler stuffed his batting gloves in his duffel bag and set the bat back in its rack. "Hey, Mr. Martell, I got a question."

"Shoot." Ruben checked to make sure he had the right scrimmage list, handed him a flyer with the schedule on it, and then watched Tyler cram it in his back pocket where it would be forgotten. Ruben made a mental note to tell Alan to follow up with an e-mail to his parents.

"Why'd you leave Boston the first time?" Tyler asked with curious, wide eyes. "Couldn't you have stayed? I bet Coach Hartner wanted you to stay."

Ruben had no idea how many times he'd been asked that very same question, often with expressions of accusation or betrayal. At least for Tyler it was so long ago that at his age it was nothing more than a curiosity.

"I've been asking him that for more than seven years," Alan spoke up. Ruben didn't have to look at Alan to know his friend was watching him with that penetrating gaze of his.

The old, familiar regret washed over him. He had faced that question from Alan the most; often with hurt in those blue eyes, sometimes anger. The anger he could handle; the hurt was something else altogether. Lately, though, the question had become more probing, and it was a whole can of trouble Ruben didn't want to open up again. Not after what happened last time.

“I needed a change of pace.” It was a bullshit answer then and it was a bullshit answer now. Looking back on it, he wouldn’t have made the same choices. But damned if he knew what choice he would’ve made. He’d done the best that he could to make things right and sometimes it felt like he’d failed on every point.

Tyler grimaced and stuck his cap on backward. “But why go to the enemy? Dad says you’re a traitor.”

“I’m a traitor, huh?” Ruben laid his elbows on the long counter and tried not to smile at Tyler’s earnest expression. Kids could be amazingly blunt at times.

“Yeah, but he forgives you, ’cause you didn’t trash talk,” Tyler assured him.

Alan snorted and Ruben finally lifted his eyes to meet Alan’s gaze. There was a challenge there, one Ruben hadn’t seen in years, and it left him flustered. What the hell did Alan want? He knew why Ruben had left. It might have been unspoken, but he damn well knew why. And if Alan wanted to hash it out after all this time…. Ruben tamped down on the little spike of hope before he let himself start dreaming again.

“There was plenty of trash talk on both sides, but not in public—just between friends,” Ruben said. “As for why, they made me an offer, a good one that I would’ve been a fool to pass up. And Tampa was closer to my family in Puerto Rico.”

Ruben could see another question forming on Tyler’s lips and he waved him off, gesturing to where his mom sat in her car. “Go on. Your mom’s waiting, and don’t forget to give her the schedule.”

“Yes, sir.” Tyler shifted his bag onto one skinny shoulder, and Ruben felt his moodiness lift a little. He’d been like that once, spending his endless summer days practicing, playing, and reveling in the heat and sweat of the game with dogged persistence. He had to admit he’d enjoyed teaching another generation the love of the game. It wasn’t where he’d thought he’d be at this point in his life. Until recently he was sure he was right where he belonged, but now he had doubts.

“You keep hitting the cage the way you’ve done today and you could be the next Nomar,” Ruben said as Tyler got to the door.

“Who?” Tyler gave him a blank look over his shoulder.

“Kid, you’re breaking my heart. Get out of here.” Ruben shooed Tyler out again and watched him get into the car with his mom.

"I think he's a little too young for Nomar, Ruben. He has other baseball heroes."

"I'm surprised it's not you," Ruben shot back, crossing his arms over his chest. "He definitely had a bad case of starry eyes when he first started coming here."

"I think I've given him enough hell over the state of his equipment that the hero worship has tarnished." Alan grinned, a wicked curve of his lips, and his eyes glinted with challenge. "You do realize your team doesn't stand a chance against mine, don't you? I have the best batting lineup in the county."

"Keep telling yourself that, Hartner. With Sammy and Adam pitching on my team, your boys won't even get a chance to hit."

Alan snorted a laugh and Ruben's heart did a little flip like he was in high school all over again. Alan's square face was framed with the start of a beard several shades lighter and redder than the shaggy chestnut hair that threatened to fall into his eyes. Alan needed a haircut more often than not and Ruben's fingers itched to brush it back. And his eyes drove Ruben crazy. They were an intense, crystalline blue that made it seem sometimes like his gaze was cutting right through the bullshit to the heart of the matter.

Ruben went back to fussing over the flyer for the pitching camp he was running at the end of the season. Three days on an island in the lake with a bunch of eleven- and twelve-year-olds. What had he been thinking? Last year had been a logistical nightmare, even if everyone had fun. He wished he could summon up the same enthusiasm this year, but it was buried deep under a mile-high pile of disillusionment.

"You've been pretty quiet all day," Alan said as he returned to putting away the equipment. "What gives?"

"Nothing I want to get into at work." Ruben shut down the program before he got so fed up with the flyer that he erased the whole thing. "I'm going to go tinker with the pitching machine that keeps stalling. We might have to think about getting a new one."

"Hey." There was a wealth of concern in that one word. Ruben paused and looked back at Alan, who studied him with his brows drawn together. He didn't press and Ruben was grateful. He didn't feel like getting into all of the drama and bullshit right now. Ruben had never been very good at hiding anything from Alan, and it irked him sometimes. "Do you want to come by for dinner tonight? The boys want me to break out the grill."

Ruben hesitated. He wasn't good company, he knew that, but the thought of being at the big, empty house alone tonight daunted him. He should've found a smaller place when Karen moved out with the kids. At least Alan and his boys would fill up the silence for a time. "Sure. I'll bring the beer."

FROM the backyard, Ruben heard the roar of a major battle taking place, the high-pitched gleeful shrieks of young boys mixed with Alan's shouts of defiance. He grabbed the six-pack from the passenger seat and went around the side of Alan's house to investigate. It might be safer to take refuge on the deck and watch the chaos until they noticed he'd arrived.

Ruben slipped through the gate and stopped with a laugh at the sight of the full-blown water war taking place. Alan had barricaded himself behind the picnic table turned on its side, and his three older sons were attempting to swarm him with water guns. None of them saw Ruben come in. The boys were too intent on getting to their victim and Alan in holding them off.

Alan jumped up with a roar, water balloons in both hands, and Brett, Mikey, and Seth scattered with another round of shrieks. Alan tossed his first round of ammunition, catching both Mikey and Seth, though Brett danced out of reach with a taunt before Alan reached down to grab his second round.

Ruben grinned, setting the beers and his phone on the deck with a wicked sense of bubbling anticipation. It pulled him out of the downward spiral of nagging regrets and the sense of hopelessness that had dogged him for the past couple of weeks. It was impossible to remain depressed around Alan and his sons.

The youngest boy, Matt, was with Alan, attempting to carry the water balloons off one by one. He was soaked to the skin, breaking most of the balloons as he hugged them to him while trying to toddle away. The only one not wet was Alan, and that couldn't be allowed.

Humming to himself, Ruben unwound the garden hose from its neat coil under the back faucet. Matt grabbed another water balloon, caught sight of Ruben, and let out a crow of delight. Ruben held a finger to his lips and beckoned to him as he turned on the water. Oh this was going to be so good.

"Unca, Unca!" Matt yelled, dropping the water balloon and waving his chubby hands as he toddled toward Ruben as fast as his short, fat legs would take him.

Alan twisted around, looking for Matt, and his gaze fell on Ruben as he pointed the hose at him. He had just enough time for his eyes to widen before Ruben turned the nozzle on full blast with a wicked laugh. The stream of water caught Alan square in the chest, and he shouted as the boys whooped in delight.

"You double crossing—" Alan cut himself off before he let loose the slew of curses that would've once dominated his tirade. Ruben snickered and kept the hose on him as Alan's boys came in with their water guns to finish him off.

Alan grabbed a water balloon and threw it at Ruben, who sidestepped it with a chuckle. "Your pitching sucks, Hartner," Ruben taunted.

"Yeah? Dodge this." Alan grabbed more ammunition and barreled forward with the burst of speed he'd once used to steal bases.

"Whoo-hoo!" Brett shouted, turning his water gun on Ruben. "Get Uncle Ruben too!"

Ruben cursed under his breath and took a step back even as he knew it was too late. Alan pelted him with the water balloons and then tackled him to the ground. Of all the fantasies he'd had over the years of Alan taking him down like this, none of them had involved water balloons or four shrieking boys in the background.

He stamped on his libido and pulled the trigger of the nozzle as Alan tried to wrest the hose away from Ruben. Water, just above freezing, went everywhere, soaking them both and Ruben let out a startled shout from the shock. He relinquished the hose and shoved Alan off him with a laugh.

"You do realize I'm the only one at this madhouse without a change of clothes, right?"

"You'll dry out in the sun. There's a nice breeze coming off the lake." Alan sat up and gave him a friendly shove back. "You should've stayed out of it if you didn't want the consequences."

"Please. You all would've involved me the moment you saw me, unless I took refuge in the house."

Alan grinned, his entire expression engaging, and for a moment the familiar camaraderie was there, the kind they'd had before things had gotten to be so complicated. Ruben missed that, the friendship without old guilt, the enjoyment of being in Alan's presence without his feelings being muddled by sexual tension and longing for more.

He only had himself to blame for any awkwardness between them. He never should've kissed Alan that night, no matter how much the memory of that kiss had been seared into his brain.

"That was awesome, Uncle Ruben," Mikey said with a look of delight lighting up his face. "Did you see Dad's face when he saw you?"

"I couldn't miss it." Ruben pushed himself up, grimacing as his shoulder popped and twinged. He rolled it, but there didn't seem to be any damage beyond what years of pitching had already done. He was old and battered enough without adding to it.

He ruffled Brett's hair before he could dodge him, then hugged Seth and Mikey, who didn't feel like they were too old for embraces. Matt had gotten distracted by something on the ground and was currently crouched in the grass, his diaper sagging down and his finger in his mouth. They were good kids. Alan had been busting his ass to give them back the sense of security the older ones had lost after their mother's sudden death.

Ruben missed this. The hole had ached a little more each and every day these past couple of weeks. He'd brought his phone with him, waiting for his own kids to ping him for FaceTime. Once again Jessica and Jonah were late. He'd tried their phones, even tried the house, but no answer. He hated feeling like Karen was restricting his access to his kids and tried to stop those negative thoughts as soon as they came. But lately, he'd been having a harder time getting out of the rut he'd fallen into.

The divorce had been a good thing, as much as Ruben wished there hadn't been heartache and anger all around. But once things had settled down and the kids had seen how much happier he and Karen were, how they'd been able to become friends again, they'd relaxed. However, losing his kids to the near bottom of the East Coast still hurt. Then to lose his career on top of it had made for a rough couple years.

"Hey, you okay?" Alan nudged Ruben's elbow with his own.

Ruben pulled himself out of his depressing thoughts and met Alan's concerned gaze. "Yeah."

"It's not your shoulder, is it?"

Ruben forced a smile and got to his feet. "Despite last year's surgery, my shoulder is faring better than my knees. I'm good." The memory of being forced out by younger, stronger men had ceased to sting a while ago. The rehab hadn't helped him get his fastball back up to speed, and neither had the surgery. Alan's offer of a partnership had given him something to work toward instead of pining for a career that had slipped away.

Besides, he couldn't complain. He wasn't the only one who'd had to quit playing professionally. At least his kids still had both their parents, even if one was in Florida and the other in Vermont. Alan had been forced to do it all on his own, and Ruben hadn't heard him bitch once about how his life had been turned around inside out.

"Then what is it?" Alan asked in a low voice as he stood up as well. He shrugged out of his wet T-shirt and tossed the thin cotton over his shoulder. Ruben looked away from his broad shoulders and trim waist, squashing the familiar tug of longing. "You used to tell me everything, Ruben."

There used to be a time when Ruben could tell him everything, but he wasn't about to pressure Alan with the stupid, unrequited love whine. He knew where Alan stood when it came to the two of them and that was okay. Ruben's "what ifs" were all his own. But if anybody would understand how much Ruben missed his kids, it would be his best friend.

"I will," Ruben assured him. "Just not now. Later, when the boys are in bed. Right now I just want to chill and break out the grill."

"I'll hold you to that." Alan turned his gaze on Matt, who was attempting to run and hold onto his falling diaper at the same time. "First, I have a renegade to take care of before he decides to strip naked."

Ruben chuckled and slipped off his own shirt to drape over the deck railing. "Jonah is the same way, so good luck. It doesn't change as they get older, it only gets more inappropriate."

Chapter 2

"MATT, Seth, say good night to your uncle and let's head upstairs," Alan said as he stepped out onto the back porch.

Matt immediately stuck his lower lip out in a sulk and looked to Ruben for rescue, as Seth protested, "Mikey and Brett get to stay up. I wanna stay up too."

"Zip it," Alan cut in before Seth could really get started. His son was a champion debater at four years old, and if Alan gave him a chance, he'd find a way to successfully argue for a later bedtime. "They'll be following soon. When you turn six you can stay up an extra half hour too."

"No, no, no, no, no." Matt clung to Ruben's shirt with one chubby hand and swatted at Alan with the other. "Bed bad. Bad bed."

"Let me." Ruben stood up and secured his arm around Matt's waist. The imp let out a squawk when he realized he'd been betrayed and tried to wiggle out of Ruben's embrace. "I haven't put them down in a while."

Alan was about to tell Ruben he didn't have to bother, but something about the set of his mouth and the slump of his shoulders stopped him. He knew how much Ruben missed his own kids and now that it was getting close to their summer visit, the house must seem extra cold and quiet. If Ruben wanted to listen to Matt and Seth's last-minute wrangling, who was he to stop him?

"You don't have to twist my arm. One story, that's what they get. Don't let the hooligans tell you anything else."

"I was a pro at this when you were still freaking out about your first diaper change." Ruben snagged Seth as he tried to make a dodge for the lawn and scooped him up as well. "Gotcha, little hooligan."

Seth began giggling, and that was enough to pull Matt out of his sulks. He ceased struggling and patted Ruben's cheek. "Unca? What's hool'gan?"

"You are." Ruben blew a raspberry on his neck, and Matt shrieked with laughter before Ruben did the same to Seth.

Alan watched them go with a sense of relief and grabbed a deck chair. As soon as the boys were in bed, he planned to get some answers out of Ruben. For as close as they were, sometimes Ruben could be maddeningly distant. He stewed and brooded until he made some crazy-assed decision that seemed to come from nowhere, leaving Alan feeling like a bombshell had been dropped on him. Alan refused to let that happen again.

From the stairwell, Alan heard Matt's shriek of "noooooo," and chuckled. It was kind of nice to share bedtime duty with Ruben. Alan knew he'd been leaning more on his friend than he should. He didn't want to take advantage of Ruben's willingness to help just because there were some nights when he found being a single parent a little daunting. He didn't know how Cassandra had done it all those times Alan had been on the road.

"Dad?"

"I'm right here, buddy." Alan waved to Brett to show him he hadn't left the back deck. Brett was getting better about not freaking out when he couldn't find him, but he still had his moments. The uncertainty came from having his mom there one morning, celebrating the newest member of their family, and gone the next. Alan couldn't begin to imagine his son's confusion and heartbreak.

And Alan still couldn't think of Cassandra without a twist of guilt that made him ache. She'd deserved better than a husband who traveled so often and spent far more time with his best friend than with her.

"Okay." Brett waved back and returned to playing whatever game it was that he'd devised with Mikey.

The bedroom light overlooking the deck came on and Alan glanced up as Ruben closed the blinds. Lately, it seemed like Ruben was drifting further away, and Alan couldn't figure out what to do to stop it. Sometimes, he just wanted to go back to how they'd been before Ruben had gotten it into his head to kiss him. That was when everything went weird. Alan still didn't know what Ruben had been thinking, and he'd tried to blame it on the postgame celebration, but that didn't explain his own reaction to that spontaneous kiss.

Admittedly, it had been hot. Alan had noticed other men before and had always dismissed it, telling himself that he was just comfortable enough with who he was that he could notice. But Ruben was in a league all his own, and Alan had seemed to notice that more often. Didn't matter; they had both been married at the time, and Alan had made it clear it couldn't happen again. It was too late, though—the damage had been done. He couldn't stop himself from looking at Ruben differently, thinking things he shouldn't, wanting to explore more until he thought the guilt would eat him alive.

When Ruben had left for Tampa, it had been a relief at first. Alan had seen it as a chance to get back to the friendship they'd had without the awkwardness of emotions and desires they didn't need. Yeah, right. He'd missed Ruben with a painful ache that had left him confused and lost. When the relief faded, he'd been hurt and angry that Ruben hadn't discussed the move with him first. They were best friends.

It didn't help that Alan obsessed over him going. He wanted to know what Ruben had been thinking. He wanted to know why, yet he was still… a little afraid of the answers he might hear.

"Got it! No, dangit!" A shout from Mikey drew Alan's attention from his brooding thoughts, and he stood up to see what they were doing. The fireflies had emerged, their gentle light blinking on and off as Mikey and Brett chased them on the back lawn. Alan smiled; he'd loved doing that on lazy summer nights too. "Make sure you let them out of the jar before you go to bed, guys."

"Uh-huh," Brett said, showing Mikey how to cup his hands around the insect and transfer it to the jar, where a couple others were already incarcerated.

"It tickles." Mikey giggled.

Alan let them play for a little longer, his thoughts returning to Ruben. Something had happened recently, something that hurt him. He was pretty good at hiding it, but Alan had known him long enough to recognize the signs, the inward air of preoccupation, the defensive tightening around his dark-brown eyes. There was a time when Alan believed Ruben would tell him anything, but then he'd switched teams and Alan realized how wrong he'd been.

Still, when Ruben had come back to play in Boston, their friendship had been stronger than ever. He'd been there for Ruben through his divorce, and Ruben had helped him to keep it together after Cassandra's sudden death. Then Ruben had been injured and he'd leaned on Alan throughout his painful rehab and coming to terms with the realization that his career was over. They'd built a place for themselves in this bustling town off Lake Champlain.

There had been only one other incident between them, which should have been a good thing, they'd moved on, yet it continued to bother Alan like poking at a sore tooth. He couldn't figure out Ruben's mindset then or now, whether he'd ever wanted to kiss him again, or if it had been a random moment of temporary insanity. Alan had thought of kissing Ruben; hell, he'd thought of a lot more, but after the way he'd shut Ruben down cold twice, it was asking for trouble to even consider the notion. He needed their friendship too much to risk fooling around with it.

Alan called Mikey and Brett in, then sent them running upstairs to get ready for bed. He followed the noise of their stampede and stopped in the doorway to Seth and Matt's room. They were settled in their bed and crib, their attention focused on Ruben, who was reading to them from *Fox in Socks* and managing the tongue twisters far better than Alan could.

Alan leaned against the door to listen as well. He loved the sound of Ruben's voice, the faint lilting accent he still had even though he'd lived Stateside since he was eighteen. Whenever he'd visit his mom in San Juan, he'd come back with his accent a little stronger for the following weeks. Alan trailed his gaze over Ruben—the warm brown of his skin, the close-cropped mass of black curls, the dark shadow along his jaw. His friend was a good-looking man, though Alan was pretty sure he'd have the same reaction to him even if he was scarred, ugly, or put on sudden weight.

"Uncle Ruben?" Seth sat up, interrupting Ruben's story.

"Yeah, little man?" Ruben shut the book, keeping the place with his finger, and focused his attention on Seth.

"Did you know my mommy?"

Alan went still as shock jolted through him. Mentally, he told Ruben to find a way to drop the subject. Every time he thought of Ruben and Cassandra in the same sentence, it brought a wave of remembered guilt and shame. It didn't help that deep down, he wished he and Ruben had gone further. Even three years after the last incident, Cassandra was still a hot-button topic.

Ruben shifted in the chair and set the book aside as Matt sat up too, his blue eyes widening. "Mama?"

"Yeah, I knew her. She was a good lady. She liked to smile." Ruben paused, cocked his head, then half turned to glance at Alan in the doorway. He had an uncanny knack for knowing when Alan was nearby; even if he remained silent, somehow Ruben always knew.

"Did she love me?" Seth asked, and Ruben turned back to him. Alan's son had such a hopeful look on his face that Alan couldn't blame Ruben for not being able to respond, even as the sharp edge twisted deeper. The boys should be asking him these kinds of questions, not Ruben.

"Very much," Ruben replied softly.

"Me?" Matt asked, climbing to his feet and clinging to the railing of his crib. "Me?"

"Absolutely." Ruben rose to lay Matt back in his crib. "Your dad and all of you boys made her very happy."

There were times, like now, when Alan wished Ruben had remembered that detail the night he'd kissed him. All of those crazy urges he'd had as a teenager had been left in the past until then. Alan had been comfortable, secure with his career, his family, his friendships… and Ruben had turned that all upside down with one incredible kiss.

"I can take over from here." There was an edge to Alan's voice he tried to hide from the boys, but from the way Ruben stiffened, Alan knew he'd heard it. There was so much left unsaid between them that they'd gotten used to listening for the subtle nuances in their voices. And the weight of all those unsaid words seemed especially heavy tonight. "Why don't you grab us a couple beers and wait for me downstairs?"

"Sure." Ruben smoothed Matt's blankets and ruffled Seth's hair. As he passed Alan, their gazes clashed. Alan had the hot temper—it came and went in a flash of lightning—but not Ruben, Ruben let things smolder until they couldn't be held back anymore. And from the look in his eye, that simmering kind of heat that had gotten them into trouble before had been building for a while.

Maybe it would be best for them both if Ruben went home. Alan would calm down before morning and things would go on as they always had. Alan sighed and closed his eyes. And then there would be yet another thing unspoken between them. If they kept this up, they'd end up not talking at all, and that thought brought a sharp, aching pain. He'd lost his career and his boys' mother; he couldn't lose Ruben too.

"Daddy?"

Alan looked at Seth, who had a worried frown, and forced himself to smile. "Yeah, Seth?"

"Are you mad?"

The last thing Alan wanted was for the boys to think they couldn't talk about their mom, not that Seth could remember her all that well, and to Matt she was a picture and stories. It was his responsibility to keep the memories of her alive in their minds. He needed to do a better job if his younger ones were turning to Ruben instead of him. Perhaps he'd paid too much attention to Brett's anxieties and not the others'.

"No, I'm not mad."

He put away the book Ruben had left out and tucked the boys in. They didn't ask any more questions, and Alan wasn't sure how to volunteer the answers. He paused in the doorway and looked back at them. Matt had already kicked his blanket off and Seth had curled onto his side, resting his fist on his cheek. "You know you can talk about your mom anytime you want, right?"

"Yeah, I know," Seth mumbled. "Love you, Daddy."

"I love you too." Alan flipped off the light, then crossed the hall to check on Mikey and Brett, who scrambled for their beds when they spotted him. He got them settled as well, half of his mind on Ruben waiting downstairs. He listened for the sound of the door, both hoping to hear it and knowing he'd be disappointed if Ruben did leave.

After good-night kisses and an admonishment to remain in bed, Alan left them to go to sleep and went downstairs to look for Ruben. He found him on the back porch, sipping his beer and staring out over the lake. The breeze coming off the water leached the heat out of the day, leaving it pleasant. The sun was almost gone, and lights were coming out along the shore in a glittering strand. Alan paused and tried to let the peace of the scene sink into him, but the confused welter of emotions roiling inside him wasn't making it easy.

Ruben opened another beer and held it up for Alan without turning around. Alan took it, though he had no interest in drinking. No matter how he said this, it was going to sting, and they both knew it was coming so there was no point in hedging. They'd had this conversation once before. "Ruben, I don't want you talking about my wife."

Ruben closed his eyes, his heavy brows drawing together as he pressed his lips tight. "They asked. What was I supposed to say? They're young; they don't know what's taboo and what isn't. They've got friends at Miss Sarah's who have mothers, and they know theirs is gone. They're still trying to make sense of it; of course they're going ask questions."

"You know what you were supposed to say and you knew I was standing right there, so there was no reason for you not to turn it over to me."

"Why're you being so hardheaded?" The line between Ruben's brows deepened. "You know I cared about her too. Cassandra was a friend. You're not the only one who carries around guilt for what happened between us."

Alan couldn't believe Ruben was arguing about this. There was no room for disagreement here. It was a boundary issue, one that Ruben had clearly crossed, and he knew he was wrong. But when he looked up at Alan with an expression that was both stubborn and aching, it made Alan bristle and put his defenses up.

"You tell them to talk to me." Alan stuck his thumbs through his belt loops. "I'm serious. This isn't something I'm going to back down on."

Ruben set his beer bottle down with a deliberate motion that made Alan's senses tingle. Of all the times for him to dig in his heels…. Alan wished he'd picked any other topic than this. When Ruben turned to face Alan, there was a hot, reckless mood in his dark eyes. "Why?"

Alan blinked and then scowled at Ruben as he stood up. "What you do mean why? That's a dumbass question. You know why."

"Why does it bother you this much?" Ruben pressed, stopping in front of him, close enough that Alan could smell the crisp, clean scent of his aftershave. "Not to be cruel, but she's been gone for two years. There's nothing we can do that'll hurt her anymore. So I have to ask myself why you still feel so guilty when I mention Cassandra."

All Alan could do was stare at Ruben, scrambling to find words. "I don't think we should be discussing this."

"Why not?" Ruben said, taking another step closer, making it hard to think. Alan's skin pricked with electricity, and he had to stop his gaze from drifting to Ruben's mouth. That would be a bad idea. That was how all this had started in the first place, with Alan watching Ruben's mouth, the way his lips moved as he rambled on about one of his favorite topics. "You've been pushing lately, asking questions I'm not sure you really want answered."

Alan scrubbed a hand through his hair and moved away to set his beer down. He needed some space between them so he could think.

"Okay, you're right, I have, and I'm still waiting on an answer for why you left."

Ruben barked a disbelieving laugh and put his hands on his hips as he stared at Alan. "You're unbelievable, you know that?"

"What?"

"I left because I knew if I didn't I'd be tempted to kiss you again." A jolt of electricity lanced through Alan at those words. "And I didn't want to get between you and Cassandra any more than I already had. I figured distance would be good for us, but I was wrong, wasn't I?" Ruben said with a pointed glance.

Alan felt the instant flush in his cheeks. "That was a mistake on my part, and right now is not the time to get into it." This wasn't why he had invited Ruben over. Whatever was bothering him had nothing to do with their past. Did it?

"I think it is, because it's still eating at you. If it was nothing more than hormones and alcohol and whatever other excuse you come up with for what happened between us, if it hadn't meant anything, then I think it would've faded by now."

The confused jumble of emotions spiked and surged, fueling Alan's temper. He couldn't get a handle on his own feelings. Who was Ruben to say how he did and did not feel?

"Will you stop bringing that up?" Alan glared at him, his jaw clenching. After all this time of not talking about it, it was a shock to hear it all being alluded to now. "Seriously, Ruben, it's time to let it go. It was a mistake. A huge one. One you started."

Ruben flinched, and this time he was the one who looked away. Alan knew he was going to regret those hot words later on, but right now the bubbling guilt, anger, and confusion had ahold of him.

"Yeah, you're right, I did, and I apologized. I never should've kissed you. You keep asking why I left the team. You know damn well why. I left because you made it clear nothing was going to happen between us, and I—"

Alan wished that Ruben hadn't stopped himself there, before he told Alan how deep his feelings ran, or what the hell had been going through his mind that night or afterward. "You what?" Alan snapped, stepping toward him again. "Jesus, Ruben, I didn't ask you to leave town because of it. Nothing could come of it. We were both married. We both had kids. What the hell did you expect?"

Ruben leaned closer, and Alan's heart began to pound, his breath shortening. His gaze went to Ruben's lips and then jerked back to Ruben's eyes. "Why does it bother you, Alan? Am I too close? Do you still think about those two nights when you're alone in bed?"

He did think of them, more often than he needed for peace of mind. His mouth went dry and his thoughts skittered back to the memory of how the desire had risen hot and hard between them.

"I do," Ruben said, echoing Alan's thoughts. "I remember your rough kisses and the way your hands gripped my shirt."

Alan stared at him, trying to speak, but the words tripped on his tongue. Ruben moved closer still and Alan's whole body stirred. "I remember how you tasted and that little urgent sound you made just before you came."

Alan stepped back, shocked into moving by hearing it said so baldly. Even though Ruben had been responsible for the first incident, the second had been all Alan's doing. At least Ruben hadn't thrown that in his face. The memories flooded through him: the dizzying pleasure of having Ruben's cock in his hand, feeling him move as Alan stroked him, hearing him moan, and having the intense, forbidden pleasure of knowing he was making his best friend that crazy.

"I think you should go," Alan said and turned away from Ruben to let him through the door. He needed to think, and right now neither one of them was thinking very well.

"Yeah, I think you're right," Ruben said softly and pushed by him. Alan bit back the hot swell of disappointment and refrained from calling him back. They both needed to clear their heads before they did something they'd both regret. Again.

Alan sank down into the nearest chair and rested his elbows on his knees as he heard the sound of Ruben's car starting. His body still thrummed and his thoughts were full of the memory of Ruben's scent, the heat of his nearness. As the sharp edge of his desire faded and his emotions cooled, he realized that he never did get to talk to Ruben about what was bothering him.

"Dammit," Alan groaned and dropped his head in his hands.

Chapter 3

THE sun beat down on the diamond and the air had dust kicked up from dozens of cleats. Though it was warm, it wasn't as humid as it would be back in Florida. Most winters, Ruben couldn't figure out how he'd ended up in Vermont, of all places, but he loved the summers, even if they were too short. He loved the mist on the mountains on quiet mornings and the view from his house of the picturesque lake. Even more than that, he loved the community in this small town and their passion for the local Little League teams.

Ruben looked around at the ring of expectant young faces covered in sweat, all with streaks of dirt embedded into their uniforms. Was there any better sport than baseball? Despite everything that had been dragging him down and his argument with Alan, it hadn't been hard to throw himself into the scrimmage, not with all these boys looking to him and his assistant coach, Laurie, for direction.

"That was a great scrimmage, guys. You keep that heart when the games begin, and we'll take this the whole way."

"Coach Hartner has got real good hitters on his team," Sammy said as he looked back at Alan's team, huddled by the other dugout.

"And we have good hitters on ours too. Don't let him psych you out, now." Ruben tugged on the bill of Sammy's cap. "Besides, if you keep pitching the way you do, you'll leave them swinging at nothing but air."

"Hey, Coach, you gonna do the game ball this year?" Christian chimed in, setting his glove on his head like a makeshift baseball cap. Ruben refrained from shaking his head as he struck a pose. The kid was a good player when he focused on the game instead of midfield song and dance antics. His biggest hurdle was the need to be constantly doing something.

"Absolutely." Ruben retrieved one of the balls they'd used in practice, the pristine white of the leather all but gone behind ground-in dirt. He signed it and tossed the ball to Laurie to sign as well. He gave one ball away at the end of every scrimmage and game, and made sure all the kids got one over the course of the season. "Okay, this ball goes to Parker. You've showed the most improvement since we started practice and you kept your head in the game today."

"Wicked!" Parker's face lit up as he caught the ball, and his teammates congratulated him before racing off to raid the cooler for their drinks and snacks. For a few minutes there was nothing but chaos as parents packed up their folding chairs and tried to get their kids' equipment sorted out. Ruben glanced across at the other dugout and picked out Alan's familiar figure as he shoved spare bats into the duffel bag.

Ruben pressed his lips together. He really owed Alan an apology. It seemed like every time he turned around he was fucking up another relationship. He needed to accept the fact that even if he could get Alan to respond to him—and damn he wasn't blind, he'd seen the heat in Alan's eyes last night—it didn't matter.

He had expected Alan's rejection, but even knowing it was coming, even knowing why, didn't stop the sting. He'd set himself up for more heartache last night. How long could he be in love with Alan before he realized his friend was never going to return the same feelings? Alan did not want that kind of relationship from him. He needed Ruben to be his friend, not his lover.

Over the past few weeks, he'd felt out of control, pitching wildly in the hope of getting some kind of a reaction out of Alan. If he kept it up, the only thing he'd accomplish would be to make Alan move right on out of his life. He had to get a handle on his life again, one way or another. He had to move on.

"Hey, Coach!"

Both Ruben and Alan turned, and for a moment their eyes met as Ruben's heart did its funny little dance. Ruben turned toward Sammy, who was running up to him, waving Ruben's phone. "You got a call."

Ruben's heart leaped and he grinned as he heard the familiar tone he'd set for FaceTime with his kids. "Thanks." He tapped the screen and his daughter's face appeared, her brown hair caught up in a messy ponytail. "Hey, Pumpkin."

"Hey, Dad." Jessica beamed, showing the flash of dimples that she hated. "I'm not bothering you, am I? Do you have a game?"

"This is a perfect time. We just finished a scrimmage against Uncle Alan's team."

"Did you win?"

"You know it, though he gave us a good fight." Ruben walked toward the dugout so he could see her face better without the glare of the sun. "I missed you last night. Were you having fun?" He kept his tone light. He didn't want to lay any guilt or pressure on her for the missed time.

"Yeah, Jonah spent the night at his dork friend's house, so Mom took me and the girls out to a movie. It was kinda boring, though. It was so girlie."

Ruben couldn't stop the grin. Despite Karen's best efforts, Jessica was still Jessica, and she was a tomboy down to her toes. He was sure that would change in a few years when she discovered dating, especially with the influence of two older stepsisters she adored, but for now he was glad she was still as rough and tumble as always.

A shadow fell across the doorway, and Ruben glanced up to see Alan's silhouette blocking the sun. He leaned against the rough wall of the dugout, arms crossed over his chest, and Ruben sensed his gaze on him. He really needed to apologize for how he'd behaved last night.

"Sometimes a little girlishness isn't a bad thing," Ruben said, turning his attention back to Jessica. "It's good for you and your mom to have a little time with your new sisters. So, are you all ready for your trip to London?"

Emotions flickered across Jessica's face, excitement and guilt, making Ruben want to ease the conflict in her eyes. "Yeah, mostly. I want to go, but I want to see you too. Maybe you could meet us there," she suggested with a hopeful note in her voice.

"You know I can't." Ruben's heart ached more as Jessica's face fell. "You're going to be staying with your aunt. Besides, I wouldn't have time to get a new coach for the team. Another time we can plan an overseas adventure of our own."

"I know." Jessica sighed and flopped back on the bed. "Am I going to get to see you at all this summer?"

"Of course you will. As soon as you land you'll be heading my way for the rest of the summer. And I'm going to talk to your mom about sneaking a week off in October to go to Disney to make up some of the time. I'll call her later on today. But if we do that, you'll have to keep your grades up."

Ruben was hoping the suggestion wouldn't lead to an argument with Karen. They both had worked hard to get through their resentments and hurt to present a united front for their kids. And in the past two years he thought they'd managed to become friends again. Still, she wouldn't like the thought of them taking off school, and he had to get over the thought that he was being taken advantage of before he called her or it could get messy.

They had joint custody, and ever since his surgery it seemed like his time was getting shaved off in little ways. First there was the wedding at the end of last summer that cut the visit short. Then there had been the few days taken off over winter break, so they could get used to the holidays as a blended family. Now they were going to be in London for three weeks of his summer. Ruben got it; sometimes life happened. Still, he wasn't going to let his time with his kids be whittled away until they became strangers. Sometimes he considered moving back to Tampa.

Alan and the boys flashed in his mind. Damned if he wouldn't miss them just as much. Maybe a move would be a good idea, though. He would be able to truly share custody. Now that he and Karen got along better, perhaps they could live in the same state without recriminations. And it would be easier to let Alan go.

"I can keep my grades up, and Jonah's such a nerd you know he'll be good."

"Stop calling your brother a nerd and a dork all the time," Ruben said, and Jessica wrinkled her nose. "Don't forget, we're visiting your *abuela* in August. You'll be quite a world traveler this year."

"That's true." Jessica's face lightened from its preteen moodiness. "I gotta go. I have a softball game with my friends, but I'll call tonight. Tell Uncle Alan and his monster squad I said hi."

"He's right here." Ruben turned the phone around so she could see Alan, and he waved.

"Hey there, Pumpkinhead."

Ruben looked back at the screen and blew Jessica a kiss. "Have fun at the game, and I'll talk to you and Jonah tonight." When the screen went black, the icy bleakness settled over Ruben again. He wasn't going to have his kids with him for another month.

"What's this about London?" Alan asked, coming to sit beside him on the bench. "Jonah and Jessica aren't coming next week?"

Ruben shook his head, turning the phone over and over in his hand. "Karen's sister is in London for a year, and she invited them to come and spend part of the summer with her. It's a pretty big deal. Jonah's going to love all the museums and history, and Jessica is dying to go to a real tea and to see a rugby match."

As many times as Ruben pointed out all the positive aspects of the trip, his heart just wasn't buying it. He wanted his time with his kids.

"I'm sorry, Ruben, that blows. I know how much you miss them."

Ruben's chest ached at the empathy in Alan's voice. He always understood when Ruben needed him the most. Ruben should've confided in him sooner about the change of plans. It didn't only affect Ruben—Brett would miss out, too, since he and Jonah were the same age and they usually had a blast together. But talking about it would've made the situation undeniably real.

"I feel like a selfish bastard, because I really wanted to say no," Ruben admitted.

"Understandable, but you didn't, because you love them and you want them to be happy." Alan laid his hand over Ruben's. "I know it's not the same, but you're always welcome at our house."

"Even when I act like a jackass, like I did last night?" Ruben had come on too strong, said too much, and pushed every single one of Alan's boundaries. He wasn't sure if it was because he'd gone over there already moody or if Alan's obvious shame over their past had pushed him to that point. In the light of the morning, he had to remind himself that Alan was a good man. One of those men who took his commitments seriously, and to break that commitment to Cassandra over some hard kisses and heated groping would have been a big deal. It wasn't that it meant nothing. It just meant couldn't happen again, in Alan's mindset.

"You weren't the only one who acted like a jackass. I shouldn't have jumped down your throat like that. I was there, I heard them ask you, and you were honest with my kids." Alan squeezed his hand and then let go, leaving Ruben to miss the warmth of his grip. "It was a knee-jerk reaction on my part."

Ruben waited to see if he would add anything else, if Alan would discuss what led to that knee-jerk reaction, but his friend remained silent. That made him ache too. "I've said it before, but I'll say it again: I'm sorry I screwed things up for you when I kissed you. I shouldn't have done it."

Alan shot him a strange look and then a smile quirked the corner of his lip. "You know, you have said that, but you haven't actually ever apologized for kissing me."

Ruben spread his hands and shrugged. "That would've been a lie. I might have run away to give us both some space, but I won't lie to you. I'm not sorry I kissed you. It was an amazing kiss. But if I had been thinking, I wouldn't have done it."

Alan frowned and stared at his hands. "Ever?"

"No, not that. But I would've waited until we were single. I know you're not like me, but I still wanted to know if maybe there could've been something."

Alan's frown deepened, and Ruben waited for him to change the subject. This was the most they'd ever talked about it other than saying it shouldn't have happened. He rested his elbows on his knees and looked out at the now quiet baseball diamond. It seemed fitting that the conversation should be happening here, in a place that connected their old life with their new one. In the distance he could hear the sound of kids playing on another field. The dust had settled and the air was heavy with the scent of dry grass.

"Did you know then that you were gay?" Alan finally asked, glancing at him sideways.

"I…. I'd known for a while. Knowing it and facing it are two different things." Ruben took a sip of water from his bottle and grimaced. It had gotten very warm. He hesitated, wondering how much he should share with Alan. He knew his friend hated that he kept things back, but he wasn't sure how much Alan really wanted to know, despite what he'd said.

"Did you have thoughts about other guys when you were younger?" Alan asked.

"Yeah, but I convinced myself it was a phase and wrong. And I convinced myself that if I ignored them, those thoughts and feelings would go away. For a while, it almost seemed to work."

Alan's expression was faraway, and Ruben wondered if he was imagining what it had been like for him then, the fear and shame of being different.

"Realizing how my feelings for you were changing helped me to face who I was," Ruben admitted. When Alan still didn't say anything, he continued. "I wanted people to know me, the real me, then if they liked or hated me, at least they liked or hated me for real reasons and not because of some mask I was wearing."

"I think to those who knew you the best, the change wasn't all that profound," Alan said, looking at him, his blue eyes solemn. "You were the same Ruben that threw a scary fastball and an evil knuckleball. You were the same Ruben that enjoys all the old black-and-white movies that you shanghaied me into watching on the road; the same Ruben who loves his kids passionately, who can hold on to a grudge for way too long. And you are the only man I know who can pull off wearing white slacks in the summer without looking like an ex-porn star. Who you were attracted to didn't change you, even if it changed some people's perception of you, and it definitely didn't make you any less my friend."

Ruben nodded, and though he was grateful for Alan's support, he was left feeling a bit frustrated, as if Alan wasn't hearing what he was trying to say.

"I'm sorry if I made you feel like you couldn't talk to me or that you had to go to another team after that kiss," Alan continued. "I didn't want you to go."

"You didn't make me feel like you didn't want me around, or that I blew our friendship." Ruben leaned down to zip up the bag at his feet and then looked to see if anything else had been left behind in the dugout. The next team would be coming soon. "I knew that we couldn't be anything more than friends, and I needed time and space to deal with that. Stupid, I know, but there it is."

"It's not stupid, Ruben."

Alan searched Ruben's face as silence fell between them, and then he smiled. "I'd always wanted to know what was happening with you when you left for Tampa, what you were thinking about me, how you felt. But I admit, at the time I was a little afraid of the answers. I guess the curiosity has gotten to me lately and I have been pushing you."

A cautious hope welled up inside of Ruben. He had waited so long to have these conversations with Alan, but every time he'd tried, he'd been blocked. He'd waited for Alan to see him as something more than a friend with whom he'd had the occasional indiscretion.

"You know, I admire you for coming out," Alan said. "I know it wasn't an easy decision, and I'm not sure if I could've made the same decision if I were in your situation."

"It was something I needed to do. Living a lie was turning me into somebody I hated." Ruben glanced at Alan and let his gaze linger on Alan's face. "Personally, I think you could do anything you set out to do. Look at everything you've accomplished in the past two years, what you've taken on without whining."

"I haven't had time for pity parties." Alan's expression became serious. "The only reason I kept it all together is because of you. It can be overwhelming, and when it is, you're there, calm and collected. It keeps me going."

"I love you."

The words slipped out of Ruben without thought and hung in the air like droplets of sun streaming through the shadows of the dugout. Alan grinned and clapped him on the back. "I love you too, man. You know that."

Once again the moment fell away, as Alan hadn't heard him. Of course they loved each other, as friends, as brothers; only Ruben meant he was so damn in love with Alan he couldn't see the end of it. He'd been in love with him for years and nothing had changed it, not leaving or coming back.

Ruben heard cars pulling up and doors slamming as kids tumbled out for the next scrimmage. He got up and slung the equipment bag over his shoulder before grabbing the cooler. "I'm going to the cage for a bit. I can drop off the bat bag for you."

"I'm grabbing the boys from Miss Sarah's and then I'm coming by for a few hours since we have that birthday party tomorrow." Alan grabbed the equipment he'd left outside the dugout. "I'll set up Matt's playpen in the office so he can have his nap, if you don't mind the hooligans being there."

"You know I don't." Ruben started to trudge out of the dugout, and Alan caught his arm.

"Hey, why don't you come by for dinner again?"

As tempting as the thought was, Ruben knew it would be a bad idea. With the mood he was in, he just might start something with Alan—either another argument or what Alan referred to as "the incidents." The reckless, on-edge feeling from the night before still had ahold of him. "Not tonight. I need to call Karen and work out a plan for the rest of the summer. See if I can talk her into a mini vacation later on this year."

"I don't like the thought of you being there alone." Alan frowned, his blue eyes darkening. "Not when I know you're still upset."

Ruben looked down at Alan's hand on his arm. It still amazed him how often Alan initiated small touches like this, while seeming to be oblivious to everything else. He couldn't seem to stop himself from reading too much into things. "It is what it is, Alan. I lived a lie and I hurt Karen, hurt myself. But we did get Jessica and Jonah out of it, and neither of us regret that. Don't worry about me. I don't plan on being alone for the rest of my life."

Chapter 4

BRETT helped Seth from his booster seat as Alan eased a sleeping Matt out of his car seat. His youngest slumped against Alan, a dead-to-the-world, sweaty weight and he didn't stir as Alan nudged the door shut. The kid could sleep through anything. He played hard and slept equally hard.

The cooler air in the batting cage was a welcome relief after being in the sun most of the day. Ruben was on the phone. He waved to him from the office and pointed at the playpen he'd already set up in the cramped confines.

"Thank you," Alan mouthed as he eased Matt down and covered him with a light blanket.

Ruben gave him a distracted smile and continued talking in rapid Spanish. Alan heard Jessica's and Jonah's name, but for all the smattering he'd picked up of the language from hanging out with Ruben all these years, he never could understand him when he was talking to his mother.

Alan paused at the door and looked back at Ruben. He'd taken the time to shower and change, though he still had faint stubble on his cheeks. His black curls gleamed, threaded with the occasional silver that thickened a bit at the temples. The summer sun had only deepened the golden-brown of his skin. He looked… sexy. Well, except for the furrow on his brow and the downward turn of his mouth. Alan couldn't figure out why he was still single. Alan had been too busy taking care of the boys to date, but Ruben didn't have that excuse. Though based on his comment earlier, he was probably looking, and that left Alan with an unsettled feeling.

Ruben glanced up, caught his gaze, and raised one heavy, dark brow in a silent question. Alan shook his head and left. He checked on Michelle, who was running the front desk, and took a quick scan of the main room to make sure all of his sons were accounted for and not into any trouble before starting to put away the equipment they'd used for the scrimmage.

As he cleaned off the catcher's gear, his thoughts kept returning to last night. He had been so certain Ruben was going to kiss him again. He'd lain awake for hours thinking about it afterward, trying to downplay the niggling disappointment. He was crazy to even consider the fantasy, but that hadn't stopped him from thinking about it or going over past memories in detail.

Ruben had a point: Why did it bother him so much to hear him mention Cassandra? It wasn't because of the kiss or the heated exploration that Alan had initiated another time, though they definitely played a part. If it had been just about the physical aspect, Alan thought he might've been able to put the incidents behind him. If it had been just the physical, it never would've gone beyond that first kiss.

Alan had missed Ruben when he left. Missed him like something vital had been cut out of his life. He'd been pissed and hurt in a way he knew was more than missing a friend. He and Ruben had a connection that went beyond friendship, an emotional intimacy that didn't belong when they were both married to other people.

That was why he felt so guilty, because he'd allowed it to continue, and that was more dangerous than the stolen kisses.

Alan sighed, rolled up the canvas bag they used to carry the equipment in, and stored it away in the locker. He wanted to talk to Ruben about it, but he wasn't sure what it meant and he didn't want to stir things up that might be better off left alone. They had a good thing going with the business, their friendship. The only thing that would make it perfect was if Jessica and Jonah could be here for the summer.

"Dad, can I use a cage?" Mikey called over the din of the other kids.

Alan crooked a finger at him. Mikey came over, his face twisted in a grimace because he already knew the answer. "What do you think?"

"I've gotta wait my turn. But, Dad—"

Alan cut him off with a shake of his head. "Whining isn't going to work, buddy. These kids paid to be here, and their parents are coming to pick them up at a specific time. It wouldn't be fair to take that away. You'll get your chance. You just have to be patient."

Mikey nodded with a huge sigh. "Yes, sir."

"You don't have to sound so resigned over it," Alan said with a chuckle. He pulled Mikey close with an arm around the back of his neck and gave him a gentle noogie.

“What’s that mean?” Mikey squirmed away. “Resigned?”

“Oh-my-God-my-life-is-so-bad.” Alan made a shooing motion. “Now go, hit up the arcade for a bit. Hey, and go tell your uncle you want him to come over for dinner.”

“Okay.” Mikey changed directions and headed toward the office. Maybe it was wrong of him to use his kids to strong-arm Ruben, but Alan didn’t feel bad about it at all. He recognized the signs of a major brood coming on. And when Ruben brooded, he often made life-changing decisions without talking to anyone first. Like signing with Tampa. Or when he asked Karen for a divorce. Or even when he returned to Boston. It wasn’t that they were necessarily bad decisions, Alan just wanted to be braced for whatever was going on in that man’s head.

Given the situation, Alan wouldn’t be all that surprised to find out Ruben had decided to move back to Tampa to be close to his kids, or maybe even go to his family in San Juan. That would still be closer to Jessica and Jonah than Vermont.

Alan frowned and stared at the office door. Ruben wouldn’t make a decision like that again without talking to him first, not now. They were business partners. That involved all kinds of logistics. Though if Alan had to choose between being closer to his kids and the batting cage, there would be no argument. His frown deepened as the worry grabbed hold of him. His boys would be devastated if Ruben moved to Florida, especially Matt. They all looked at him as if he were another member of the family.

“Dad, are you mad?” Mikey asked as he came out of the office. He stopped when he saw Alan’s face.

“No, why?” Alan asked, pulled out of his spiraling thoughts.

“You’re making a scowly face at the door.” Alan watched Mikey’s expression change, as if he was making a catalogue of recent transgressions in his mind. “I didn’t do anything.”

“Uh-huh.” Alan couldn’t help teasing him and grinned when Mikey’s eyes went all wide and innocent. “Spare me the excuses, buddy. I’m just messing with you. Cage Three has opened up. You can go hit for a while if you want.”

“Wicked.” Mikey started to race off and then dropped to a fast walk when he realized Alan was still watching him.

“Hey, Mikey. What did your uncle say about dinner?”

Mikey jammed a batting helmet on his head. "He said to tell you, 'You win.' Does that mean he's coming over?"

"Yep. Thanks, buddy."

Alan took one last glance at Ruben's door then went back to work. There was no sense angsting over a maybe. He'd talk with Ruben later. They'd had a good conversation earlier, just like the talks they used to have on a regular basis. Open and honest, not holding anything back, and Alan wanted to see them continue.

RUBEN shook his head as Mikey shut the office door. Alan was too used to getting his way. Ruben had a hard enough time saying no to him, but it was even harder with the boys, especially when it was such a little request. He knew Alan well enough to realize that if he sent one kid in, he'd send them all. So if Ruben wanted to talk to Karen, he'd better do it now instead of later. He glanced at Matt, who still slept in his playpen, his thumb planted in his mouth. Ruben got up and gently removed his thumb before returning to his desk to make the call.

"Disney, Ruben? Really?" Karen said when she answered and Ruben winced. He should've called before Jessica had a chance to tell her. "During the school year? Don't you think you should've talked to me first before you mentioned that to your daughter?"

Ruben tamped down his initial surge of irritation at her tone. She already sounded exasperated, and they fed into each other's moods too well.

"You're right. I should've. I was just throwing out possibilities," Ruben said, tapping a pen against the stack of invoices on his desk. "I also told her it would be based on how they were doing in school. They can't have missed days or dropping grades if they are going to take some time off. It was a 'we'll see' plan, not anything definite."

Ruben refrained from pointing out that Karen hadn't talked about London with him first, either. They'd both learned early on in their split that things went so much smoother when they didn't snipe at each other.

"I just want some more time with them this year," he continued. "I'm not blaming you for the craziness last year, but I'm really missing them. They're growing up so fast."

"I know, Ruben. I'm sorry," Karen said, her voice softening. "What if instead of missing school in October, they extend their winter break and stay in Vermont for some skiing after Christmas? They'll still miss a few days, but nothing gets accomplished at that time of the year anyway."

"That's the teacher in you talking." Ruben considered her suggestion. On the one hand, he'd have to wait a little longer to see them, but if they extended their holiday visit, then Alan and his boys could go skiing too. Jessica and Jonah would like that. "I think that's a good idea."

"That should make the kids happy. They've done Disney several times. It's not really a novelty anymore. They rarely get their winter sports and they complain about that."

"Are you all set for London?" Ruben tossed the pen in the cup holder and settled back in the chair. No matter what he did, he couldn't seem to calm the restlessness inside of him. He needed to do something, anything; this waiting was really getting to him.

"Yes, now that the passports have come in. I was beginning to worry. Thank you for not freaking out about this." Karen hesitated, apology tingeing her voice. "I jumped on the chance, and I know it really puts a damper on your summer."

"Like you said, it's a good opportunity for them. So I'm trying not to be a selfish bastard over it." The cramped office was crowded with pictures from their baseball days, many of just Alan and Ruben, but the desk was reserved for pictures of their kids. Ruben stared at one of all six of them, lined up like stairsteps, with Jonah and Brett looking like fraternal twins, one darker, one lighter.

"I was thinking… I know it's last minute, but why don't you come down for a few days before we go?" Karen suggested. "It'll give the kids a welcome surprise. They've been bummed too, despite their excitement for the trip."

Ruben pulled out his calendar as the idea grabbed ahold of him. "I think I could do that if we got Michelle to cover my time here at the cage. Laurie could easily handle the missed practices. But I'd have to be back in time to get ready for Opening Day. It's a big deal around here. Let me talk to Alan and see what he thinks."

Karen was silent a moment, and there was a strange hesitance and curiosity in her voice when she spoke again. "I don't know if you realize this, but you talk about him like he's your significant other."

Ruben thought about what he and Alan had built together, and how they interacted with Alan's kids and with Jonah and Jessica when they were visiting. "I suppose I do in some ways." Sometimes it seemed like in just about every way except one.

The phone went quiet again and Ruben braced himself for accusations that he had no defense for. "Was he the one you left me for?" She didn't sound upset, more reflective. Ruben supposed that the years since he dropped the bombshell and her happiness with her new marriage had mellowed her hurt.

"No. Not in the way you think. I was in love with him, still am, but we're not together. He's not interested in me like that, though there are times when he's given me hope. You'd probably get a kick out of watching me pine. I left because I was living a lie and you deserved somebody who could give you everything."

"Damn, Ruben, you still know just what to say, don't you?" Karen said with a light laugh.

"Not always." Ruben glanced at the playpen as Matt stirred. "I'll call you tomorrow about coming down after I talk to Alan tonight. What do you think about them staying later in August too? They can come back the week before school starts."

"A week? Back-to-school shopping is our big thing. We make a long weekend out of it."

"You mean you're not going to do a shopping extravaganza while you're in London?"

"Well…." Ruben heard the smile in her voice. "Maybe, but that's not going to get them set up for school. I suppose we can split the back-to-school shopping this year. How's that?"

"I think that works," Ruben said, tucking the phone under his ear as he got up. Matt yawned and rubbed his eyes. "Thank you for being so understanding." They both wanted what was best for Jessica and Jonah, and that was having both of them in their lives. He should've known she would work with him instead of letting his disappointment build up false anxieties in his head.

"We've both said and done things we regret. I know this last year has been crazy, but we both need to make some sacrifices, right?" Karen replied.

Matt pulled himself to his feet with a little whimper and silently held up his arms to be picked up. "Hey there, big guy," Ruben murmured and gathered him up, smiling as Matt burrowed into his arms. He was always a cuddle bug when he first woke up. "We do. Thanks again, Karen."

He hung up the phone, then kissed the top of Matt's tousled head. "I think we need to change your diaper and go find your dad."

Matt pulled his thumb out of his mouth and patted his damp little hand against Ruben's mouth. "No. Hush."

Ruben chuckled and shifted Matt in his arms. "What? I'm not allowed to talk to you, sleepyhead?"

"Talk bad. Bad. Bad, Unca." Matt blinked sleepy blue eyes up at him and continued to pat his mouth in an unmistakable gesture that Ruben should shut up and let him enjoy his drowsy state. Ruben considered tickling him and then decided against it as he sat back down behind the desk and pulled up the budget program. He knew very well that moments like this ended too fast as kids grew up.

Chapter 5

ALAN could not concentrate on the movie. The house was silent, the boys long since asleep. He was enjoying the intimacy of the quiet time with Ruben, both of them relaxed at the end of a long day, the comfortable familiarity of having Ruben near, that was all, nothing else.

To be honest, the only reason he was watching the movie at all was because it had been Ruben's turn to pick. If his friend could tolerate Alan's comedies, then he could return the favor, even if this was another Bogart film. Alan was beginning to suspect Ruben had an ongoing mental lovefest for the man. He crossed his arms as a little pang hit him. He didn't get what was so sexy about a man in black-and-white anyway.

It was a little harder to concentrate tonight, though. They were both stretched out on opposite ends of the wide couch, their legs tangled together, and Ruben kept rubbing his palm along Alan's shin. Every time he felt the hand move, Alan's thoughts scattered and his body stirred. Ruben seemed to be unaware not only of what he was doing, but the effect it was having on Alan as well. Instead, Ruben was watching the screen as if Bogart was a godsend.

It was irritating.

Alan nudged him in the side with his big toe. "What is the Maltese Falcon, anyway? This isn't going to be another one of your weird endings, is it?"

Ruben kept his eyes on the screen, but he quirked his lips in a smile of anticipation. "Just watch and see. You talk too much, Hartner." This time he moved both of his hands along Alan's foot, and Alan was hyperaware of every bit of skin those long fingers touched.

A few more minutes passed and Alan shifted, turning his body alongside Ruben and draping an arm over his legs. His thoughts drifted to the conversation they'd had after the scrimmage, more specifically to Ruben's last statement. He didn't plan on being alone… that could mean one to two things. Either he was interested in someone or he was considering moving away.

Alan wanted to ask if Tampa was on his mind, but was afraid of the answer. He couldn't fathom what kept Ruben in Vermont. He caught a lot of flak from fans in the area who had long memories of his defection. Friendship was one thing, being uncle to Alan's kids was another, and the business… but none of those were really reasons to stay.

Alan shifted through possibilities until his mind settled on one that irritated him even more than Bogart did: Stuart, with his super cool trendy looks, metrosexual suaveness, and the hot eyes he gave Ruben whenever he came to the batting cage on some excuse or another. There was no reason for him to lurk other than he was trying to hook up with Ruben. Now that he thought about it, the two of them had been hanging out more often.

"That guy came around when you were holed up in the office on the phone today," Alan said.

Ruben stole a quick glance at him and then went back to the movie. "That guy? I need a little more to go on."

"You know, Mr. Cool, your new buddy." Alan reached for his beer bottle and drained the last of the contents. He considered getting up to retrieve another round, then decided against it. He was too comfortable sprawled out with Ruben.

"You mean Stuart?"

"Yeah, he mentioned something about heading to Burlington to see some new indie film." Alan hadn't heard of it, though he was sure it was something Ruben would probably enjoy. He didn't see what Ruben got out of the friendship; the other man didn't even like baseball. There had to be something seriously wrong with him. "I told him you had plans for tonight. I meant to pass along the message but I forgot."

Ruben looked at him with what looked like a laugh playing about his lips and raised his eyebrow. "Was this before or after you sicced your kids on me?"

"After, thank you very much. Besides, you had plans even before I sent in Mikey." Alan poked Ruben with his toe between his ribs, where he had that one ticklish spot. Ruben grabbed his foot and moved it onto his lap.

As Ruben turned his attention back to the movie, the need to know if Stuart and Ruben were heading toward domestic bliss clawed at Alan until he couldn't remain silent any longer. "So are you two seeing each other?"

Ruben hit pause on the remote and swung his head around, his eyes wide. "No, just friends. It's nice to talk to someone else who's also gay." Ruben's gaze lingered on Alan's face. "He's way too young. I'm not looking for that."

There had to have been some lovers over the years since Ruben and Karen split. Sometimes Alan wished he could tell his brain to shut up and stop wondering. So what if Ruben had had some hot flings. He was entitled. He wasn't a monk, for God's sake.

There had been rumors since Ruben came out, occasionally with his name linked to one man or another. Most often, though, the rumors centered around Alan and him. Alan had shrugged off the gossip and focused on his sons instead. Hell, the rumors had been flying even before Ruben came out. If there was one thing Alan had learned while in the majors, it was not to let the media eat him up. It could be an out-of-control machine, and addressing it often only fueled the issue.

Now that he thought about it, Alan hadn't heard of Ruben dating in the past couple of years. He'd never heard Ruben's name connected with another man's other than his own. And in a town like this, where he was a minor celebrity, that was no small feat. But there had to have been others.

The thought brought with it a surge of irrational jealousy that Alan had never experienced in all the years when they'd both been married and struggling with the emotions raging between them. Odd, now things had quieted, that it should bother him so.

"I'll call Stuart when I get back into town," Ruben said and unpaused the movie.

Alan frowned, took the remote, and stopped it again. "What do you mean when you get back?"

"I'm taking a few days off to see Jessica and Jonah before they head to London." Ruben furrowed his brow and stroked Alan's skin with his fingertips. "I was going to see if you'd take me to the airport. It shouldn't be a problem, should it? I didn't see any other events planned at the batting cage."

"When?" Alan asked, left with the stunned, unsettling feeling that he'd been hit by a fastball. It was just a visit, and not the first time Ruben had visited Tampa, but Alan was certain there was more to it than that. Ruben had been so down lately, like he was only going through the day-to-day motions. He only seemed to liven up when he was coaching or to relax on nights like this, when it was late and they were both feeling mellow.

"At the beginning of the week. I want to give Laurie a chance to take the lead the next practice so I'm not leaving her feeling like I dropped the ball." Ruben searched Alan's face and cocked his head. "Don't worry, I'll be back to helping you rein in rug rats soon."

Alan's frown deepened as that touched on one of his uncertainties. "I know I lean on you all the time with the boys. I don't want you to feel obligated to—"

"Hey, no, don't be an idiot," Ruben cut in and reached down to touch Alan's hand. "I was talking about work, not about the boys. I love them. They're not an obligation in any way. I like helping out with them, even when they make me miss my own troublemakers."

"Okay." Alan reached for the remote again. "I just worry sometimes."

"Don't." The movie flicked back to life, but Ruben's attention remained on him. "How about you? It's been a couple years now… have you thought about dating?" Ruben asked, looking back at the TV, though Alan got the sense he wasn't really paying attention, it just gave him something to watch other than Alan.

The question caught Alan by surprise. So much had been going on, he hadn't really considered dating. He'd been wrapped up in making sure the boys felt centered and secure, getting the batting cage off to a strong start, and reconnecting with Ruben. The time had kind of flown by.

"I… no, not really." Brett's teacher from last year was hot and single. She had hit on him a couple of times, and they'd almost hooked up one night, but Alan hadn't really been into it. "I don't know, it would have to be someone pretty special. It's not just me anymore, it's my boys too. I'm not looking to bring a bunch of women in and out of their lives. Maybe if I find the right person, but I'm in no rush."

"I'm in no rush either. I know what I want and I'm really not interested in chasing after anything else." Ruben squeezed his foot and turned his attention back to the movie, leaving Alan to ponder his words and the disappointment he thought he'd seen in Ruben's expression.

Alan knew what he wanted too. He wanted a partnership, a friendship, not just somebody to lie next to. He wanted somebody his kids could love too, someone they trusted. Somebody who gave them the attention, and sometimes discipline, they needed, the way Ruben did. It also left Alan wondering about what Ruben did want, if there was a certain kind of guy who pushed his buttons.

The movie continued, but Alan had completely lost track of what was going on. His brain wouldn't let him relax, which was probably a good thing. He could almost fall asleep right here on the couch, curled up next to Ruben. That had happened a few times over the past several months, and he really needed to put a stop to it before the boys got confused or came to expect Uncle Ruben at the breakfast table.

"So I was thinking about what you said, about why I got so bent out of shape the other night," Alan said, giving Ruben another poke. This time Ruben stopped the movie altogether. Alan's heart jumped when he looked at him with those oh so serious dark eyes. Sometimes it was very hard to concentrate when Ruben looked at him like that, like all of his attention was focused on him.

Ruben cocked his head and stilled his hands. "You mean about Cassandra?" he asked, his voice cautious.

"Yeah." Alan fiddled with the drawstrings of the thin cotton pants he'd put on before they started their movie. "What you said made me think about why it bothered me so much."

"And?" Once again Ruben stroked Alan's ankle in a light caress that made him feel all wobbly inside.

"It bothers me because it meant more than it should've. I mean, it was just a kiss and a little fooling around. Stupid guy stuff when your adrenaline's up and you've had a few too many beers, right?" Ruben's gaze became shuttered and Alan felt a little panging ache in return. He sat up straighter and leaned toward Ruben. "So if it was just that, I should've been able to let it go and move on, but I couldn't. I felt like I was continuing to betray her long after we fooled around, because I had a hard time not thinking about it."

Ruben sat up too, untangling his legs. Alan still couldn't read his expression, and he was afraid Ruben was about to leave without a word. He should've kept his fat mouth shut instead of stirring the pot. There was a reason they hadn't talked about this. "Wait. Don't go."

"I'm not." Ruben turned to face him and something in his gaze made Alan's pulse skip a couple beats. "I think a part of the problem is that when I kissed you it was so sudden, there was no warning, it came and went like lightning and you were able to dismiss it."

He leaned forward, placing his hands on either side of Alan's hips as he moved into his space. Alan's breath came a little faster as he sank back against the cushions, feeling a little light-headed. "And the second time?" Alan asked.

Ruben curved his lips in a secret smile as he hovered over Alan. "If I recall, the second time, both of us were too pissed at each other to think straight. I was actually expecting you to punch me when you showed up at my hotel room, not kiss me."

"Well, that had been the plan." Only Ruben had opened the door only in his boxers, with a defensive look in his eyes Alan had never seen directed toward him before, and all of his intentions, his plan to demand answers, had crashed to the floor as they'd reached for each other with bruising hands and lips.

"Instead you kissed me," Ruben said. "Both those times we'd buried it, we'd rationalized it away and we'd focused on our commitments. This time it's going to be different."

Alan kept flitting his gaze to Ruben's lips, the sexy way his mouth formed words. His heart was doing a running-man dance in his chest, complete with crazy flips. "Because neither of us is involved?" Alan managed to say as Ruben closed the distance between them too slowly.

"Yeah, that, and because this time you know I'm going to kiss you." Ruben smiled in a way that made it hard to think. "So if you don't want it, you'd better tell me now."

Alan slid his hands up Ruben's arms and felt the strength in his biceps, the heat of his body. This was a mistake. This would open up closed doors and bring in a whole other dimension to their relationship that Alan wasn't sure he was ready for. Yet he couldn't voice any of those excuses. "What are you waiting for? Kiss me, already."

Alan lifted his head as Ruben came down, and they met in the middle. At first it was just a brush of lips that made him tingle and seek more. He pressed his lips to Ruben's, and they moved, nibbling, exploring without the devouring insanity that had poured through them both before.

Ruben cradled the back of Alan's head in his hand as he slanted his mouth and parted his lips in a silent invitation that left Alan dizzy. Alan curled his fingers into Ruben's arms as he accepted without hesitation and deepened the kiss, aching to taste him again. This tender exploration was so different from last time, and still so damned good.

Alan breathed him in as Ruben's hard weight settled over him. He stilled his tongue and wrapped his arms around Ruben, memorizing the incredible sensation of feeling muscle against muscle. He had not fully appreciated the difference last time; he'd been in too much of a frenzy of frustration and need.

Ruben skimmed Alan's side with his fingers, where he had gone a little soft over the past two years. Before Alan could start to feel a little self-conscious about that, Ruben stroked his tongue over Alan's and all he wanted was a little more of everything.

He tightened his arms around Ruben and turned them both so they were side by side and Ruben was trapped between the back of the couch and Alan's body. He made a sexy sound, like his breath was caught in his throat on a groan. He made Alan crazy, set him on fire inside and out. He drove his tongue into Ruben's mouth as he pushed his knee between Ruben's legs and slid it up until it rested between his thighs.

Ruben broke away and groaned, "Damn, Alan. You can kiss me like that anytime you want."

Alan closed his eyes, touched his forehead to Ruben's, and slid his hand along Ruben's leg, hiking it higher over his hip. His hands would've been trembling if he wasn't touching Ruben. He'd never felt this shaky before and it didn't help his state of mind to feel Ruben's slight trembling in return. He breathed in Ruben's scent as he pressed closer, fitting against his friend like he belonged there. His groin ached and Ruben's own arousal was unmistakable as he circled his hips and ground them against Alan's.

They were both panting as if they were in the middle of a race. Alan slid his hand under Ruben's T-shirt, running his fingers over smooth, lean muscle. Ruben turned his head, and the scrape of his stubbled cheek on Alan's skin made him shiver with excitement and the ache for more ramped up. He tugged Ruben's shirt off and then shifted so Ruben could do the same to him.

They should stop or take this elsewhere; one of the boys could wake up and come searching for him. "Ruben," Alan said in a low voice, pulling back slightly.

"No, not yet." Ruben kissed him again, his lips hot and urgent, and Alan fell into it. A little longer wouldn't hurt. He'd be able to hear them if they woke up. They never did anything quietly.

Ruben scratched through the hair on Alan's chest and then found his nipple. Alan shivered with a groan against Ruben's mouth. His friend paused and then circled his fingers before rolling the hard nub between his thumb and forefinger. A shot of electricity went straight to Alan's cock at the rougher play. He liked the harder hands, the muscles instead of curves, the masculine scent of him.

Alan broke the kiss and dragged his tongue down Ruben's throat, feeling the tingle from the rasp of his stubble. He lowered his head, searching until he found Ruben's own peaked nipple. He pulled and sucked, then rubbed with his tongue, and Ruben let out a strangled groan, rocking his hips. "You have a wicked mouth."

Alan wondered what it would be like if he did this elsewhere. The thought of his mouth on Ruben's cock filled him with a strange mix of confusion and desire. He wasn't sure if he'd like it, but he'd definitely like hearing Ruben moan some more, and the thought of Ruben's mouth on him made Alan's mouth go dry with want. The fantasy seared into his brain as his cock throbbed as if to say "yes, please."

Ruben was so fucking sexy. They shouldn't be doing this. Instead of stopping him, the conflicting thoughts only seemed to spur him on more.

Ruben shifted, pushing Alan back a bit and moving under him. Alan's heart jumped as he settled between Ruben's thighs and pressed his cock right against Ruben's hard bulge. "Oh fuck yeah," he panted, rocking his hips, pushing harder against him and rubbing their cocks together. The thin pants he wore didn't provide much of a barrier, and Alan could feel the heat coming off of him, noticed every throb of Ruben's cock.

Ruben's head fell back against the cushion with a soft moan, his lips slack with desire, his gaze burning as he stared up at Alan as if he was trying to commit every detail to memory. Alan knew he'd never be able to forget this any more than he'd been able to forget the first two times they'd screwed around. "Again," Ruben gasped, fumbling with the drawstring to Alan's pants.

Alan obeyed, thrusting and grinding against him. Oh fuck, that was good. He felt like he had years of pent-up sexual tension running through him in a fever. Ruben arched up against him and then slid his hands down the back of Alan's boxers. He dug his fingers into Alan's ass, guiding him to move with quick, hard rocks against him.

"Yeah, just like that. Just like that, Alan."

They stared at each other as their bodies moved together, and it just felt so damn right, so much better without the guilt and shame. Alan wasn't sure if they were making a huge mistake or not, but right now neither his heart nor his body cared. He dipped his head down and kissed Ruben tenderly, thoroughly, and it filled him with an aching sweetness.

Ruben's pants changed to deep moans broken off in the back of his throat and he tensed. Alan felt like his entire body was oversensitized and on edge as his balls tightened and his cock tingled. Then the tension shattered and they ground against each other, riding out the quick, hard waves of their orgasm, and a strangled whimpering groan fell past his lips.

"Remembering how you make that sound has haunted me for the past three years," Ruben said under his breath.

Alan chuckled and rubbed his cheek against Ruben's. He remained on top of Ruben, his eyes closed, feeling sweaty and sticky and fucking amazing. Ruben stroked the back of his neck, sending an aftershock up and down his spine.

"I…." Ruben stopped himself, and Alan wondered if he was going to say he loved him. They'd been saying it for years, but sometimes Alan wondered what Ruben actually meant by those words. And as soon as he started to question, it always caused a little surge of panic. Ruben couldn't possibly mean them the way Alan thought he sometimes wanted to hear them.

He did love Ruben, no doubt about that. Ruben was truly his best friend, the kind of friendship he'd wished he'd had with his wife, but it had never quite gone to that level. There had always been something missing. Now that he had Ruben back in his life, Alan didn't want anything to come between that friendship. Fooling around with Ruben the way they had just done could really fuck that up.

Alan opened his eyes to find Ruben staring at him, and once again those dark eyes were unreadable. "I suppose I should go," Ruben said, shifting and gently pushing Alan off him.

Letting Ruben leave would definitely be a mistake. That was how it had ended the last two times they'd indulged in a heated moment, with one of them leaving and then both of them overthinking.

Maybe Alan wasn't sure how to quite process the fact that they'd gotten down and dirty on his couch. It had been scorching hot, and parts of him would like to repeat the experience, often. But he did know that he wanted to remain close to Ruben for a bit before he went home, instead of shoving Ruben out the door or letting him run. He didn't know what would happen after this, but he wanted to figure it out with Ruben and not apart from him.

"Don't." Alan grabbed Ruben's hand and gestured toward the silent, dark TV. "I still don't know what's going to happen with the falcon thing. And you love this movie."

Ruben sighed and rubbed a hand over his hair. "Nothing is going to happen, Alan. It's a MacGuffin."

"It's a what?"

"It's something that doesn't exist. Everybody's chasing it, but nobody's going to get it." Ruben gave him a sad smile, stood up, and turned away.

"How come I get the feeling you're not talking about the movie?"

"It's nothing. Sorry." Ruben waved his hand at the TV. "I know I've been moody lately, acting like I'm in the throes of a midlife crisis. Sometimes I feel like there have been too many changes in the past few years, other times like there haven't been enough."

Alan could relate to that. Maybe in the morning he'd have a minor freak-out over what had happened between them, but even if he did, he refused to let it affect their relationship. This time was going to be different. They'd find a way to figure it out.

"Come on, we'll get cleaned up. I've got something you can borrow, and we can restart the movie." Alan caught Ruben's hand, and this time Ruben looked at him. Alan squeezed his hand. "I want you to stay."

"Okay," Ruben replied, a ghost of a smile flicking across his lips. "If you really want me to stay, I swear I won't disappear on you."

Chapter 6

THE pounding of multiple feet roused Ruben out of a sound sleep. He was lying back against Alan on the couch, his hand over Alan's arm, which was curled around Ruben's waist. Alan's cheek was pressed against the back of Ruben's shoulder as they spooned. Sleepy instinct had him rubbing back against Alan's groin, and his friend's morning wood perked up even more, sending a jolt of pure electricity through Ruben.

Another rush of feet thundered overhead, waking him up fully, and Ruben smiled. He hadn't been awoken by that kind of a commotion since the last time Jonah and Jessica stayed with him. As details of the night before came filtering through his consciousness, the noise of feet came racing down the stairs.

"*Dad*?"

Ruben sat up at the sound of Brett's terrified voice, and behind him Alan stirred. Upstairs, Matt began to wail.

"I'm in the living room, chill out," Alan called back, his voice husky. "What's wrong?"

Brett came barreling into the room, followed by Mikey. The panicked confusion on Brett's face turned to relief when he saw Alan and Ruben on the couch. "I thought you left!"

"Brett, have I ever disappeared on you?" Alan held out his arms, and Brett burrowed into them, for the moment his big-brother cool-guy façade gone under the fears of a little boy who'd already lost one parent. Ruben knew Alan would pay anything to help Brett get over his lingering anxieties.

"No, but I couldn't find you," Brett said, his voice muffled against Alan's shoulder. "You weren't in your room and it was so quiet."

Ruben sat up, tugging on the waist of his borrowed sleep pants and caught Alan's flush when he noticed. What a mixed-up, crazy morning. He ruffled Brett's hair as if it was no big deal he was there and stood up. He really hoped Alan wouldn't freak out on him over last night. He could handle Alan pulling back to think things through, but he wasn't sure he could deal with a "what the fuck did we do" moment.

"Hey, Mikey. I think we'd better get Matt before he upsets Seth," Ruben said, smiling at the other boy. "Want to help?"

"Guess so." Mikey glanced at his dad and brother, then gave Ruben a gap-toothed, impish smile. Ruben knew that smile. Mikey wanted a deal. "If I help, will you make blueberry pancakes for breakfast?"

The boys didn't seem to think it strange at all to find the two of them half-naked, asleep on the couch. Ruben gave Alan a cautious glance, waiting for a negative reaction from him, but so far it wasn't happening. Alan lifted one shoulder in a shrug and then turned his whole attention to Brett, who still clung to him.

"Maybe. Do we even have blueberries?" Ruben asked as he headed up the stairs with Mikey.

"Uh-huh, Dad bought them yesterday. Uncle Ruben?" Mikey tugged on his hand and stopped on the top tread.

"Yeah?"

"I was a little worried too," he admitted with a frown. "Sometimes when I hear the door shut and I didn't know Dad was going outside, it scares me. What if something happens to him?"

Oh boy. Ruben's heart ached for Mikey and Brett both. And like Alan, he wished he could do or say something that would make it all better.

"Stop it!" Seth yelled at Matt from the bedroom. "Wanna sleep! Bad Matt."

Ruben peeked into Matt and Seth's room. Seth had half buried himself under the blankets with his hands over his ears, glaring at Matt, who was standing in his crib, still screaming. He stopped crying when he saw Ruben and began jumping up and down. "Bad! Bad! Bad!"

Ruben crouched down and looked at Mikey straight in the eye. "I know it's scary because of your mom, Mikey. But your dad is going to do everything he can to make sure he stays with you guys. That's why he quit baseball, because as much as he loves the game, he loves you even more."

Mikey looked thoughtful at that. "Yeah, Dad really loves baseball."

"Exactly." Ruben smiled. "So, he's doing the best job he can do to take care of himself and you boys. And I promise you, no matter what happens, he'll make sure you are taken care of and loved, okay?"

"Okay." Mikey grinned at him. "Sooo… pancakes?"

"Bad! Ba—" Matt stopped his chant and lifted his arms. "P'cakes? Up! Unca up!"

"You know, I'm very curious about your brother's favorite word." Ruben eyeballed Seth and Mikey as he picked up Matt, who laid his head on Ruben's shoulder. "You might want to stop telling him he's bad all the time."

"But he is!" Mikey protested. "He's always taking my toys."

"And he screams." Seth sat up with a grumpy expression.

"I seem to remember one of you flushing my car keys down the toilet when you were Matt's age." Ruben pointed at Seth, then turned his finger on Mikey. "Then another one of you flipping over the couch and breaking the new TV. Matt's being a boy, just the way you were being boys. You're going to give him a complex if you keep telling him he's bad."

Mikey and Seth exchanged looks and Mikey sighed with childlike exasperation. "Fine. We won't tell him he's being bad when he's bad. We'll let Dad tell him."

Ruben's lips twitched as he tried to hold back a smile. "Fair enough."

Seth huffed, lay back down, and pulled the blankets up to his chin. "It's not wake-up time."

"Pancakes?" Mikey asked. "Please? With extra blueberries?"

Ruben laughed and motioned to the door. "Fine, hooligans, you win. Now go turn on the coffeepot while I get Matt cleaned up, and then we can make pancakes."

"Whoo-hoo!" Mikey took off and bolted down the stairs. Seth groaned and curled into a ball, turning his back to Ruben and Matt.

"Not hungry. Wanna sleep."

Ruben left him alone. The smell of breakfast cooking would get Seth up without an argument. He took his time getting Matt cleaned and dressed to give Alan a chance to talk to Brett. At least that was what he told himself. The reality was, he was uncertain. He didn't know how Alan would react to what had happened the night before, or to the boys finding them this morning. He wasn't sure if this changed anything between them or not.

He wanted a change, wanted to feel like he wasn't stuck in limbo any longer. Only, he had the feeling that despite what had happened, Alan wasn't all that keen on change. He seemed happy with the way things were.

Ruben made his way downstairs, holding Matt's hand, only half listening to his babble. Alan had pulled on his shirt, and he tossed Ruben his when he came into the living room. Alan's cheeks reddened again, and he looked away. "Mornin', Matt."

"Blocks!" Matt toddled off to his pile of cardboard building blocks with an absent wave to his dad. From the kitchen, Ruben heard sounds of silverware clattering and the scent of brewing coffee.

"He has his priorities," Ruben said to break the silence between them.

"Apparently."

"How's Brett?" Ruben asked as he tugged on his shirt.

"Better. I wish he wasn't so anxious. I don't know how else I can help him." Alan glanced toward the kitchen. "He's afraid he's going to forget about Cassandra."

"You won't let that happen." Ruben sat next to him and tried not to read too much into it when Alan shifted. "Mikey admitted he gets worried, too, about something happening to you. I think the only thing you really can do is give them as much stability and support as possible, which you already do."

"Yeah." Alan scrubbed a hand through his hair, and it seemed like he was avoiding meeting Ruben's gaze. "They get a lot of that from you, not just me."

"I love them. They're family to me as much as Jessica and Jonah." He loved Alan, but Alan didn't seem to hear those words past the friendship level.

"They love you too," Alan said softly, his brows still drawn together in concern.

"Have you given any thought to trying counseling again? I know they went for a bit those first several months, but it might not be a bad idea to send Brett and Mikey back," Ruben suggested.

"I have thought about it. They didn't like the last guy much. Maybe they'll respond better to someone different."

"It can't hurt." Ruben wanted to touch him, to slide his arm around Alan's shoulders to give him what comfort he could, but he settled for bumping his knee to Alan's in silent support.

Alan glanced at him, his gaze unreadable. "Brett wanted to know if you were coming over for another sleepover."

A chill gripped Ruben when Alan looked away again, fiddling with a crayon left behind on the coffee table. "What did you say?" he asked, trying to make his voice sound as normal as possible.

"I said I didn't know, but probably not before your trip." Alan cast him a sideways glance.

That was honest, Ruben could appreciate that, and he owed Alan the same honesty in return. "Alan, I don't know if I can pretend nothing happened and go back to the way we were."

Panic flickered across Alan's face, and then he nodded, still rolling the crayon around with the tip of his finger. "I need to think about it. We can talk when you get back. Okay?"

Ruben took a deep breath and then let it out in a rush. It wasn't a "hell no" or even a shutout. Time to think was not too much to ask for. He knew the exact struggle Alan was having about who he was and what he wanted. Besides, last night Alan had admitted that their first kiss had meant something. Ruben had waited years to hear that; he could wait a little longer. "Okay. Do you want me to leave?"

"Are you crazy?" Alan gestured toward the kitchen as he gave Ruben a mock glare. "The boys would declare mutiny if I tried to make the pancakes. No way are you leaving."

"Aye-aye, Captain." Ruben allowed himself to relax when the rejection he'd feared didn't happen.

"Seriously, though," Alan said as he glanced at him again with a look of entreaty. "I don't want you to go. We'll figure this out."

"Okay." This time Ruben smiled and stood up. "Well, then, I'd better get started before they really get hungry. I'll take the pancakes if you'll cook the bacon."

Chapter 7

THE airport was quiet and sleepy even late in the morning. Ruben had zipped through the baggage line and gotten his boarding pass with no problem. The security line was nonexistent. Alan missed the days when family could've gone back and hung out at the gate until boarding time. At least in this quieter airport, Ruben could stay with them until it was almost time to go.

"Lunch?" Alan suggested as Ruben strolled toward them, pulling a rolling carry-on with one hand and slinging his computer bag over his shoulder with the other.

"Sounds like a plan." Ruben stuffed his boarding pass away in the bag and caught Seth's hand as he started to wander off. "Stay close, little man."

Alan cast him a sideways glance before turning toward a restaurant he knew the boys would like. It would've been a better idea to leave them behind at Miss Sarah's, but Alan told himself they'd want to see Ruben off. However, Alan suspected that both he and Ruben were taking advantage of the boys' presence to avoid talking about what happened several days earlier.

Ruben hadn't brought up the latest incident once and seemed completely at ease with him. In fact, he'd seemed a little more relaxed the past couple of days. He was probably looking forward to his visit with Jonah and Jessica. Maybe it was just Alan who was using the boys as a buffer.

He couldn't deny that being with Ruben had been an incredibly erotic experience, even more so than the taboo touches from before. This time he'd gone into it with his eyes wide open. But it scared him too, because it changed everything. Like Ruben said, they couldn't go back to the way things were. Hell, Alan should've understood that from their very first kiss. Nothing went backward, no matter how hard they both tried.

Alan hadn't allowed himself to consider the possibility that he might be gay too, even after his history with Ruben, or his teenage musings. He wasn't sure if his reactions meant he had been buried deep in the closet, or if he was bi, or if it was just Ruben he reacted to like this. His biggest fear was that he'd start something with Ruben only to find that he couldn't commit to it, he could handle short-term experimentation only, and not the day-by-day realities of being a gay man. If he started something and then tried to take it all back, Ruben would leave for sure, and Alan wouldn't blame him.

If… if they took this further, then his family was going to freak out, but Alan had distanced himself from them years ago. Neither he nor Cassandra had wanted their boys confused and hurt by his family's ultraconservatism about anything different. He also wasn't worried about the community, since it was a pretty open-minded and tolerant place. Considering the rumors about them in the media over the years, half the town probably already gossiped about the possibility of them being a couple. He had been concerned at first about how his boys would react, but Brett and Mikey had seemed to view Ruben's presence there in the morning as perfectly acceptable. Ruben had been a part of their extended family for so long it might not be that much of a shock to the boys.

No, the biggest worry eating at him was if it didn't work out and Ruben disappeared from their lives. Then the boys would be devastated. Alan would be devastated. So he just didn't want to rush things.

"You've barely said a word all day," Ruben said as the waitress led them back to a booth. "What gives?"

"I'm wondering what's going through your mind, whether you're planning any life-changing decisions," Alan admitted.

Ruben shot him a startled look and waved at Seth to get into the booth first. "Should I be?"

Alan shrugged and passed over the booster seat. "You've been known to do them on occasion." He just wished he could get his mind to shut up and stop speculating about whether Ruben was going to decide to move to Tampa. It could be a totally baseless worry. He'd never even raised the question with Ruben. Maybe it was time he did, when they were alone next.

Ruben's expression relaxed, and he held up his hand as if making an oath. "Those days are behind me. I promise, no big changes without talking to you first. We are a team, after all."

"Damn right." They bumped fists, and Alan pushed his worries aside as he got Matt settled in the high chair. The restaurant was pretty empty, and the other three boys were happily occupied scribbling on their menus with the complimentary crayons. "So, do you have any plans while you're down there?" Alan asked after they ordered.

"No, nothing too hectic. I don't want to wear them out before their trip. I'll probably take them to the beach most of the time, maybe catch a ballgame one night."

Alan thought of Ruben running through the waves in his bathing suit, the warm brown of his skin getting even darker. He used to be able to dismiss those images easily, but it had been getting harder to do so for a while, and he found himself lingering over them instead. He wondered if Ruben thought of him like that and was filled with a rush of confused warmth. It was like he was a teenager all over again, trying to make sense of his sexuality only to discover he might've been lying to himself for most of his life.

"Is Jonah coming back with you?" Brett asked, stealing a crayon from Seth and holding it out of his reach when he protested.

"Not this time," Ruben replied, as Alan gave Seth and Brett his "behave in public or else" look. If he could keep the inevitable squabbles to a minimum until they got back to the car he'd consider this outing a win.

Brett grimaced and handed back the crayon. "Uncle Ruben, you think maybe his mom would let him get Xbox Live, so we get to play together and talk and stuff?"

"It's a possibility, but I'm not making any promises. He'll be visiting later in the summer, so you'll get to see him then. And we are all going to Puerto Rico again." Ruben moved Seth's drink out of the way as the waitress returned, loaded down with plates.

"Dip it?" Seth asked, pointing toward the bottle of ketchup, and the next few minutes were busy with getting the boys settled with their meals before turning to their own.

Alan didn't have much of an appetite. It was crazy to feel like he was missing Ruben already, and he didn't want to tell him that either. Ruben needed this time with his kids, and Alan didn't want to do anything to shadow that.

Their hands brushed as they both reached for the pitcher of iced tea, and a little shock went through Alan. Their eyes met and Ruben smiled, a kind of secret smile he'd given Alan off and on over the years.

"Are you having a staring contest?" Mikey asked, clambering to his knees and waving his hand in front of Alan's face. Alan looked away, feeling his cheeks flush. "Can I play too? Betcha I can win."

"Betcha you can't," Brett retorted.

"Ha! Just watch me!"

"You can try after you finish your burgers, guys." Ruben pointed to their plates and the barely nibbled on burgers. "You've killed the fries, so why not try the rest?"

Yep, bringing the boys was a mistake. There were things he wanted to say to Ruben before he left. Or at least attempt to say. Maybe it wouldn't come out pretty as he fumbled through trying to explain how he was feeling, but he was pretty sure Ruben would understand anyway.

All too soon lunch was over and they were standing by the security barricade. Alan watched Ruben say good-bye to Brett, Mikey, and Seth, with so many things he wanted to say he was rendered incapable of speech, period. Ruben leaned close and gave Matt a raspberry on his cheek, making him squirm and giggle in Alan's arms.

Their eyes met again, and Alan caught Ruben in a hard hug. It felt damn good to have Ruben's arm around him too. He pressed his cheek against Ruben's. "I don't want you to be an experiment," Alan whispered, then kissed his cheek, still holding onto him.

Ruben nodded, turned his head, and brushed his mouth over Alan's in a quick kiss that sent a shocking thrill through him and left him wanting more. Then he was gone, striding down the walkway to the short security line, and it felt like he was taking Alan's heart with him.

Alan glanced down at Brett, who was watching him with round eyes. "Dad, is Uncle Ruben your boyfriend? 'Cause that would be kinda cool. He could have dinner at our house, like, every night."

"What's a boyfriend?" Mikey asked, his expression curious.

"It means they like hang out all the time, dummy, and make kissy noises." Brett shot Mikey a withering look, and Mikey glared right back at him.

"I'm not a dummy, you're the dummy. 'Cause they already hang out all the time. Duh."

"Enough, you two. For the love of God, enough." Alan motioned to them to cut it out and then lifted his gaze to watch Ruben disappear on the other side. He sighed. "Your uncle is my friend. And we're all lucky he puts up with us. Come on, let's get you yahoos home."

RUBEN pulled up in front of the home that Karen had bought with her new husband, a sprawling two-story farmhouse that could accommodate both sets of kids. From what Karen told him and what he'd been able to glean from Jessica and Jonah, they all got along fairly well, though Jonah was having a harder time adjusting to the many changes that had happened in his short life.

Jessica was his tough girl. Jonah was far more sensitive and kept things locked inside. He brooded, just like Ruben. Excited, Ruben got out of the car and bounded up the front steps. He couldn't wait to see them both again. He had so many ideas for what they could do over the next few days, but mostly he just wanted to see them and talk to them and just be a family again.

The excitement intensified as he rang the bell, then heard Karen call out, "Jonah, would you get that for me, baby?" Ruben grinned and adjusted his baseball cap at the pounding of familiar footsteps, then the door was flung open. Jonah's hazel eyes widened through a mop of dark hair.

"Dad?" Jonah cried out, and Ruben's eyes stung as he held out his arms.

"Yeah, Jonah, it's me."

"Dad!" Jonah cried out and threw himself at Ruben. "Jessie, Jessie, Dad's here!"

"Daddy!" Jessica bolted down the steps, jumping the last two, and raced to join them. "What're you doing here?"

"I missed you two something crazy, so your mom and I decided I should come down for a quick visit before you two go off on your big adventure."

For several minutes it was hugs, misty eyes, and babbling from all of them. When Ruben straightened, Karen was standing in the hallway, watching them with a smile. "Hey, Ruben."

"You're looking good," Ruben said with a smile. In fact she looked more content than he'd seen her in years. It was good to see her and not feel the dull edge of guilt that usually accompanied it. Karen was right where she wanted to be.

"Thanks. I have their overnight bags packed, so they're all ready to go. Are you staying at your usual place?"

"Yep." Ruben tugged the bill of Jessica's ball cap and ruffled Jonah's hair. "Go grab your stuff and say good-bye to everyone."

The kids went barreling off, making a racket. At the top of the stairs, Karen's two stepdaughters appeared, leaning over the railing and whispering.

"How are Alan and his boys doing?" Karen asked with none of the defensive tightness that would've been in her gaze even a year ago.

"Good. The boys are getting big." Ruben glanced around for Dave, Karen's new husband, but didn't see him. "How are Dave and the girls?"

"The girls are dying of excitement over the trip. Dave, not as much. He's not going to be able to stay with us the entire time. Big project at work." She glanced up at the ceiling at the clatter of footsteps running from one end of the hall to the other. "I wanted to tell you, and I expect that you'll hear an earful anyway, but I'm going to have another baby."

Ruben's gaze fell to her flat stomach and then back up to meet her eyes. "You are? What are you doing going to London?"

She laughed and shook her head. "Ruben, it's a long ways off and I'll be okay. God, you never change. Dave and I both wanted one more, the girls are excited, but I think Jonah hasn't warmed up to the idea yet. I thought you should know."

"Thanks." Ruben glanced up as Jessica came tearing down the stairs again, breathless, her ponytail swishing. She gave her mom a hug and a kiss then bounded over to Ruben, dancing from foot to foot.

"Can we go to the pizzeria for dinner?"

"Sure, but first, let's check in, drop our bags off, and let Uncle Alan know I've gotten here safely. He wanted to say hi to you both."

"Cool. Can I talk to the monster squad too?" Jessica turned toward the stairs and raised her voice. "Come on, Jonah! I'm hungry."

Jonah came down the stairs, still blinking back tears, and went and gave his mom a hard hug. Oh yeah, there was something bugging him, maybe several things, and Ruben vowed to have a good long talk with him over the next few days and worm it out of him.

THE beach was a little quieter on a weekday, but not by much. Ruben kept his attention roaming between Jessica, who was frolicking in the edges of the surf, and Jonah, who wandered, collecting bits of shell and other interesting things in his bucket. Jessica had been enjoying the last couple of days full tilt, bubbling with excitement over spending time with him, the upcoming trip to London, and giddy over the chance to have a baby in the house. She had adored taking care of Matt when he was a newborn. She was a natural big sister.

Ruben returned his gaze to Jonah, who had settled in the sand to examine his findings. Jonah would be a good big brother too. He was patient with Alan's younger boys. He and Brett butted heads more often, but that was because they were the same age and best friends. When he'd asked Jonah how he felt about it all—the trip, the new baby—all he'd gotten in return was a shrug and "it's okay."

This morning, though, something new had upset him, and he'd hardly said a word all day. This might be the last chance Ruben had to talk to him alone before he left in the morning. "Not so far out, Jessica," he called as he started walking toward Jonah.

His daughter waved to him and came in closer by a few feet, then a few feet more when Ruben shouted again. He plopped down next to Jonah, watching Jessica's silhouette against the blazing sun. "Did you find anything interesting?"

Jonah nodded and pulled out a sliver of shell worn smooth by the pounding surf. The iridescent colors were especially brilliant, and it had been whittled down to almost a crescent shape. "Looks like a moon, don't it?"

"Yeah, you're right. That's pretty cool. It's definitely a keeper."

Ruben didn't ask what was bothering Jonah—that had yielded nothing but denials and silence. Instead he talked about small things, making comments about Jonah's treasures, the best methods for making a sand castle, and tactics for surviving the zombie apocalypse. Bit by bit, Jonah warmed up to the conversation and offered tidbits of his own.

"Dad, are you sad about not playing baseball anymore?" Jonah asked, touching the scar on Ruben's shoulder from the surgery.

"Sometimes, but I haven't really lost the game. I still can play for fun, and I love coaching. When I miss the big games, I go watch one and think about all the things I have instead."

"But it's not the same. It's all different now," Jonah said, digging his plastic shovel into the sand and then examining what he pulled up.

Ruben watched Jessica in the water, his heart aching for his son. "Change can be difficult, Jonah, but life is all about change. Sometimes I get sad watching you and Jessica grow up. I miss you as babies and toddlers, but I love watching what you've become and wondering where you're going to go from here. If I spent all my time being sad because I miss four-year-old Jonah then how can I appreciate eight-year-old Jonah?"

"I guess so." Jonah let the sand pour out in a trickle. "Hey, Dad, do we really get to come see you after London? Promise?"

"I promise. The whole rest of the summer you're going to be with me. And there's going to be lots of things going on—there's the pitching camp, and Brett's very excited about seeing you again and going swimming with you."

"I hate him!"

Ruben stared at Jonah, surprised by his vehemence. Jonah stared at the ground with a fierce scowl on his face, blinking rapidly. "What? Who do you hate? Brett?"

"Yes!" Jonah's face crumpled and a fat tear rolled down his cheek. Ruben brushed it off and Jonah swatted his hand away.

This made no sense. Except for the minor squabbles typical between friends, the two boys had always gotten along. "I thought he was your best friend," Ruben said carefully, trying to think of what might've precipitated this outburst. "I didn't hear you two arguing when you were talking yesterday. What happened?"

"I hate him, 'cause you're going to stop being my dad and start being Brett's."

"Whoa, wait a minute. Where did you get a crazy idea like that? I'm always going to be your dad." Another tear rolled down Jonah's nose, and he dashed it away angrily. Ruben rubbed Jonah's back and then slung his arm around his skinny shoulders. This time Jonah didn't push him away.

"I Google-Alerted your name 'cause I like seeing all the cool news stuff that sometimes comes up about you. And this morning there were these pictures of you and Uncle Alan and you were being all kissy-face, icky lovey, like Mom and Dave, and there's going to be no room for me anywhere anymore."

It must be hard for Jonah to be with his sister and two older stepsisters, who were not afraid to speak their mind and speak it loudly. Add in the excitement of a new baby, and he must feel lost in the crowd. Then throw in the swerve with Ruben and Alan, and he probably thought nothing was stable anymore.

"Jonah…." Ruben searched to try to find the right words to say to reassure his son that no matter what happened between him and Alan, if anything happened between them, he'd still be his dad. "I love you. I've loved you since before you were born. I loved you all those years when I was on the road so often and it was just you, Jessica, and your mom. And I loved you when your mom and I got divorced and she took you two back to Tampa. Nothing is ever going to change that."

"Promise?"

"I swear it. I love Alan's boys too, and your mom loves your stepsisters. That's the neat thing about love, Jonah: the more you love, the more you have to give away to others. But if you hide it away and hold onto it out of fear and not wanting to share, that can make love get sickly. Do you understand?"

Jonah thought about it, leaning into Ruben's side. "I think so."

"What makes you happier? Being friends with Brett or saying you hate him like you just did?" Ruben asked, lowering his head next to Jonah's.

Jonah's shoulders hunched. "Being his friend."

"What about when we have FaceTime at night? How do you feel when we get to talk versus when you're upset and ignore it when I call?"

"When I talk to you." Jonah looked up at him, his face solemn. "Sometimes, I feel mean when I don't want to talk, and then I cry 'cause I miss you and I want to take it back."

"I get sad when I miss you too, and I'm happy when I talk to you. Life is crazy sometimes. Like I said, you can't stop it from changing, but you can enjoy each day as much as possible, okay?"

"So if I love Dave too, then it's not bad, it's okay?"

"It's absolutely okay. He makes your mom happy, right? He treats her well and he's good to his daughters and you two. I think those are very good reasons to love him." Jonah heaved a big sigh and smiled up at Ruben. "Do you feel better?"

"Yeah, thanks, Dad."

Ruben hugged him. "Thank you for talking to me. Now, why don't we go check on your sister before she decides to go body surfing without us?"

"Yeah, okay." Jonah set his pail under their beach umbrella. "Dad, does this mean you're going to marry Uncle Alan like Mom got remarried?"

Oh boy, what was it with kids stabbing right at the heart of an issue? "Actually, despite what you may have read online, Alan and I are just taking things a day at a time, no rush. Mostly we're friends, and that's not a bad way to start a relationship."

"I love Uncle Alan, and so does Jessie," Jonah offered as they headed across the hot sands to the shoreline.

"He feels the same way about you two."

"Wow, I didn't know I loved so many different people. Are you sure there's enough to share?"

Ruben laughed and squeezed Jonah's shoulder. "I'm absolutely positive."

The past few days had been amazing, and Ruben had soaked in every minute with his kids. It didn't matter where he was: if he was in Tampa, he felt like half his heart was left behind in Vermont with Alan and the boys, and when he was back home, he felt the same way about Jessica and Jonah.

This was like when he'd been on the road, working that hectic, grueling schedule. Only then he had been able to see his kids more often, and now his relationship with Alan was maybe turning into everything Ruben had dreamed of. He knew Alan was worried that he was frustrating the hell out of Ruben, but Ruben had already been through this stage, trying to figure out what he really wanted out of his life. He knew Alan had concerns that Ruben would get it in his head to move back to Tampa, and damned if there weren't times when he was tempted. But when Alan said he didn't want Ruben to be just an experiment, Ruben had vowed to himself to see this through to the end.

Alan was worth fighting and sticking around for. When he got back, Ruben was going to make a stand and show Alan what he really was choosing if he chose him. And he would make the most of every moment he had with his kids when they were together.

"Jonah."

"Yeah, Dad?"

Ruben crouched down at the water's edge and smiled at him. "Thank you for talking to me. You helped remind me about what's important."

"I did?" Jonah scrunched his face together as he thought about it. "Was it about the love stuff?"

Ruben laughed and hugged Jonah to him again. "Yeah, buddy, it's about the love stuff. You know that no matter where I am, I love you whole bunches, right?"

"Totally." Jonah flung his arms out as wide as they would go. "You love us this much and more."

"You've got it, little man."

Chapter 8

WHEN Ruben emerged from the airport, he found Alan waiting for him by the curb, leaning against his SUV and studying the open binder he held in his hands. Ruben paused, his heart doing the Charleston. Even after all these years, whenever he saw Alan after a few days' absence, he still got that little thrill of awareness, the feeling he was coming home.

"So, you ready for the annual town exhibition game Saturday?" Ruben asked, setting his carry-on down. "My shoulder is all rehabbed now; you're not going to be able to walk all over me like you did last year."

Alan glanced up and the corners of his eyes crinkled with his smile. "Well, look at you, Mr. Florida. Looks like you had plenty of sun while we were stuck with rain up here."

"It was beautiful. Hot, but beautiful."

Alan tossed the binder onto the backseat through the open window, then went to open the hatch on the back of the SUV. Ruben felt a little awkward as he put his bag in the back. Normally, Alan would've hugged him. He was that kind of a guy—he hugged, he backslapped, he drove Ruben crazy with all those small, innocent touches.

Apparently he'd done some thinking over the past few days. Ruben's thoughts went back to what Alan said before he left, that he didn't want Ruben to be an experiment. He'd taken it as a plea for more time to process what was happening between him, but now he wondered if it meant Alan really wanted to step back altogether and go back to being only friends.

"Come on," Alan said, slamming the hatch shut. "If we hurry, you'll just make your practice. Laurie will be happy to see you."

Ruben slid into the seat and buckled himself in as Alan rolled off down the access way. "She said practice went well, but I'm sure the boys were antsy; Opening Day weekend is coming up fast. Who are you playing on Sunday?" he asked to distract himself from his disappointment. Both days were utter chaotic fun, Saturday with the demo game, team pictures, and parade, then Sunday with every team getting a chance to play at some time either in the morning or the afternoon.

"Eddlington's team. We have one of the first slots, right before they start the picnic feast."

"We're not on until after lunch, so I'll be able to watch."

"That's cool, it'll give me a chance to grab Mikey beforehand. I think Brett is playing right after you."

It was easy to sink into the familiar talk of juggling schedules, maximizing their time together without even thinking about it. Still, nagging at the back of Ruben's mind was the sinking thought that Alan might want to go back to the way things were. If that happened, Ruben didn't know how to start letting go of that dream for both of their sakes.

"How are Jonah and Jessica doing?" Alan asked as they headed north. "It sounded like you were having a fun visit."

"Jessica is doing well. Nothing much fazes her. She misses your monster squad." Ruben watched the countryside go by, the white glare of the sun in Tampa replaced with the cool green of the mountains. He let the scenery settle and soothe him. "Jonah is having some problems adjusting."

"What, with the new stepfamily?" Alan asked, a note of concern creeping into his voice. "I guess when you think about it, not that much time has passed since the divorce."

"That, and having his summer routine changed and Karen's pregnant. That's playing into it as well."

"Wow. That's a lot to take in."

Ruben debated whether he wanted to get into the rest of it with Alan, but he wasn't likely to get another chance soon without them being interrupted. It was just the two of them and a long ride ahead.

"He was also worried that I was going to stop being his dad, that Brett would replace him."

"Where did he get a crazy-assed idea like that?" Alan asked, and Ruben caught his glance out of the corner of his eye.

"Some damn pictures a blogger posted from the airport." Ruben knew he should've warned Alan about it, but that last day had been hectic. That was probably just an excuse; Ruben hadn't wanted Alan to find out about it until he had a chance to be with him to run damage control if he needed to. "And a nice piece speculating on the length of our relationship."

Ruben turned to look at Alan to gauge his feelings, but Alan was hard to read sometimes.

Alan let out a breath and his hands tightened on the wheel before they relaxed. "Well, there were rumors going on about us before there was anything to talk about. I guess you could say we've finally given them something to actually discuss."

"Yeah, I guess so. I'll send you the link. The pictures came out rather nice." Though Ruben would've preferred that the intimate moment would've been left out of the media. His emotions about Alan were too raw right now to share with anybody else.

"I know I said we'd talk when you came back," Alan said. A chill touched Ruben's stomach, and he nodded without looking at Alan. *Please, don't let it be a complete step backward.* He couldn't go on pretending the love he had for Alan was just friendship. "And I've been giving it all a lot of thought."

Thinking about it was better than the alternative. Ruben wished he had something to do with his hands, anything. "I know it's a lot to consider."

"It is, because it doesn't affect only me. Honestly, I'm scared of fucking this up, Ruben, I really am. I don't want to lose our friendship. I need it. I need you, and the boys need you too." Alan stole another glance at him, and this time Ruben met his gaze.

"I've been thinking about it too. I had a good conversation with Jonah, and it helped me put some things into perspective. We're not going to lose our friendship. Neither of us would let that happen. If you decide you can't pursue this and I have to take a step back to regroup, then I will, but it doesn't mean I can't be your friend, it just means I need to learn to let go of the idea that we could be something else."

"I'm not asking you to let go," Alan said quietly.

A wild surge of hope leaped up in Ruben's chest. "You're not?"

"No, I just want some time to figure it out. It feels like everything is happening so fast. I know it's not, maybe it's been building for a long time, but to me, it's like suddenly we were one way and the past was the past, and now it's all different. I'm thinking of you differently, and it's kinda blowing my mind."

Ruben remembered those days when he first realized he was falling for Alan—the stress of trying to bury the inappropriate thoughts, the ache of wanting to be closer and being afraid, the realization that the map he'd laid out for his life was completely altered because the mask he'd built for who he thought he was had been stripped from him.

And he sure as hell hadn't come to any conclusions overnight, either, or even over a long few days apart. It had been a painful, liberating, slow revelation, and he couldn't deny Alan the same time to wrestle with his feelings and identity.

"Take all the time you need, Alan. I'm not going anywhere."

Alan flashed him a smile that lit up his whole face. Damn, he just made Ruben crazy. He reached over and squeezed Ruben's hand. "That's all I need to know."

"GET a home run, Dad!" Brett shouted from the stand as Alan walked toward home plate.

Immediately, another familiar voice piped up. "Strike him out, Uncle Ruben!"

Alan glanced at his boys, who sat next to Miss Sarah, and pointed at Seth, who grinned impudently back at him. Ruben laughed and called back from the pitcher's mound, "Don't you worry, little man, I've got your dad's number."

Adjusting the straps on his batting gloves, Alan tried to get into the zone. Maybe it was just an exhibition game, where all the Little League coaches in the county made two teams and started off Opening Day weekend with a blast, but whenever he faced off against Ruben, neither of them held back. Last year he'd gotten the best of Ruben, but he knew it was only because of the surgery. That hadn't stopped the locals from enjoying the hell out of the contest, and the two teams had been itching for a rematch all year.

He tapped the edge of the plate with his bat three times and hopped from foot to foot in his old routine, getting himself geared up. Ruben might go easier on the less experienced batters, but he'd bring his A game for him. Alan lifted his bat and stared at Ruben as a frisson of awareness sizzled through him.

They had faced each other more times than Alan could count, both in practice, while they were on the same team, and as rival players when the stakes were much higher. As Ruben leaned forward, his razor concentration on the catcher, his entire face focused, Alan felt the jolt of heat that had become impossible to ignore. Ruben was sexy when he was so intent. It made Alan want to march over and kiss him until all that attention was focused on him instead.

Ruben gave a slight nod, then straightened, his entire body still for a moment until that long leg came up. Alan steadied the bat, his heart thumping from more than just adrenaline. He remembered that leg hugging him as they'd rubbed against each other on the couch last week.

Alan let out his breath in a rush as the ball came screaming toward him. He swung, but his rhythm was off and he knew he'd missed even before he finished the motion. The crowd groaned and Ruben grinned, a wicked curve of his lips. "It's too early in the game for you to get psyched out, Hartner," he called.

"I'm just getting started." Alan pointed the bat at him. "Don't forget what happened in Boston." Ruben's gaze narrowed as he leaned forward to study the catcher again. No, Ruben wasn't likely to ever forget Alan was the one who had shut down his no-hitter. He had been hopping mad.

And today Alan's focus was all wrong, just like it had been all wrong that night in Boston. Alan had kept getting distracted by all of Ruben's little mannerisms and he'd screwed up every time he'd stepped up to the plate, striking out swinging until the frustration had built up to the breaking point in the ninth inning, when he'd smacked that damn ball right over the Green Monster.

Only that wasn't the most distracting memory that kept flitting through Alan's head. It was what had happened later, when Alan went to Ruben's hotel room, still filled with the same frustration from the game, the same ache of losing his best friend to another city, another team.

He'd showed up at the hotel room, and Ruben's eyes had been hot and furious as he stared back at him. They'd almost been black in the dim light coming from his room. He'd warned Alan not to press him, but all Alan could think was he didn't want to be shut out anymore.

Ruben's gaze caught him again with a rough jolt as he straightened. Alan remembered the feel of those firm lips, those hard hands on his body as they'd pulled their clothes off with impatient tugs, stumbling their way to the bed.

The ball sailed across the plate, and Alan blinked as the crowd roared. "What're you doin', Dad!" Brett yelled at the top of his lungs over the ump calling strike two. "Stop daydreaming and swing the bat."

Alan chuckled as he heard his own oft-repeated words shouted back at him. If he didn't get his head on the game, he was going to be the laughingstock of the town for the rest of the weekend and his sons would never let him hear the end of it. "Come on, Alan, you don't have to make it that easy for him," the catcher said with a snicker.

He tapped his bat on the plate again, forcing his gaze away from Ruben. Those memories were hitting him hard. And he was consumed with thoughts of inviting Ruben up to his bedroom tonight, undressing him, and taking it slow and easy as they explored one another. Ruben hadn't tried kissing him once since he came back, keeping to his promise to give Alan space, and it was making him absolutely nuts.

Ruben's leg came up and Alan narrowed his focus on the bat in his hand and the ball that came toward him. It was slower than the last two pitches and seemed to almost dance in the air between them. Alan swung, cursing himself even as he did. Ruben hadn't thrown a knuckleball in a long time.

He connected and knew it was no damn good. The pop fly was caught easily by the shortstop and Ruben came jogging forward as the end of the inning was called. "Didn't get enough sleep last night, Alan?" he called teasingly, and Alan narrowed his eyes. Oh no, he was not going to be the only one who had a hard time concentrating today.

"Just remembering *The Maltese Falcon*," Alan said, patting Ruben's back as he came to an abrupt halt. "Makes it a little hard to stay focused."

Ruben turned to look at him, his gaze hot and intense, and Alan knew he'd gotten under his skin. He was learning to recognize the little signals from Ruben that gave away his interest, like the way those eyes of his would darken even more, or the way he'd kind of lean in toward Alan. "Good movie," Ruben said, after a minute examination of Alan's face. "Good memories associated with it."

"Good, hmm?" Alan let his gaze rake over Ruben and grinned wickedly as the other man shook his head in bemusement. "I can think of many other adjectives."

Ruben leaned closer still and lowered his voice. "You're a damn tease, Hartner. I never would've thought that of you."

"Goes to show you don't know everything about me yet." Alan backed away toward his dugout with another grin, spreading his hands wide. "Kind of exciting, isn't it?"

RUBEN watched Alan saunter off. Even though no one had gotten on base from Alan's team, it felt like the other man had come out on top. He looked down at the dust coating his feet and grinned. It had been hard during the past week to pretend that the night on the couch had never happened, to stop himself from stealing kisses good night or confessing once again that he loved him. It seemed like his patience was finally paying off.

Still, though, despite Alan's words and the simmering sexual tension between them that was impossible to deny, Ruben didn't want to rush things. He'd let Alan make the next move when he was ready, and in the meantime he rather looked forward to discovering this new, playful side of his best friend.

"Hey, Martell, you going to stand there daydreaming all day? We've got a game to finish."

Ruben felt his cheeks heat as he joined the other coaches on his team in the dugout. The rest of the game went by in a blur as the coolness of early morning gave way to the lethargic heat of midday. Ruben had no other opportunity to talk to Alan again as they rushed from the game to change into their uniforms for the team pictures, followed by the parade down Main Street. The excitement of the kids was palpable, as most of the town had lined up to watch. There were four big festivities in the county during the year; this weekend for the All-Stars was one of them.

He didn't get a chance to see Alan again until at the end of the day, when he was herding the boys into the SUV. "You want tacos?" Alan asked as he buckled Matt into his car seat. "I prepped everything before I left the house this morning."

"Can't, I promised Laurie and her husband pizza, and she's already giving me enough grief for the way I let you distract me earlier." He'd had a hard time getting his equilibrium back to find the plate again in the second inning.

Disappointment flashed across Alan's face, but he shrugged it off with a smile. "Tomorrow night, then?"

"You won't be able to keep me away." Ruben leaned closer, daring to tease him a little in return. "Maybe we can watch another Bogart film."

Alan's cheeks flushed and his eyes brightened. Ruben stole a quick, hard kiss, the first time he'd touched Alan like that since the airport. Brett and Mikey started snickering. When he pulled back, Alan was staring at him. His gaze dropped to Ruben's lips, and then another, slower smile crossed his lips. "Tempting offer. I'll let you know."

Ruben's heart jumped and a hot surge of awareness made his mouth dry. It was probably a good damn thing he wasn't hanging with Alan tonight; he'd need every bit of concentration for tomorrow's games.

He stuck his head through the SUV window and tugged on Brett's cap. "If I don't get to see you tomorrow before your game, good luck."

"You too, Uncle Ruben."

Matt kicked his legs and waved his chubby hand. "Bye, bye, bye!"

"Hey, Uncle Ruben, are you gonna kiss my dad again?" Mikey asked, looking at him curiously.

Alan snorted under his breath and slid into the driver's seat, his eyes dancing with suppressed laughter, which was a much better sight than the conflict Ruben had seen in them too often. "You're going to leave me to field all the questions now," Alan said low enough so only Ruben would hear.

"Yep, Mikey, is that okay with you?"

Mikey considered the question with a tilt of a head. "Do I get more pancakes?"

"Cork it, Mikey," Alan ordered, snapping on his seat belt. "You are not bargaining my kisses for breakfast. That's between me and your uncle. And you, don't encourage him. Mikey doesn't need it."

Ruben winked at Mikey, ruffled Seth's hair, and then propped his elbows on the open window frame next to Alan. "Sweet dreams, Hartner. I hope the memories don't keep you up all night."

Chapter 9

ALAN was damn grateful he had one of the first games of the day. He'd had an impossible time getting the boys down after the excitement of the previous day. And he'd lain awake way too late, thinking of Ruben, wishing he were in the bed with him and not a couple miles down the shoreline in his own lonely bed. It was hard to worry about whether or not this was going to work when he was coming to the realization they were already deep into a relationship, and that two quick kisses since the night on the couch were not nearly enough to satisfy him.

His thoughts had turned from memories to what might happen the next night when Ruben came over, to what Alan wanted to happen. Those thoughts had kept him on the edge of sleep for hours and as a consequence, he was running late.

"Dad! I can't find my baseball cap!" Brett shouted down the hallway.

Alan let out his breath in a huff of exasperation and hauled Matt out of the bathroom before he could get into the toilet paper rolls again. "Brett, I told you to put all your equipment together last night. Check the closet in your room and hurry up."

Matt let out an ear-piercing scream as Alan shut the bathroom door. "No," Alan said firmly. "They're not blocks and you cannot dress up in them."

"Bad! Bad, Dad." Matt glared at him.

"Whatever," Alan muttered and returned to getting dressed. He wasn't sure how the heck he was going to finish getting the boys together and out the door on time this morning. They were still wired. He really wanted to give Ruben a call to see if he'd come over to help, but he had his own things to take care of this morning.

"Daddy, how come I don't get to play?" Seth stood in the doorway, the only one ready, dressed in his T-Ball uniform from earlier in the season. "I want to play too."

"Don't worry, little man. The second season will be starting soon. I've already signed you up for it." Alan tugged on his team T-shirt and grabbed his own cap. "I bet they'll have something going on at one of the empty diamonds. If you're good and ask Miss Sarah nicely, maybe she'll take you and Matt there."

The house phone rang and Alan ignored it in favor of catching Matt up in his arms. "Let's get you changed hooligan, and then we're good to go. Seth, would you be my big helper and check Matt's diaper bag for me, make sure there are extra diapers in there?"

"Sure," Seth said and took off to his room at a run.

"Dad!" Mikey yelled from somewhere downstairs. "Phone!"

"Tell them I'll call them back." If it was anyone that he cared to talk to they would've called him on his cell phone.

"It's Aunt Dawn and she wants to talk to you now."

Alan's thoughts immediately darted to his parents. He only spoke with them on birthdays and holidays. He talked to his sister a little more often as she tried to bridge the gap between him and the rest of his family. Something must be wrong for her to call early on a Sunday morning. "Bring the phone up."

"Whoohoo! Found it," Brett hollered and Alan heard him go barreling down the stairs. He winced, half expecting a collision with Mikey. They were crazy, the lot of them, like a troop of monkeys high on sugar and they were going to drive him mad.

He set Matt in his crib and grabbed the clothes he laid out for him the night before as Seth upended the diaper bag on the floor. This was getting to be one of those mornings where he understood those old Calgon commercials. "Seth, for the love of God, put everything back in there neatly," Alan said, striving for a patience that was eroding fast. "Please. We have to get moving."

Mikey, still in his pajamas, came in carrying the phone. Alan bit off a swear word. "Get dressed now. If you're not ready the next time I see you then you get no video games tomorrow and you're helping me with extra chores." He turned his attention back to Matt and tucked the phone between his shoulder and his ear. "Hey Dawn, is everybody okay?"

"I just sent you a couple of pictures to your cell and I want you to explain them," Dawn said, her voice tense. "Before I have to explain them, please tell me it's just another misunderstanding like the others."

"Now is not really a good time." Alan finished getting Matt dressed and crouched down to help Seth get the diaper bag together. "The team's first game is in less than an hour and I still have two hooligans to corral."

"It's important," Dawn insisted.

Alan pulled his cell phone out of his pocket and went down the hallway to check on Brett and Mikey's progress. Brett sat on his bed, his cap on his head and his baseball glove in hand as he watched Mikey scramble into his clothes. Finally. "Okay, I'm checking it now."

He pulled up her text message and an image appeared of him and Ruben in a close embrace with Matt between them, his hand on Ruben's cheek, the picture from the airport that Ruben had told him about. Alan stared at the photo and a rush of warmth filled him, chasing away the irritations of the morning.

He didn't know why he'd been so reluctant to look at the pictures. He'd thought about it, but never went looking for them. The photographer had caught Ruben's profile and the expression on his face—like he was right where he wanted to be—made Alan's heart swell and a smile come to his face. The second picture was taken a mere moment before the too fleeting kiss and was a wider shot with Brett, Mikey, and Seth arrayed around them in the airport.

"Well?" Dawn asked.

His old automatic response, that Ruben was just a friend died on his lips. He wasn't sure yet how to define what they were but they sure as hell weren't just friends. "Nothing I say is going to make a difference because Mom and Dad are going to hate it no matter what."

"That's putting it mildly. They are going to freak out. What about your boys? They're right there. You're in public."

Alan stiffened and stuck his cell phone back in his pocket as he gestured to Mikey to hurry up. "My boys are doing just fine and what's going on with me and Ruben is nobody's business but our own. For crying out loud it's not like we're doing anything illegal."

"What about Cassandra's parents?" Dawn asked, trying a different tactic. Alan rubbed his temple before it started to ache. Dealing with his family always set him on edge and Dawn was the most reasonable one.

"You may be surprised to hear this, but her parents are far more open minded and loving than ours." Which was why the boys had a much more extensive relationship with them, but maybe he should talk to them and let them know what was new in their life.

"Look sis, I appreciate your concern and I know you're caught in the middle, but I really don't give a damn what Mom and Dad think. I'm sorry, I know it hurts you. I know you want us to be a happy family, but it's never going to happen. I'm not living the kind of life they want me to lead and when they hear of this that'll be the end. I'm not willing to change to suit them or to teach my sons that being different automatically means you are less. We've been over this."

"I know, but this is different. How long have you been carrying on with Ruben? The blog insinuates that it's been for years. Were you still married?" With each statement Dawn's voice rose a little higher and Alan's heart sank. He gestured for Mikey and Brett to head downstairs then went to retrieve the other boys.

"It doesn't matter." Alan cut off her protest and continued. "Seriously, at this point it doesn't and I'm not going to discuss it with you because the sticking point is that I'm in a relationship with another man. And to make matters even worse, he's not a white man. Mom and Dad are going to have to deal and if they don't, if they cut me out even more completely than they already have, that's on them. I'm not turning my back on Ruben because they're close-minded bigots. God help me, I still love them, but that's what they are."

Alan slung the diaper bag over his shoulder and picked up Matt from his crib. "And on that note, I'm letting you go because I have a game to rush to and I still need to drop the boys off first."

"I don't understand," Dawn sighed. "I'm trying to, but I just don't get it."

"There's nothing to understand. Call me again in a few days when you've had a chance to think about it." Alan followed Seth down the stairs and gave Brett a grateful smile when he saw him carting the equipment out the door to the waiting SUV.

"Believe me, I will." Dawn sighed again, a wealth of worry in that sound. "I love you."

"I love you too."

Alan hung up the phone and tossed it to Mikey. "Put that back for me, little man." He loaded the kids in the SUV and paused to get his equilibrium back after that call. He was pretty sure Dawn would come around, just as he was absolutely certain his parents would completely cut him off. The feeling had been pretty mutual for years. Alan brought up the picture of them at the airport again and stared at the expression on Ruben's face. He had his boys, Ruben and a baseball team waiting for him. He didn't need anything else.

By the time he got to the field his assistant coach was already there, watching the team members go through their drill and barking out commands to hustle more. To his relief, Charles Eddlington's team was just arriving so he wasn't all that late.

"They're enthusiastic this morning," Charles commented after he set his own boys to their drills and walked over to Alan. "I just hope they stay focused; they get excitable during the first game."

"They'll settle down once the game starts." Alan looked over his shoulder as he felt a familiar gaze on him and met Ruben's eyes. The black and gray of his uniform stood out among the others, and Alan found himself smiling. The bastard looked completely rested, while Alan was frazzled from lack of sleep, the hectic morning and the conversation with his sister.

Charles cleared his throat and Alan turned back to the other coach, who was watching him with amusement. "You need to stay focused and not let Martell distract you," Charles said with a shake of his head. "Unless you want a repeat of yesterday's entertainment."

"Point taken. No more distractions." He'd tried to get under Ruben's skin and it had backfired on him, big-time. His team deserved his full attention during their opening game. "We'll give you a good game."

"I'm counting on it," Charles replied with a clap on his shoulder and trotted off to the opposite dugout. Alan watched the drills continue for a bit before calling his team in. They crowded around him, some anxious, others excited, but by some miracle all of them were paying attention.

"Now, they have a couple of good pitchers," Alan said without any preamble. "Watch how that ball leaves the mitt and don't swing at just anything. Got it?"

"Yes, Coach!" came the chorus of voices.

"You guys have everything you need to play a good game. I want you to do your best, play fair, and you'll make me proud." Alan held out his hand and the kids piled theirs on top. The excitement in the air was palpable.

"Who are you?" Alan barked.

"Green Mountain Boys!"

"How do you play?"

"Fair and hard!"

"And what do we do best?" Alan finished.

"Play ball!"

The group broke up with cheers as Eddlington's team scattered across the outfield, taking up their positions. Alan walked over to the chain-link fence separating him and Ruben, waving to Brett and Mikey, who sat in the stands. Ruben's eyes seemed even darker, accented by his uniform, and after his long, lonely night, Alan couldn't get within two feet of him without feeling a little surge of awareness.

"Good luck," Ruben murmured, holding up his fist to the gap in the links.

"You too." Alan tapped his knuckles against Ruben's, and his stomach fluttered in response. "I hope you slept well."

A smile crinkled the corners of Ruben's eyes. "I could've slept better," he admitted. "I should've known taunting you was a bad idea. Are you okay?"

"Yeah, just had a hard time getting the boys moving this morning. They were in rare form." Alan hesitated. He really didn't want to get into it there, but talking to Ruben was second nature. "Dawn called this morning. She saw the picture the blogger took."

Understanding and sympathy softened Ruben's expression. "I'm sorry."

"Don't be. It was a good picture." Alan had wasted regrets over his parents for years and decided not long after Brett was born there were some things not worth wasting his emotions over. The explosion of their relationship was finally coming to a head, leaving him free to walk away with no lingering filial guilt.

Ruben searched his face, his fingers tightening around the chain links. "Yeah, it is a good picture."

The scent of grilling meat filled the air, and over Ruben's shoulder Alan saw the local eateries setting up for the crush of players and spectators later. "Will I see you at lunch?"

"Probably not. I'll have to get my own team psyched up and ready to play. I'll grab something before your game ends."

Alan nodded and glanced down at the clipboard in his hand, quelling the little spurt of disappointment. The schedule today was a little crazy, and after they participated in both their games, then watched Brett's, they were going to be worn out. He wanted to ask Ruben if he still planned on coming over later, but he wasn't sure it was going to happen. For the past week, they'd spent almost no time together outside of work. Every time he brought up a chance to see each other in the evening, it was gently shot down. Ruben was taking his zeal to give him some space too damn far.

"I'll see you at Brett's game, then." Alan turned toward his team as his assistant coach handed him a list of the batting order.

"Hey, Hartner." Alan glanced back over his shoulder and was warmed by Ruben's grin. "We still on for tonight?"

"Wouldn't miss it." With a much lighter heart, Alan turned back to the game.

"I THOUGHT they would never get to sleep," Alan said with a sigh as he sat next to Ruben on the back deck and set the baby monitor on the low table between them. "You'd think after the past two days they'd pass out the moment their heads hit the pillows."

"They were pretty wound up, but I think you can expect them to sleep hard for the rest of the night." Ruben was pretty spent himself, with a kind of relaxed languor after a long day in the sun. He lounged in his deck chair, listening the hum of insects around the lake and the song of the frogs. He wanted to talk to Alan about the conversation with his sister, but he didn't want to introduce any tension into the calm night. They were both mellow and he wanted to keep it that way, enjoying Alan's company instead of worrying about other people intruding on their lives. Alan looked happy and that was all Ruben needed to know. There would be other days for serious talks, knowing the two of them; they'd be spending half the night going over the games play-by-play.

"Did you get a chance to speak to Jessica and Jonah today?" Alan asked, popping the top off a beer. He took a long drink, staring out at the moon shining on the dark water.

"Yeah, they made it to London safe, and they're having a good time reconnecting with their cousins. Jessica is eager to try some real fish and chips, and Jonah is dying to see the Tower of London."

"That sounds like your two. I miss them. At least we still have the trip to San Juan together." Alan scrubbed a hand over his face and leaned back in his chair to take another long drink. "With no worries about your mom freaking out over a blog."

"My mom loves you. She thinks you keep me grounded and she would be right," Ruben said, taking a beer for himself. Alan did not deserve to be harassed by his own family and their relationship was still in such an uncertain stage. He felt like they were on the cusp of starting an amazing run together and it scared him that a phone call could possibly stall them. "I wish I could've spared you that."

"As long as Dawn eventually comes around, and I think she will, I'm okay. She's more upset knowing there is going to be a break in the family than because there is a picture of us kissing online. The only reason my parents kept in contact with me this long was because of the boys and I try to limit that because they don't need to hear my parents' stupidity. We're all better off without that."

Ruben looked over at Alan's profile, his gaze tracing over his familiar face. Alan glanced at him and smiled, and Ruben's heart did that quick two-step at the easiness of that smile. Alan disarmed him completely and once again Ruben pushed his worries aside. He held his beer toward Alan. "True, I'd rather talk baseball anyway."

Alan clinked his bottle against Ruben's. "Well, here's to us, the underdogs once again."

"Won't be the first time we started out losing and ended strong." Ruben chuckled and took a sip. "Though, if you ask me, Brett's team is the one to beat this year. They were very together today. I'm pretty proud of him."

"Yeah, he's one hell of an outfielder. Doesn't hit too bad either." Alan grinned. "Though I swear, I think the play of the day should've gone to Sammy. That kid almost went horizontal through the air to make that catch and get the out. How often do you see a move like that? Horizontal, Ruben. He leapt off that pitcher's mound like something out of *The Matrix*. It blew my mind."

"What about that triple Tyler made in your game?"

Alan shook his head, turning his beer bottle in his hands. "These kids amaze me. I thought I'd miss it more—the old life, you know. And there are times I do, but when I watch these kids play the way they played today, I realize how happy I am right here, doing this."

Ruben smiled, feeling his heart expand once again in his chest. Alan glanced his way again and then paused with his head slightly tilted. "What? You're giving me that look again."

Ruben brushed his fingertips over Alan's arm and took his hand when Alan offered it. "What look is that?"

"With your eyes all soft…. I don't know, there's something about it, always catches me hard."

"I'm so in love with you, Alan."

Alan's eyes widened, then he laughed under his breath softly in a wondering sort of way and shook his head. For some reason, maybe because he was too tired, Ruben didn't have it in him to be stung or defensive. "What's so funny?"

"You love me?" Alan sat back in his chair, set his beer down, and tightened his grip on Ruben's hand.

Ruben stared at their clasped hands. "I've been telling you that for years. Maybe I wasn't using the right words. I love you with everything that there is in me."

Alan laughed that funny little laugh again and turned his head to study Ruben's face. There was a smile around his lips and he was rubbing his thumb across the back of Ruben's knuckles. "I get it. God, I've been so blind, let myself worry about so many other things, big and small. And there you were the whole time, always there, loving me, being there for me when I needed it…." He trailed off with another shake of his head and squeezed Ruben's hand. "It's you. It's always been you."

Ruben's heart started to pound, and he suddenly found it difficult to swallow. "What are you saying?"

Alan's tender smile broadened into a grin. "The same thing I think I've been trying to say for a long time too." He lifted Ruben's hand and pressed a hard kiss to his knuckles. "I'm so in love with you, Ruben Martell. I have been since I don't know when."

Ruben's heart stopped then sprang back to life with a rapid pounding. He'd wanted to hear those words for so long that it was a little surreal now. He leaned across the space between them and slid his hand around the nape of Alan's neck. Relief, elation, and the ache of how much he loved Alan caught him up, stole any more words right out of his mouth. And then there was no chance to speak because Alan was kissing him.

He sighed into the kiss, smiling against Alan's lips, his heart still flipping with happy little jumps. "Come upstairs with me," Alan murmured.

“Are you sure?” Ruben asked, pulling back slightly, though his body argued against it.

“More sure than I have been about anything in a long time,” Alan admitted. “I’ve been going crazy thinking about you, about us, about how good it felt to be with you on that couch. I want that again. I want to know everything there is to know about you. And even more, I want to wake up beside you every morning for the rest of my life.”

Again, Ruben found himself incapable of speaking. He stood up, drew Alan with him, and with their hands still linked, led him upstairs. They paused in the doorway to Alan’s bedroom and Alan brushed his lips over the nape of Ruben’s neck, sending a hot shiver rippling through him. “Say it again, Ruben.”

“I love you.”

Lips curved against his neck, and Alan slid his arms around his waist and pulled him closer. “I’m listening this time. I know what I want, and it’s you.”

MARGUERITE LABBE has been accused of being eccentric and a shade neurotic, both of which she freely admits to, but her muse has OCD tendencies, so who can blame her? Her husband and son do an excellent job keeping her toeing the line, though. Together with Fae Sutherland, Marguerite has found a shared passion for stubborn men with smart mouths. With her solo work she often likes to explore darker themes as well.

When she's not working hard on writing new material and editing completed work, she spends her time reading novels of all genres, enjoying role-playing games with her equally nutty friends, and trying to plot practical jokes against her son and husband.

Visit Marguerite's web site at http://www.margueritelabbe.com.

CPSIA information can be obtained at www.ICGtesting.com
Printed in the USA
LVOW10s0704220913

353506LV00001B/24/P